The Devil'

Simon McCleave is a multi-million copy bestselling author. Before writing crime novels, he worked in television and film. He was a Script Editor at the BBC, a producer at Channel 4 and a Story Analyst in Los Angeles. He worked on films such as *The Full Monty* and television series such as the BBC Crime Drama *Between The Lines*. As a script writer he wrote on series such as *Silent Witness*, *Murder In Suburbia*, *Teachers*, *Attachments*, *The Bill*, *Eastenders* and many more.

# Also by Simon McCleave

## DI Ruth Hunter

## The DC Ruth Hunter Murder Case Series

## The Anglesey Series – DI Laura Hart

*The Dark Tide*
*In Too Deep*
*Blood on the Shore*
*The Drowning Isle*
*Dead in the Water*

## Psychological Thrillers

*Last Night at Villa Lucia*
*Five Days in Provence (June 2025)*

# Simon McCleave

# THE DEVIL'S CLIFF KILLINGS

CANELO CRIME

 Penguin Random House

First published in the United Kingdom in 2020 by Stamford Publishing

This edition published in the United Kingdom in 2025 by

Canelo Crime, an imprint of
Canelo Digital Publishing Limited,
20 Vauxhall Bridge Road,
London SW1V 2SA
United Kingdom

A Penguin Random House Company
The authorised representative in the EEA is Dorling Kindersley Verlag GmbH. Arnulfstr. 124,
80636 Munich, Germany

A CIP catalogue record for this book is available from the British Library.

Paperback ISBN 978 1 83598 177 1

This book is a work of fiction. Names, characters, businesses, organizations, places and events are
either the product of the author's imagination or are used fictitiously. Any resemblance to actual
persons, living or dead, events or locales is entirely coincidental.

Cover design by Tom Sanderson

Printed and bound in Great Britain by Clays Ltd, Elcograf S.p.A.

Look for more great books at
www.canelo.co | www.dk.com

*For Andy, Cat, Tom, Millie and Merlin*

# PROLOGUE

*Summer 2019*

Even though it was starting to get dark, the evening was warm and the air close. Rosie Wright was enjoying her sixteenth birthday party. Her next-door neighbour, Steven Haddon, had let her use the old barn and disused farm buildings on the far field of his farm. Haddon Farm. Steve was cool. If she was honest, Rosie had a bit of a 'dad crush' on him. His daughter and her best mate, Emma, teased her about it.

*Eww. Stop flirting with my dad, you freak!*

Rosie never thought her parents would agree to a party and a sleepover – but they did. *Literally amazing!* Especially given how messed up and dysfunctional they were. There was all sorts of crap going on at home.

Seven of Rosie's closest girlfriends were sleeping over and they had managed to smuggle cider, wine and weed along in their bags. They were going to get wasted. Emma said it was going to be better than those stupid American 'sweet sixteen' parties she had seen on MTV with ball gowns, tuxedos and limousines. They were just fake, shallow losers.

Rosie had lived in Capelulo, a small village in Conwy County at the northern tip of Snowdonia Park, all her life. Her taid had told her the name Capelulo was Welsh for 'the meeting of two semicircles'. She couldn't remember why. In fact, now that she thought of it, wasn't that actually Dwygyfylchi?

Looking up at the fiery evening sky, Rosie squinted as the edges of the cumulonimbus clouds started to deepen into a shade of tangerine. It was beautiful. Suddenly, two black crows squawked and flew up from the nearby field, headed for the trees. It made her jump. They looked like they were conspiring. She hated crows.

A scream of laughter brought her attention back to her friends, who were dancing to music that blared from a speaker. Billie Eilish. They knew every word and sang at the tops of their voices. Eilish was an uber-cool, sexually ambiguous, anti-glamour goddess who talked about mental health, anxiety and the reality of the chaotic world of Generation Z. But Rosie and her friends were annoyed. They had discovered Billie long before the rest of the world. They didn't care that the grown-ups thought it was self-indulgent misery music. She was theirs and the fake, airbrushed, arena-filling pop princesses could go and fuck themselves.

Rosie got to her feet, feeling the dust and stones under her pink Converse trainers, and took a long toke on a spliff. The thick smoke was hot in her throat. She coughed, choked and stumbled overdramatically to get her friends' attention. It was her party and she wanted to make them laugh. It had the desired effect as her friends howled in hysterics at her antics.

'Fake baked!' Emma yelled.

Rosie's eyes watered – she couldn't see anything for a second. Then she laughed and did the peace sign at her friends. 'Drugs, man,' she said in a Californian accent. They all shrieked and giggled.

'Ems, have you got a corkscrew?' Kara choked with laughter. 'Beth bought a bottle of wine with a fucking cork in it! What a cock!'

Kara was Emma's younger sister – but only by fifteen months – and often hung out with her and her friends.

'What a cock!' Beth yelled. She was already hammered.

Rosie picked up another log and chucked it onto the fire. Embers flew up momentarily like fireflies darting in the air. She got out her phone and wandered away.

Rosie had something important to do that night, and it was making her anxious.

'Where are you going?' Emma asked.

Rosie shrugged, holding up her mobile. 'Over to the yard to get signal.'

'Don't spend all night on your phone, slag!' Emma teased her.

Rosie gave her the finger as she walked away. She and Emma had known each other since they were five, and Emma was like a sister to her. They told each other everything. Even Rosie's dark secret that no one else knew about.

The air inside the barn was thick, muggy and hot with a characteristic summer smell of hay and dry wood. The girls' rucksacks, sleeping bags and pillows were stacked together just inside. Rosie's distinctive green rucksack lay beside her fashionable Vans bag.

The barn was still and unnervingly quiet. A fly buzzed past her ear and she instinctively flicked it away. Putting her hand on the warm wood of the central columns, she glanced around. She felt another twinge of anxiety. Even though she was slightly drunk and high, her senses began to feel heightened.

Pacing the entire length of the barn, splinters of pink skylight speckled in the dust and particles of hay that hung in the air. She scanned left and right. The ground floor of the barn was empty. Gazing up at the hayloft, she could see the steps were retracted.

Walking out of the far end of the barn, Rosie could see the fading sunlight. The cool air felt lovely on her face as she took a deep breath.

In front of her were a few old farm sheds that had been boarded up because they were now unsafe, some rusty machinery and an uneven yard of concrete and stones. A long steel farm gate was wide open. She couldn't remember if it had been open when they got there. Now she thought about it, it had definitely been closed.

*That's weird.*

To the left, a dirt track cut through the fields. As it trailed off into the distance, Rosie knew it was over a mile up to the main road. She could see the magnificent green sweep of fields heading down into the deep basin of Sychnant Pass. The Afon Gyrach river snaked its way past about a third of a mile away. West of that were the dark wooded areas of Bryn Dedwydd. Welsh mythology claimed there was a two-thousand-year-old yew tree in the woods that was haunted by the ghost of a Celtic prince who had been betrayed by his brother. Rosie and Emma used to play up there when they were younger until one day they saw a man watching them. But that was years ago.

Rosie could feel her nerves starting to jangle as she tried in vain to get a phone signal.

*Come on, come on!*

Further up the road, Rosie could hear the sound of an approaching vehicle. A cloud of dust seemed to surround the car as it neared. She squinted – she couldn't see the driver from that distance.

Walking over to the gate with a frown, Rosie shielded her eyes from the low glare of the setting sun.

*I can't see a bloody thing.*

The car came thundering around the corner as the noise of the tyres crunching on the hard dirt track increased.

*Christ! Someone's in a hurry!*

Rosie took a couple of steps backwards as the car drew up dramatically beside her.

It was only as the dust settled and Rosie leant down and peered inside that she could finally see who was inside the car.

# CHAPTER 1

It was eight o'clock in the morning. Detective Inspector Ruth Hunter and Detective Sergeant Nick Evans of the North Wales Police were speeding their way through Snowdonia Park, heading for Capelulo. A teenage girl had been reported missing in the early hours. There was still no sign of her.

Ruth looked at the intel on her phone. 'Rosie Wright, aged sixteen. A group of friends went out to camp in the neighbour's barn and she just disappeared.'

Even though some of these cases turned out to be runaways, they had to treat it seriously. And that meant the clock was now ticking.

'A teenager goes missing. Nine times out of ten it's a boyfriend, girlfriend, parents, they've run away or something else irrational.'

Ruth frowned at Nick's casual attitude.

'Yeah, let's not forget that the other ten per cent find their way onto tabloid front pages or TV programmes like *Britain's Most Shocking Crimes*,' Ruth said darkly.

Nick nodded.

*He's been preoccupied all week*, Ruth thought.

Ruth looked out at the stunning scenery. They dropped down into the Sychnant Pass, *Bwlch Sychnant*, which linked Conwy to Penmaenmawr via Capelulo, with a range of mountains looming over them. Past that would be the town of Conwy itself and then the cold, dark expanse of the Irish Sea.

*Now that's a proper view*, she thought.

When she was feeling particularly disgruntled, all Ruth had to do was look out at the scenery of Snowdonia and she'd feel at least a little better. She reminded herself that a few years ago she would have spent the day mopping up the bloody damage of gang and drug violence in Peckham, South East London.

*Those days are gone. Thank God.*

The transfer to North Wales Police Force hadn't been quite as straightforward and stress-free as she'd expected. Her colleagues in the Met had taunted her that she would be chasing stolen tractors and arresting sheep rustlers. Far from it. Instead, she had dealt with several high-profile murder cases since her arrival. However, on a day-to-day basis, her quality of life was significantly better.

Slowing down as they entered Capelulo, Ruth could see a beach in the far distance and then a thin strip of dark blue sea on the horizon. It was a spectacular view in any well-seasoned traveller's book. The grey stone houses and narrow roads showed her that this was another small, tight-knit Snowdonia community. Everyone knew everyone's business. Sometimes that was incredibly helpful in an investigation. However, it also meant that in times of crisis, the community could close ranks defensively and no one would tell the police anything.

If Rosie Wright was a genuine missing teenager, Ruth hoped that this type of community would help them find her. And quickly!

As the track became increasingly bumpy, they spotted a sign – *Haddon Farm* – and a cottage next door.

'I think we bust a cannabis farm out here a few years ago,' Nick said, half to himself as he got out of the car.

'You think?' Ruth frowned.

'When I was drinking, I couldn't remember one day to the next,' Nick admitted. 'I was in a blackout when I nicked some people. We'd go to trial and the brief would have to remind me who they were.'

'The CPS must have loved you,' Ruth said sarcastically, but she was glad to see Nick's ongoing sobriety. She had seen too many good coppers drink themselves to death when she was in the Met. The combination of alcohol and macho bravado was a treatment for PTSD and trauma, with lethal results.

A patrol car, with its distinctive yellow and blue marking and *HEDDLU – POLICE* lettering, was parked outside the small cottage where Jason and Kathy Wright, Rosie's parents, lived.

Knowing that there was no time to lose, Ruth marched up the neat stone path. The front garden was immaculate, with a small wooden sign that read *Hazel Cottage*. You could learn a lot about people from the way their houses and gardens were presented. Ruth desperately needed a ciggie, but she would have to wait. She had promised her girlfriend Sian that she would cut down, and Nick had been designated as Sian's spy in the quest for her to quit.

A young, male uniformed officer, gawky and ginger-haired, stood outside the front door and nodded at her. 'Ma'am.'

Ruth and Nick showed their warrant cards. 'DI Hunter and DS Evans, Llancastell CID. What have we got, Constable?'

'The daughter, Rosie Wright, went missing from a field about a mile up that way. She's sixteen. Friends and family have been searching for her all night. We've had a look around and there's no sign of her anywhere, ma'am,' the constable explained at speed. Everyone was acutely aware of the time pressure.

Ruth would make sure they checked again. There had been several times in the Met when missing children and teens had been found hiding under beds, in wardrobes or even in attics. Those cases never surprised her. Living in the squalid, dysfunctional and sometimes violent flats of Peckham's estates with addict or alcoholic parents was horrific. She didn't know how some of the children survived the experience. Some of them didn't.

'What about a FLO?' Nick asked. A police officer would be appointed as the family liaison officer to provide an ongoing line of communication between the family and the police.

'My sarge said to wait for you guys to get here, sir,' the constable explained.

Nick nodded. It sounded sensible to wait until they could establish if it was likely that a crime had been committed. 'Okay, thank you.'

The officer pushed open the door, and Ruth and Nick walked in purposefully. The house was tidy and smelt of air freshener and coffee. Coats hung neatly from hooks in the hallway. Boots, shoes and trainers lined up tidily. A small patterned rug covered the wine-red tiled floor. Instinct told Ruth that there was some order and normality to the Wright family as far as first impressions went.

It was the first ten minutes that normally gave Ruth a clue as to whether there was something to worry about. And there was always a slight apprehension before meeting the family. How were they going to react to her as a detective? Some were hostile and overemotional. Some were stunned and quiet. And some simply pretended that it wasn't happening.

As Ruth and Nick came into the long kitchen, they saw a woman sitting at the table, her fingers pawing at a mug of tea. Kathy Wright.

A female uniformed police officer, tall with dyed-black hair in a ponytail, rested against the kitchen counter. She looked over as the detectives came in.

'Ma'am,' the officer said as she instinctively straightened. Probably young, ambitious and keen to impress CID officers whenever she could. Ruth knew the type.

Ruth showed her warrant card. 'Thank you, Constable. We'll take it from here.'

The officer nodded and made herself scarce.

Kathy Wright was in her early forties but looked older. Her hair had been dyed so blonde that it was just this side of white. It was cut into a fringe that made her face look more severe than it actually was. Even though Kathy was overweight, she squeezed into skinny jeans that were finished off with immaculate pink trainers. Ruth knew she was being judgemental but as she looked at Kathy, she remembered Hannibal Lecter's analysis of Agent Starling in *The Silence of the Lambs*: she was only a generation away from poor white trailer trash.

Kathy had made an effort with her appearance, but Ruth didn't know if this was a sign of anything darker. It did pose the question that if she was frantic in the search for her daughter, why had she gone to so much trouble? But in Ruth's experience, some people were just like that. They tried to create a sense of normality and routine as if nothing had happened.

Kathy looked up from the table, smiled and blinked. *She doesn't know what bloody day it is, poor woman*, Ruth thought. Kathy had that horrible vacant look Ruth had seen so many times before. Shock, disbelief, terror, denial. It was all there.

'Mrs Wright? I'm Detective Inspector Ruth Hunter and this is my colleague, Detective Sergeant Nick Evans. Can we sit down?'

Kathy nodded. 'Of course, sorry. Yeah. It's Kathy.' She lifted her mug to take a sip of tea, and Ruth could see that her hands were trembling slightly.

'Is your husband here?' Nick asked.

'He's gone out with some others to look…' She didn't finish her sentence. She couldn't because that would make what was happening real.

'Kathy, I know that this is a very difficult time for you. I can't imagine what you're going through,' Ruth said in the gentle voice that was her trademark. Ruth had been through something similar with her own daughter Ella last Christmas, but it wasn't the time to explain that to anyone. She needed to keep it nice and simple. 'We just need as much information as we can get. The more you can tell us, the more likely it is we can get Rosie home safely.'

Kathy nodded, but Ruth could see the tears welling up in her eyes.

'Shall I make us a cup of tea?' Nick suggested quietly.

Ruth gave him a knowing smile. 'Yes, thanks. That's a good idea.'

Taking the kettle to the sink, Nick filled it up as Ruth got out her notebook. She glanced up at the fridge, which was covered in magnets, photos and drawings. Even in those few seconds, she deduced that the Wrights had two children. Rosie and a brother who was a couple of years older.

*On the surface, this is a nice, normal family*, Ruth thought. And that meant alarm bells were starting to ring.

However, all families had their secrets, despite what some of them would have you believe on social media. Maybe there was more to this.

'I know you've already told my colleagues, but could you run through what happened last night for us?' Ruth asked, keeping her voice soft.

Kathy shifted awkwardly in her chair. 'Rosie went with Emma from next door up to one of Steven's fields. It was her birthday.'

'Steven?' Ruth asked.

'Steven is Emma's dad. Steven Haddon. He owns the farm next door,' Kathy explained. 'There were about seven of them going to sleep up at the barn.'

'How far is that from here?' Nick asked.

'I don't know. Less than a mile. Ten minutes' walk, I guess.'

'What time did Rosie leave?'

'Emma called for her about six.'

'And that was the last time you saw Rosie?' Ruth asked.

Kathy nodded and bit her lip for a moment. The emotion was getting to her again. That's how it worked. It would come in overwhelming waves that then subsided for brief moments before rolling back with a vengeance.

Ruth looked at her with real empathy. 'It's all right, Kathy. Take your time.' She didn't mean it. She needed as much information from her as quickly as possible.

'Steven... and Jill came and knocked about ten o'clock. Emma and her friends said they couldn't... they couldn't... find Rosie,' Kathy explained.

'And then what happened, Kathy?'

'We all went up there in Steven's Jeep. We were looking around, but she wasn't there. We came back. I rang everyone I could think of, but no one had seen her.' Kathy's hands began to shake as she tried to get her breath.

'And then you called us? Around two o'clock this morning? Is that right?' Ruth said, looking down at her notebook.

Kathy nodded and said, 'Yeah. That's right.'

'I know this is difficult, but could you let us have a recent photograph of Rosie?'

Kathy thought for a moment and then said, 'I've got one on my phone from a few days ago?'

Ruth pulled out her contact card and handed it to Kathy. 'If you can text me that now, I can circulate it this morning.'

Kathy nodded and flicked through her phone. Nick came over and placed two mugs of tea down on the table.

'Here we go,' Nick said.

'Thanks,' Ruth said as her phone buzzed with the photo. She opened the image. There she was. Rosie Wright. Sixteen. Long blonde hair, black T-shirt, jeans and pink Converse trainers. She didn't look like she had a care in the world.

'We'll need a description of what she was wearing,' Nick said as he sat down at the other end of the table.

'The same jeans and trainers as in the photo I sent you. And a luminous green T-shirt with "Billie" written on it. You know, the singer Billie Eilish. She loves her,' Kathy said.

Ruth nodded. She didn't know who Kathy was talking about, but that didn't matter. Sipping her tea, she looked around the kitchen. From the photos on the fridge and the wall, Jason Wright didn't seem to get much of a look-in when it came to family days out. Maybe he was always working? Or maybe he was just one of those dads that were very hands-off.

'Have you noticed anything different about Rosie or her behaviour in recent days?' Ruth asked, now refocusing.

'No. She's been the same… Bit moody, but she's a teenager,' Kathy said with a shrug.

'Anything at home that might have upset her or given her a reason to not want to be here?' Ruth asked.

Kathy clearly took slight exception to Ruth's insinuation. 'No, no. Everything's fine. She's been talking about only having two weeks left at college. You know, she was excited about the summer holidays with her friends. They're all going to Leeds Festival together.'

'Anything bothering her at school? Friends, bullying, anything like that?' Nick asked.

'No. She moans about it, but she actually likes going to school. She's doing really well.'

Ruth could see that Kathy was proud of her daughter, which was more than could be said for lots of parents she met in her line of work.

'Relationships of any kind? Boyfriends?' Ruth asked. 'Were there any bitter exes who wouldn't take no for an answer?' She had seen insanely jealous teens do all sorts of hideous things to ex-girlfriends and -boyfriends.

'No. Not that she's mentioned. A couple of boys at school that she likes, but nothing that I know of.'

'Thank you.' Ruth could feel her pulse start to quicken. Her instinct was that there was now a concern that Rosie was genuinely missing. It was a judgement based on her initial impressions of the family and the portrait Kathy Wright had painted of her daughter. She wasn't ruling out the possibility that Rosie had run away, but she seemed happy and in a stable home.

Ruth shot Nick a look – in a second she could see that he was thinking the same thing.

They might be dealing with an abduction.

And that meant they were now racing against time. Finding Rosie safe – and soon – was their priority.

'Does Rosie have access to a computer or a laptop?' Ruth asked with a growing sense of urgency.

Kathy nodded and gestured to the stairs. 'It'll be in her bedroom. Do you want me to get it?'

'No, that's fine. We'll get it before we go,' Nick said.

'Kathy, I'd like to organise a family liaison officer for you. Is that okay?' Ruth asked as she looked over at Nick, who would get working on it immediately.

'I don't know what that is,' Kathy said. She looked confused.

'They're a police officer. They will come and be with you. And they'll be here permanently to keep you informed of everything that's going on while we're looking for Rosie,' Ruth explained.

Kathy nodded as she processed this. 'Yeah, of course.'

Ruth's eyes were drawn to a large family photo on the wall. Rosie was with her parents and a slightly older teenage boy who must have been her brother. 'Is it just you, your husband and Rosie that live here, Kathy?' Ruth asked.

'Yeah. My son Gareth lives over nearer the coast,' Kathy said. 'He's a few years older than Rosie.'

'What does Gareth do?' Nick asked.

'He's doing an apprenticeship at college. Training to be an electrician,' Kathy explained.

There was the sound of movement and a tall man in his forties walked in. He had thick greying hair, a pale complexion and dark, hooded eyes. It was Jason Wright, Rosie's father.

'Mr Wright?' Nick asked as he looked at them.

'Yes,' Jason Wright answered in a thick North Wales accent.

'We're detectives from Llancastell CID,' Nick explained.

'Right, I see. And you're sitting here drinking tea? You should be out there looking for my daughter!' Jason thundered.

Nick shot Ruth a look – he'd obviously gone to the same charm school as many of the other farm workers she had met up here.

'As I was explaining to Kathy, we need to get as much detail as we can to help with the search for Rosie,' Ruth explained calmly. It was clear who wore the trousers in this household.

Jason nodded and looked at them all. 'Well, I can't sit around here waiting. I need to keep looking for her,' he snapped.

'Mr Wright?' Ruth said.

'What?' he replied in a withering tone.

'Just to confirm, you were here with your wife all last night? Is that right?'

'No, no. I was at the pub,' Jason explained.

'Oh, right. And what time did you get back?' Nick asked.

'Half seven, eight. Right, I'm going back out there.' Jason shot Nick a look. 'I'll leave you ladies to your tea.'

Ruth looked at Nick as they got up to go.

'I'll get the computer. Can you get all CID officers in for briefing in an hour?' Ruth said, now feeling the pressure of the developing investigation.

The abduction of a child was horrendous for everyone involved – and some people never recovered.


*Sixteen hours*

Having updated Superintendent Jones, Detective Chief Inspector Drake and the North Wales Police media desk over in St Asaph, Ruth called a briefing for CID officers. So far no sightings, no answer from Rosie Wright's phone, no contact. They all agreed it looked like a case of abduction – and so now the clock was ticking.

Up on the wall, the screen showed the photo of Rosie Wright that her mother had sent Ruth earlier. She was smiling with a broad, playful grin. That's what photos of missing kids and teenagers showed: happiness, innocence and a complete ignorance of the darkness that awaited them. Birthday parties, a day out, a holiday. And that's what crushed Ruth's heart. Other officers kept a professional distance; they said they needed to be objective and unemotional to do the job properly. Not Ruth. In her experience, the more she cared, the more she focused on getting the right outcome for the victims and their families.

Behind her, a detailed map of Snowdonia and the North Wales coast had been attached to the incident whiteboard. A red pin marked the location of the village of Capelulo and Haddon Farm.

As the senior investigating officer, SIO, Ruth gathered some papers and headed to the screen and whiteboards to lead the briefing. Half a dozen CID detectives, who had been sitting and chatting, quietened.

Everyone knew how this worked.

Find the missing person quickly or all the statistics showed that they would be dead or never found. The first forty-eight hours were decisive. After a week, they'd be trawling rivers, lakes and looking out for shallow graves.

'Okay, guys, if we can get going quickly on this, please. As you know, time is absolutely crucial here. Rosie Wright, aged sixteen, left home at six yesterday evening with her friend, Emma Haddon. The Haddons own a farm here.' Ruth pointed to the map. 'Rosie and Emma met with five other girls from their school. The plan was to drink, listen to music and sleep out in a barn, which is just under a mile from the Wright's home. At around nine p.m., Emma noticed that she hadn't seen Rosie for a while, but when she went in search of Rosie, she had disappeared. We don't have a specific time, but Emma thinks that it was about eight o'clock when Rosie had mentioned that she couldn't get a signal on her phone and was going to try the other side of the barn where there are disused farm buildings and a yard. That was the last time Rosie was seen. Luke?'

DC Luke Merringer, with his expanding waistline, ginger hair and goatee, stood up. Ruth had known Merringer for a couple of years, and she was fond of him. He was passionate about the job and why they did it. 'We're trying to trace Rosie's mobile phone. At present, the phone has not been used since five o'clock yesterday afternoon. If Rosie was trying to call someone after eight last night, she didn't get through. Tech are trying to see if there are any GPS apps switched on and see if the number has hit any masts in the area and then triangulate.'

'What about social media?' Ruth asked.

'I've looked. At the moment, there's nothing I can see that stands out, but we need access to her Snapchat and Instagram accounts. It's going to take a while to get those. I'm working on getting her phone records sent over now,' Merringer said.

'Okay, thanks, Luke. I'm interviewing Emma Haddon in a minute. What about the other friends, Sian?' Ruth asked.

DC Sian Hockney shifted in her seat and looked down at her notes. 'Boss, I spoke to Beth Miller and Kara Haddon this morning. Kara is Emma's younger sister. They confirmed Emma Haddon's version of events. Rosie Wright was up there with them for a couple of hours, then she seemed to vanish into thin air. They didn't see her go anywhere and they didn't see anyone else around.'

Ruth nodded. 'Thank you, Sian.'

Sian gave her a slight smirk. 'Boss.' She and Sian had made love that morning so they both had a lightness and glow about them. She was glad that there was now an unspoken acceptance of their relationship amongst most of the CID officers.

'Someone must have seen something. Rosie Wright didn't just disappear. How did she leave the field? Where did she go? She's sixteen, so if someone snatched her, then there would have been a struggle. I'm guessing she would have screamed. What about the house-to-house, Dan?'

DC Dan French, early thirties, slim and clean-cut, had only just joined them from Uniform so was essentially a probationer. So far, he seemed very keen and was starting to show himself to be a good copper. 'Uniform are doing a house-to-house at the moment, boss. No one saw anything out of the ordinary.'

'Okay. We've got dog units heading up to the fields now. Nick, can you go and talk to the Haddons next door? See if you can get a picture of what the Wrights are like as a family,' Ruth said.

'Boss.' Nick nodded.

Ruth looked out at the CID officers for a moment. 'As far as I can see, Rosie Wright was a happy sixteen-year-old girl with everything to live for. Stable home, doing well at school, lots of friends. There's nothing I can see that would suggest she has run away. And that means she may have been taken from that field, or somewhere around there, against her will. The next forty-eight hours are absolutely vital, so I want us to go out there, do our best work for Rosie, find her and bring her back alive.'

Ruth's impassioned plea clearly had an effect on the officers. She could sense the determination in the room. Anything that involved kids always had that effect. It's why they did the job.

–

Twenty minutes later, Ruth was striding down a corridor towards the lifts on the sixth floor of Llancastell Police Station, where CID was housed. She had managed to smoke a cigarette outside and down a coffee before getting ready to interview Emma Haddon. The nicotine and caffeine had sharpened her mind. She looked up and Sian was coming the other way. She gave Ruth a cheeky wink.

They stopped for a moment.

'Did you enjoy your breakfast?' Sian said with a knowing smile. She wasn't talking about her cornflakes.

'Yes, I did enjoy it, thank you very much.' Ruth grinned back at her and touched her hand for a moment. They were still at that stage where a touch of a hand could give a buzz and quicken the pulse.

Sian scrunched up her nose and sniffed the air before glaring at Ruth. 'I thought you were cutting down on the smoking?'

*Shit.* 'I am. I will.' Ruth gestured along the corridor. She didn't have time for another lecture. 'Emma Haddon's waiting for me.'

Sian nodded but still seemed a little annoyed. 'See you later, boss.'

Ruth turned and went into the interview room where Emma Haddon was sitting with her father, Steven. The room was stark, virtually windowless and generally inhospitable. Ruth wished they could have had access to the family suite, but Child Protection were using it.

Even though Steven Haddon was sitting, Ruth could see he was a man-mountain. Well over six foot, he was very handsome, with a neat greying beard and a lined, sun-worn face.

'Mr Haddon? And it's Emma, isn't it?' Ruth asked with a kind smile as she sat opposite them. 'Thank you for coming in.'

They both looked concerned, which was to be expected. 'No problem,' Steven said.

Ruth looked over at Emma. 'My name's Ruth and I'm trying to find out where Rosie has gone. So is it okay if I ask you some questions which might help me do that?' she asked in a voice that was verging on maternal.

Emma nodded and looked at her father for reassurance.

'She hasn't really slept,' Steven said as he put a comforting hand on her shoulder. Emma flinched for just a second as if her father's physical contact had startled her. Ruth noticed but didn't let on.

*What was that about?*

'Of course. You must be very worried about Rosie.' Ruth looked down at her notebook. 'So you picked Rosie up from her house at around six yesterday?'

'Yes,' Emma whispered with a nod.

'How did she seem?' Ruth asked.

'She was in a good mood. It was her birthday,' Emma said uncertainly. She didn't seem to know what Ruth was asking.

'She wasn't nervous about anything? Or upset?' Ruth clarified.

'No, no. She seemed really happy.'

'And then you walked up to the field and the barn on your dad's farm. And that's about a mile, is it?' Ruth asked.

'Just under,' Steven said. 'Takes about ten minutes to walk up there.'

'Thank you. And that's where you met your friends? I have a list here, but there were seven of you, including you and Rosie?'

'Yes.'

'And what did you do then?'

'I built up a firepit and lit it. We put our stuff in the barn. Put some music on, you know?'

'Were you drinking alcohol, Emma?' Ruth needed the full picture and to know what kind of state the girls might have been in.

Emma shot a slightly anxious look at her father.

'Don't worry. I was sixteen once. Just tell her the truth,' Steven said with a nonchalant shrug.

'We just want to find Rosie, so we need to know everything that happened while you were up by the barn,' Ruth said gently, implying there would be no judgement if they were drinking. They were teenagers. And that's what teenagers did.

'Yeah. Some of us were drinking a bit.'

'And it was nearly nine o'clock by the time you realised that Rosie was missing?' Ruth asked, clarifying what she had read in Emma's preliminary statement.

'Yeah. I went into the barn to see if I could find her.'

'And when was the last time you can remember seeing Rosie?'

'I think it was about eight. She went to the other side of the farm to get a signal on her phone.'

'Do you know who she was trying to call?' Ruth asked.

'I think she was texting someone or on Snapchat. But I don't know who.'

'Did she seem agitated or upset?' Ruth asked.

'No, nothing like that. Just annoyed 'cos she couldn't get a signal. So, she tried over by the yard because the signal is better over there,' Emma explained.

'And you didn't see her again?' Ruth asked.

Emma shook her head and began to look a little teary. She put her hand to her eyes and wiped a tear away with her palm.

'Sorry…' Emma sniffed as she tried to hold it together.

'It's all right, Emma. I know this is really upsetting for you,' Ruth said. She could see how difficult it was for the girl. It must have been terrifying to be Emma's age and have your best friend vanish off the face of the earth. 'Did you see anyone else up there? Anyone you knew, or anyone you didn't recognise?'

Emma sniffed and shook her head. 'No, no one. We… didn't see anyone else until we came back.'

'Was there anything worrying Rosie? Or had she seemed different recently?'

'No. She was just the same… Nothing seemed to bother her,' Emma explained.

'College was okay?'

'Yeah, she was really smart. The teachers loved her.'

'Any boyfriends or relationships?'

'No. A few lads had asked her out, but she said they were immature. She had a bit of a thing for older men…'

*Is that something to look at?* Ruth thought.

'What about home? Was she happy at home?'

Ruth could see the change in Emma's face as she glanced up at her father. Ruth waited for a moment as her question hung in the air.

*Now that's struck a chord…*

'Emma? Was Rosie happy at home?' Ruth asked a little more urgently.

'No… not always…'

'Why not?' Ruth asked. It was the first hint that something was wrong in Rosie's life.

'Her dad's a prick,' Emma spat under her breath.

It was uncharacteristic of Emma, from what Ruth had seen so far, and it was said with a degree of emotion.

'Emma!' Steven said. 'You can't say that.'

'Well, he is a prick, Dad. You don't like him. You said he was a wanker the other day.' Emma was getting angry. Steven looked embarrassed, but what his daughter had said was clearly true.

'It's all right. Do you think you could tell me why you don't like Jason Wright, Emma?' Ruth asked.

'He's just… nasty. You know? Shouts at Rosie and her mum. He's horrible,' Emma said.

Ruth looked over at Steven. 'Do you have much to do with your neighbours, Mr Haddon?'

'Sometimes. Kathy, Rosie's mum, she keeps herself to herself but she seems friendly enough. Jason works for me. He's my farm manager. Most of the time he's okay, but he's got a temper on him,' Steven explained.

'Is he ever violent?' Ruth asked.

Steven shrugged. 'Not that I know of…'

'Yeah, he is. He tried to stop Rosie going out once and dragged her by the arm. She had bruises on her wrist and her shoulder hurt.'

'Was that the only time he has been violent to Rosie?' Ruth asked.

'I think so. She threatened him so she said he had stopped speaking to her for the last few weeks.'

'Threatened him? What do you mean?' Ruth asked.

'She said if he ever touched her again, she would call the police and have him arrested.'

# CHAPTER 2

*Eighteen hours*

The clouds now obscured the sun that had been shining through the window as Ruth finished another coffee. In her gut, she could feel the growing tension of finding Rosie before something horrible happened. And the fact that the clock was running was making everyone tense.

Even though it was summer, the sky was slowly becoming a uniform steel grey. Sitting down in her chair, Ruth arched her back to stretch it. Her thoughts went back to lying in Sian's arms earlier that morning. Warm and safe.

Ruth had a daughter, Ella, and even though she was now in her early twenties, Ruth remembered how difficult she had been when she was sixteen. Sometimes Ella had been rude, emotional and selfish. Was Jason Wright grabbing his daughter's wrist a sign of anything else other than frustration? But the portrait that Emma and Steven Haddon had painted of him didn't sit comfortably with her.

Ruth's train of thought was broken by Nick knocking at her door.

'How was Emma Haddon?' he asked.

'Worried and upset. But I wouldn't expect anything else.'

'Yeah, I spoke to the mum, Jennifer Haddon, earlier.'

'Anything interesting?'

'She's a MILF – I would.' Nick grinned.

'What is wrong with you?' Ruth asked, rolling her eyes. She was used to Nick's laddish humour and knew it was a front.

'According to most people, everything.'

'Correct me if I'm wrong, but aren't you and Amanda having a baby soon?' Ruth asked.

Nick and his girlfriend Amanda had only been together since Christmas, so Ruth assumed that the pregnancy wasn't planned. Nick hadn't said as much but he had seemed shocked. He was clearly in a happy place now, which was in stark contrast to where she had found him when she first arrived in North Wales. She was pleased for him. However, she could see that the responsibility of the pregnancy weighed on him sometimes.

'I was just looking. Anyway, the lovely Jennifer and Kathy Wright aren't close but get on okay. However, Jason Wright isn't winning any popularity contests in that house anytime soon.'

'What did Jennifer Haddon say?' Ruth asked.

'She described Jason as "a controlling bully",' Nick said.

Ruth nodded – it fitted with the picture she had too. 'Emma Haddon told me that Jason Wright had bruised Rosie's wrist and hurt her shoulder. He sounds like a nasty piece of work.'

'Yeah, I got that general impression too. We need to interview him asap, don't we?' Nick asked.

'I think a voluntary interview today might be sensible.'

At that moment, Merringer came thundering across the incident room towards them. He must have been in a hurry as he had one side of his shirt hanging out of his trousers. That's what she loved about Merringer: his slightly nerdy gawkishness.

'Boss, call from SOCO. They've found blood at the yard at Haddon Farm. They need you there as soon as,' Merringer said breathlessly.

*Christ! That doesn't sound good.*

Grabbing her jacket, Ruth looked at Nick. 'Let's go.'

'You smoke, I drive? I know,' Nick said with mock resignation.

It was their little saying that had somehow come about since they started working together a few years ago.

'Just don't tell anyone I'm smoking,' Ruth said as they went.

'It'll cost you,' Nick said, arching an eyebrow.

'I won't tell Amanda that you're a sleazebag that flirts with every attractive witness you meet?' Ruth suggested.

Nick nodded. 'Seems fair. You're on, boss.'

–

Ruth and Nick sped from the A55 down to Capelulo. In an abduction case like this, Ruth knew that everything had to be done with speed and sharp focus. A missed lead, clue or piece of evidence could be catastrophic.

Passing the sign to Abergele, Ruth looked out at the flat, dry farmland that stretched away to the south until it hit the ridges of Snowdonia Park. Due to the heat haze, the northern mountains and hills of Snowdonia were a blurred, undulating shape on the horizon. As Nick and Ruth turned west, the larger headland of Penmaenmawr came into view. To her left, Ruth could see a smooth arc of green hills and uplands extending east to west.

Nick knew the area nearby because of the Fairy Glen Waterfalls, which he had visited on a school trip. They were over twenty-five feet high, and the water fell down a ragged rock face that had been formed during the last ice age. It was the Victorians that had given the falls their name after a series of fairy sightings in the 1880s.

As their car bumped along the farm track, Ruth wound down the window. The scent of tree blossom mixed with the thicker smell of farmland. She reached into her bag to get a cigarette.

'That's four today, boss,' Nick said, reprimanding her.

Ruth gave him the finger. 'Fuck off, Dad!'

'Charming.' Nick raised his eyebrow sardonically.

Sheep and lambs moved out of their way and scuttled towards a wooden gate and wire mesh.

Up ahead, they could see two marked patrol cars and the SOCO forensic van parked in a field. In the distance, a uniformed officer was taping off the scene with blue-and-white evidence tape. This was now a crime scene.

Nick and Ruth pulled off the track, parked in the field and made their way towards the barn. A few local rubberneckers had already arrived to see what was going on.

*How long will it be before the bloody press arrive?*

By the main gate, there were already some candles, flowers and a teddy bear. Messages that had been written or typed had been stuck to the wood of the gate with *#FindRosie* featuring on many of them.

A female uniformed officer was standing beside the tape about twenty yards from the barn.

'Are you running the duty log, Constable?' Ruth asked.

'Yes, ma'am,' the Constable replied.

Ruth and Nick showed their warrant cards. 'DI Hunter and DS Evans, Llancastell CID. No one comes in or out of this crime scene without signing in, Constable.'

'Yes, ma'am.'

Ruth looked over at the locals, who were deep in conversation. 'Could you politely ask our bystanders to move back from this area, Constable? Just in case we find anything else.'

'Will do, ma'am.'

*Haven't they got anything better to do with their time?* Ruth thought.

Ruth and Nick ducked under the tape as a man bounded over to greet them. As he pulled down his mask, she could see it was the chief forensic officer, Alexander Travis. They had worked together on the Andrew Gates case at Christmas.

'Afternoon, Alex,' Ruth said. 'What have you found?'

Alex held up a small plastic bag that contained seven pink pills. 'My junior officer just found this over by the firepit.'

Ruth took the bag and looked at the contents. Each pill had a heart shape stamped at its centre. She knew what they were. 'Ecstasy?'

'At a guess, yes. I'll test them at the lab,' Alex said.

'Looks like Rosie and her friends were up here to do more than just drink a bit of cider,' Nick said.

'You've found some blood?' Ruth asked.

'Yeah. Over by the courtyard gate, through the barn,' he explained, gesturing to the grisly discovery.

'Is it human?' Nick asked.

'Not sure. One of my officers is just running it through the precipitin test.' Alex pointed to an officer in a forensic suit and mask by the van.

A SOCO handed them white forensic suits, nitrile masks, shoes and purple gloves, which they snapped on.

As they entered the large barn, the wind picked up a little, and the thick timber joists and frame groaned. Glancing around, Ruth saw the wooden ladder that had been pulled down to access the hayloft.

'Anyone been up there?' Ruth asked.

'Yes. We didn't find anything,' Travis explained.

The air in the barn was warmer and thicker than outside. A couple of flies buzzed and swirled by the stained window.

'Out here,' Travis said as he guided them through the barn and out the other side into the sunlight.

They came out into an uneven stone yard that was covered with the remnants of dry mud and straw. The yard was bordered by a semi-circle of derelict outbuildings and feed sheds. Ruth glanced at the rusting farm equipment that rested sadly against boarded-up wooden doors.

'Apparently, this is the old part of the farm. It hasn't really been used since they modernised in the Nineties,' Travis explained.

'Perfect place for a party,' Nick said.

'Didn't have you down as a closet raver, DS Evans,' Ruth quipped.

Travis stopped by the long steel gate that led out to a track road, which disappeared into the fields.

It was then that Ruth spotted what Travis wanted to show them. A small patch of blood that had left a dark stain on the stone. It was now marked with a yellow plastic evidence tag.

Squatting down, Ruth looked at the blood. It was definitely fresh.

Then she followed her eyeline across the bloodstain and over the dirty surface of the yard towards the gate. She spotted something that didn't look right underneath an old rusty farm trailer that was about ten yards away.

Walking over, Ruth took a torch from her pocket. She crouched down again and used her torch to look underneath.

More blood? A lot more blood.

'Nick, can you help me move this?' Ruth said with some sense of urgency as she stood and grabbed the trailer.

'Course,' Nick said as he went and took the other end.

Giving it a yank, the trailer rolled back a few yards. Underneath where it had stood was an enormous blood stain that covered an area of at least six feet by four feet.

*Jesus Christ!* It looked like a good few pints of blood. Ruth's heart sank.

'This is not good, boss,' Nick mumbled grimly as he crouched down to get a closer look.

'No, it's really not,' Ruth said.

*If this is Rosie's blood, then something very violent and horrific happened here*, Ruth thought.

'And this blood is fresh too. No more than a day or two,' Travis said as he inspected it.

'It rained three or four days ago, if I remember correctly, so that narrows down the time frame,' Ruth said, thinking out loud.

'If this is human blood, I would like to get in a blood pattern analyst. Something doesn't quite add up at the moment.'

There was movement and a SOCO officer strode purposefully out of the barn. The officer removed his mask so as to speak clearly.

'Sir, the test came back as positive for human blood.'

Ruth and Nick exchanged a look – it wasn't what they wanted to hear.

'Thank you, Martin. I'll be with you in a minute,' Travis replied quietly. 'I'll check this patch too, but my educated guess is that it's the same.'

Travis looked at them both as his mind processed the test results.

'What does this tell us, Alex?' Ruth asked.

'At first glance, I think it would have taken three to four pints of blood to create a blood stain of that size and consistency,' Travis explained. 'So, whoever's blood this is was either dead or unconscious when they left this farm.'

# CHAPTER 3

*Twenty-three hours*

Ruth looked out of the windows of CID. It was still light, and specks of the white and orange lights of Llancastell twinkled in the distance. They had just passed the summer solstice. When she was younger, Ruth always loved how the evenings seemed to go on for ever. However, today time seemed to be racing away and it was close to being twenty-four hours since Rosie Wright went missing.

Striding over to the incident whiteboards, Ruth looked up at them. At the centre was a large printed copy of the photograph of Rosie Wright. It struck her how much Rosie looked like her mother. The blue eyes, slim nose and rosebud mouth were identical from what she could remember from her meeting with Kathy Wright. Rosie had posed for the photograph with an over-the-top grin and the fingers on her left hand showing the peace sign. She looked the epitome of youthful joy and carefree exuberance.

*Where the hell is she? What has happened to her? And why?*

Forensics wouldn't be able to match the blood sample from the barn to Rosie's DNA until later that night or even the morning. However, Ruth's instinct told her that it was Rosie's blood. And that meant Rosie was either in serious danger or worse.

The house-to-house and search of the farm had turned up nothing. Rosie hadn't used her phone since she disappeared. The dog unit and local volunteers had searched the nearby woods and heathland. A police helicopter had completed a ten-mile-radius search with thermal imaging cameras and found nothing. Of course, if Rosie Wright was lying dead in a shallow grave or in a river somewhere, the cameras wouldn't pick anything up. Even in summer, a dead body will be stone-cold in four to five hours.

Social media was already awash with the story. Of course, exposure had its pros and cons. Press coverage meant that the public were aware of Rosie, what she looked like and the fact that she was missing and might have come to harm. However, the downside was that every crazy, nut and attention-seeking lunatic came out of the woodwork. That meant time spent on false leads and real leads missed.

Ruth's train of thought was broken by movement. Nick was still at his desk on the other side of the room.

'Get yourself home, Nick,' she said.

'Will do in a minute, boss.'

'Haven't you got a pregnant girlfriend at home?' she asked.

'Why do you think I'm here?' Nick replied with a grin.

'Bloody hell. And there's me thinking you're a thoughtful man in recovery,' Ruth joked, and then she looked at him for a moment.

'What?' Nick asked.

'It's scary, isn't it?' Ruth said.

'What's that?'

'Bringing a child into the world. Probably worse if you see what we see every day,' Ruth said.

'It's all scary. I haven't had a proper girlfriend since I was about twenty. And as for bringing up a kid…' Nick puffed his cheeks at the thought of it.

'You'll be a great dad. I promise it'll be the best thing you ever do with your life,' Ruth said.

Nick nodded, smiled and came past to look at the boards. It was clear Nick wasn't going to be drawn any further into a long conversation about the meaning of life.

'If she's still alive, we're running out of time, boss,' Nick said.

Ruth looked up at the map of Capelulo and the surrounding area.

'I know… This is the only way from the farm up to the main road,' Ruth said, pointing to a track on the map.

'Yeah. There's just that track that we came down today.'

'Okay. And if that blood turns out to be Rosie Wright's, then she was either dead or unconscious when she was taken from that yard.'

'From what the esteemed Mr Travis said.'

'So where did she go? Who took her? And how did they leave Haddon Farm with no one seeing anything?'

They both looked at the map for a moment – there was only one way in and one way out: the track that led down from the main road.

–

Sam Fender's 'All Is On My Side' was playing from somewhere inside Ruth's home as the last remnants of daylight faded outside. It was late, and Ruth and Sian were cuddling in the kitchen as Ella walked in.

'Oh, God, get a room!' Ella exclaimed, hiding her eyes in feigned horror.

'We've got a room,' Ruth smiled. Sian had moved in over six months ago. Somehow Sian had come into her life and woken her from a five-year relationship coma. And as far as she was concerned, Sian was the sexiest woman who had ever walked the planet.

Sian placed her hands on Ruth's hips and moved her sideways to get to the fridge.

'I demand more booze!' Sian boomed, attempting to mimic Richard E. Grant in *Withnail and I*. She grabbed some wine and poured them all a large glass. Holding up the bottle, Sian frowned. 'There's not a lot in a bottle, is there?'

'Not the way you drink it,' Ella teased.

'You are aware that it's not pop?' Ruth said as she put her arm around Ella's shoulder and escorted her into the living room. Through the open patio doors, the sky was moving from a dusty purple to darker hues of blue.

For a moment, Ruth looked at the sky. Rosie Wright was out there somewhere, and it sent a shiver down Ruth's spine. She would grab four or five hours' sleep and be back looking for her at dawn.

'Come on, mush, I need to talk to you about something,' Ruth said to Ella, trying to maintain some kind of normality.

'Oh, good. That sounds ominous.' Ella rolled her eyes and slumped into the soft armchair.

'It's nothing horrible,' Ruth reassured her.

'Are you two going to have a baby or something hideous?' Ella groaned.

'No. Nothing like that. I mean, I don't know but that's not it.' Ruth was getting flustered and had been thrown off track.

'You don't know?' Ella pulled a face.

'Ella, can you just listen for a moment? Your dad has sent me two emails and he wants to know if he can get in contact with you,' Ruth explained. Ruth had seen the emails earlier in the week and it had been weighing on her mind just how she was going to break the news to her daughter.

Ella frowned as she took this in and then bristled. 'Why?'

'He's your dad. He's coming to the UK this summer and I guess he would like to see you,' Ruth explained. She knew how little contact Ella had had with her father, and his request would seem confusing. It made Ruth angry, but she didn't want that to influence Ella.

'What do you think?' Ella asked. She had understandably been thrown by the news.

'It doesn't really matter what I think,' Ruth said. She had to allow Ella to do what she wanted and not let her own annoyance cloud the issue.

'It does to me,' Ella said.

Sian came in with glasses of wine, which she handed around. She quickly picked up on the slight atmosphere.

'Sorry. You guys in the middle of something?' Sian said, gesturing that she could leave them to it.

Ella shook her head. 'No, no. Mum's probably told you that my dad's been in touch.'

Sian looked over at Ruth, who gave her an imperceptible nod. 'Yeah, she mentioned it.' Sian looked back over at Ella. 'Must be confusing for you?'

'I don't know. I don't know my dad. He's a stranger and that's down to him, isn't it?' Ella was clearly struggling to process everything.

Ruth was glad that Ella trusted Sian enough to share how she was feeling. Sian took her wine and sat at the far end of the sofa.

'Look, I know your dad has not been there for you. And that might make you feel upset or angry. And that's completely understandable. So if you didn't want to see him, no one would blame you. But you only have one dad. And the older you get, the more that kind of thing becomes important to you,' Ruth explained calmly.

There was a moment where Ruth's words seemed to hang in the air.

'You miss your dad – Grandad – don't you?' Ella asked, picking up on the subtext of Ruth's words.

'Yeah, a great deal. It's just something to bear in mind, that's all,' Ruth said.

Ella took a long swig of wine and then said, 'Maybe I should just ring him?'

That wasn't what Ruth was expecting her to say. To be honest, she couldn't predict how her daughter was going to react.

'Are you okay ringing him?' Ruth asked, uncertain of how a phone call would leave Ella feeling.

'Maybe if I just spoke to him and let him explain why he wants to see me, then I would know how I felt about it,' Ella shrugged.

*Bloody hell, what a sensible and astute way of looking at it*, Ruth thought. She would never have had that kind of insight when she was Ella's age. It was rare for her to have that kind of insight as she approached fifty, for God's sake. It was her daughter's rational behaviour that made her so proud of Ella.

'That sounds like a very mature way of handling it, Ella,' said Sian as she looked up from the laptop that she had just opened.

'Do you have the number?' Ruth asked.

'Yeah, it's in my phone from years ago. Remember I wanted to call him a few Christmases ago?' Ella reminded Ruth.

'Take the landline up to your room and ring him from there.'

'It's not my room, it's the spare room.'

'It's your room for as long as you want,' Ruth said.

Ever since the traumatic events of last Christmas, Ella had stayed in the spare room and Ruth made it clear she needn't ever leave.

Ella paused and then nodded. 'Yeah, I will. Then I can talk to you guys afterwards.'

Ella went over and gave them both a kiss.

'Love you, darling,' Ruth said, hugging her closely for a few seconds longer than she normally did. Rosie Wright's disappearance had reminded her how precious Ella was. She was so proud of her daughter that sometimes it felt a little overwhelming.

Ella looked at her. 'You okay, Mum?'

'Yeah. Rough day at work,' Ruth said quietly.

Ella grabbed her wine. 'I'll be back down in a bit.' She disappeared upstairs.

For a few moments, Ruth sat back and drank her wine and listened to the music. Her phone buzzed.

Snowdonia News @ Snowdonia News Online

What had happened to that smiling, innocent sixteen-year-old girl that was so full of life a couple of days ago? The sound of children playing in a nearby garden broke her train of thought. The air from outside was still warm and there was the smell of the remnants of someone's barbeque.

'You okay?' Sian asked as she tapped away at the laptop.

'Yeah. Fine,' Ruth said, still deep in thought. 'I just hope this is a good thing for Ella. If Dan lets her down or hurts her, I will castrate him.'

Sian smirked over at her. 'Which wouldn't take long, from what you've told me.'

Ruth gave a snort of laughter as Sian wiggled her little finger to show the size of Dan's manhood. 'Yeah, I forgot I told you that.'

'I've been looking at city breaks in the autumn for us,' Sian said, gesturing to the laptop.

'Great. Something to look forward to.'

'What about Berlin? Third to the sixth of November?' Sian suggested.

Ruth noticeably bristled. She couldn't help it. Sarah, the love of Ruth's life, had gone missing on 5 November 2013; it would be six years this year. There was no reason for Sian to have that date etched on her mind. But rather than help take her mind off the anniversary, she knew it would ruin their time away.

Sian had already clocked the sudden change in Ruth's face and body language.

'That's when Sarah went missing, isn't it? Sorry...' Sian said quietly.

'It's all right. Not the best of weekends,' Ruth said.

'It's fine. We'll just go another weekend,' Sian said, forcing a smile.

The tension in the room was palpable until Ruth's phone vibrated with a message. It was an email from the chief forensic officer.

'Oh, no,' Ruth muttered under breath as she read the update.

Sian gave her a quizzical look. 'What's the matter?'

'DNA test from the lab. The blood we found at the yard today belongs to Rosie Wright.'

'Oh, God, that's horrible,' Sian said.

'I thought it probably did, but I just hoped I was wrong,' Ruth explained.

'What does that mean?'

'There was a lot of blood. From what the chief forensic officer said, we could now be looking for a body.'

–

It was approaching eight o'clock and Nick and Amanda were standing together to one side of the church meeting room. There were around twenty-five other alcoholics chatting and laughing as they drank tea and ate biscuits.

'I'm a bit nervous,' Nick admitted as he finished his coffee.

'Really? But you love the sound of your own voice,' Amanda teased him.

He gave her a sarcastic smile, but as he looked into her big dark brown eyes, he couldn't believe how lucky he had been to have found her. Despite the mess of last Christmas, and the dark secret that they kept between them, he loved her so much that it frightened him sometimes. But there was another part of him that was utterly terrified of all the responsibility that would soon fall at his feet. He was having to act like a grown-up for once.

'I'll speak up so that Junior can hear,' Nick said as he placed his hand gently on Amanda's bump. She was six months pregnant.

'If I sneak out, do you think they'll notice?' Nick said with a grin.

'Go and enjoy your birthday,' she said as she gave him a kiss. She was referring to his AA first birthday. He had been sober for a year – to the day – and he knew that was a miracle.

'Maybe I'll just go and get a biscuit,' Nick said. He really was feeling nervous now.

Amanda gave him a playful shove towards the front of the room. 'Just go and sit down, you knob.'

Walking up to his seat, Nick sat down next to Charlie, who was the group leader. Charlie, in his sixties, was a semi-retired architect who had over twenty years sobriety under his belt. Charlie was known as 'Posh Charlie' because of his public-school accent and fondness for natty suits.

Opening the meeting, Charlie welcomed everyone and thanked Nick for coming to do the main share. It was traditional for AA members to do their first main share on their one-year anniversary. It meant talking to the group about your life for about half an hour. People would touch on their childhood, talk about their first introduction to alcohol, how it progressed to alcoholism, how they got sober and how they continue to stay sober in recovery.

Charlie handed the meeting over to Nick, who took a moment as he looked out at everyone. The room was still and his mouth went dry.

'Hi, my name's Nick, and I'm a very grateful alcoholic.'

'Hi, Nick,' the room responded.

'And I'm feeling a bit nervous about doing my share for the first time. But it's a miracle that I'm sitting here because for a long time I couldn't stay sober for a day, let alone a year.

'As my sponsor said to me, "When you drink, your life will just keep getting worse. When you stop drinking, your life will get better and better." And he was right.

'As many of you know, I've been around the rooms for many years. I've done what I call the old "AA hokey cokey". You know, "In, out, in, out, shake it all about." The AA revolving door. I would come into the rooms completely broken, determined to stop drinking. Then after a few weeks, or even a few months, I'd think to myself, "It wasn't that bad, was it?" I'd always been sober for a few months, so I would reckon I could have a drink and control it. "It will be different this time." Two days later, I'd be drinking vodka for breakfast and thinking, "Oh, bollocks, those bastards in AA were right. It is never going to be different."

'As an idea, it's so simple. If I put alcohol into my system, I have no control over how much I drink and no amount of alcohol will ever be enough until I black out and then pass out. Then I wake up the next day, feel like I'm going to die and so I start again. It's not a lifestyle choice. It's not a matter of willpower. It's an overwhelming, destructive addiction. And this place, these rooms, the friendship, support and love I have found in here, is the reason I am sober today.'

Nick could feel his voice go a little with emotion. He didn't mind. No one would judge him here.

Amanda gave him a smile and a wink.

–

The evening's heat had kept the garage unbearably warm as Ruth wandered through the clutter. Ella and Sian had gone to bed half an hour before, and Ruth made her excuse of watching television for a bit longer.

She stepped in between boxes of books, DVDs and CDs that she still hadn't unpacked since moving her stuff up from South London. An untouched toolbox rested on a nearby shelf. The only time she had ever used it was to get a screwdriver to try to remove a cork from a wine bottle. The lawn mower was the one thing in there that ever got used, and she could smell the warm grass from its collection box.

At the far end, over by the fuse box, Ruth had created a small work area for her own private investigation. She had made sure that the table, chair and the photos and maps on the wall were hidden from the garage doors. She didn't want Sian to see it. And that made her feel guilty, but it helped Ruth deal with the events of 5 November 2013; a day that would be etched in her memory for ever. It was the day that Ruth's partner, and the love of her life, Sarah Goddard, vanished into thin air. Sarah had left their home and boarded the 8:05 a.m. train from Crystal Palace to London Victoria. The CCTV footage showed her getting on the train, as she always did. But she never got off. They examined CCTV at London Victoria station millisecond by millisecond. Every frame of CCTV on the line between Crystal Palace was scoured. Every station scanned.

Sitting down at the rickety wooden table, Ruth put down the cold bottle of beer she had just opened and wiped her cold fingers across the sweat on the back of her neck. Glancing up at the wall, her eyes rested on a photo of Sarah. Glastonbury, June 2008. When Ruth took the photo, they had been watching Amy Winehouse singing 'Back to Black' on the Pyramid Stage. With a straw cowboy hat and boho Seventies sunglasses, Sarah beamed her radiant smile with a cigarette in one hand and a pint of cider in the other. It had been a magical afternoon.

Pushing her teeth together, Ruth felt the pain come as it had done so many times before. And then tears, which she wiped away with the back of her hand. It was so bloody unfair. What would she give for the door to open and Sarah be standing there? Anything. Everything. They had had such a beautiful life together, and not knowing what happened to her was unbearable. She simply disappeared off the face of the planet. She had not moved out. Not quit her job. Not met someone else. Not decided to cut ties with Ruth. Not had a terrible accident. No note, no clues, no contact with friends or relatives.

Two passengers remembered seeing her chatting to a man as commuters were squeezed together in compartments. She now knew that man could well be Jurgen Kessler.

Moving her eyes to the left of the wall, she looked at the CCTV image of Kessler. A German banker, he was tall, blond, blue eyes behind fashionable glasses – archetypically Teutonic.

Next to the CCTV image, a news story from the *Telegraph* newspaper. Last year, police in Germany had linked Kessler to two murders in Berlin. He had disappeared but had been spotted entering the UK on a false passport in August. He then tried to get a job at Bournemouth University before his fake ID was spotted. Since then, Kessler had vanished again.

Ruth knew that the key to Sarah's disappearance was Jurgen Kessler. And she was going to track him down, however long that took.

# CHAPTER 4

*Thirty-five hours*

Ruth had arrived at Llancastell nick at the break of dawn and briefed Superintendent Jones and DCI Drake on the developments in the Rosie Wright case. Now that her disappearance was becoming national news, Jones and Drake were keen to show that North Wales Police were moving heaven and earth to find her. It was the typical kind of political bullshit she had come to expect from Jones. She had seen him cover his arse before.

Ruth had an old sergeant in the Met called Terry 'Uncle' Harrison who she worked with in Battersea CID in the days when Battersea was rough and moody and hadn't been gentrified into South Chelsea. Harrison had a very dim view of senior management in the Metropolitan Police Force. He said he knew how to spot a candidate for the senior ranks early in someone's police career. They would be the officer who was most likely to be tying their shoelaces when a fight broke out during an arrest, or who would have the bus timetable handy so they knew the exact minute to push you underneath one.

DCI Drake was different. He was a copper's copper. Even after the Macpherson report labelled the police force as 'institutionally racist', Ruth knew that change had been slow. As a black officer, DCI Ashley Drake would have had to be smarter and work harder than his white colleagues to rise through the ranks. And in her book, that showed great integrity. Drake was essentially the antithesis to Jones.

Drake's wife, Paula, had been battling breast cancer, and even though Drake never mentioned it, Ruth could see his preoccupation. She made a mental note to ask him about how she was the next time they had a moment alone.

By the time Ruth had sat down to conduct the North Wales Police's press conference, she was already aware that someone had leaked the discovery of the blood at the barn.

BBC Wales @ BBC Wales Breaking News

Sources claim that a significant amount of blood was discovered at Haddon Farm by forensic officers yesterday.

Ruth was fuming but had no reason to think it had come from Llancastell CID. It could have been any of the SOCOs or uniformed officers who had been at the farm yesterday afternoon. The leak could have even originated from the forensic lab. It wouldn't be the first time. Either way, Ruth was angry that the discovery was trending on social media. It should have been information that they had control over.

However, Ruth had to admit that a social media explosion often helped a case like this. Rosie's face was all over the Internet. A Twitter campaign of *#FindRosie* had gone viral with over a million likes and retweets. A Facebook page had been set up by school friends.

Looking out at the assembled journalists, Ruth took a moment. Kerry Mahoney, the chief corporate communications officer for North Wales Police, who had come up from the main press office in Colwyn Bay, sat next to her. Ruth had met her before and had her down as a patronising bitch. Mahoney came from the new school of thought that believed the media needed to be controlled and even manipulated. Mahoney believed in media blackouts and vague press releases. In contrast, Ruth believed this new policy ignored two key reasons why they should keep the media fully informed and up to date. First, the public had a right to know what was happening in their communities, especially if there was any threat to their safety. Second, it was a fact that the police stood a better chance of catching criminals if they used the media to appeal for witnesses.

On the table in front of Ruth were several small tape recorders and microphones. *Here we go*, she thought. It didn't seem that long ago she was doing a press conference in the hunt for Andrew Gates at Christmas. The thought of that case made her shudder.

'Good afternoon, I'm Detective Inspector Ruth Hunter and I am the senior investigating officer for the investigation into the disappearance of Rosie Wright. Beside me is Kerry Mahoney, our chief corporate communications officer. This press conference is to update you on the case and appeal to the public for any information regarding Rosie's disappearance on Monday evening between six p.m. and nine p.m. Rosie's family are understandably very worried, and we are looking for any information that can help us bring Rosie back home safely.

'At this stage in the investigation, we know that Rosie was with friends on a farm in Capelulo. She was last seen at around eight p.m. The area where she went missing is very quiet, so if you saw anything out of the ordinary, however insignificant you think it might be, please contact us so we can come and talk to you. I have a few minutes to take some questions.'

'Can you confirm that a significant amount of blood was found at the farm yesterday?' a reporter asked from the front row.

*Bloody great! I don't want to have to talk about this now. Nor do I want anyone to think that this is now a murder case!*

'All I am prepared to say is that there is a thorough forensic examination taking place of Haddon Farm. If there is anything significant, then we will let you know,' Ruth explained. She wanted to make sure that the media continued to report this as a missing teenager story.

'If a significant amount of blood was found, are you now treating Rosie's disappearance as a possible murder?' asked another reporter.

*For fuck's sake! Did you not just hear me? Let's wrap this up, I've got a teenager to find*, Ruth thought.

'I can only reiterate what I've already told you. As far as we are concerned, Rosie Wright is missing and we are doing everything in our power to find her and bring her home safely,' Ruth said, but she knew she sounded a little irritated.

'From the forensic investigation so far, do you think that Rosie is still alive?' a television reporter shouted from the back of the room.

Ruth couldn't help but glare at him for a second. 'Right, thank you, everyone. No more questions.'

As Ruth stood and gathered up her files, she noticed Mahoney giving her a slightly conceited look. She could see that Ruth was a bit rattled and she was judging her.

*Oh, fuck off, you smug bitch! Go and write a press release. I've got a proper job to do.*

Thirty minutes later, Ruth was back in her office ploughing through paperwork so she could get out and continue the search for Rosie. Checking her watch, she could see that Rosie had been missing for over thirty-six hours. They still had no concrete leads, and it was frustrating her.

Losing concentration on the job in hand, Ruth ran theories around her head. Rosie Wright was a well-adjusted teenager from a seemingly normal home. Haddon Farm was the end of the road. Rosie hadn't been abducted from a dark city street or walking home from school. Therefore, it wasn't a random abduction. Rosie Wright had been targeted by someone who had contact with her, or had seen her, prior to Monday night.

A tweet flashed up on her phone from the Media Team at St Asaph: *ITV Wales Breaking News – North Wales Police appeal in search for missing teenager Rosie, aged sixteen.* At least the press conference was generating the right kind of publicity.

Nick came into her office and handed her a coffee. 'Thought you could do with this, boss.'

'Cheers. Anyone spoken to the FLO?' she asked. It had been the FLO's job to break the news to Jason and Kathy Wright that Rosie's blood had been found at the farm. She couldn't imagine how terrified they must have felt hearing that news.

'The FLO said that Kathy Wright went to bits. They've had a GP out to give her something to help her sleep. Jason Wright was very quiet and uncommunicative,' Nick explained.

*Uncommunicative?* Ruth thought. There was something about Jason Wright that just didn't sit right with her. Did his erratic behaviour suggest that he was hiding something?

'I'll go and see them this afternoon,' Ruth said.

'Oh, and we've found the press leak. One of the SOCOs admitted she had told her brother about the blood and he happens to be a journalist,' Nick said.

'I hope Travis gives her a proper bollocking!' Ruth growled, but then her attention was drawn to the screen on the wall of CID, which was showing the BBC News channel.

Ruth got up and took two steps out to watch the news feed. It was the tail end of the morning news, and the male and female anchors sat together on a red sofa. The photo of Rosie Wright appeared behind them on a screen.

'*The search for missing teenager Rosie Wright continues in North Wales today,*' the male anchor said solemnly.

A map of North Wales appeared on the screen with the location of the farm circled.

'*Rosie was with friends when she went missing from the Cape-lulo area of Snowdonia some time on Monday night,*' the female anchor continued. '*Police will resume their search of the local area this morning with the help of dog teams and helicopters with thermal imaging equipment. Local volunteers have been helping police in their search for Rosie, who has been described as a happy and fun-loving teenager by friends and family. In a press conference earlier today, the police dismissed reports that a significant amount of blood had been found at the scene and stressed that they are continuing to treat this as a missing persons inquiry.'*

Sian looked over at Ruth and approached.

'Nothing of you from the press conference? You didn't get your fifteen minutes then?' Sian teased her.

'Thank God. I look like shit,'

'Not from where I'm standing,' Sian replied flirtatiously under her breath.

Ruth felt a twinge of guilt as Sian smiled at her. There was still an emotional hangover from spending time thinking about and mourning Sarah the previous night.

Merringer arrived with printed pages. 'Boss, routine PNC check on the family. It seems that Gareth Wright has several convictions for possession.'

Ruth nodded. 'Maybe Gareth supplied his sister and her friends with those pills?'

'I also did the usual check of the Sex Offenders Register. There is a Martin Hancock that lives close to Capelulo. Aged forty. Suspended two-year sentence for downloading and possession of indecent images. Lives on his own,' Merringer explained.

Ruth nodded and glanced over at Sian. 'Sian, can you go and talk to this Martin Hancock? He's on the register and lives locally. And take DC French.'

# CHAPTER 5

*Forty hours*

Ruth was feeling the time pressure of the case as she and Nick arrived at Haddon Farm. There were still no solid leads and they were hurtling towards the dreaded forty-eight-hour mark. She knew that after that point, the team at CID Llancastell would begin to lose hope of finding Rosie alive.

Where the bloody hell was she?

The area was still and virtually deserted except for two uniformed officers who were there to prevent the rubber-neckers from trampling on the crime scene. The flowers, candles and messages had doubled since the last time Ruth had been there.

In the distance, a police search adviser, Polsa, had organised uniformed officers to conduct a fingertip search of the dark woodland. The stillness was broken by the deep bark of a German shepherd search dog with his handler.

Before work that morning, Ruth had googled Capelulo and looked at the map. Lying close to the north-western tip of mainland Wales, it was just south of the massive headland called the Great Orme. The word *orme* was said to have had a Scandinavian origin. The story went that a Viking raiding party saw the rock rearing up from the mist in front of their longboat and, mistaking it for a serpent, they fled in terror.

Ruth wanted to revisit the area to see where Rosie had gone missing from. She wanted to walk the scene so it was clear in her head. Were they missing something? At the moment, they were struggling to come up with any decent hypothesis for what had happened to Rosie. The blood in the yard suggested she had been attacked. But then what? Had someone dragged her from the farm and taken her away? How? By car? And why? They had none of the key ingredients – motive, means and opportunity. All they knew was that it wasn't a random attack. So, who had contacted or had seen Rosie in recent days or even weeks?

Ruth closed her eyes for a moment, letting the air freshen her face. She found that sometimes, in the quiet of a crime scene, she could think and feel clearly what might have happened.

*Come on, Rosie. Where are you? We're running out of time. What happened to you?*

Standing in the yard by the boarded-up farm sheds, Ruth looked down at the ground and the bloodstains that were now covered and numbered with yellow plastic forensic tags. Some of the blood-soaked straw had been scattered by the wind. Had Rosie struggled and been stabbed before being bundled into a car? If that had happened, there would have been some spots of blood. But here they had pints. Why?

Ruth looked over at the barn. On the other side, the girls had been out of sight as they sat by the fire pit, drinking, dancing and giggling with music blaring. They wouldn't have seen or heard a thing.

Turning back, Ruth looked over the meadows and the river that snaked through them in the distance. She brought her thoughts back to the long steel gate and the track that led away up through the fields. How did anyone take Rosie from the farm without being seen? None of it seemed to fit together into a coherent theory.

Walking back through the barn, the sound of the wind was amplified by the wood of the roof. In several places, the wind whistled through the gaps in the timber. The smell of hay was strong, and now there was also the faint scent of the chemicals the SOCOs had used out in the yard.

Emerging from the barn, Ruth looked down at the fire pit where the girls had congregated on Monday evening. The logs were black. A loud noise took her attention into the sky as two Canada geese flapped overhead.

She imagined Emma and her friends. The music, the drinking and the howls of laughter. Teenage girls hadn't changed that much since she was young. She would have been their age in 1985. It would have been Duran Duran or Wham. And it would have been Battersea Park or down by the river at Wandsworth. Cider, music and dancing. Pink ra-ra skirts, *Choose Life*, lace in their hair just like Madonna. *Like a virgin…*

A gust of wind blew a tousle of her hair as she came back to the present. If Rosie had been attacked in the yard, her friends would have been oblivious. It was too far away. Peering from where she stood, the track through the fields was clearly visible. Could they have missed a car coming down to the yard? It was still somewhat light at around eight o'clock. She wasn't sure.

The sound of footsteps on the grass approached.

'Penny for them, boss,' Nick said, looking around.

'Whoever attacked and took Rosie would have taken a huge risk of being seen if they had come down the track? Why would they do that?'

Nick looked over from where they stood. 'A car coming down there would have been visible for a while.'

'So, they either took that risk, or they came and left from a different direction,' Ruth said.

'How? There's no other way of getting a vehicle down here. Even a four-by-four would struggle across those fields.' Nick said.

'Tractor or quad bike?' Ruth suggested.

'Maybe? Still noisy and visible.' Nick said.

'And they had an unconscious or dead body with them.'

'How tall is Kathy Wright roughly?'

'Short. Five foot two, five foot three.'

'I've seen the photos on the fridge. Rosie was about the same height and probably a stone lighter. She can't have been more than six or seven stone.'

'So, she could have been carried away, at least for a while.'

The blue-and-white police tape rustled noisily in the wind as Ruth gazed around at the landscape.

Then she spotted something that sparked an idea. 'The river?'

Nick followed her gaze. The river was about a third of a mile from where they stood.

Did someone take her to the river and escape that way?

'Actually, you're right. I know someone who used to take a canoe on the Afon Gyrach.'

'Let's see how long it takes to walk there,' Ruth said as she pulled out her phone and started the timer and began to make her way to the river.

'Carrying Rosie would slow you down.'

'If you're a big bloke, carrying six stone over your shoulder isn't going to slow you down that much,' Ruth said as she marched onwards.

Nick glanced back at the barn and the farm buildings. 'If you walked in a straight line, the girls' view is blocked by the barn all the way.'

Ruth met his glance. Were they on to something? Or was this just an elaborate distraction? They couldn't afford distractions and time was running out for Rosie.

As the lowlands dropped and then dipped sharply at the river's edge, Ruth stopped the timer on her phone. 'Five minutes, and we weren't racing. It's not long to keep out of sight if you have a boat waiting.'

About twenty yards to their left, Nick spotted a small area of sand and pebbles where the river bent right. It was essentially a tiny beach. He jumped down and inspected the ground.

'What is it?' Ruth could see that Nick had found something.

'Drag marks. Someone has pulled a boat onto this beach. You can still see the marks in the sand.'

'Do we really think that someone attacked Rosie in the barn and then took her away on a boat down the river?' Ruth wasn't sure that this hypothesis felt right.

Nick shrugged. 'It would explain why no one saw anyone arriving or leaving. It would explain why house-to-house has thrown up nothing and why Traffic haven't found any vehicles leaving the area at that time.'

It was a good point, Ruth thought as she looked down at her phone. 'We need SOCO down here now before it rains and those drags marks are washed away.'

—

Glancing around at the immaculate front garden, Sian and DC French made their way up the neatly paved steps to Bluebell Cottage, where convicted sex offender Martin Hancock lived.

On the way there, Sian mulled over a dream she had had the previous night. There were flashes of it still in her mind. She couldn't recall much, but she did remember that in it Ruth had been in bed with her previous girlfriend Sarah. It wasn't surprising after their conversation about the dates in November and going to Berlin. It was always going to be like that. It was worse than Sarah being dead because there was always the remote possibility of her being alive somewhere. What the hell would they do if she was alive? What would *she* do if Sarah just turned up on the doorstep one day? She knew all that when she agreed to move in with Ruth. However, sometimes it did make her question if she had done the right thing.

Pushing those thoughts to one side. Sian found herself surprised at the pristine condition of the garden and cottage. Hanging baskets were full of the tumbling purples and pinks of fuchsias. As she rang the doorbell, Sian could hear classical music from inside the house. A moment later, the door opened and a man in his forties looked at her. He was greying, hand-some and took care of himself. He was dressed in a blue shirt and jeans.

'Mr Hancock?' Sian asked. She knew that sex offenders came in all shapes and sizes, but even she was surprised by how she found Hancock. 'I'm DC Hockney, and this is my colleague

DC French. We're from Llancastell CID,' she said, raising her warrant card.

'I thought it wouldn't be long before you knocked on my door,' Hancock said with virtually no hint of annoyance. 'Come in, please.'

Hancock showed Sian and French in. The house smelt of coffee and expensive aftershave. Inside, the cottage was decorated in a shabby chic style with fashionable cushions in all shades of blue. Like the outside, it was immaculate. A copy of that day's *Mirror* newspaper lay on a nearby desk with the headline: *Police Intensify Search for Rosie* and a photograph of Rosie.

'Would you like coffee?' Hancock asked.

'No, thank you. Just a few questions to help us with an ongoing missing persons inquiry,' Sian explained.

*My gaydar tells me that a well-groomed man, living on his own with such attention to home furnishings is unlikely to be heterosexual,* Sian thought.

Hancock gestured them to sit on the Tiffany-blue sofa in the living room. 'Please, sit down.'

'Thank you,' French said.

Sian and French took a seat next to each other as Hancock sat opposite them on another pristine matching sofa. It was a pleasant change from some of the rat-infested drug houses Sian had attended in recent weeks.

'I'm guessing that it's about the missing girl? Rosie, isn't it?' Hancock asked.

'Yes, Rosie Wright. Did you know her?' Sian asked. Hancock certainly wasn't skirting the issue.

'Not really. I knew her by sight, that's all,' Hancock said. 'Pretty girl. It's been all over the news. Poor family.' Sian wasn't sure that she was buying his compassion. It felt a little phoney.

'Could you tell me where you were between six and nine on Monday evening?' French asked.

'I was here,' Hancock explained.

'Can anyone confirm that?' French asked, looking down at his notepad and clicking his pen.

'No, I'm afraid not. There was an opera on BBC Four and I stayed in to watch that,' Hancock explained.

*Watching opera? That was an alibi first.*

'Did you see anyone or speak to anyone on the phone?' Sian said.

Hancock shook his head and gave a half-smile. 'Not a soul. Obviously, it would be better for me if I had an alibi, but I just don't.'

*It's not something to smile about, you prick. A teenage girl has gone missing*, Sian thought to herself.

'And if I talk to your neighbours, they'll confirm what you told us?' Sian asked.

'I've no idea. One side are geriatric and keep themselves to themselves. The other side are homophobic and seem to think that they're going to catch AIDS by making eye contact with me.'

'Okay. Thank you,' French said, putting away his pen and notebook.

'You do know that I was convicted of possessing photos of boys, well, young men actually. I have no interest in teenage girls. It's just not my thing,' Hancock explained with a lack of emotion that Sian found chilling. The full details of Hancock's conviction hadn't come through yet, so this *was* new information, but it matched her deductions.

Sian got up to go. 'We might need to talk to you again at some point, Mr Hancock.'

'I'll be here. All day, every day. I've been out of work for six months. Not much call for a psychotherapist with a conviction for possession of indecent images.'

Hancock seemed almost bitter about the fact that he couldn't get work and showed no hint of remorse. His whole manner was a little creepy.

'Where did you used to work?' Sian asked.

'Rhoswen Prison. Actually, I was a counsellor on the Young Offenders wing,' Hancock explained.

Sian remembered that Kathy Wright was a prison officer at HMP Rhoswen. It might well be a coincidence, but she was going to ask.

'So you knew Kathy Wright, Rosie's mother, then?' Sian said as she and French shared a look.

'Not really. I tried not to interact with her, if I'm honest,' Hancock said, his eyes widening at the mention of the name.

'Why?' Sian was now intrigued by his reaction.

'People were scared of Kathy Wright. Nasty little woman. Even the top cons gave her a wide berth,' Hancock explained.

### Forty-two hours

By the time Ruth and Nick had arrived at the Wrights' home, a legion of photographers and other members of the national press had begun to camp out. Vans with satellite dishes, journalists talking to cameras, and a whole battalion of telephoto zoom lenses all trained on the cottage. Ruth knew that Rosie's disappearance was big news, but even she was surprised by the extent of the media coverage.

Jason Wright stood in the garden surrounded by about a dozen locals who were all armed with leaflets carrying Rosie's photo. As Jason approached them, he gave Ruth a withering look and said, 'I suppose I should give you one of these.' He handed her one of the leaflets.

'We are doing everything we can to find Rosie, Mr Wright.' Ruth tried to make eye contact but Jason had already turned away. Did he just have a problem with the police or was he avoiding her for a darker reason?

'We'll look for her ourselves,' Jason growled as he went back to the growing group of locals and dogs that were about to mount a second search of the area.

He projected the image of a terrified father searching for his daughter, but Ruth's instinct told her that Jason Wright knew more than he was saying.

Ruth gazed down at the leaflet. It had been printed with a colour photo of Rosie and read:

Help us find Rosie Wright.

We are appealing for the public's help in finding missing teenager Rosie Wright, aged sixteen years. Rosie went missing on Monday evening from the Capelulo area.

As they headed towards the front door, Ruth handed the leaflet to Nick.

'I'm still not convinced about the father,' Ruth said quietly.

'Yeah, he seems to be avoiding us like the plague,' Nick said.

The FLO, PC Laura Bennett, let them in and they came purposefully into the living room where Kathy was sitting, looking distraught.

'She said you've found blood!' Kathy exclaimed, pointing at PC Bennett with panic in her voice. 'But no one will tell me anything.'

Ruth sat down opposite her. 'Kathy, we have found some blood up by the yard...'

'But is it Rosie's? Do you know if it's my Rosie's?' Kathy garbled desperately. Her eyes darted around as she tried to process the news.

'Yes. We have tested it and Forensics have confirmed it is your daughter's blood,' Ruth said gently.

'Oh, no...' Kathy sobbed as her hands shook. 'Oh, please God... no...'

'We are doing everything we can to find Rosie and get her back safely,' Ruth explained gently.

Kathy wiped the tears from her face as she took a deep breath. 'But... someone's hurt her. Someone's hurt Rosie—'

'It doesn't change anything.' Ruth said firmly. 'And we're doing everything we can to find her.'

Ruth's frustration was growing. They were heading towards the forty-eight-hour mark and they had no viable leads. The extensive search of the farm and the surrounding area had given them nothing. The drag marks from the riverbank had proved inconclusive. It really did seem that Rosie Wright had vanished into thin air.

Knowing that three-quarters of female murders were carried out by partners, family members or someone the victim knew, Ruth had to concentrate the investigation close to home. And that was difficult with everyone so raw with emotion.

'Kathy, we would like you to do a press conference, if you think you're up to it? It can be very powerful,' Ruth said.

'Yeah, of course. We'll do anything you think will help,' Kathy said, nodding as she dabbed her eyes and sniffed.

'We would need Jason to be with you,' Ruth explained to her.

'He's organised for locals to help the police to search again,' Kathy said quietly.

At that moment, a young man came into the room. Gareth Wright was tall, skinny and wearing a grey tracksuit. He looked clean and smelt of aftershave.

When he saw Ruth and Nick, he stopped dead and eyed them suspiciously. He looked back at the door, clearly regretting having come in.

'You must be Gareth? Is that right?' Ruth asked, knowing full well who he was.

'Come and have a seat next to your mum, please, Gareth,' Nick said in a way that implied he had no choice.

Gareth glared at them. 'What you talking to us for? Why aren't you out there looking for Rosie?'

'Please, Gareth. Just have a seat for a moment?' Ruth said gently. 'We know how difficult this must be for you.'

Gareth sat on the sofa next to his mum. She smiled at him and patted him on the shoulder reassuringly, as if he was still at primary school.

*Mummy's boy*, Ruth thought instantly.

'Can I get anyone a tea or coffee?' Kathy asked.

Ruth was going to suggest that the FLO could do that but she was outside having a ciggie. Plus, it would allow them to talk to Gareth on his own.

'Two teas. White. No sugar, please, Kathy. Ta,' Ruth said with a kind smile. She wondered how long it would take Kathy to sort out the tea in her confused state.

There was an awkward moment once Kathy had left as Gareth fidgeted nervously, staring at the floor.

'You must be very worried about your sister, Gareth?' Ruth asked.

'Yeah, of course,' Gareth mumbled with a frown.

'Can you think of anyone that would have wanted to harm Rosie?' Nick asked.

'No,' Gareth responded as if that was a ridiculous question.

'Must be hard on your mum and dad too. They must be very upset?' Ruth said.

Gareth didn't respond and just nodded while continuing to look down.

'Your mum and Rosie must be very close,' Ruth asked.

Gareth grunted, 'Yeah, they are.'

'What about your dad? Do you get on all right with your dad?' Nick asked.

'No. No one gets on with him.' Gareth huffed and sat back on the sofa. 'I'll go and help Mum with the teas.'

Ruth gestured for him to stay seated and said, 'I'm sure she'll be fine. Why does no one get on with your dad?'

'He's never really here. He's just... I dunno... moody,' Gareth explained.

'Does Rosie get on with your dad?' Ruth asked.

'No.' Gareth was definite about that. 'No way.'

'Did they row?' Nick asked.

'Yeah. All the time. She said she couldn't wait to go to college and move out. Then she would never have to see him again.'

'I know you've already given us a statement, but where were you on Monday evening?'

'Just out. Driving around with mates. We went to a pub out by Corwen for a bit,' Gareth said. 'Then I went back to my place.'

'Do you know which pub?'

'The Ship or something. I'm not sure.'

'And the pub will confirm that you were there?' Nick asked.

'Yeah, course. Why you asking me all this? I didn't have nothing to do with Rosie going missing, did I?'

'Just one more thing, Gareth. I see you've had some dealings with the police in the past?' Ruth said.

'Just a bit of weed. Everyone does it round here.'

'We found a bag of what looked like ecstasy tablets up at the barn. We think that Rosie and her friends planned to take them on Monday night. Do you know where they might have got them?'

'Me? No, nothing to do with me. Pills are not my thing. Some of them are only fifteen! I wouldn't be getting involved in that.'

At that moment, Kathy came back in with a tray of teas and some biscuits. She put them down on the table with a clatter. Ruth noticed that her hands were shaking a little. Must be the growing anxiety. She knew how that felt from when Ella had gone missing at Christmas. It was a living hell.

Ruth smiled over at Kathy and said, 'I'd like to take a look at Rosie's bedroom. It might give us some clues.'

Kathy nodded and pointed to the stairs. 'It's the bedroom straight over at the top of the stairs.'

'Thank you,' Ruth said as she and Nick got up and began to walk up the stairs. The wood creaked a little underfoot. Ruth looked at some holiday photographs that had been enlarged, framed and hung on the wall.

'What do you think?' Nick asked in a hushed voice, gesturing downstairs.

'He's a bit of a wanker but I don't think he's got anything to do with Rosie's disappearance,' Ruth whispered back.

'I got the feeling he's hiding something,' Nick said as they put on their purple latex forensic gloves and went into Rosie's bedroom.

Ruth nodded. 'There's something off about him. But I don't know what he's not telling us.'

Rosie's bedroom was a little untidy, with clothes and schoolbooks strewn on the dark red rug by the bed. Some of the things were pink and girly and Ruth assumed still there from when Rosie was younger. The smell of deodorant and sweet perfume still lingered. Used mugs, bowls and empty cans of drink were lined up on her desk.

As Ruth glanced around for clues as to what had happened to Rosie, there was a stillness that was absolute. No sound, no breeze, nothing. An eerie feeling that this was a room that was now static and lifeless like a photograph. For some reason, Ruth felt a chill down her back, as if she instinctively knew that Rosie wasn't ever coming back to this room. It was in these moments that the enormity of the job got to her. A victim's room, frozen in time. Clothes that would never be worn, books never read, a bed never slept in again. Ruth's world was full of tragic rooms like this.

Nick crossed the room to look at the scattered papers and books on her desk as Ruth continued to survey the room from the doorway. What had happened to Rosie? She had been attacked by someone at the farm. They had taken her from there, dead or alive. Nothing pointed to it being a random attack. So, who wanted to harm Rosie Wright? A row with a parent or sibling that got out of hand? Someone she had met online who had groomed her? Neighbours or a local who had watched her from a distance before making their move?

Moving across the carpet, Ruth went over to the pine wardrobe. She opened it and saw a couple of dresses, cardigans and coats hanging in a neat row.

Ruth's eye was drawn to a long rainbow-coloured flag that had been stuck to the inside door of the wardrobe. Above that, a rainbow heart sticker that had the letters *LGBT* in the middle.

Nick came over and looked at what Ruth had found. 'She's gay?'

Ruth nodded. 'Looks that way.'

She didn't know if that had any bearing on why Rosie had disappeared, but if Rosie had been in any kind of relationship, it was likely they were looking for a girl rather than a boy.

# CHAPTER 6

*Forty-four hours*

'We just don't have any solid leads,' Ruth admitted as she and Drake marched along the corridor from his office.

'Nothing? Anything from the press conference?' Drake asked.

'Lots of possible sightings, suspicious neighbours and the usual cranks. None of it is viable. And it's wasting time,' Ruth explained as they walked briskly around the corner.

'That's the risk we take with a press conference,' Drake said.

'We know she was taken from the farm, that she was injured or worse…' Ruth said. She could feel herself getting increasingly exasperated.

'How was she taken?' Drake asked.

'We don't know. There are vehicle tracks all over the road to the farm. We're looking at the possibility that she was taken away along the river,' Ruth said.

'What about the parents?'

'Mum, Kathy, is in bits. Not sure about the dad. I think he's hiding something, but his alibi at the pub checks out,' Ruth explained.

'Problem is that whoever took her could be anywhere by now,' Drake said darkly.

Ruth looked up to see the duty sergeant coming the other way. He was clearly looking for her.

'Ma'am. An Emma Haddon and her father are downstairs. They want to talk to you so I put them in Interview Room One,' the duty sergeant explained.

'Thank you,' Ruth said as she stopped at the stairwell to go downstairs.

Drake looked at her. 'My instinct is that we focus on her life close to home. Family, friends, college. I really don't think that Rosie Wright was snatched by a total stranger. And someone in her life knows something they're not telling us.'

–

Ten minutes later, Ruth entered the interview room, where Emma and Steven Haddon were already sitting waiting for her. Emma glanced up as Ruth came over and immediately seemed worried. Her face was scrubbed of make-up. She looked very young and very tired.

'Hi there. I understand you wanted a word?' Ruth said as she sat down and gave them a benign smile across the table.

Emma, whose leg was jigging, looked up at her dad for guidance.

'Emma has a couple of things that she needs to tell you about Rosie. She didn't tell you last time because she had promised not to. But she knows this is very serious, so I told her to come and talk to you,' Steven explained. 'She would like to talk to you alone, if that's okay?'

Ruth nodded. 'If it's an informal chat, that's fine.' Anything else would require an appropriate adult.

Steven went to the door and gave Emma a supportive nod before leaving.

Ruth gave Emma a kind smile across the table. 'Emma, you don't need to worry. But I do want you tell me anything you know about Rosie and her life. Even if she asked you not to. We all want to find Rosie and get her back safely, don't we?'

Emma nodded as she took a breath. 'Yeah. Sorry…'

'You don't need to be sorry, Emma. You're Rosie's friend. And good friends sometimes keep secrets. But this is different now, so you need to tell me everything. Is that okay?'

Emma looked up at her for a moment. 'Rosie had met someone online that she was talking to. Hayley.'

*Now we're getting somewhere*, Ruth thought. Instinctively, it felt important.

'Do you know who she was, where she was from?' Ruth asked.

Emma shook her head and said, 'I think Rosie said Rhyl. Rosie really liked her.'

'Rosie was gay, wasn't she?'

Emma frowned. 'How do you know that?'

'So, was this a romantic thing?'

'I think so. They were talking and they definitely liked each other,' Emma explained.

'Anything else? Surname, age?'

'I think she was a couple of years older because she could drive. And Rosie said that she was going to come up to meet us at the farm on Monday,' Emma explained.

Ruth's ears pricked up.

*That's the first thing we've heard that sounds like a lead*, she thought.

'Hayley, the girl that Rosie had met online was going to come and meet you all on Monday night at the farm?' Ruth repeated back to clarify. There was now a link between Rosie's online 'friend' and Monday night.

'Yeah, it was like this big surprise. Rosie was really excited. Except Hayley was meant to be there by seven, but she didn't turn up. Rosie thought she had got lost because we were in the middle of nowhere. When Rosie went off, she was trying to phone Hayley to see where she was.'

'And that was the last time you saw her?'

'Yeah...' The reality of the thought appeared to hit Emma and she began to choke up.

'And that was about eight o'clock?' Ruth asked in a hushed voice.

'Yeah. About then…' Emma started to cry and wiped a tear from her eye. 'I'm really sorry. I should have said something before.'

'Don't worry, Emma. This is really useful. Any idea what site they met on?' Ruth asked.

'I think it was Billie Eilish's fan site, but I'm not sure?'

'Did Rosie's mum and dad know she was gay?'

'No. No way. God, they would have gone mad. They're both homophobic racists.' Emma sneered as she said it.

'So, when you went to pick up Rosie from her house at six there was no mention to her mum that she was meeting anyone?'

'Her mum?' Emma asked with a frown.

'Kathy Wright said the last time she saw Rosie was when you came to pick her up from her house at six?' Ruth was now confused but getting the distinct feeling that Kathy Wright had been lying to them.

'No. Her mum wasn't there. She must have been out because her car wasn't there either.' Emma paused. 'But it's not a big surprise that she said so.'

'Sorry? What's not a big surprise, Emma?'

'That woman lies about everything,' Emma explained disapprovingly.

*Forty-five hours*

It was early afternoon by the time Nick got to Llancastell Sixth Form College. Built originally in the Sixties as a technology college, the buildings at the front of the site looked like they needed revamping.

While Nick had stayed at Ysgol Dinas Padog and done his A levels in their sixth form, some of his mates had gone off to Llancastell Sixth Form College. He envied them as it was far more laid back than being at school, and students only had to be on site when they had classes. They spent the rest of the time smoking weed or going to the pub.

Nick had found his way up to the politics department where he met George Xavier, head of politics and Rosie's form tutor. The bright classroom was on the first floor and had high ceilings. Walls were decorated with coloured world maps and political posters from history – Nazi propaganda, Soviet Cold War, all the way through to Brexit.

Xavier was in his mid-twenties, olive-skinned with fashionable black hair and a beard. Nick imagined Xavier had lots of admirers within the female population of the college.

'I can't believe it. Doesn't feel real, you know?' Xavier took a breath. He was clearly feeling emotional about Rosie's disappearance.

'No...' Nick nodded sympathetically, but he was keen to get the information he needed as quickly as possible. He glanced up at the large wall clock. Its second hand clicked rhythmically as if to emphasise the passing of time and the growing tension that came with it.

'A lot of students that knew Rosie haven't come in today. It's understandable. Some of them have gone over to Capelulo to help with the search,' Xavier explained.

'Of course. How would you describe Rosie?' Nick asked, getting out his pen and notepad.

'Very intelligent, earnest, funny. She would do anything for anyone. She was... lovely,' Xavier said sadly.

'What about recently? How did she seem at the end of last week?' Nick asked.

Xavier took a moment and sat forward in his chair. 'Actually, she wasn't herself in recent weeks. She seemed worried or preoccupied about something.'

'Do you know why?' Nick asked.

'No. I asked her, but she said it was nothing. I guessed it was something to do with home,' Xavier said.

'What makes you think that?'

'I assume you've met Rosie's parents?'

'Yes.'

Xavier clearly thought it prudent not to take his comment too far. 'I don't think she was happy at home.'

'Why do you say that?' Nick asked.

*Come on, mate. I haven't got time for you to be vague today!* Nick thought.

'Just some things she would say in form time. You can't help overhearing what students are talking about. Her relationship with her brother, I forget his name—'

'Gareth.'

'Gareth. Yes. I think it was a big problem. I don't know what he was getting himself into, but it didn't sound good.'

'What do you mean when you say "it didn't sound good"?' Nick asked. Was there more to this?

'I just overheard Rosie telling her friends that her brother was going to end up going to prison or get killed. She said he was a "nasty little chav" and she wanted nothing to do with him,' Xavier explained.

–

By the time Ruth got back to her desk, she had several emails from the media office down in St Asaph. That morning's national newspapers and television stations were dominated by the search for Rosie.

Ruth was aware that they still needed to have a more in-depth interview with Jason Wright, but he was leading the volunteers. It would be difficult to prise him away from that to ask him some difficult questions without creating a shitstorm. But they also didn't have time to tread on eggshells. She could feel the tension in her stomach.

Ruth's phone vibrated and she looked at the latest news on Twitter:

BBC Wales @ BBC Wales Breaking News

> More than 150 family and friends of missing Rosie
> Wright are taking part in a second mass search of
> local countryside in North Wales two days after she
> vanished #FindRosie

Ruth had asked French to use Traffic and ANPR, Automatic Number Plate Recognition, to see if he could find out where Kathy Wright had been late on Monday afternoon. It might give them a clue as to why she had lied and would give them the upper hand when they confronted her about her deception.

Ruth looked up to see Sian approaching. They shared a smile.

'What happened with Martin Hancock?' Ruth asked.

'He doesn't have an alibi. He was watching opera on BBC Four,' Sian said, raising an eyebrow.

'Was he now? What do you think?'

'Instinct says he's not involved. He got nicked for having photos of teenage boys. I'd put him on the back burner for the minute,' Sian explained.

It made Ruth's life so much easier that Sian was a good copper.

'Thanks, Sian.'

'There was something, boss. Hancock used to work with Kathy Wright at HMP Rhoswen.'

'Right. Did he know her?' Ruth asked, intrigued by the connection.

'Not really. He said prisoners were scared of her and that she was "a nasty little woman".'

Ruth frowned. 'Doesn't sound like the Kathy Wright I've met.'

'This is the opinion of an effete paedophile, so I wouldn't give it too much thought,' Sian said.

'Effete?' Ruth said teasingly.

'Good word, "effete".' Sian grinned back.

'Thanks, Sian,' Ruth said as Sian turned to go back to her desk.

Wandering over to where Merringer was working at a computer, Ruth could see that he was trawling through CCTV footage.

'Luke, what have we got?' she asked.

'In her statement, Kathy Wright told us that she had been to the Tesco on the Llancastell industrial estate prior to returning home last Monday. I got the CCTV from the supermarket sent over. And look who we find sitting in the car park at six p.m. when she was said she was at home.'

Ruth could see Kathy Wright's black Ford Focus parked. Squinting a little, she could see a figure sitting in the driver's seat. It was definitely a woman. But there was also someone in the passenger seat.

'She wasn't alone, boss,' Luke said.

'Yeah. Can we get a look at who that is?' Ruth asked, wondering about the nature of Kathy Wright's clandestine meeting and why it meant she needed to lie in her statement.

'Here we go,' Merringer said, playing the footage forward a few minutes. 'Unfortunately, he's wearing sunglasses and the quality isn't great.'

The man wearing the sunglasses was short and stocky. On the CCTV footage, he got out of the car and then disappeared out of the camera's range.

'What about getting into the car?' Ruth asked.

'Nope. This van blocks the camera for that.'

'I don't suppose we get to see what car he was driving?'

'No, boss. He wanders this way towards more shops and then he's out of range of the CCTV.'

'I think I might need to pay Kathy Wright a visit,' Ruth said.

# CHAPTER 7

*Forty-seven hours*

Winding down the window, Ruth sucked on her cigarette for a second and blew out the smoke in a long plume that was then violently thrashed away by the wind rushing past the car.

In terms of percentages, she knew that Rosie Wright's disappearance was now likely to be a murder case. That didn't mean she had given up hope of finding Rosie alive. However, there had been no sightings, nothing significant found on social media and no suspicious activity on Rosie's phone. With no solid leads and time marching on, the statistical chances of them finding Rosie alive were diminishing with every hour that passed. And they only had one hour left before the dreaded forty-eight-hour mark and all the dark implications of the data that came with it. Ruth felt uneasy.

Instinct told her to keep the investigation close to home. The likelihood of a random stranger snatching Rosie from the farm was incredibly remote.

Something else occurred to her as she slowed behind a tractor for a moment. They needed footage of the locals who were helping to search for Rosie. In the past, there had been various cases where the killer had helped police in the search for their victims. She assumed they got a sick thrill from being in the middle of the chaos and fear they had created. If whoever had attacked and potentially killed Rosie was hiding in plain sight, she wanted footage to see if it could provide any clues.

An hour earlier, Ruth had seen that the social media trolls had started. There were comments trending about Kathy and

Jason Wright. Nothing intelligent. Just the usual toxic stuff about murderers in these cases often being close to home. Jason Wright had the look of 'a paedo'. There was 'always something weird' about Gareth Wright and how he had been expelled from school for drug dealing so was 'probably paedo scum'.

Ruth's thoughts turned to Kathy Wright and her liaison in the supermarket car park. Her immediate assumption was that it was some kind of affair. However, lying about when she saw her own daughter for the last time was repugnant.

By the time Ruth pulled up outside the Wright's cottage, it had started to rain heavily. Undeterred, photographers and members of the press had sought refuge under brightly-coloured umbrellas, waterproofs, nearby trees or in the press vehicles that were amassed at one end of the lane.

Kathy Wright was sitting at the kitchen table in her usual spot when Ruth was shown in by the FLO. Now looking tired and drawn, Kathy wore virtually no make-up and was dressed in a grey and pink tracksuit.

Ruth sat down and looked over at her. There was a stillness as Kathy shifted in her chair and sat upright.

'I know I should be out looking for her, but I wanna be here. I don't want her to come home and for me not to be here,' Kathy mumbled as the tears began to stream from her eyes. Her shoulders juddered as she wept, trying to catch her breath.

'It's whatever you need to do, Kathy,' Ruth said as she gave her a compassionate look across the table.

'I don't think she's coming home though. Do you?' Kathy took some tissues that PC Bennett, the FLO, had handed her, wiped her face and then blew her nose.

'I promise I will do everything in my power to find Rosie.' Ruth waited for a moment. 'And for that to happen, you have to tell us the truth, Kathy.'

Kathy frowned as Ruth's comment hung in the air.

'What do you mean?' she asked.

'We know you weren't here at six o'clock on Monday. And we know that you didn't see Emma when she called for Rosie,' Ruth said quietly. She was experienced enough to know that these types of situations needed a softly, softly approach.

'Eh? I was here. What are you talking about?' Kathy asked, looking over at her.

Fishing into the A4 envelope she had in her hand, Ruth pulled out a still from the car park CCTV and slid it over the table for Kathy to look at.

She looked at it and then mumbled, 'Shit.'

'Why did you lie to us, Kathy?'

'Why do you think?' Kathy sneered. Now on the defensive, all the grief and anguish of the last few minutes was gone.

*Jesus! Was that all an act?*

Ruth wasn't sure whether the grieving mother routine had been for show, but the change was marked.

'Who is the man in the car with you?' Ruth asked.

'Andy,' Kathy mumbled.

'Andy who?'

'I've no idea,' Kathy said dismissively.

Ruth snorted. 'Come on. You don't know?'

'It's first names only. That's the deal.'

'Deal? Are you and this Andy having an affair?'

Kathy shook her head, but seemed completely unfazed by the conversation. 'No. It's just sex. No questions asked. Meet someone, drive somewhere, have sex, end of.'

'How did you meet?'

'One of them websites for married people.'

'Does your husband know about this?' Ruth asked.

'No, of course not. And I'd like it to stay that way.' Kathy said, looking directly at Ruth – it almost felt like a threat.

Maybe Martin Hancock was accurate in his description of Kathy Wright. She had certainly shown a very different side to her character when confronted. And that also threw up questions about her relationship with Rosie.

71

The cafeteria at Llancastell Police Station was quiet – just the distant metallic sounds of cutlery and chatter from the kitchens. Picking up the tray of coffees, Nick headed back over to the table where he was talking to Kara Haddon, Emma's sister. Steven Haddon sat next to her with a concerned look on his face.

Although they had already taken preliminary statements from the girls, Ruth had asked Nick to talk to them all again. There was a growing feeling that they had missed something in Rosie's life that would explain the attack and her disappearance.

'Thanks,' Steven said as he put sugar in his coffee.

Nick watched Kara as she just gazed at the mug of coffee. She was wearing a Billie Eilish tour T-shirt and grey jogging bottoms. He could see the shock of the previous couple of days was taking its toll, especially as she was only fourteen.

'Kara, there's just a few things we need to clarify about Monday night with you. Is that going to be all right?' Nick asked, trying to be as sensitive as he could.

Kara looked up at him and pushed her dark ringlets out of her face. 'I wanted to help look for Rosie today but Dad wouldn't let me,' she said, looking up at her father.

'I just think you've been through enough in the last couple of days, Kara. We all have. And there are lots of people out there looking for Rosie who are trained and know what they're doing,' Steven reassured her.

'You dad's right, Kara. You're probably better off at home,' Nick said.

'Where is she?' Kara asked in a virtual whisper.

'That's what we're trying to find out. And the more detail we have about Rosie, her life and what happened on Monday, the more likely it is that we'll find her safe. Is that okay?' Nick asked.

'Yeah, of course,' Kara said as she looked down and began to pick at her fingernails.

'So, it was your sister Emma who first noticed that Rosie was missing at around nine o'clock?' Nick asked.

'Yeah, Rosie went over to the yard to get a signal because it was crap where we were sitting,' Kara explained.

'Do you know what time that was?'

Kara shook her head. 'No, sorry. Quite a long time before though. She was gone for ages.'

'Would you say she was gone for about fifteen minutes?'

'No, it was more than that. Probably half an hour or more. We just thought she was talking to Hayley.'

'The girl she had met online?' Nick asked. Ruth had briefed him earlier.

'Her girlfriend,' Kara said, determined to show them both that she wasn't fazed by saying this. 'They had been talking online for ages.'

'Ages? Can you tell me roughly how long?' Nick asked.

'Last few months, I think.'

'Do you know her surname?' Nick asked.

'No, sorry. Just Hayley.'

'Anything else that might help us find her?'

Kara thought for a second and then said, 'She worked in a pub in Rhyl. The Mill something. The Mill Arms?'

Nick looked down at his phone and quickly googled pubs in Rhyl. 'The Millbank Arms?'

Kara nodded. 'Yeah, that's it.'

'You're sure?'

'Yeah. After Rosie and Hayley had met up, she and Emma said if we got a train up to Rhyl, Hayley would serve us in the pub and we could get free drinks.'

The fact that Rosie had seen the girl in person was news to Nick. 'You're sure they met up? Emma seemed to think that they had just been talking online?' Nick asked.

'No, they definitely met up in Chester a couple of times. Rosie told me on Monday when we were sitting around,' Kara said.

'And this Hayley was meant to be coming to meet you all at the farm?' Nick asked.

'Yeah. It was this big thing and Rosie was really excited. Except Hayley was late or something. Some of us were making jokes, saying that Hayley didn't exist and that Rosie had been talking to some forty-year-old paedo online,' Kara explained.

'Kara!' Steven said, looking at her.

'What? That stuff happens, Dad. Don't be naïve.' Kara looked over at Nick and shook her head at her father's perceived innocence.

'So, Hayley never turned up. And Rosie went over to the yard to try to call her to see where she was?' Nick asked.

'Yeah. She said that Hayley was driving. Oh, and then she said she hoped Hayley's "dad" wasn't bringing her over. And she made speech marks with her fingers, you know, and laughed?' Kara demonstrated the speech marks with her index and middle fingers.

Nick didn't like the sound of that. 'What did she mean by that?'

'When Rosie went to meet Hayley in Chester, Hayley told her that she was being picked up by her dad. When Rosie came out of McDonald's, she saw Hayley getting into a car down the road. But she was pretty sure it wasn't her dad.'

'Why do you say that?' Nick asked.

'There were three men in the car. And they were all pretty young. Like twenties. And the guy driving the car was Asian. Rosie said they must have been Hayley's friends.'


*Forty-eight hours*


Ruth tramped across the dark green fields away from Capelulo and out towards Pensychnant Conservation Centre. She needed to speak to Jason Wright, who, given Kathy's false statement, was now the last person to see Rosie at the house before she left.

The rain had stopped, which was something. Now the sun was starting to set, but it was still baking hot. Putting her hand to the back of her neck, Ruth could feel the sweat. She took off her coat and slung it over her shoulder.

Up ahead, a long line of police officers in high-visibility jackets, volunteers and locals were scouring the area for anything that would give them a clue as to where Rosie had gone. Digging with sticks and poles, a few of the figures had crouched to inspect anything of interest in more detail. She noticed that many of the locals had dogs with them, and once in a while the tranquillity of the heathland was broken by a series of barks.

Catching her breath, Ruth looked back at where she had come from. The tiny white buildings of Capelulo village were dwarfed by the towering grey mass of Conwy Mountain and the Carneddau mountain range behind that. It looked like it could be somewhere in Austria.

Striding forward, Ruth began to make ground towards the search party whose progress was slow and painstaking. She soon identified Jason Wright, with his worn black baseball cap, and approached.

'Mr Wright!' Ruth called.

Jason looked over and made it clear he wasn't impressed to see her. 'Come to help?' he said sarcastically.

'I just need a few minutes to clarify a couple of things with you,' Ruth explained.

'Oh, yeah? I've told you everything I know already.'

'It seems that your wife was mistaken about what time she actually arrived home from work and the supermarket,' Ruth said.

'Not a surprise. I don't know where she is half the time these days,' Jason muttered under his breath.

'Well, it seems that you were the last person to see Rosie at the house and we need to establish a timeline of her movements.'

'Why? She went missing from the Haddons' farm, didn't she? What difference does it make?' Jason grumbled with growing anger.

Ruth had had enough of Jason Wright's shitty attitude. 'Everything that Rosie did on Monday, and in the days leading up to Monday, matter, Mr Wright! We know what we're doing. I understand that this is an incredibly difficult time for you and your family, but I'm asking for your help,' Ruth said as she looked him in the eye.

Jason nodded and looked a little chastised. 'Yeah… I'm sorry.'

For a moment, Jason looked out at the police officers, the dogs straining at leashes and the volunteers. The enormity of it all seemed to hit him.

'I can't imagine what you're going through, but we all want the same thing.' Ruth said. 'We want to find Rosie safe and well and bring her home.' Of course, she knew all too well what Jason Wright was going through. She still didn't know what had happened to Sarah, and that was six years ago now.

'I'm not going to give up until I find her,' Jason said in a determined voice.

For the first time, Ruth saw some genuine emotion in his face. That's how some people dealt with situations like this. Block it out and get angry until reality hits them.

'So, when did you see Rosie on Monday?'

'I came in for a break from work at about four. She was definitely home then.'

'You saw her?' Ruth asked.

'No. The extractor fan in the bathroom was still running, so I assumed that she'd had a shower. I could hear music from her bedroom, I think,' Jason explained.

'You didn't see her?'

'No. Like I say, I knew she was in but I didn't see her.' Jason started to sound frustrated.

'Did you hear her? Moving around upstairs? A door closing, footsteps?'

'I don't know. I don't think so,' Jason said, now clearly annoyed.

'And you think there was some music but you're not certain?'

'Yes. I don't know now. It's the same every day so I can't remember what happened on Monday.'

'According to your statement, you then went to meet friends at the Royal Oak pub down the road?' Ruth asked.

'Yeah. I go there every Monday. They had a band playing in the garden.'

'And they'll vouch for you, will they?'

'I don't see why not,' Jason growled.

'Okay. Could you tell me when you actually last saw Rosie in the house?' Ruth asked patiently.

'Must have been Sunday evening. Yeah, she came down and asked my wife if she could borrow some moisturiser. Then she was upstairs for the rest of the evening,' Jason explained.

'Do you know if your wife saw Rosie on Monday?'

'I thought she saw Rosie before she went out with Emma,' Jason snapped.

'What about in the morning before she went to work and Rosie went to college?' Ruth asked.

Jason shook his head. 'No, no. Kath gets up at five to go over to the prison. She wouldn't have seen Rosie.'

Ruth frowned and took a moment. 'That means that neither you, nor your wife, saw Rosie at your home on the Monday? Is that correct?'

'Yeah. That's what it sounds like, doesn't it?' Jason said with a heavy degree of sarcasm.

# CHAPTER 8

*Forty-eight hours*

Nick knew Rhyl from when he was a kid. It was known as the Welsh Blackpool in the Eighties and Nineties. Not any more. It had become a byword for a cheap, dilapidated seaside resort. His dad had brought him and his mum there every summer. They would have a great time at the aquarium, on the beach and in the arcades. After she died from ovarian cancer when he was eight, they never went back.

Now the fairground was closed, and the Sun Centre and Sky Tower were boarded up and derelict. Rhyl was now a town with a sleazy and dark reputation. The B&Bs were full of refugees and migrant workers. On the road into town there was a large green sign: *Welcome to Rhyl*. Nick noticed that someone had thought they were hilarious by scrawling *Twinned with Kandahar* underneath.

Heading along the beach road, Nick looked at the sad, faded red frontages of the closed amusement arcades and bowling alley. It didn't look like it had changed much since the 1980s. Dark red iron shutters protected the doorway to a club called Fusion. Two men sat in the doorway of the King Casino, drinking. He knew that could have been him if he hadn't managed to stop when he did. He hoped they found a way to stop drinking their lives away.

Turning right, he made his way into the middle of Rhyl. Slowing outside a cheap-looking hair salon, Nick spotted the Millbank Arms where they believed 'Hayley' worked. It was a large brewery pub set back from the road with all sorts of deals for food and drink – *Curry and a Pint: £5.*

Nick parked the car and looked at his watch. Rosie Wright had been missing for two full days, and they weren't even close to getting a breakthrough.

Striding towards the pub with a sense of urgency, Nick realised that he had only been in a pub once since he got sober. He was glad that he had no thoughts of alcohol these days. He didn't want to go back to the days of drinking vodka for breakfast. The sweats, the shakes and the crushing despair and anxiety. And that's where one drink would take him. That's what the men he had seen down by the casino didn't understand. It only takes one drink to set the wheels of alcoholism in motion. And then a thousand drinks wouldn't be enough.

As Nick approached, he got the thick waft of booze and fried food that seemed to surround pubs like the Millbank Arms. For a moment, he was transported back to lovely, warm days in the pubs of Llancastell. Alcohol gave him a sense that nothing in the world mattered. That was the appeal. What would it be like? To sit down and have a few drinks just to take the edge off?

Nick pushed that thought from his mind, opened the door and glanced around. There were less than a dozen people in there. A family sitting in a corner on phones and not talking. Three people sitting at the bar; they'd probably been there all day.

Two shaven-headed men, who were nursing pints nearby, stopped talking and looked at him. In places like this, people had an instinctive sense if someone was a copper.

Showing his warrant card to the young barman, Nick said, 'DS Evans, North Wales Police. I'm looking for Hayley.'

The barman took a moment. Nick guessed he was wondering what Hayley could have done to have the police asking after her and was deciding whether he was going to lie to protect her.

'It's all right. She's not in trouble. Just a couple of questions,' Nick reassured him.

The barman finished pouring a pint of lager and Nick looked at it. He was flooded by a wave of the associations. A chilled pint outside on a summer's day. Wouldn't that be nice? For a fleeting second, his brain told him that it would be amazing. But that's not how the day would end. It would end in vodka, disaster and blackout.

The barman scoured the pub and frowned. 'She's serving food. Might be in the kitchen. I'll go and get her.'

The barman disappeared and Nick waited. The three customers sitting at the bar hadn't said a word since he showed his warrant card. He rested on the bar and smiled at them.

'The sun's out. You should go and sit in the garden,' Nick said. Their skin was milky white, even at the height of summer.

They looked at him blankly. He glanced up at the television mounted on the wall that was silently showing horse racing on Channel 4.

Then, out of the corner of his eye, Nick spotted a figure hurrying across the car park at the side of the pub. A young girl, about seventeen, dressed in the black and white clothes of a waitress. The barman had tipped her off.

*Wanker.*

'Shit!' Nick muttered as he ran to the door and headed to where he had seen the girl.

'Hayley?' he shouted over at her as she gingerly stepped over a small brick wall and out of the car park. Her dark hair had been partially dyed blue and she wore heavy eye make-up. The girl glanced over, sprinted down a side road and out of sight.

'For fuck's sake!' Nick growled as he set off behind her. He got to the corner of the road, but she had gone. She had vanished into thin air.

Feeling his anger rising, Nick strode back to the pub, crashed through the door and went to the bar.

*I'll fucking show you*, he thought as the red mist descended.

The barman, who was pouring another pint, looked anxious but was trying to hide it as he avoided his gaze.

'Right, dickhead—' Nick thundered.

'You can't call me that,' the barman said as he turned off the beer pump.

Before he could react, Nick had reached across, grabbed him by the shirt and pulled him towards him. His face was now about six inches away from his own.

*Don't fuck with me! I'm not in the mood.*

'Yeah, I can. You either tell me Hayley's surname and give me her address, or I nick you, put you in cuffs and drag you back to Llancastell Police Station for wasting police time and obstructing an investigation! Then I'll bounce you around an interview room and put you in a cell for the night.' Nick pulled a face. 'And a word of advice. You might want to clean your teeth because your breath is horrendous!'

The barman nodded and within two minutes Nick was back in his car with a name and an address scribbled on a beermat. He was soon trawling the narrow roads of West Rhyl, which DCI Drake had recently informed Llancastell CID had the highest crime rate in Wales, including Cardiff and Swansea. The area stretched from the town centre along the coast, from Edward Henry Street to Fairfield Avenue, and inland as far as the railway station. It was known for drugs, prostitution and violent crime. However, the roads, now bathed in warm sunshine, were quiet except for some kids riding their bikes.

Nick found the house the barman had given him for Hayley Collard. He parked, got out of the car and moved slowly around the outside of the house. The front garden was full of rubbish, a rusty old cooker and a pile of car tyres. Curtains were pulled across every window. It was a shit tip.

Going back to his car, Nick opened the boot and took off his tie. He pulled a grey hoodie out of his gym bag and put it on over his shirt. He grabbed his sunglasses and ruffled up his hair. It was his best attempt at trying to hide the fact that he was police and scaring Hayley away immediately.

Pushing the sunglasses back on the bridge of this nose, Nick strolled casually up to the front door. There was no doorbell, so he knocked on the stained UPVC panel. The thud of dance music came from somewhere in this house as a door was opened. And then some shouting in a foreign language that he didn't understand.

As Nick went to knock again, the door opened about two inches. It was on a safety chain. A dark-skinned man in his twenties, shaved head and dark eyes, looked at him and raised his chin as if to say, 'What do you want?' He could have been Middle Eastern, but Nick wasn't sure.

'Hayley around?' Nick mumbled.

'Nah, bro. You a friend of Hayley?' the man asked. His accent was thick Mancunian.

'Sort of…' Nick said as he nodded. 'Friend of a friend, you know?'

'You looking for business then?' the man asked.

Nick now knew that Hayley worked as a prostitute. Even though he had encountered teen prostitution before, it still made Nick uncomfortable and angry.

'Yeah, maybe. How much, mate?'

'Fifty. No fucking weird shit,' the man said and then looked him up and down. 'You isn't plod, are ya?'

'No, mate… Fifty's good. You sort me out with some white as well, yeah?' Nick asked. *White* was the local street name for cocaine.

'Yeah, bruv. It's all good. I can do that. Hayley ain't here so come back in half an hour and I'll get her here.' The man closed the door in Nick's face abruptly.

What was Hayley's connection with Rosie Wright? Was Hayley and Rosie's relationship genuine? Or was there a far darker reason for Hayley trying to befriend Rosie?

Walking around the corner, Nick rested against a wall in the sunshine and got out his phone. He needed uniformed backup from Rhyl. He didn't want Hayley disappearing again. He wanted her back in Llancastell to find out what she knew about Rosie's disappearance.

Twenty minutes later, two squad cars had arrived and were now parked close to the house but out of sight. Two uniformed officers had gone to the street behind in case anyone decided to do a runner over the back wall.

Signalling to the cars, Nick made his way to the front door and knocked again. There was silence. No more dance music and no more foreign accents. Maybe they had twigged that Nick was a copper and weren't answering.

Eventually, the chain rattled and the man's face appeared. 'Sorry, bro. Hayley ain't around. Maybe later, yeah? You want me to hook you up with that white?'

'No, I want you to open the door,' Nick said, showing his warrant card.

'You fuckin' joking, man?' the man shook his head and kissed his teeth.

'I'm not joking. Open the door.' Nick could feel his pulse quicken. He didn't know how this was going to go, but he needed to check Hayley wasn't inside the house for starters.

'See your search warrant, pig.'

'You've just offered me drugs and the services of a prostitute, *mate*. I don't need a search warrant!' And with that, Nick kicked the door hard. The chain broke and the door hit the man in the face. He went reeling to the floor.

*Oh, dear! I hope that didn't hurt*, Nick thought.

Nick and the uniformed officers spent the next ten minutes searching the house, which was filthy and stank of weed. The bedrooms upstairs had old, stained mattresses on the floor where the prostitutes worked. Downstairs, the kitchen was covered in drug paraphernalia. Scales, needles, plastic bags.

However, Hayley was nowhere to be seen and no one knew where she was.

Sipping at her hot coffee, Ruth knew that they had passed the forty-eight-hour point in their search for Rosie. She stared at the two large photos of Rosie that were prominent at the centre of the whiteboards in the incident room. One of them featured her dressed in a cream bridesmaid dress with a silver necklace. She was wearing heavy eye make-up that made her eyes look big and white. Her lips glistened in the light of the camera flash. She didn't look innocent. In fact, if anything, she looked a little sultry. Neither a child nor an adult. Aware of everything in the adult world, just not sure how to deal with it or how to fit it into her changing life.

Then it hit Ruth. A quick flash of an image of Sarah in her bridesmaid dress at a friend's fashionable Hampstead wedding seven years earlier. She looked beautiful. And now Ruth was filled with the unwanted memories that seemed to be out of her control. A slow dance at the wedding reception to Etta James's 'I'd Rather Go Blind'. A lingering kiss.

From behind, Sian gave her a surreptitious squeeze on the hip.

'You okay, boss?' Sian asked.

It made Ruth jump. 'Yeah,' Ruth said unconvincingly as she looked at the maps, writing and photos on the scene boards. She felt guilty. As though thinking about her time with Sarah was somehow cheating on Sian. She knew that didn't make sense, but that's how she felt.

Now back in the present, Ruth knew she was feeling tired and frustrated. Pointing at the bridesmaid photo, she turned to Sian. 'Where the bloody hell is she?'

'I wish I knew.' Sian showed her some printed sheets. 'Results from Tech. Nothing on the laptop we took from the home. A few emails from college about homework. I looked at her Snapchat and Instagram accounts. Just what you would expect from a sixteen-year-old girl. Selfies, friends, music stuff.'

'Nothing regarding Hayley Collard?' Ruth asked. Nick had already debriefed Ruth about his trip to Rhyl.

'Nothing. No mention of her anywhere that I could find. However Rosie and Hayley contacted each other, we couldn't find it,' Sian explained.

At that moment, Nick approached. 'Boss, PNC and criminal record check on Hayley Collard. Shoplifting. Possession of class A drugs. And three counts of soliciting. One when she was thirteen.'

Ruth shook her head. She had heard and seen it all before, but the idea of a teenage girl selling sex to grown men still sent a shiver down her back.

Nick was looking at the printout and said grimly, 'It's the usual story. Addict parents. Grew up in care. Foster parents, running away, children's homes and then petty crime.'

They shared a look. It was Ruth's favourite topic when she drank too much and became maudlin. The endless cycle of poverty, abuse, addiction and crime that passed from generation to generation, and that no one seemed to be willing to tackle. It was their job to hold it together as best they could.

Ruth let out an irritated noise, then snapped. 'We've got nothing. No motive, no suspects, no leads.' She could feel herself welling with a mixture of frustration and sadness.

'We've got Hayley Collard. It's the one thing that doesn't add up on that night,' Sian suggested.

'It doesn't give us anything. Rosie was friends online with a teenage prostitute. So what? Tonight is Rosie Wright's third night away from her home. We don't get many teenage girls that come back after that!' Ruth said sharply. It was starting to get to her.

Ruth could see that Nick and Sian were a little surprised by her outburst.

'Ruth? Can I borrow you?' Drake appeared at the door and beckoned Ruth to come over. There seemed to be some sense of urgency in his manner that Ruth thought was unusual.

Walking down the corridor towards Drake's office, Ruth took a moment to compose herself. She felt bad for snapping at Sian.

'Everything all right, boss?' Ruth asked, wondering why there was the need for all the cloak-and-dagger stuff. Was she in some kind of trouble?

'Yeah. I need to borrow you for a bit,' Drake explained.

Ruth didn't like the sound of that. Why hadn't he spoken to her in front of everyone else in briefing? She had a sinking feeling in her stomach.

'I've been meaning to ask you how Paula is, boss?' Ruth asked, now remembering that she was still suffering from cancer.

Drake slowed for a moment. 'The chemo is working. But it's making her very ill. She's lost her hair...' he said sadly.

'I'm sorry to hear that,' Ruth replied.

'Main thing is, the cancer hasn't spread. That's what I was worried about,' Drake admitted.

Ruth nodded. 'Tell her that I'm thinking about her.'

She had only met Paula twice, but she seemed to be a woman with a real zest for life and an infectious laugh. It was horrible to think about what she was going through.

'Thanks, Ruth,' Drake said as they arrived at his door.

At the table on the far side of Drake's large office were two detectives. One was a middle-aged man, thickset and wearing a worn-looking navy suit. The other was in her thirties, Asian and pretty. The detectives looked up as Ruth entered and Drake closed the door.

'Have a seat, Ruth,' Drake said gesturing to a chair on the opposite side of the meeting table to the two detectives. 'This is our SIO on the Rosie Wright case, DI Ruth Hunter.'

'Hi there,' Ruth said, a little annoyed and even concerned about why they were meeting. They didn't look like officers from the IPCC.

'DI Lyon and DS Buckley are officers in the Regional Prison Investigation Team,' Drake explained.

Ruth frowned. *What the hell does any of this have to do with the RPIT?* Then the penny dropped. Kathy Wright was a prison officer. The two must be connected, mustn't they? But how?

Lyon shifted in his seat and moved a folder to the centre of the table. 'The RPIT has had Kathy Wright under surveillance for the past six months. We believe that she is running a team of prison officers who are smuggling drugs and mobile phones into HMP Rhoswen.'

*What the—?* Ruth's mind whirred with the information, trying to piece it together. Did this have any bearing on Rosie's disappearance?

'We didn't realise that Kathy Wright was Rosie Wright's mother until we put two and two together this morning,' Buckley said.

'Do you think the two things are connected?' Ruth asked.

'We're not sure,' confessed Buckley.

Ruth looked up at Drake and then said with a sense of urgency, 'Boss, we need to get Kathy Wright in now and find out if what she's doing at Rhoswen has resulted in Rosie being harmed.'

'It's not as simple as that,' Drake explained as he leant on his desk and picked up his coffee. The phrase *cool as a cucumber* must have been invented for Drake.

'Why? We're running out of time if we want to find Rosie alive,' Ruth snapped. 'What the hell are we waiting for?'

Drake shot her a look. Ruth didn't normally challenge Drake with that kind of resolve, but when a young girl's life was at stake, she was compelled.

'At the moment, we're still at the evidence-gathering stage. And we don't have enough to arrest and hold her or any of the other prison officers. If we alert her that she's being watched, then we lose everything,' Lyon said.

Ruth snorted. She couldn't believe what was being said. *Fuck evidence-gathering!*

'Jesus Christ! A sixteen-year-old girl was attacked and abducted ten minutes from where she lives. She's either dying or dead. We have no idea who took her or where she is. But we can't interview the mother because she's smuggling stuff into a prison!' Ruth exclaimed angrily.

'That's not quite the full story, Ruth,' Drake said calmly.

Lyon took an A4 photo out of an envelope and slid it over the table for Ruth to look at.

*Now what?*

'Do you know this man?' Lyon asked.

Ruth looked. She instantly recognised the shaved head, the perma-tan and expensive teeth.

'Curtis Blake.' Ruth nodded. They knew all about Curtis Blake, the Liverpudlian gangster that Llancastell CID had dealt with when he had made county-lines inroads into North Wales. 'An officer from our CID ended up dead after crossing paths with Curtis Blake. There are plenty of detectives here who would like to see him hang,' Ruth said.

'Curtis Blake was transferred from HMP Wakefield to Rhoswen for his own protection. There's a turf war in Merseyside as gangs try to divvy up Blake's empire. It seems that Blake has ruffled a few feathers in Rhoswen in the past couple of months as he's decided that he's now running the show there. We believe that might have brought him into direct conflict with the old-time criminals who were running things before and with Kathy Wright, their inside girl,' Buckley explained.

'Maybe Blake threatened to harm Kathy's family if she didn't do what he wanted her to do?' suggested Ruth.

Instinctively, Ruth felt this was a solid lead. There was now definite motive.

Lyon nodded. 'That's a distinct possibility. And if she called his bluff or didn't believe him, then maybe that puts him in the frame for Rosie's disappearance.'

'However, we do need to tread carefully. There is no compelling evidence against Kathy Wright for the supply of drugs and mobile phones at Rhoswen. At least nothing that we would get past the CPS. And Kathy Wright has a missing teenage daughter who has been seriously harmed or worse,' Drake explained.

Ruth knew what Drake was getting at, but she had a teenage girl to find. Everything else was secondary to that. 'No. I'm sorry, but we don't have time to tread carefully, boss. If we have any kind of lead on why Rosie was taken, we need to move on it now.'

Lyon leant forward. 'If we drag Kathy Wright in for questioning for a crime that she turns out to be innocent of while the whole country is watching her and her family's terrible anxiety over Rosie, then it's a huge PR disaster for not just North Wales Police but the entire force.'

'Bollocks to PR! This is a girl's life we're talking about,' Ruth thundered.

*How bloody dare they see this in terms of PR!*

Drake shot Ruth a look to keep a lid on it.

Buckley looked around at them all with an air that suggested she had a solution. 'As far as we know, Kathy Wright has no idea that she is under surveillance. We're confident there will be something at her home that would help us caution or even arrest her, but we can't get enough for a search warrant.'

'Why not?' Drake asked in disbelief.

'We've constructed what we believed was a solid ITO twice now. And twice we've been turned down by the magistrate because there were no reasonable or probable grounds for the search,' Buckley explained. An ITO stood for Information To Obtain, which was a document filed by a police officer to a judge seeking authorisation to obtain a search warrant, often to look for evidence of an offence.

'We can search the property,' Ruth said, thinking out loud.

'Sorry, I'm not following.' Lyon frowned as he looked over at Ruth. Buckley smiled at Ruth; the two women were on to something.

'We can search the Wright's property as part of our investigation into Rosie's disappearance. Kathy and Jason Wright are due to do a press conference with me here at eleven tomorrow morning, so they won't be at the property. If DCI Drake agrees, I'm sure that you could "observe" some of our officers from CID giving the Wrights' home a thorough search. If they are looking for clues to Rosie's disappearance but happen to stumble across something else, that is just coincidence. But it will be admissible in court as it is covered by our search warrant,' Ruth explained, feeling energised and rather pleased with herself.

Drake looked over and gave her a nod to show he was impressed.

'Perfect,' Lyon said as he nodded at Buckley.

*Now we're getting somewhere,* Ruth thought.

# CHAPTER 9

Having arrived home twenty minutes earlier, Sian came into the garage in search of a screwdriver. The arm of the sofa had slumped again, dropping her drink to the floor, and she was determined to fix it.

*It's just a waste of good alcohol.*

Sian's head was still full of the Rosie Wright case. Not only from work, but it was the major news story on the various BBC radio stations she had listened to on her way home. At the moment, CID didn't really have any clear motive, means or opportunity. Did that mean Rosie Wright had been taken by a total stranger? Of course, it wasn't impossible. It was just unlikely.

Stepping over Ruth's boxes that were still full of DVDs, CDs and books, she saw a toolbox. *Brilliant.* But inside, there was only a large hammer, tacks, nails and a long-handled metal tool – she had no idea what that was or what it did.

Where would she find a screwdriver? Balancing as she stepped over another box, she headed to the far end of the garage. The smell of grass from the lawnmower was stronger, and the air seemed thicker and warmer back there. *Still no bloody screwdriver.* Maybe she would go and get a cold beer and sit on the patio instead.

Turning to go, she spotted something through the cheap metal shelving unit that seemed to sit in the middle of the garage space for no apparent reason. A small table and chair.

*What the hell is that doing there?* The chair was tucked neatly under the table and there were photos and maps stuck to the wall.

Approaching slowly, a realisation dawned on Sian. Her fears were confirmed. The wall was a little shrine to Sarah and Ruth's ongoing investigation into her disappearance. There were half a dozen or so photos of Sarah at festivals, weddings and bars. A map of London with Crystal Palace and London Victoria marked with red pins, as they would be if this was Llancastell CID. To the right, photographs of the CCTV from Crystal Palace station and London Victoria on that day in 2013.

And then what Sian knew was the darker side of the disappearance. A police Photofit of the German banker Jurgen Kessler, who passengers saw talking to Sarah on the train that morning. A man that Berlin Police wanted in connection with two murders. His blank expression and dead eyes behind glasses looked cold and creepy.

Closing her eyes for a moment, Sian felt the emotional pain in the pit of her stomach. She couldn't compete with a ghost. A ghost that in the rose-tinted perspective of ever passing time was perfect in every way.

–

The sun was beginning to drop by the time Nick and Amanda began to walk up to the impressive Caernarfon Castle. It had taken them an hour to get there, but it was worth it. It was the most impressive of all of Wales's castles, Nick thought, even knowing that it was technically an English construction.

Amanda reached for his hand as they ambled along the cobblestones. The warm summer breeze blew from the Menai Strait, giving it the salty sea smell of holidays. Wasps hovered noisily over a bin where ice cream wrappers and cans of drink had been discarded.

As they looked up at the imposing thirteenth-century turrets, Amanda smiled and said, 'Are you going to bore me with everything you know about this castle?'

'Do you want me to bore you?' Nick smiled back.

'Of course,' she said, squeezing his hand.

'Okay, it's medieval and was built by the dirty English scum and their king, Edward the first, at the end of the thirteenth century.'

'Racist.'

'Now, there was a Roman fort on it before and—'

Amanda interrupted him, 'Actually, on second thoughts, no. Can we just walk around and just look at it?' Amanda said.

'Oh, fine. Be ignorant. Prince Charles was here when he became Prince of Wales in 1969.'

'Okay, that's vaguely interesting,' Amanda teased and then pulled him by the hand. 'Come on. Before you break out in full-blown tedium-itis.'

As they walked, Nick looked over at the forty or so boats that were moored up along the marina and around the actual harbour. From here, cruises would take tourists over to Anglesey or inland to look at the Snowdonia mountain range. The castle's reflection stretched out lazily across the water and only stopped where the water was shallow and small pebbled beaches had begun to appear at low tide.

Amanda frowned, stopped and put her hand to her pregnant bump.

'You okay?' Nick asked, already concerned.

Amanda smiled. 'I think Junior just kicked!' There had been movement before, but this was the first time the baby had kicked properly – a look of joy spread across both their faces.

'What?' Nick beamed and put his hand on her bump. A moment later, the unmistakable kick of their baby. 'He did it again!'

'He? He? You're such a bloke.' Amanda hit him playfully.

'I've just got a feeling. And I can tell he's definitely a left kegger.'

'A left what-er?' Amanda asked, rolling her eyes at his banality.

'Left-footed. All the best rugby players are left-footed. Dan Carter, Jonny Wilkinson…'

'Bloody hell. That's what I love about you, Nick. You can go from boring old man to moronic juvenile in the blink of an eye.'

'As you said, that's what you love about me,' Nick quipped.

He wished evenings like this would go on for ever. He loved being under this fairy tale castle with Amanda, but he also felt a twinge of fear. What if he just didn't have it in him to be a responsible dad and partner? 'Doesn't it scare you?'

'What?' Amanda asked as she looked at him. 'Having a baby?'

'Yeah,' Nick mumbled quietly. He wasn't quite sure how much to reveal about his true feelings.

'Of course. It's terrifying. But that's how everyone feels, especially the first time,' Amanda explained.

'Do they?' Nick asked. He came from a culture where no one really talked about how they felt about anything. Especially men. It wasn't the done thing to rock up in the pub to watch the rugby and try to discuss your anxieties about becoming a father for the first time.

Amanda's phone buzzed and interrupted Nick's train of thought. She checked it and frowned. 'My dad? Which is weird.'

'Why?' Nick asked. She rarely mentioned her dad and all Nick knew was that he had walked out on her and her mum when she was a teenager and was now in prison. He wasn't even sure why.

'Well, he doesn't text me a lot, does he?'

'No. But what's he doing with a mobile phone in prison anyway?' Nick asked.

'They moved him to an open prison last month,' Amanda explained.

'Near here?'

'Cheshire, so not far,' Amanda said.

'Will you go visit him?' Nick asked.

'I should do. I haven't seen him since I was pregnant.'

'Does he know?'

'Oh, yeah. And he's happy for me. But it's always a bit difficult, you know?'

'Does he know I'm a copper?' Nick had been out with a couple of girls who had had to hide the fact that he was on the job from their less than salubrious families.

'Yeah. I've told him about you.'

Nick waited a moment. He knew all about difficult relationships with fathers. It had only really been in the last year that he and his father had had any kind of proper relationship. But that's what sobriety had given them both.

'You never talk about why he's in prison,' Nick said, wondering how Amanda would respond to this.

'No,' Amanda said, and his question hovered in the air between them.

'It's fine. We don't need to talk about it,' Nick said eventually, breaking the tension.

'No, I want to... I spent so much of my adult life being dishonest and secretive... I want us to tell each other everything.'

'No, I get that. My motto used to be "If in doubt, lie. And then lie again",' Nick admitted. He still struggled to tell the truth if lying made it easier.

'So, my dad mounted the pavement in blackout and killed a middle-aged woman walking along, minding her own business. He got seven years,' Amanda explained awkwardly.

'That's terrible,' Nick said, although he had seen a lot worse.

'He woke up in the police cells again. He was a regular. He thought he'd been arrested for drunk and disorderly. He just had no memory of it.'

'Is he an alcoholic?' Nick asked.

'He doesn't think he is. But yeah, I would say so.'

'Alcoholic dads. Another dark thing we have in common. Nature or nurture?' Nick said.

Amanda looked at him for a second. 'Will you come and see him with me?'

'Of course.' Nick nodded. He would do anything for her.

Amanda walked over and pecked him on the lips. He put his arm around her and pulled her in gently as they kissed passionately.

*Two days, two hours*

It was gone nine thirty and the light in the garden was fading fast. Dragging on a ciggie, Ruth looked out at the fields. The dry summer had taken its toll and the grass looked faded and patchy. The distant sound of children playing somewhere – shrill yells and screeches of joy. It brought a sharp reminder that Rosie Wright still hadn't been found. Was Curtis Blake involved? Was he using Rosie to apply pressure on Kathy Wright? That would be a far better scenario in the short term than any sexually motivated abduction. Blake would need Rosie alive – and that gave Ruth a glimmer of hope.

A noise on her phone signalled that a new email had arrived. It was from Steven Flaherty, her Missing Persons liaison from the Met. He had been Ruth's point of contact at the Met from the day that Sarah had gone missing and had been incredibly patient and supportive ever since.

The sight of his name always made her stomach clench.

Hi Ruth,

We've had information that a man bearing a striking resemblance to Jurgen Kessler interviewed for a job as an economics lecturer at Edinburgh University two days ago. Something made the admissions team suspicious and they photocopied the passport, which was for an Austrian national called Matthias Schürrle. However, something must have spooked the guy as he disappeared and failed to show for a second interview with the faculty head.

I'm waiting for the documents to come through from Edinburgh Police. I've contacted Interpol in Vienna to see if we can track down Matthias Schürrle and see if it's a stolen identity.

I'll ring you when I have more information.

Kind regards,

Steven

Ruth took a few seconds to process the new information. She felt a little shaken, as she did whenever anything like this happened. Kessler had tried to get a job at Bournemouth University. Now he had been spotted in Edinburgh. What was he doing? Why was he hiding out in the UK? There had to be less conspicuous options?

Ella came out with two mugs of tea and a plate of biscuits. Putting them down, she sat at the table next to her mother.

'You okay?' Ella asked.

Ruth knew that the colour had drained from her face, but it wasn't the right time to talk about Kessler. 'Yeah, fine.'

'I made you a tea,' Ella said as she shifted the chair.

'What are you after?' Ruth asked sardonically as she put her phone away.

'I'm not after anything,' Ella replied defensively.

There was a pregnant pause, and Ruth knew that Ella was itching to ask for some kind of favour. Maternal instinct was never wrong.

'Go on then?' Ruth said with an encouraging smile.

'Dad's moved his flight from Sydney forward,' Ella said.

'When is he coming?' Ruth asked, fearing what was coming next.

'Day after tomorrow.'

'And you're sure you still want to see him?' Ruth asked. She was concerned that seeing her father after all this time might destabilise her. Especially if Dan did his usual trick of disappearing again.

'I think I would really regret it if I didn't. We spoke for nearly an hour last night,' Ella explained. Ruth could see all the hope and joy in Ella's face, and it angered her that Dan had been so absent in her life.

'Good. I'm glad you're getting on,' Ruth said. There was part of her that didn't want Ella's dad swanning into her life, but she knew that was selfish.

'He's hilarious,' Ella said with a smile.

The one thing she always loved about Dan was his caustic sense of humour. She had to give him that at least. 'Yeah, he is.'

After a few seconds, Ella gave her a meaningful look and said, 'Would you meet him when he comes over?'

'No fucking way!' Ruth exclaimed. It was an instinctive reaction.

*This is the man who left her to bring up Ella on her own with virtually no contact and no support. He can go fuck himself.*

'Why not?' Ella asked. Ruth could see she was upset.

*Because he's a selfish prick!*

'Why would I? You know what he did to us, darling?' Ruth said through gritted teeth.

'He's my dad. And I've never seen my own parents in the same room together. I know we'll never play happy families or anything like that. But it would mean so much to me to see you two together,' Ella explained.

Ruth knew that to say no would be selfish. And anything that helped Ella feel better about her childhood had to be a good thing.

'Okay. But let me think about it,' Ruth said.

Ella looked at her and smiled. 'Thank you.'

'I didn't say yes,' Ruth protested as her phone buzzed. It was another update from Twitter and the #*FindRosie* feed. She was frustrated that they would have to spend tomorrow pussyfooting around rather than hauling Kathy Wright in for questioning at the crack of dawn.

*It's bloody political and PR bullshit*, Ruth thought angrily, even though she had compromised and agreed to a search of the Wrights' home. Time was ebbing away at a frightening pace. If the Blake lead proved to be a dead end, Rosie could be in the hands of someone who might not wait another day to kill her and dump the body.

Ruth's train of thought was broken by the sound of footsteps coming through the patio door. Sian approached with a bottle of beer in her hand. 'What are you going to think about?' Sian asked. She seemed to be a bit drunk.

'Ella would like me to meet her dad when he visits,' Ruth explained.

Sian frowned and noticeably stiffened. 'Right.'

'Is that okay?' Ruth asked, sensing the tension.

'Yeah, of course. I'm just surprised after all that you've told me about him,' Sian said.

Ruth looked at her – she had definitely been drinking. And more than normal.

'Ella just wanted to see me and him talking. That's all. Are you okay with that?' Ruth asked.

Sian nodded and spun on her heels, 'Not really my business, is it? I'm just going to get myself another drink.'

Ruth and Ella watched Sian go and then shared a look. She wasn't happy.

# CHAPTER 10

*Two days, ten hours*

It was early morning but Incident Room One was already bust-ling with noise, movement and the odd crack of laughter. Ruth grabbed her lukewarm flat white and documents and headed for the front of the room. Drake was already there, leaning back on the table as he casually surveyed the meeting. She might be the SIO on the case, but they were now on day three. The media was going nuts and Drake knew they needed a breakthrough.

Social media was awash with people being highly critical of North Wales Police's failure to find Rosie Wright or to make any significant steps to finding out what had happened to her. Ruth had already read a Twitter thread from that morning:

Scott Chamberlain @ ScottChamberlain1981

#FindRosie After the Andrew Gates debacle last Christmas, I smell another North Wales Police fuck up! They couldn't find their way out of a paper bag with a map!

Tracie @ NorthWalesExpress

#FindRosie Where is Rosie? The North Wales Police aren't getting anywhere. No wonder her poor dad and the locals have taken matters into their own hands to look for her. We're thinking of you.

'Morning, everyone. If we could get started,' Ruth said loudly as the room settled. She realised that she sounded irritated. Maybe she was? She was definitely frustrated.

The morning sun was fully risen and cast shadows across the sixth floor carpet. It was also beginning to heat up. A small plastic fan had been dug out from somewhere and whirred on a desk nearby.

*All that's doing is blowing around hot air*, she thought. That was the problem with being in a Seventies tower block with no proper air conditioning. Only the custody suite, where suspects and prisoners were processed, was air conditioned. *The bloody irony.*

Drake stood and put his hands on his hips as he faced the room. He had told Ruth that he wanted to kick today's briefing off.

'Right, guys. It's day three of our search for Rosie Wright. I know you are all working flat out, so thank you. But we also know that the statistical chances of us finding Rosie Wright alive are decreasing every hour that she is missing. This is an innocent sixteen-year-old girl who was attacked and taken. I want us to do our best work for Rosie and her family. And that means hard work and concentration. We're working long hours, and I know that's difficult—' Drake walked over and pointed to the photo of Rosie dressed as a bridesmaid '—but let's keep focused and get her back safely, eh?'

Inside, Ruth felt buoyed by his words. She could see in the faces of the CID officers in front of her that it had had a palpable effect. Drake had a natural charisma that made him a brilliant leader, and she hoped he stayed in CID and wasn't lured by the power of senior management.

Now Ruth had the complete attention of the room, she went to the scene boards. 'Okay, this is what we know. Last Monday evening, Rosie Wright went with her friend Emma Haddon to join other friends at these farm buildings and a barn on Steven Haddon's farm.' She gestured to the map of the exact location. 'She left her group of friends at around eight p.m. to find a better signal for her phone over by the yard. At around nine p.m., Emma went to look for Rosie, but she had vanished.' Ruth then pointed to a SOCO photo of the patch of blood by the gate in the yard. 'A significant amount of her blood was discovered by the gate to the yard. The volume suggests that she was attacked and was either badly injured or possibly dead when she was taken from the area. One theory is that Rosie was taken away by some kind of boat along the river there. Nick, have SOCO been down there?'

'We'll have something concrete tomorrow morning,' Nick replied.

'Good. What about this girl, Hayley?' Ruth asked.

Moving from the table that he was leaning on, Nick went over to the computer and clicked. A police photo of Hayley Collard came up on the screen. 'This is Hayley Collard, aged seventeen. We believe that Rosie and Hayley had formed a relationship online. They had met secretly in Chester. However, when Hayley claimed that she was being picked up by her father, Rosie said that she saw Hayley getting into a car with three young men, one of whom was Asian. We tracked Hayley down to Rhyl, but when I tried to question her, she ran.'

'You have that effect on women, Nick,' quipped Sian. Ruth rolled her eyes, but a bit of humour was welcome this early in the morning. She was also glad that Sian was less frosty than she had been the previous evening.

Nick gave her the finger and forced a smile. 'Thanks, Sian. We've discovered that Hayley Collard has previous for solicitation and is working as a prostitute in West Rhyl. According to Rosie's friends, Hayley was meant to be driving over to meet them on Monday night. As far as we know, Hayley never arrived. We also suspect that Rosie was trying to contact Hayley when she left her friends to go to the yard.'

'Thanks, Nick. Sian, what have we got?' Ruth asked.

'Technical Forensics have checked Rosie's laptop and gained access to her social media accounts. There's nothing on any of these that gives a clue as to why she was attacked. We checked the Sex Offenders Register and came up with a Martin Hancock, who lives in Capelulo. He doesn't have an alibi, but he was charged with the possession of indecent images of young men and has no history of violence.'

Looking at her notes, Ruth then glanced over at Merringer. 'What about the Wright family, Luke?'

Merringer clicked on the computer to show a photo of Jason Wright. 'Jason Wright. Works as the farm manager on Steven Haddon's farm. He doesn't get on with Rosie, and Emma Haddon claims that he has been violent with her. The general consensus is that he's unpleasant and has a nasty temper.' Merringer clicked and a photo of Kathy Wright appeared.

'Actually, Luke, let me deal with Kathy Wright in a minute. What about the brother?' Ruth said.

A photo of Gareth Wright appeared on the screen next. 'Gareth Wright. Twenty-one. Lives nearby with a friend. Has previous for possession and dealing weed. No history of violence though. Again, his relationship with Rosie isn't good,' Merringer said.

Ruth nodded as she moved back to the centre of the room again. 'Thanks, Luke. As some of you know, DCI Drake and I met with officers from the Regional Prison Investigation Team last night.' Ruth clicked the computer to bring up a photo of Kathy Wright. 'This is Rosie's mother, Kathy Wright. She works as a prison officer at HMP Rhoswen. The RPIT have had her under investigation for the past six months as they believe that Kathy is running a team of prison officers smuggling drugs and mobile phones into Rhoswen.'

There were some mutters around the room. It wasn't surprising. This started to change the picture of the Wright family and possibly what had happened to Rosie.

'However, things at Rhoswen have changed in recent months.' Ruth clicked and a photo of Curtis Blake appeared on the screen. There were louder murmurs within the room.

Llancastell CID and Blake had previous. Even though Ruth had brought Nick up to speed on the phone after her meeting with the RPIT, she could see his face had turned to thunder. Nick and Blake went way back, and Nick's personal vendetta against Blake had sometimes got the better of him.

'Curtis Blake was transferred to Rhoswen a couple of months ago. It seems that Blake has decided that he is now going to be running things at Rhoswen, and that includes the smuggling and sale of drugs and mobile phones. If Kathy Wright is running the team of bent prison officers, that means Blake has to either deal with her or get his own person. If he wants Kathy Wright to work for him now, that means either money or intimidation. And we all know what Blake is like.' Ruth moved the presentation on to the next image. A tough-looking man in his sixties, shaved head, prison-regulation grey sweater. The side of his face was badly swollen and bruised. A dark six-inch slash from his eye socket to his lip had been stitched up. 'This is Frank Cole. Cole ran things at Rhoswen until Blake arrived. This is what happened to Cole in the prison gym last week.'

'Boss, if Blake wanted to take Rosie to gain leverage over Kathy Wright, why was there so much blood? Blake would need Rosie fit and well, wouldn't he?' Nick asked.

'I don't know, Nick. Maybe they came to take her and she fought them off? She was going to scream. Something went wrong. And all this is supposition at the moment,' Ruth said.

Drake got up from the table, signalling that he wanted to speak. 'The intel we've had from the RPIT appears to be the strongest line of inquiry that we have. However, let's not take our eye off other lines of inquiry until we have concrete evidence.'

'I am running a press conference with Jason and Kathy Wright this morning in the Media Room. Sian and Merringer, I need you to meet the FLO and uniformed officers at the Wrights' home at ten. As far as anyone is concerned, you are looking for anything to help with the search for Rosie. However, you are unofficially looking for anything that might help the RPIT in their investigation of Kathy Wright at Rhoswen. The RPIT officers will be with you as "observers",' Ruth said. 'Nick, I need you to swing by the college again. At the moment, we have no idea what Rosie Wright was doing last Monday. Was she at college, at home or somewhere else? Thank you, everyone. Back here at six, please.'

*Two days, fourteen hours*

It was ten o'clock when Ruth walked into the second press conference in as many days, now with Jason and Kathy Wright. As she sat down and looked out, Ruth saw it was standing room only. Journalists from around the country were clamouring for news about Rosie.

Pushing his chair back from the table, Jason immediately folded his arms. It was a bit late to give him some body language tips or media training, but he looked angry and anything but the concerned father. *Twitter trolls are going to have a bloody field day with him*, Ruth thought. Twenty minutes earlier, Jason had asked Ruth whether the press conference was really necessary and if it ever resulted in anything meaningful. Ruth had reassured him it was worthwhile, but she really wanted to ask why he wasn't willing to do anything to get his own daughter back.

Their appearance instigated a surge in the bustling noise in the room. In the old days, Ruth remembered the deafening noise of cameras clacking rhythmically.

*Nowadays, everything's all bloody digital*, Ruth thought.

Kathy Wright had hardly said a word since she arrived at Llancastell Police Station an hour earlier. If their hypothesis about her and Curtis Blake was true, and she suspected that her criminal activity had resulted in Rosie's disappearance, then she would be feeling overwhelming guilt. However, why didn't she just come clean? A couple of years in prison for the drug and phone smuggling in exchange for help to find her daughter?

Sensing the growing tension in the room, Ruth knew it was time to begin and could feel the nerves in her stomach. Ruth shifted to get comfortable on the chair and cleared her throat. *Here we go again.*

'Good afternoon, I'm Detective Inspector Ruth Hunter and I am the senior investigating officer on this case. I want to update you on developments in the search for Rosie Wright. First, I would like to reiterate my message from yesterday that our search for Rosie continues unabated and we are using all available resources to find her. Second, I would like to extend my thanks to the local communities in Capelulo and the wider Snowdonia area who have assisted with our search efforts so far. The sheer number of people who have shown support during the public searches has been incredible. I would ask that all planned public searches are coordinated through us so they dovetail with the extensive search operation the North Wales Police are running. Finally, I would urge anyone who has any information as to Rosie's whereabouts to come forward immediately. We do not have any further information that we can share with you at the moment, and I will not be answering any questions at this stage. Beside me are Rosie's parents, Jason and Kathy, and they would like to say a few words.'

Kathy looked at her and shifted awkwardly in her chair as she moved towards the microphone. Her voice was trembling and quiet. She looked broken. 'Rosie, we just want you back with us at home. You're not in trouble. We just want to make sure you are okay. If you can, please give us a call or a text – just to let us know you are safe. We all love you and want you back home with us. If you are Rosie's friend and you are sheltering her or you know anything, please get in touch.'

Kathy looked over at Ruth to signal that she had finished. Ruth glanced over at Jason Wright, who continued to stare grimly down at the floor as if he would rather be anywhere else but there.

Climbing the stairs, Sian and Merringer had already conducted a thorough search of the ground floor of the Wrights' home. So far, they had found nothing that helped them with the search for Rosie or Kathy Wright's possible involvement in the smuggling of drugs and phones at Rhoswen.

While Merringer checked the bathroom, Sian wandered into the main bedroom. It was small, tidy and dominated by a double bed with a subtle, floral duvet. A wedding photograph sat on the windowsill. Beside that was Kathy's dressing table with perfumes, jewellery and a hairbrush. On the wall above the bed was a small wooden cross. It seemed incongruous to Sian; neither Kathy nor Jason Wright seemed to be the religious type.

For a split second, Sian remembered what she found in the garage last night: Ruth's little shrine to Sarah's disappearance. It made Sian feel stupid and sick to her stomach. How were they meant to build any kind of life with that going on, for God's sake? Maybe they wouldn't be able to. Maybe it was time to move on. She had spent the morning swinging between anger and being hurt and upset.

Trying to focus on the job in hand, Sian opened the door to the large pine wardrobe and flicked through Kathy's clothes. Shoes, boots and trainers were lined up neatly at the bottom.

Merringer entered, holding something in his hand.

'Found something?' she asked.

He held up a green packet of pills: Microgynon 30. 'Isn't this a contraceptive pill?' Merringer asked.

Sian nodded. 'Yeah?'

'Prescribed for Rosie Wright?' Merringer said with a frown.

Sian knew that Merringer was curious as Rosie was allegedly gay. 'Some women use the pill to help with heavy or painful periods,' she explained.

'Oh, right…' Merringer said as his face blushed.

Merringer looked suitably awkward as he nodded and left. She smiled to herself. Even though he had two daughters, Merringer was a bit clueless when it came to anything like that.

A few seconds later, Merringer popped his head back round the door and looked past her as if he had seen something.

'What's up?' she asked him.

'You know that wardrobe's not flush to the wall?' he said gesturing to the wardrobe she had just looked in.

'We're not here to feng shui their furniture, Luke,' Sian quipped.

'Funny,' Merringer said.

Sian took a step to one side and looked at the wardrobe closely. He was right. There was a six-inch gap between the back of the wardrobe and wall. It might be nothing, but...

'Let's have a look,' she said, peering into the darkness behind the piece of furniture. There wasn't much light, so it was difficult to see anything, but it did look like there was something behind there.

Merringer clicked on his pocket torch and handed it to her. 'Here you go.'

'Ta,' she said as she moved the torch's beam and saw that a bag had been squashed between the wall and wardrobe. It might have fallen down there from on top of the wardrobe, or had something been deliberately hidden? 'Yeah, there's something there.'

'Let's move it out.' Merringer grabbed the wardrobe with both hands and edged it out slowly about two feet.

Sian crouched down and grabbed what looked like a black and grey canvas gym bag. Pulling it out onto the floor, she straightened out the handle before reaching for the zip and opening it.

Inside were plastic bags of bound fifty-pound notes. Sian looked up at Merringer – *bingo*.

'How much is there?' Merringer asked.

Sian flicked through them. Each packet contained one thousand pounds' worth of fifty-pound notes.

'About twenty grand,' Sian said.

'Bloody hell,' Merringer said as he crouched down to get a better look.

*What the hell are the Wrights doing with twenty thousand pounds hidden behind a wardrobe?* The intel about Kathy's smuggling business at the prison looked like it could be spot on.

--

It was baking hot by the time Nick had parked in the visitor car park at Llancastell Sixth Form College. It was the height of the exam season and the corridors were relatively quiet. As he climbed the stairs, Nick got a waft of food cooking somewhere. *Either the cafeteria or food technology classes*, he thought.

It had been nearly twenty years since Nick had been in this part of the college. Even though Nick had stayed on at Dinas Padog for his A levels, he had started dating Laura Foley who was doing English Literature, English Language and Art A levels at the college. She was a year older than him, which was pretty cool when you were seventeen. They bonded over The Stereophonics and Manic Street Preachers' albums that Nick claimed made him feel proudly Welsh. Both their childhoods had been dysfunctional, so maybe that's what drew them together. Laura had gone off to Liverpool University and after a few months they had drifted apart. However, the thought of her twisted his stomach.

Laura had got hooked on drugs at university and quickly became a heroin user. On a beautiful August evening in 2003, Laura had overdosed and died in the house she shared in Toxteth with three other smackheads. Nick couldn't bear to think of her like that.

Finding Rosie's form room empty save for George Xavier, Rosie's form tutor, Nick asked if he could have another word. Bringing over his laptop, Xavier sat down opposite Nick at the front of the classroom. For a moment, Nick still had the image of Laura in his head, but he had to focus. He tried to put her out of his mind.

Glancing up at one of the wall displays, Nick noticed one that had lettering spelling out, 'Wonderwall', with a photo of Liam and Noel Gallagher either side. The wall had students' work all over it.

'Wonderwall? Aren't Oasis a bit before your time?' Nick said.

'A bit. Classic songs though. Not a fan?' Xavier asked.

'They weren't even the best Beatles tribute act in Manchester,' quipped Nick. He wasn't sure he believed that, but it was a good joke.

'Ouch. Bit harsh,' Xavier said with a smile and then nodded as he found something on the laptop. He showed Nick the digital class register. 'Okay, so Rosie was in for morning and lunchtime registration.'

Nick noticed Xavier had a Glastonbury Festival wristband in amongst his assorted leather and fabric bracelets. *Who is he trying to impress?* Nick thought.

'Can you tell me what time she left college?' Nick asked.

'No. Lunchtime register is at one. Rosie had private study periods in the afternoon where she's meant to go to the library to work. But some students go to the cafeteria and just chat. Others find empty classrooms or computer rooms to go and work in,' Xavier explained.

'Isn't that a safeguarding issue?' Nick asked.

Xavier shrugged. 'Probably. I don't run the college. But I did ask the IT people to send over some CCTV from the main gate and the road outside. You can see when students leave. I've done it before when I think someone's been lying to me,' Xavier explained.

Nick nodded but suspected Xavier was showing off, trying to play amateur detective. 'Can we have a look?'

Xavier began to play the footage of the gate and road on fast-forward. The time code ran at the bottom right of the screen. It was mainly quiet, with only a couple of students leaving during the hour before the end of the college day.

At 3:10 p.m., the figure of a girl, with a rucksack on her back, made her way out of the gates. She was on her phone.

Xavier immediately stopped the CCTV on his laptop and pointed. 'I think that's her.'

As the footage played now in real time, the girl turned her head a little and Nick could see that it was definitely Rosie Wright.

'Yeah, it is,' Nick said. Then his eye was drawn to a black VW Golf that had slowed and parked outside the school gates. 'Can you stop it for a moment?'

Xavier paused the footage and Nick squinted as he looked at the car. The driver's window was down and a young man looked out as Rosie approached. It was Gareth Wright.

'That's her brother,' Xavier said as he saw what Nick was looking at.

'Yeah, I've had the dubious pleasure already. Does he normally give her a lift from college?' Nick asked.

'I'm not sure. As I said, Rosie didn't give the impression that they get on.'

'Yeah, he doesn't strike me as the altruistic type,' Nick said.

'He was at this college for a while,' Xavier explained.

'What happened?' Nick asked.

'He was permanently excluded.'

'What for?'

'Drug dealing and threatening a fellow student with a shotgun,' Xavier said, shaking his head.

'Not really head boy material then?' Nick quipped. This new knowledge did little to dispel the impression that Gareth Wright was a scumbag.

As they watched the footage play, Rosie leant down and spoke to Gareth for a moment. From the facial expressions and gesturing, it was clear that they were having some kind of argument.

Backing away from the car, Rosie then kicked the car door and the front wing in sheer fury. The door opened sharply, nearly hitting Rosie.

Nick watched closely as Gareth got out of the car. He grabbed Rosie around the throat for a few seconds and then pushed her to the ground. He was clearly shouting at her. Jumping back into the car, Gareth sped out of shot, leaving a shocked Rosie still on the pavement.

Nick and Xavier shared a look – they weren't expecting to see that.

### Two days, nineteen hours

'With all due respect, sir, there is a sixteen-year-old girl missing. We don't have time to wait to see how this investigation pans out…' Ruth growled. She was exasperated that the investigation into Kathy Wright and the alleged smuggling of drugs and phones into HMP Rhoswen was getting in the way of their hunt for Rosie.

At the head of the table, Superintendent Jones sat listening to what everyone had to say. They needed someone of his rank to decide on how to proceed.

Ruth shifted in her seat. She needed another ciggie and more caffeine. Either side of her sat Nick and Drake.

DI Lyon and DS Buckley from the RPIT sat opposite. They seemed equally frustrated at having six months of surveillance and evidence against Kathy Wright and several other prison officers blown out of the water. Ruth knew that Lyon was right. As soon as Kathy Wright was questioned about her smuggling of drugs and phones into Rhoswen, her relationship with Frank Cole and now her relationship with Curtis Blake, the game was up.

'You don't have any proof that there is a direct correlation between Kathy Wright's trafficking of drugs and phones, and Curtis Blake and Rosie Wright's disappearance,' Lyon said, looking over at Ruth, Nick and Drake.

'That's true, DI Lyon. I know you've put hundreds of hours of manpower into your case. However, do you think it is a coincidence that Curtis Blake arrives at Rhoswen, takes over the supply of drugs and phones, and the prison officer who is controlling the smuggling ring has her daughter taken by force?' Drake said, ever the diplomat in his tone and manner.

'This can't be your only line of inquiry?' Buckley asked. Ruth could see she was angry.

'You two didn't answer the question,' Nick said, getting confrontational.

Lyon glared at him across the table and sat forward. 'The theory that DCI Drake offered is complete supposition. You're just guessing that Curtis Blake is trying to intimidate Kathy Wright. Where's your evidence?' Lyon asked.

'Hey, I've seen what Curtis Blake does to people he wants to intimidate. He's a sick, evil psychopath and taking Rosie Wright is his standard MO,' Nick sneered.

It wasn't that long ago that Nick had worked a case where members of Curtis Blake's gang had posed as police officers to kidnap a rival drug dealer, Gary Parsons', wife. Blake had warned Parsons that he was dealing on his turf and that he needed to leave Merseyside or he would regret it. When Parsons ignored the threats, Blake chopped off four of Sonia Parsons' fingers just to show how serious he was.

'Again, that's subjective,' Buckley pointed out, much to Nick's annoyance.

'Look, we understand how much work has gone into the investigation at Rhoswen. But the link between Kathy Wright and Curtis Blake seems to be our most viable line of inquiry,' Ruth explained.

Jones pulled his seat forward. Ruth knew that he found these types of meetings and having to make a decision difficult. Making a decision meant that Jones could choose the wrong one and could therefore be culpable if something didn't go to plan. If he left it to others, then he could clear up the mess afterwards but claim he was not responsible. The more she dealt with Jones during her time at Llancastell, the more she resented his insipid nature and spinelessness. He was the worst kind of slick politico, and, as far as she was concerned, he had no place in the police force.

'First, the fact that drugs are getting into Rhoswen is not a huge surprise. We know demand is so high that they're throwing drug-filled rats over the walls there,' Jones said.

However unpleasant the story, Ruth had heard that dead rats were being hollowed out, filled with drugs, stitched up and tossed over the prison's walls into the recreation area. There were no ends to how inventive criminals could be to get drugs into a prison. She had heard of everything from drones to pigeons and tennis balls to hollowed-out dildos. The mind boggled.

'Is there some kind of compromise that we can reach here?' Jones asked, gesturing with his hand like some well-rehearsed politician.

Lyon shrugged and looked over the table. 'DCI Drake, what's the minimum that you need on your end?'

Drake turned his head to look at Ruth. 'Ruth, what do you think?'

'We need to talk openly to Kathy Wright. We need to persuade her to be honest about her relationship with Curtis Blake. Has he threatened her or her family?' Ruth said.

'And that ruins our case and hundreds of hours of work!' Lyon growled.

'Do you suggest that we wait until Blake has Rosie Wright's ear or fingers cut off and sent to her family before we actually do anything?' Ruth exclaimed.

Drake looked at Jones. 'Sir, given the amount of time Rosie has been missing, we do need to talk to Kathy Wright.'

'Once you've spoken to her, she can't go back to work,' Buckley said.

'Put her under house arrest,' Nick suggested. 'She doesn't go anywhere near the prison. The staff at Rhoswen are none the wiser. They think she's off because of Rosie. The FLO,

PC Bennett, makes sure that she has no access to a phone or computer in the coming days. We follow her even if she goes for a piss.'

Jones nodded. 'I think Nick has a good point. What do we think?'

Drake nodded. 'It works for us, sir.'

Lyon looked at Buckley, who nodded. 'Okay. It might work for us in the short term,' he said reluctantly.

Jones gathered together his papers. 'Thank you, everyone. Ashley and Ruth, keep me posted.'

As she headed for the door, Ruth's phone buzzed and she answered it. 'DI Hunter.' Ruth couldn't help but smile at the news she was hearing.

'Boss,' Ruth said.

'Ruth?'

'Sian and Luke have just found twenty grand hidden in a bag at Kathy Wright's home,' she said.

'I'd like to see how she's going to explain that,' Drake said, raising an eyebrow.

# CHAPTER 11

*Three days missing*

HMP Applethorn was a category-D prison in the East Cheshire countryside. The open prison was the final step for many prisoners before they settled back into society, with a far more relaxed environment including a farm and allotments that were all run by the prisoners.

It was close to dusk by the time Nick and Amanda arrived to see her father, Tony. The prison still had a strict security system for visitors. Nick felt overly protective as a female prison officer frisked and searched Amanda. But once they were beyond that, it felt like a different world. He had been to the old Victorian prisons over in Liverpool and Manchester that seemed to have come out of some dark Dickensian novel. Whereas Applethorn looked clean, modern and comfortable.

Tony met them in the gardens, which were neat and well tended with colourful flower beds. Nick was surprised at how tall he was. Maybe six foot four. He was rakishly thin with a Roman nose and thin glasses. He and Amanda gave each other an unconvincing hug in greeting. Nick noticed that Tony's clothes seemed to hang off him. They said very little as they made their way over to a table, which overlooked the garden and the Cheshire countryside beyond that.

Glancing out at the vista below, Tony started to clean his glasses. 'You know, for the first couple of years, I forgot what it was like to look out at a view or a sunset. Not that I'm complaining... Anyway, you okay, Mand?'

'Yeah... First grandchild on the way,' she said as she smiled and patted her stomach.

'It's nice to meet you, Tony,' Nick said. The awkwardness was getting to him and he felt compelled to say something.

'Mand's told me a lot about you, Nick,' Tony said.

'Oh, dear. Well, none of it's true, I promise,' Nick joked, and they all laughed. At last the ice was starting to melt.

'A copper, eh?' Tony said.

'Twelve years on the job now.'

Tony nodded thoughtfully. 'Neither of you have chosen an easy career path, have you? Fair play to you both.'

'A pair of do-gooders, eh?' Amanda said with a smile.

Amanda still had a couple of months left working for the Llancastell Child Protection before she was off on maternity leave. If he was honest, Nick worried about her being around the horror and tragedy that went hand in hand with her job, especially as she was pregnant. However, she had assured him that she had coping mechanisms, particularly now she was sober.

After a moment, Amanda pushed her hair out of her face and behind her ear. Nick knew it as a tell. If Amanda felt nervous about what she was about to say, she pushed her hair behind her ear. He told her never to play poker because she would get cleaned out. She did it in AA meeting sometimes when she shared or had been asked to read something to the group.

'I was surprised to get your text, Dad,' Amanda said.

'Yeah. It was about time that I saw you. Especially with all that's going on for you.' Tony looked at his nails for a moment. 'I also wanted you to know that I've got cancer. But before you say anything, it's prostate, they've got it early and I'm not going to die, which will disappoint some people on the planet.'

'I'm really sorry, Dad,' Amanda said as she reached across the table and touched his hand for a second. Nick could see how uncomfortable the gesture made Tony. Guilt had that effect on people. He could also see how gaunt Tony's face was – he was skin and bone all over. Maybe it was Nick's suspicious nature, but Tony didn't look like a man who had had an early diagnosis of prostate cancer.

'No need to be sorry. It just made me think, that's all. I've had to live with what I've done, and that's been fucking hard. And I know I've got amends to make to those that will allow me to. And you're one of them, Mand,' Tony said.

'Thank you, Dad. That means a lot.'

'I wish your mum was around, you know?'

'I know. When do you get out?' Amanda asked.

'Three months.'

'You gonna be all right?' she asked.

'Yeah. It's just one day at a time, isn't it? Two days that I can't do anything about. Yesterday and tomorrow. It's taken me this time being banged up to realise how lucky I was and still am. Learn a bit of gratitude, you know?'

Nick's ears pricked up. He knew someone in the fellowship when he heard one. 'How long have you been going to the meetings?'

At first, Tony looked angry, even indignant. Feeling that he had either overstepped the mark or got it wrong, Nick was going to apologise. He kicked himself for being some kind of born-again AA zealot.

However, Tony's face changed and he said, 'About a year, I suppose. There was a good meeting at the nick I was in in Warwick. You?'

Nick nodded. 'Early days. You know, keep coming back, keep listening.'

Amanda caught Tony's eye. 'Me too, Dad.'

Tony took this in and scratched his chin. 'Really?'

'Yeah. It's where we met. Well, sort of,' Amanda explained.

Tony shook his head. 'I didn't think you'd be telling me that tonight, Mand. But if you're looking out for each other, I guess that's a good thing.'

Nick watched as Tony moved his hand and put it on top of his daughter's for a moment. He could see how unsure Tony was, but Amanda gave her father a reassuring smile.

'We're gonna be fine, Dad. Don't worry.'

# CHAPTER 12

*Three days, twelve hours*

Built in 2010, HMP Rhoswen was a new super prison for mainly category-A prisoners on the North Wales coast. With over two thousand inmates, Rhoswen was the biggest prison in Wales and was heralded a decade ago as a modern and progressive flagship for the UK's penal system. But it hadn't quite worked out like that.

As Nick pulled the car into the visitor car park, Ruth was searching through the social media response to the Wrights' press conference.

'We don't have time for this to be a wild goose chase,' Ruth said.

'It's Blake. It's his MO. And that means Rosie is being held until Kathy Wright does what she's told,' Nick said with confidence.

'You always think it's Blake, Nick. But if it's not, we're running out of time,' Ruth said, aware that she sounded annoyed. She couldn't help it. Rosie was still missing and progress was agonisingly slow.

Ruth wondered how their meeting with Rhoswen's governor, Gordon Holmes, would go. She knew that Holmes's liberal views on prison life had made him a target for the right-wing press. He was open in his belief that prisoners should be referred to as *men* and not *offenders*. They were housed in *rooms* and not *cells*. Holmes wanted Rhoswen to be truly rehabilitative. He was fond of quoting Nelson Mandela's ideas about freedom and justice: 'As I walked out the door towards the gate that would lead to my freedom, I knew if I didn't leave my bitterness and hatred behind, I'd still be in prison.'

With a full-sized Astroturf football pitch, gyms, education area, workshops, sports hall, Rhoswen even had a wellbeing and multi-faith centre.

However, Rhoswen had had more than its fair share of teething problems since its opening. There had been delays in the completion of certain sections of the prison. And the relaxed regime seemed to have had the opposite effect on the prison population. Violence within the prison was above average, as was the number of prisoners who tested positive for drugs.

Getting out of the car, Ruth remembered the last time she had visited HMP Rhoswen. It had been an ill-fated day with the serial killer Andrew Gates last December. The very thought of Gates made her shudder. Back then, the ground had been scattered with snow and the car park was icy. Now, the summer sun was blazing down on them and the air was warm and still.

Glancing around at the series of new box-shaped buildings that had been highlighted with stripes of red, blue, green and yellow, she thought that HMP Rhoswen could be mistaken for one of the modern academies she had seen in her time in South London. In fact, the only giveaway to the buildings' true purpose were the bars on the windows. Sardonically, she thought some South London academies could have done with bars too.

Ruth's train of thought was broken by the sound of a car door shutting nearby. DI Lyon and DS Buckley had parked close and now strolled over to meet her and Nick.

*Right, let's get on with this.*

'Welcome to HMP Premier Inn,' Nick said acerbically.

'I wonder where they went wrong?' Lyon asked, gesturing to the modern prison blocks.

Nick shrugged. 'I think it's too late by the time they get here. You can change a child or a teenager's views on what's right and wrong. But some forty-year-old villain who's spent half his life inside isn't going to change because he's got a nice library, a yoga class and some positive slogans on the wall.'

'Unfortunately, I think you're right. Some of the men in here were going to prison from the day they were conceived. We just pick up the pieces,' Buckley said with a world-weariness.

Ruth wasn't listening. In fact, she was getting frustrated that the others were having a casual debate over modern justice and the penal system.

*There's a teenage girl missing, tied up somewhere or worse – get a move on!*

Ruth could tell she was becoming too emotionally involved. But that's how she worked, and she wasn't going to change now.

Looking around, the four of them headed over to the security entrance and then inside. The reception area had brightly-coloured seats and a large slogan painted on the wall: *Big journeys begin with the small steps.*

Within ten minutes, they were sitting with the governor, Gordon Holmes, in the prison's main conference room. It was all glass and clean angles and wouldn't have looked out of place in the advertising agencies of London's West End. Even though he was in his early fifties, Holmes had a boyish face, a mop of greying hair and intense blue eyes.

Holmes was disappointed but not surprised that some of his prison officers were under investigation by the RPIT. However, he was annoyed that it had taken them this long to bring their suspicions to him. Lyon and Buckley assured him that they were planning to make their suspicions known to him as soon as they had enough concrete evidence to make arrests.

Ruth brought their attention back to Rosie's disappearance – they were still working against the clock. 'Look, we're invest-igating the disappearance of Rosie Wright,' Ruth explained. 'That's what's important here. And she's been missing for nearly four days.'

'It's horrible. I feel so sorry for Kathy. I've told her to take as much time off as she needs,' Holmes explained.

'Unfortunately, we believe that Kathy Wright is at the centre of the prison officers who are smuggling in drugs and phones,' Lyon said.

Holmes shifted uncomfortably in his seat and frowned. 'Kathy? Really? I'm shocked.'

Ruth looked at him. Was he shocked or had he had his suspicions? She couldn't tell.

'One theory is that Curtis Blake is somehow involved in her daughter's disappearance,' Nick clarified.

'Although we don't have solid evidence of that,' Lyon explained.

Nick shot Lyon a withering look, 'Which is why I described it as a theory.'

'I wouldn't put anything past Curtis Blake. He's been here five minutes and thinks he runs this place. I know some of my officers feel intimidated by him being here,' Holmes explained.

'The suspicion is that Kathy Wright was supplying drugs and phones to Frank Cole. As you know, Cole was severely injured in your prison's gym. Blake would want Kathy to continue to organise the smuggling. He has a history of intimidating people by getting to their families,' Ruth said.

'And this information has to stay within these four walls. We don't want any of your officers to know about the investigation. Not until we can confirm who is corrupt and who is not,' Buckley said.

Holmes nodded sternly. This was all happening on his watch, and Ruth could see how uncomfortable it had made him. 'Of course. Anything to get Rosie back.'

'We need a surveillance team to put a hidden microphone in his cell. We also need a table in the visiting area to be fitted with a hidden bug and for Blake to be assigned that table for any visitors. I want to monitor every conversation Blake has with anyone. We need continuous access to your CCTV.' Ruth gestured to the folder she was carrying. 'I have a RIPA authorisation with me from Superintendent Jones at Llancastell.'

RIPA was the Regulation of Investigatory Powers Act, which regulated the use of surveillance within the UK.

Holmes looked at everyone in the room. 'Yeah, that's fine. No problem.'

'Looks like we're all in agreement then?' Ruth said as she got her paperwork together. It was progress, but it felt like wading through mud.

–

It was mid-morning when Sian and French took the turning to Penmaenmawr from the North Wales Expressway. Ruth had sent them to get an explanation from Gareth Wright about the altercation with Rosie outside the sixth form college, as well as nail down his vague alibi for the time of his sister's disappearance.

It was burning hot, and even though she was wearing sunglasses, Sian squinted at the sun's rays that glinted on the windscreen and the car's bonnet. Penmaenmawr was a small town a few miles from Capelulo, up on the North Wales coast. It had been a quarrying town in the past. Now it was known for its stunning Snowdonian scenery. The Penmaen-mawr Mountain stood above the sea immediately to the west of the town. It had once stood at a magnificent 1,600 feet above sea level and had been the site of a fortified prehistoric settlement. However, as the result of devastating quarrying in the nineteenth century, the mountain now had a distinctive flat peak – the rock face was made from the hardest granite in the British Empire. Within a few decades, quarrymen reduced Penmaenmawr from a majestic mountain to a stumpy bump, just under 1,000 feet high. The granite was taken by boat to Scandinavia and mainland Europe to build roads and buildings, and over to England to build the roads and factories of Victorian Manchester.

The journey to Capelulo was only the second occurrence that Sian had spent any length of time with DC Dan French, the first being their interview with Martin Hancock. He had all the zip and energy of a rookie. However, he kept himself to himself and seemed intuitive when discussing the case.

'So, why the police force, Dan?' Sian asked, taking the lead.

'I come from three generations of coppers. I wasn't going to be anything else,' Dan said with a cheery shrug. Sian could see that he didn't seem to resent the fact that he was now in the 'family business'.

'Yeah, my taid was a policeman too. But then it must have skipped a generation because my dad was a thieving toerag,' Sian said with a chuckle.

French looked over at her and raised a quizzical eyebrow.

'Oh, nothing heavy like. We just couldn't return Christmas presents because there were no receipts, you know. That kind of thing,' Sian explained.

Turning off Bangor Road, they headed for the centre of town and soon found the small house on St David's Terrace that Gareth Wright shared with a friend.

On the road outside, a black Volkswagen Golf 1.6 was parked. French pulled over and parked behind.

'Is that Gareth Wright's car?' French asked knowingly.

'Yeah, why?'

'Golf 1.6. Fifteen plate. That's ten grand's worth of car,' French explained.

'Know your cars, Dan?'

'I was a boy racer in a previous life,' he quipped.

'And how does a twenty-one-year-old apprentice afford that?' Sian asked rhetorically. *Unless he's up to no good*, she wanted to say.

As they got out, Sian could see that the exterior of the house was covered in nasty brown pebbledash and patches of damp. The paving stones were cracked and strewn with weeds, which had flowered yellow. A plastic bag of empty beer cans and a stack of pizza boxes were next to the overflowing bin.

'Home sweet home,' French said wryly.

Sian knocked and eventually Gareth answered the door. Dressed in a T-shirt and trackies, he looked like he had just rolled out of bed.

'Gareth Wright?' French asked.

'Yeah...' he mumbled.

'DC Hockney and DC French, Llancastell CID,' Sian said, showing her warrant card.

'Is it Rosie? Have you found her?' he asked, rubbing his face and blinking.

'No, I'm sorry. Can we come in? We need to clarify a few things with you in our search for Rosie,' Sian explained.

As they went in, the house smelt of burnt toast and weed. Sian knew they weren't there to nick Gareth for possession. Not today anyway.

The living room was a tip. Cans of beer, stale food, remnants of spliffs. *Student stereotype noted*, Sian thought.

'Sorry about the mess,' Gareth said as he slumped down on the sofa.

'Can you tell us where you were at about three o'clock last Monday afternoon?' French asked as they sat cautiously on two worn armchairs.

Gareth frowned, scratched his stubble and then shook his head. 'No, sorry. I can't remember. I might have been here.'

Sian removed a still from the college CCTV and showed Gareth. 'We have this CCTV footage of you outside Llancastell Sixth Form College at three o'clock?'

'Oh, right. Yeah, I went there to catch up with Rosie when she left,' Gareth said.

'And why was that?' French asked.

Sian had clocked two rolled twenty-pound notes on the table. Gareth had been doing more than just smoking weed.

'I was going to give her a lift home,' Gareth said.

*Stop lying to us, you twat!*

'And did you give her a lift home, Gareth?' French asked.

'You've got the CCTV, mate,' Gareth sneered back.

'We watched the CCTV and it's clear that you and Rosie had a row,' Sian said.

Gareth shrugged. 'So what? Not the first brother and sister to row.'

'A row that ended up with you grabbing her by the throat and pushing her to the ground,' Sian said.

'Why you bothering me with all this shit? There's some fucking psycho out there who's got my sister,' Gareth said, giving them a withering look.

'What were you arguing about, Gareth?' French asked.

'I can't remember.'

French looked directly at him and raised an eyebrow. 'Well, if you could remember, that would be useful as Rosie went missing five hours later,' he said with a heavy dose of sarcasm.

'You know, brother and sister shit. I dunno...'

'No, I don't know,' Sian snapped. She was losing her patience. Gareth was hiding something and he needed persuading to tell them what. 'Let's see if I can jog your memory. If I get forensic officers in here to sweep that table for class A drugs, are they going to find anything incriminating? You've already got previous for intent to supply, Gareth.'

Gareth let out a sigh and then said, 'Okay. Rosie wanted me to get her and her mates some pills. I said I wasn't going to deal drugs to my little sister. So she kicked the shit out of my car.'

'Why did you grab her round the throat?' French asked.

Gareth didn't want to answer, and he tapped his foot on the carpet in frustration.

'DC French, what's it like when forensic officers search a house for drugs?' Sian asked knowingly.

'Well, they basically rip the place apart. I've seen them cut open mattresses to look for drugs,' French explained, playing along.

'And the dogs?'

'Don't get me started with the dogs...' French said, shaking his head melodramatically.

'DC French was admiring your car earlier, Gareth,' Sian said.

'That's ten grand's worth of wheels. How did you afford that? Student loan? Or do we need to get access to your bank account?'

Gareth sat forward. 'All right. Point made. Rosie said if I didn't get them the pills, she would go to our dad and tell him that I was dealing again. Which was bullshit,' Gareth explained reluctantly.

'And that's why you attacked her?' Sian asked.

'Yeah. I didn't mean to, but…' Gareth took some tobacco and skins from the table and began to roll himself a cigarette. His hands were shaking a little.

'Are you scared of your dad, Gareth?'

'He's a prick,' Gareth snorted.

'Is that a yes?'

'He's not right in the head. If you're going to talk to anyone in our family about Rosie going missing, you should be talking to him.'

Sian shot French a look – what did that mean?

'Why do you say that?' Sian asked.

'He's a fucking weirdo. Haven't you worked that out, yet? I saw the way he looked at Rosie and her friends. It was bloody creepy, you know. It made me sick when he tried to flirt with some of them. Sad wanker,' Gareth explained as he lit his cigarette.

Sian processed what Gareth had just said. They needed to have a very close look at where Jason Wright was on Monday evening.

–

As they had left HMP Rhoswen and Ruth had returned to Llancastell to debrief Drake, Nick received a call from the surveillance team in West Rhyl. They had followed Hayley Collard up to Holyhead Port with a Romanian national, Christian Vasilescu, where they were due to catch a ferry to Dublin.

Having heard all the recent intel and data coming out of Holyhead, Nick wondered if Hayley Collard was being sex trafficked out of Wales and into Ireland. Romanian gangs had taken over the prostitution and sex trade in Dublin. There had been turf wars with local gangs and Russian traffickers. The police had only just tightened up security at Holyhead, but it was still seen as 'soft' by Eastern European gangs moving human traffic between Ireland and the UK mainland.

There was an added element to the intel. An eyewitness said they had seen Rosie Wright in a van with a man with dark skin at Holyhead Port. Local uniformed police officers had gone to check out the sighting. They couldn't find the van or anyone that even looked like Rosie.

However, Nick started to put together a hypothesis. A Romanian gang in North Wales was trafficking vulnerable girls out to Dublin to work as prostitutes. They were using Hayley Collard to befriend and groom any vulnerable teenage girls that could be coerced. Rosie had been kidnapped by the gang and shipped out by ferry. The gang were taking Hayley over to Ireland that morning. It was all supposition, but it fitted together neatly.

Despite all this, Nick still favoured the hypothesis that Kathy Wright was leading a team of bent prison officers who were smuggling drugs and phones for Frank Cole. Curtis Blake's arrival at HMP Rhoswen had signalled a new regime and put Kathy Wright in a very dangerous position if Blake wanted to put in his own officer. Intimidation and violence, especially of family members, was Blake's MO. And, of course, Nick wasn't deluded enough to know that he favoured any theory that would add to Blake's time in prison.

The ferry terminal was busy. It was the height of the holiday season. Cars and vans queued in the heat, the smell of exhaust fumes and the sea was thick in the air. The dull growl of engines was broken intermittently by the caw of gulls overhead. To the right, enormous articulated lorries were parked in long rows, so close that they looked like they were interlocked as one long, metallic creature.

Taking off his sunglasses to get a clearer view, Nick parked over by the Stena ferry terminal. *False Alarm*, Two Door Cinema Club's latest album had been playing on the car stereo. Nick thought its Eighties retro sound was perfect for the hot weather.

The latest update from the uniformed officers was that Hayley Collard and her travelling companion had been followed all the way from Rhyl but had been lost somewhere in the terminal building. The next ferry to Dublin was in half an hour. Passports were not technically required to travel from Holyhead to Dublin. However, some form of ID was needed to travel, and a Romanian criminal gang would have no trouble getting hold of fake IDs. It would be a reasonable assumption to think they would be travelling under false names.

Once inside, Nick made radio contact with local uniformed officers and met them over by the ticket office.

'Morning, lads,' Nick said as he approached and showed them his warrant card. 'What have we got?'

Even though Nick knew it wasn't a desirable part of his character, he couldn't help feeling a sense of pride and superiority in being a detective sergeant from Llancastell CID when talking to the woodentops. It didn't matter as long as he didn't let it show and become an arrogant twat.

'Sarge. We've checked the passenger list. Twelve sets of male and female passengers travelling together on the next ferry,' the officer – male, blond and freckled – said. His pale skin was a Chernobyl shade of red. *Too much time in the sun*, Nick thought.

The older officer – bald, suntanned and carrying some extra timber – nodded and said, 'Checked for "Hayley Collard" and just "Hayley". Nothing, but that's not surprising. You can get a bloody fake driving licence online for fifty quid these days.' His tone was dour – he'd seen it all before.

'What about the vehicle they travelled here in?' Nick asked.

'We lost them as we came into the ferry terminal. We've checked the number plate against all the vehicles on the list. No match,' the blond officer explained.

'So, they either ditched the car or are travelling on foot? Or they've switched vehicles or plates?' Nick said, thinking out loud.

'Yes, Sarge,' the older officer said and nodded.

Then out of the corner of his eye, Nick caught sight of dyed-red hair. Dark eye make-up, high cheekbones, long silver earrings.

It was Hayley Collard.

'Shit!' Nick muttered as he moved away. 'She's over there. Red hair,' he said quietly as he gestured to where Hayley was walking past the rows of blue seats about a hundred yards away.

For a few tense seconds, they followed her across the passenger lounge – she was oblivious to their presence.

Then a baby beside them started to wail.

Hayley was being hypervigilant. She looked over to the sound and spotted them. She took off, her rucksack bouncing across her shoulders, and sprinted away. Dying her hair from blue to red had done little to conceal her identity.

'Great!' Nick immediately broke into a sprint. He felt his feet clatter against the blue carpeted floor and the hot material of his trousers against his thighs. This was not a day to go chasing suspects.

A female voice made an announcement over the loudspeaker about times for boarding the ferry.

Weaving in and out of passengers, Hayley looked back to see how far away Nick and the other officers were.

Sidestepping a mother and pram, Nick pumped his arms – he was gaining on her. She looked like she didn't know where to go next as she dodged left and then right.

Hayley made her move: over to the right towards the large glass double doors out onto the quayside. As she cut right, Nick knew immediately she was heading outside. Once there, it would be easier for her to lose them. *Shit!*

Glancing over at the blond officer, who rather annoyingly wasn't struggling for breath, Nick pointed at another set of doors.

'She's going outside!' Nick yelled. 'Cut her off that way!'

Passengers looked up from what they were doing, alarmed by the sight of police officers running and shouting.

Calculating that the quickest way to the doors was over the rows of blue seats, Nick changed direction, took a leap and hurdled three empty seats. Waiting for his foot to catch and for him to tumble into a heap, he thankfully landed on the other side and kept his balance.

*I hope someone was videoing that on their phone. It was one hell of a jump!*

Crashing through the doors, Hayley disappeared out of sight. However, Nick was now only yards behind. Following her out onto the concrete quayside, he could see the vast white Stena ferries that loomed over everything in sight.

Glancing quickly left and right, he looked for Hayley. *Where the hell is she?* His attention was caught by a metallic clanging sound. She was running up a steel walkway.

'DS Evans to all units. Suspect is heading up a gangplank to one of the ferries,' Nick said into his Tetra radio.

However, the walkway led to a large, locked metal door. Hayley tried it with all her strength.

Nick got to bottom of the gangplank and looked up at her, trying to catch his breath.

'Come on, Hayley,' Nick said, gesturing for her to return the way she had come.

'I'm not going anywhere with you,' Hayley growled at him.

'You can jump in if you want, but I'm not going in there to save you. It's too bloody cold,' Nick said sardonically.

Hayley pulled out a knife from her bag. It was a six-inch lock knife that Nick knew was popular with local gangs.

'Really, Hayley? You're going to stab a police officer? Come on, throw the knife away or you're going to get into serious trouble, aren't you?' Nick said. He was fairly certain Hayley had no intention of attacking him.

'I'll use it,' Hayley said.

'No, you won't,' Nick said. 'Just throw it away, eh?'

'I've used it before or don't you believe me?' Hayley asked.

'Hayley, this is what is going to happen if you continue to stand there waving a knife around. Police officers are going to come down here with a Taser. If they use it, it's very painful. They might send down some armed officers too. Or the dog unit. It's going to be horrible and you'll get arrested,' Nick said calmly. 'Or you can throw the knife in the water, come with me back to Llancastell, have a cup of tea and I can tell you why I want to talk to you.'

Hayley looked at him directly for a moment, rolled her eyes and threw the knife into the water.

'For fuck's sake!' she shouted to no one in particular.

'There you go. Let's go and get that tea now, shall we?' Nick said.

*Three days, eighteen hours*

After the debriefing with Jones, Ruth sent uniformed officers to pick up Kathy Wright and bring her back to Llancastell for questioning. Prior to the interview, Ruth and DI Lyon had gone over what they were going to ask her and what evidence they were going to present. Under Lyon's gruff exterior, Ruth could see that he was a thoughtful officer who was focused on why he did the job. He reminded her of some of the older officers she had worked with at the Met.

Opening the door to the interview room, Ruth saw Kathy Wright glaring back at her from across the room. She was wearing too much make-up and the top she was squeezed into was ill-fitting and tight on her arms.

'What the bloody hell am I doing here?' Kathy thundered.

Lyon looked over at her as he sat down. 'Kathy Wright, you are under arrest for misconduct in a public office, supplying controlled drugs of class A and B into a prison and conveying a list A prohibited article into a prison. You do not have to say anything, but it may harm your defence if you do not mention when questioned something which you later rely on in court. Anything you do say may be given in evidence.'

'What the fuck is going on?' Kathy shouted and looked at her solicitor. 'Say something!'

Ruth and Lyon put their folders down as they settled.

Watching her for a moment, Ruth could see the cogs in Kathy's brain whirring at a hundred miles an hour.

'Kathy, we have reason to believe that you have been smuggling drugs and mobile phones into HMP Rhoswen. You have been under the surveillance of the Regional Prison Investigation Team for the past six months,' Lyon explained.

Looking like she had been smacked across the face, Kathy sat back in her chair, trying to get her head around what had just happened.

'This is a sick joke. My daughter has been taken by some disgusting paedo and you're doing this?' Kathy said with a sneer as she moved her head to give her words more emphasis. She was a long way from the vulnerable mother that Ruth had first encountered.

'Kathy, we strongly believe that Rosie's disappearance might be linked to your supply of drugs and phones into Rhoswen,' Ruth said.

'I don't know what you're talking about,' Kathy said, screwing up her face like she had tasted something sour.

'You're denying that you are smuggling drugs and phones into the prison?' Lyon asked.

'Of course! This is bloody stupid,' Kathy said and looked to her solicitor again.

However many times she encountered it, Ruth was still amazed at some people's ability to lie despite the consequences for their loved ones.

'For the purposes of the tape, this is image two–six–seven, item reference S-I-seven-five,' Ruth said as she slid over a photograph. 'The image shows twenty thousand pounds in a sports bag that was recovered from your house. Could you tell us how it got there?'

'I've got no idea,' Kathy said.

'This isn't your money?'

'No, of course not.' Kathy sighed as though it was a stupid question.

'Can you explain how twenty thousand pounds ended up in a sports bag in your house?' Lyon asked.

'No, I can't. I'm not the only person who lives at that house. And anyone could have come into our house and put it there,' Kathy said with a shrug.

That was one of the worst things about the job: when people told the most idiotic lies. They lied and tied themselves in knots. They lied even when they knew that you knew that they were lying. It's some people's default setting.

'Come on, Kathy. If you don't tell us what's going on, how are we going to find Rosie?' Ruth asked.

*Lying to us when your daughter is out there. What kind of bitch are you?* What Ruth really wanted to do was shake her and give her a slap.

'I promise you. The money's not mine.'

'What do you know about a prisoner called Curtis Blake?' Ruth asked.

'Nothing.'

'You don't know who Curtis Blake is?' Lyon asked disbelievingly.

'For the purposes of the tape, this is image two-nine-three, item reference S-I-seven-eight,' Ruth said as she slid over a still from the prison's CCTV. The image showed Kathy talking with Curtis Blake in the recreation area. 'The image shows the suspect Kathy Wright talking to a prisoner identified as Curtis Blake. According to the time code, this conversation lasts for fifteen minutes.'

'So what? I'm a prison officer. I talk to the prisoners. It's not a big surprise.'

Ruth shook her head. She couldn't believe that Kathy was going to flatly deny smuggling contraband or having any knowledge of Blake. Her daughter's life was at stake.

'You do know Curtis Blake then?'

'Everyone knows Curtis Blake,' Kathy said, giving Ruth yet another withering look.

'What kind of relationship do you have with Curtis Blake?' Lyon said.

'Eh? I don't. I've no idea what you're talking about,' Kathy said.

'Do you know a prisoner at Rhoswen called Frank Cole?' Lyon asked.

'Of course I do.'

'What kind of relationship do you have with Frank Cole?'

'I don't have any bloody relationship with Frank Cole either,' Kathy said, shaking her head.

'And you have never brought any drugs or phones into HMP Rhoswen for Frank Cole in return for payment?' Lyon asked.

'Who told you that crap? Don't be bloody stupid!' Kathy sneered at Lyon across the table.

There was a silence as Ruth and Lyon realised that Kathy was going to deny everything until the evidence against her was overwhelming. It wasn't clear whether she was keeping quiet to protect herself, her liberty or worse, Rosie.

'What are you doing, Kathy?' Ruth asked quietly, in a tone of complete disbelief.

'What do you mean?'

'Just before we came in here, I saw this footage of you talking to Curtis Blake. You are clearly having an argument. If Blake threatened you or your family, you need to tell us. How else can we get Rosie back?' Ruth said.

'This is all bullshit. You know that. It has nothing to do with Rosie.'

'So you haven't been threatened?' Lyon asked.

'No. Everything you've said so far is complete bloody fantasy,' Kathy said.

Ruth didn't believe her. She looked frightened. Like a woman who was hanging on to the lies she was telling with all her might.

'Don't you want to get Rosie back?' Ruth asked angrily.

'Of course I do. But her going missing has nothing to do with me, so why don't you go and do your job properly?' Kathy asked. Ruth noticed that Kathy was now shaking – it was all getting too much for her.

'If you're frightened, that's understandable. There are things we can do to protect you,' Lyon said.

'Witness protection? You're having a laugh, aren't you?' Kathy snorted. 'You're looking in the wrong place.'

Ruth frowned. 'What do you mean?'

'If you'd done your job properly, you'd know all about Jason and his past,' Kathy said.

Ruth exchanged a look with Lyon. *What is she talking about?*

'Jason?' Ruth asked, slightly thrown by the complete change of direction.

'Sex with a fifteen-year-old girl. Assault. Weird shit with his sister. Long time ago. But if you want to be pointing any fingers, you should be looking at him, not me,' Kathy said, glaring at them.

# CHAPTER 13

Nick and Merringer came into Interview Room Three. Hayley had been allowed to have a shower and was now wearing a standard grey tracksuit. The room was painted white and sky-blue with one small window high up on the far wall. It smelt of cheap shower gel and coffee.

Beside Hayley sat her legal aid solicitor, a small woman with short brown hair and kind eyes.

Now she had showered and most of her make-up was gone, Nick thought Hayley looked a good three or four years younger. In fact, she was a young seventeen. Her black-and-red hair was still wet and tucked behind ears that were full of earrings and studs. Her feline eyes locked on to his for a moment with a defiant look that said, 'This is boring me, so can we get on with it?' Hayley had been in interview rooms like this a dozen times before. It didn't faze her. It was just part of the game. Seventeen, and she was already an old pro. That's what having addict parents and growing up in care did to you.

Nick put down the folder and papers on the grey plastic table and moved his chair back to get comfortable.

'Hello, Hayley.' Nick reached over and clicked the tape machine. 'For the purposes of the tape, I'm Detective Sergeant Evans. This is my colleague Detective Constable Merringer. Present as well are Hayley Collard and the duty solicitor, Carol Brown.'

Hayley was staring at the floor, but when she looked up, she gave the detectives a withering look.

'You understand that you've been brought here to help us with our enquiries into the disappearance of Rosie Wright?' Nick asked.

'Jesus, I don't know who the fuck you're talking about,' Hayley sneered and then kicked the table.

Brown leant over and whispered in her ear. Nick guessed she had told Hayley to tone it down.

'Yeah, I understand,' Hayley said reluctantly.

Nick leant forward so that his arms rested on the table. He looked at her and said, 'Hayley, at the moment, we're not interested in the drugs, prostitution or the knife. We're interested in finding Rosie Wright, that's all.'

'What's that got to do with me?'

'Because we know that she was a friend of yours, wasn't she?' Merringer said.

'Was she?' Hayley was trying to be clever and play games.

Nick gave an audible sigh and sat back. *It is going to be like that, is it?*

'DC Merringer, what is the likely sentence for threatening to assault a police officer with a knife?' Nick asked.

'Hard to say. But I do know that last month a man in Cardiff was sentenced to twelve years in prison for a very similar offence,' Merringer said, joining in with Nick's game.

'You said you'd forget about the knife, you wanker!' Hayley shouted.

'*If* you help us and tell the truth… Twelve years. Long time, Hayley. That would mean you would be just coming up to your thirtieth birthday by the time you get out,' Nick said, looking her directly in the eye.

*Don't fuck with me. I've got a teenage girl to find.*

Hayley looked at Brown, who nodded to confirm that what Merringer had said was correct. As far as Nick was concerned, he was going to make Hayley an offer she couldn't refuse in return for all the intel she could give him.

'Okay, here's the deal, Hayley. I want you to tell me everything you know about Rosie Wright. What you talked about, where and why you met. What happened last Monday night. Or you're going to spend a decade behind bars doing laundry or making signs in the noddy shop at HMP Styal,' Nick said, spelling out her options very clearly.

Hayley shrugged. 'What do you wanna know?'

'When did you first contact Rosie Wright?' Nick asked.

'A few months ago,' Hayley said.

'Where?'

'On a fan site for Billie Eilish. We just started talking,' Hayley said.

'And you're a fan of Billie Eilish?' Merringer asked. Nick was pretty sure that Merringer had no idea who Billie Eilish was.

Hayley shook her head. 'No. That's just how it works?'

'How what works?' Nick asked, although he was beginning to put some pieces together.

Hayley seemed reluctant to talk. She sat back in her chair and looked at the nails on her right hand. Nick saw that she had a small blue tattoo by the thumb on that hand – *Te iubesc*.

'Nice tattoo. It's not French, so I'm going to take a guess. Romanian?' Nick said.

Hayley frowned as if to say, 'How the bloody hell did you know that?'

'Let me suggest something to you, Hayley,' Merringer said. 'You meet and befriend teenage girls on websites for someone else? Am I right?'

'Sometimes.'

'And Rosie was one of these girls?' Nick asked.

Hayley nodded and now looked down at the floor. She was starting to lose some of the bravado she had when she started the interview.

'For the purposes of the tape, Hayley nodded to answer affirmative to the last question,' Merringer said.

Digging into an A4 envelope, Nick took out a photo of Christian Vasilescu, the Romanian man Rhyl Police had identified and seen her with. 'Hayley, do you know who this man is?'

Vasilescu was in his early thirties, with dark skin, shaved head and chiselled features. *He looks like a charming, handsome thug*, Nick thought.

'Yes,' Hayley said.

'Christian Vasilescu? Is that right?' Merringer asked.

'Yeah.'

'Would it surprise you to know that Mr Vasilescu is wanted in Romania in connection with people trafficking, drug smuggling and extortion?' Nick asked.

Hayley shrugged. 'I don't care.'

'How do you know Christian Vasilescu?' Merringer asked.

'He's my boyfriend.'

Nick and Merringer exchanged a look – how many times had they met vulnerable girls or sex workers who thought their pimps were their boyfriends?

'And why were you planning to travel to Dublin this morning with Mr Vasilescu?' Nick asked.

'To see some of his friends. They live there.'

'Are his friends in Dublin from Romania?'

'Yeah, some are. Some are Irish.'

Sipping his coffee, Nick could feel the interview losing a little focus. 'So, you befriended Rosie Wright on the Billie Eilish website for Christian. What happened then?'

'Me and Rosie started chatting and stuff. You know, about school, friends and music.'

'And I'm guessing you pretended that you went to school and lived with your parents?' Nick asked with no hint of judgement.

'Yeah. I needed to check her out. Get her talking. Trust me.'

'Check her out?' Merringer asked.

'We have a profile of what I'm supposed to look for. You know, mainly girls who are in care or with foster parents that they hate.'

'That's not Rosie Wright though, is it?'

'Some of the girls I talk to are just unhappy at home. They want to run away, take drugs, self-harm, usual shit.' Hayley explained.

'And why did you think that Rosie Wright was one of these girls?'

'From what she told me online. She said her dad was a psychopath. And that her mum and brother were both criminals. She hated being home and already had a bag ready to run away,' Hayley explained.

Rosie must have known about Gareth Wright's criminal record. However, the fact she labelled her mum a 'criminal' was surprising. Did Rosie have suspicions about what Kathy Wright was doing at Rhoswen? How? Had she confronted her mother with what she knew?

'So, you checked Rosie fitted what you were looking for and then arranged to meet her?'

'Yeah. I met up with Rosie in Chester.'

'Why?'

'To see if she would meet me in secret. You can tell a lot about someone if they're willing to meet someone they've met online on their own without telling their parents,' Hayley explained.

'And it was Christian that Rosie saw pick you up in Chester?' Merringer clarified.

'Yeah. That wasn't meant to happen.'

'And then what?'

'Christian told me to arrange to meet Rosie again. She suggested that I come and meet all her friends. I had a time and a place of where she was going to be.'

'And then what?'

'I gave all that information to Christian. That's it. That's what happens,' Hayley said.

'You didn't go and meet Rosie last Monday night?' Nick asked.

'No,' Hayley said.

'Did Christian meet Rosie last Monday night?' Nick asked.

'I don't know. He doesn't tell me stuff like that,' Hayley said.

'Come on, Hayley. What happens to the girls whose information you pass onto Christian?' Nick asked.

'I dunno. It's not my business,' Hayley said.

Nick was starting to lose patience. 'Hayley, where does Christian take the girls that you groom online for him?'

Hayley tried to settle herself. Then she looked up at him and said, 'Ireland, I think.'

'This is bullshit, Hayley! Does Christian take the girls via Holyhead to Dublin to work as prostitutes for the Romanian gangs out there?'

Hayley looked at the floor and nodded.

'Hayley, is that what's happened to Rosie?'

'I don't know. I didn't see her. I promise you, I don't know or I'd tell you.'

'Where does Christian Vasilescu live?' Nick thundered.

'I don't know!' Hayley shouted at him.

'Bollocks! Where does he live?' Nick thundered as he looked directly at her. He didn't have time for her lies.

'I know he sometimes stays up at the travellers' place on Woodburn Farm.'

*Three days, nineteen hours*

As Ruth marched through the incident room towards her office, she reassured herself that everyone was working flat out on finding Rosie.

Mugshots of sex offenders flicked rapidly across French's computer monitor, and Sian had been logging calls from the public of possible sightings and tip-offs while keeping an eye on the media. They had to wade through these to sift out anything that seemed useful. Sometimes it was difficult to know where to start. Already that day they had sightings of Rosie in Canterbury with a 'weird-looking man' in an orange baseball cap and an hour ago in a furniture lorry on the M5 near Birmingham. It wasn't until there was some kind of pattern that they could take any of these seriously. Two or three sightings in Canterbury, and then things would change.

French looked up at her for a moment. 'Boss, SOCO have come back to us about the tracks at the riverbank. They're inconclusive. There's no evidence that anyone launched a boat from there in recent days.'

Ruth nodded as she sipped her coffee. Someone must have taken Rosie by road then. She glanced up at the large monitor on the wall showing news footage of the search for Rosie with local volunteers helping police officers. Ruth paused the television and Sian looked over at her. 'Boss?'

Feeling a little unsettled by their row the previous evening, Ruth smiled and approached. Moving close to her, she took Sian's hand. 'Are we okay?' she whispered.

'Yeah, of course,' Sian whispered back but avoided any meaningful eye contact. Ruth wasn't convinced, but she wasn't going to pursue it now.

'What have we got?' Ruth asked, back in work mode.

Sian pointed up at the monitor. 'This is the BBC's footage of the search. Now if I play it forward a bit...' Sian took the remote from Ruth and played the shot for a second and then paused it again. 'There.'

Ruth looked up at the screen. Steven Haddon was standing with his black labrador talking to another man who Ruth recognised but didn't know why.

'Steven Haddon. And this here... is Martin Hancock,' Sian said.

'Our resident sex offender,' Ruth said. 'Do they know each other?'

'I don't know. And maybe Hancock was just there out of the goodness of his heart to help look for Rosie.'

'His paedophile heart?' Ruth said sardonically. 'Can you go and have a word with Steven Haddon and find out if he knows

Hancock and what they talked about. We've seen this before in Soham, haven't we? I don't want anyone to accuse us of ignoring a suspect just because he's in plain sight.'

'Okay if I take DC French with me?' Sian asked.

'Of course. How's he doing?' Ruth asked. She couldn't help worrying about new CID officers and how the job could affect them.

'Still at the very serious stage, but he'll be fine. I'll have him making inappropriate jokes before you know it,' Sian said with a knowing smile.

'I don't doubt that. Let me know what Haddon says as soon as,' Ruth said, still not certain if Sian was annoyed at her. She was certainly being a little distant.

As Sian turned to go, Merringer arrived with some computer printouts. 'Boss, I've done some digging on Jason Wright. The minor offences and cautions date back to the late Eighties and early Nineties. It's so long ago that they've been filtered from his record, which is why they didn't appear on the PNC when we checked the first time,' Merringer explained.

'What's there?' Ruth asked.

'There's a whole string of allegations that were recorded by Conwy Police at the time. Molestation and indecency. No convictions in the 1980s,' Merringer explained.

Ruth rolled her eyes and said, 'In the 1980s, judges and coppers thought a fifteen-year-old girl in a short skirt was just a "dirty little flirt" who was asking to be sexually assaulted. If a boy grabbed your tits, he'd probably get a pat on the back from the local bobby.'

Merringer nodded seriously. 'However, Wright had a conviction of underage sex with a fifteen-year-old girl in 1991 when he was nineteen. Suspended sentence so it was wiped from his record.'

'And the Sex Offenders Register wasn't until the late Nineties, so he wouldn't have gone on that either,' Ruth said, thinking out loud.

'But this caught my eye, Boss. In 1993, Wright was charged with sexually assaulting his fourteen-year-old sister, but the records show that the charges were dropped a few months later,' Merringer explained.

There was something a little unsettling about Jason Wright's pattern of behaviour as a young man. Was it something that he stopped doing? Or did he just find ways of not getting caught?

# CHAPTER 14

Parking at the main farm gates, French turned off the car engine. He wound down the window and gestured to Steven Haddon, who was standing beside an enormous green and yellow John Deere tractor. He was tinkering with something on one of the vast wheels that rose above his head at over eight feet in height. Either he hadn't heard them arrive or he was ignoring their presence. Sian knew that police officers brought out all sorts of strange and sometimes unpleasant behaviour in people.

Opening the door, she was hit by the wall of heat from outside. They'd become used to the car's air conditioning and the hot air took her breath away for a moment. The smell of the farm was thick and there was a stillness all around. It was as if everything had stopped moving or making any form of sound because it was just too hot.

Wiping his oil-stained hands with a rag, Steven turned to look at Sian and French as they approached across the dry, potholed yard. A Labrador and a spaniel got up out of the shade of the feed shed and wandered over to see who had arrived. The dogs were too hot to do much more than sniff around their ankles for a moment.

'Mr Haddon?' Sian called as she tried to navigate around a pile of cow dung.

'Afternoon,' he said as he squinted up at the sun and shielded his eyes.

Sian showed her warrant card. 'DC Hockney. Have you got a minute?'

Steven nodded and looked concerned. 'Yeah, of course. Any news on Rosie?'

'I'm afraid not,' French said as he pushed his Ray-Bans back onto the bridge of his nose. Sian wanted to remind him that he wasn't in an episode of *CSI: Miami*.

'God, what's happened to her? I just don't understand it. It's terrible,' Steven said as he shook his head.

Taking a photo out of an envelope, Sian showed him a still of the BBC News footage she had shown Ruth earlier.

'Can you tell us if you know this man, Mr Haddon?'

'It's Steven, please. Erm…' Steven studied the photo for a couple of seconds. Sian wasn't sure if he was trying to buy time before responding. 'Yeah, it's Martin. He came to help us when we searched the woodland at the back.'

Steven handed the photo back to her nonchalantly and gave her a look as if to say, 'Is that all?'

'Is Martin Hancock a friend of yours?' French asked.

'Oh, I don't know his surname. He's not a friend of mine. I've seen him down the pub a couple of times.'

'What about in the last few days? Apart from when he came to help in the search, have you seen him around?' Sian asked. If Ruth remembered what had happened in previous cases like this, the perpetrator would try to involve themselves in the chaos they had caused as much as possible.

'Not really. Look, I've heard all the rumours around the village about Martin. He's this or he's that. I'm not really interested in gossip. When I talked to him at the pub, he seemed a nice enough bloke,' Steven said.

'Thank you, Steven,' Sian said. She didn't like to point out that 'a nice enough bloke' is how virtually every infamous killer in British criminal history is described by those who 'knew' them. Most people saw genial, caring GP Harold Shipman as an all-round 'good bloke', until it was revealed he had murdered an estimated two hundred and fifty people. As Sian was once told in training, Joe Public's instinct for who is guilty of terrible crimes and who is not is about as reliable as a chocolate fire-guard.

'If you want to talk to anyone about Martin, you should ask Jason,' Steven said, gesturing to the cottage next door.

Sian and French exchanged a meaningful look – that was interesting.

'Martin Hancock is a friend of Jason's?' French asked.

'I don't know if they're friends. But I've seen them drinking at the pub together,' Steven explained.

'Thank you. We'll have a word,' Sian said as they turned to head back to the car.

It was at that moment that she noticed a dark blue Land Rover parked in one of the farm buildings. More interestingly, there were two long wooden Canadian canoes strapped to a roof rack on top. There had been mention of the possibility that Rosie had been taken away via the river; although Forensics hadn't come back with anything concrete, it was still worth looking into.

'Are those your canoes, Steven?' Sian said, pointing over to the Land Rover.

'Yes. Bloody marvellous.'

'Where do you use them?' French asked.

'Mainly off the coast. Down the Conwy Estuary and the Menai Strait. When it's like this, we sometimes canoe over to Anglesey,' Steven explained.

'What about local rivers?' Sian asked.

'The Afon Gyrach is just over there, isn't it?' French asked, following Sian's line of inquiry.

'Once in a while. It's a bit shallow this time of year.'

'When was the last time you were on the Afon Gyrach?' Sian asked.

'Last summer, I think,' Steven said.

'Thank you,' Sian said as she put her sunglasses back on and turned to go to the car.

Even though SOCO had found nothing at the riverbank, Sian wondered whether if they took a closer look at those canoes, would they be able to match samples to show they had been down by the riverside?

*Three days, twenty-one hours*

It was late afternoon and Ruth and Merringer had been driving Kathy Wright back to Capelulo from Llancastell. Winding down the window, Ruth lit a ciggie and blew the smoke out in a long plume as she processed the case.

'Do you mind?' Kathy said from the backseat.

'No, I don't mind,' Ruth replied. Merringer smiled at her little sarcastic comment.

Neither of them had any time for Kathy Wright at the moment. She was a bent prison officer who was holding out on them and putting her daughter's life at risk. Somehow, Kathy felt that her own liberty and safety were more important than finding her daughter.

Listening to the radio news for a moment, Ruth's ears pricked up.

*'Police in Edinburgh are investigating the rape and attempted murder of a woman in the city centre late last night. The police are appealing for witnesses with information to come forward. The unnamed twenty-three-year-old woman is said to have been visiting a Canadian student working at Edinburgh University. Doctors say she is in a critical but stable condition.'*

*Edinburgh? Kessler has been in Edinburgh*, Ruth thought. *Is that a coincidence?* Raping and attacking women was Kessler's MO.

Ruth sat with these thoughts for a moment and made a decision to give Steven Flaherty a call later to see if there was any link or anything that might implicate Jurgen Kessler in the attack.

Ruth knew that she needed to put her personal investigation to one side and concentrate on finding Rosie, but the similarities were hard to ignore. She needed to talk to Jason Wright and quiz him about his dark past. Could he be responsible for Rosie's attack and disappearance? They had a volatile relationship and he had been violent with her in the past. His alibi for being in the pub was vague, as were his timings for Monday night. Did the historic alleged sexual assault on his own sister also suggest what sort of person he was?

Ruth also wanted to revisit the Wrights' house and see where the money had been hidden. She hoped there would be time to have another look around the crime scene up at Haddon Farm. The clues to what had happened to Rosie were there somewhere. Had Curtis Blake threatened Kathy so that she would continue to organise the smuggling of drugs and phones into Rhoswen? Had Kathy refused out of loyalty to Frank Cole? Cole was still in the hospital infirmary with his face slashed and battered. Was that a message for Kathy as to what would happen if she didn't do what Blake told her?

Having spoken to Nick, Ruth also had to factor in a line of inquiry that revolved around Rosie's relationship with Hayley Collard. It seemed clear from Nick's interview with Hayley that she was being used by a Romanian gang to groom vulnerable girls in North Wales. Once Hayley had befriended and coerced these girls, a Romanian criminal, Christian Vasilescu, would take them on a ferry from Holyhead to Dublin, where they would be intimidated into working as prostitutes. It was clear that Hayley had targeted Rosie and tried to groom her. Had Vasilescu travelled to Capelulo and abducted Rosie? Had Rosie struggled and been injured in the kidnapping? Was Rosie now in Dublin? Drake had put a call into the Gardaí in Ireland to see if they had any intel on Vasilescu.

Parking outside Hazel Cottage, Ruth climbed out of the car and opened the rear door for Kathy Wright to get out. Merringer followed them inside.

'Right, Kathy, sit yourself down. Constable Bennett is going to make us all a nice cup of tea to start with.' Ruth smiled over at Bennett, who had already started to fill the kettle. 'This is how it works. You are still under caution. You are confined to this house and its outside areas. You will have no contact with anyone except your immediate family. No use of the phone or the Internet. If you attempt to leave this area or if you attempt to contact anyone, you will be arrested. You will then be taken to HMP Styal, where you will be housed on the vulnerable prisoners' wing on bail. I think we all know how popular prison officers are in the general prison population. So, unless you want to pick glass and faeces out of your food and worry twenty-four hours a day whether someone is going to attack you, you'll do as you're told.'

There was a moment as Ruth looked at Kathy. *What is going on in her head?*

'Do you understand all that, Kathy?' Ruth asked when Kathy made no answer.

Kathy rolled her eyes. 'Yeah.'

'I'm going to need stuff like your car keys and the spares for starters,' Ruth said.

'Car key is behind the driver's sun visor in case Jason needs to move it. Spare is in that drawer there.'

Ruth indicated to Bennett to go and retrieve it. She nodded.

'Now I need to have a chat with your husband,' Ruth said.

'Ma'am, I saw him half an hour ago on a quad bike in the field opposite here,' Bennett said.

Ruth was more than a little surprised that Jason Wright had decided to go and do some work while his daughter was still missing.

Bennett noticed Ruth's expression. 'Mr Wright said he couldn't just sit here and drink tea all day. He wanted to keep busy,' Bennett explained.

Ruth signalled to Merringer that it was time to go. As they left through the open front door, she could smell lavender and freshly cut grass. Birds chirruped from up in the tree and the sun moved out from behind a cloud and warmed Ruth's face.

She closed her eyes just for a second to get a moment's peace. How were people so devious, hostile and dysfunctional in a place like this? She had seen the families trapped in poverty and addiction on the crack-infested estates of South East London. Crime and hatred seemed almost understandable. They would have killed to live in a place like this. Perspective and gratitude were subjective things, she told herself.

'She's a cold fish,' Merringer said of Kathy Wright as he closed the door behind them.

'I don't understand why she's not telling us the truth,' Ruth said as she walked down the garden path and out into the road.

'Fear. Selfishness. Who knows, boss?' Merringer replied, putting on his sunglasses. His phone buzzed with a text. He looked at it and smiled.

'Good news?' Ruth asked.

'Yeah. We've got a place for Katie at St Mark's now. It's a big improvement from the previous school,' Merringer explained.

Ruth knew that Merringer's youngest daughter had learning difficulties and they were trying to get her into a special education school in the centre of Llancastell. She was really pleased for him.

'That's brilliant news, Luke.'

'Yeah,' Merringer said as he beamed and put away his phone. 'She'll be really happy there.'

A noise from across the road distracted them. Jason Wright was closing the steel gate to the field and securing it with a padlock.

'Mr Wright?' Ruth called.

Wiping sweat from his face on his shirt sleeve, Jason walked over. 'Any news?' From his half-hearted tone, he obviously didn't think there was.

'I'm sorry. Nothing new. There's a few things we'd like to ask you, though, if that's okay?' Ruth said.

Jason shrugged. 'Yeah, of course.'

Ruth was taken aback by his cooperation. It was about time that Jason Wright started to be helpful.

'We've noticed that you had some dealings with the police when you were younger?' Ruth said.

'Oh, that? That was nothing. Just being a bit of an idiot.'

'Sex with an underage girl isn't just being a bit of an idiot. You would have ended up in prison and on the Sex Offenders Register if it had happened now.'

'Come on! I was only a teenager and that was thirty years ago. How does this have anything to do with Rosie?' Jason said, getting angry and indignant.

'And a fifteen-year-old girl is a child,' Ruth said.

She was getting annoyed at his levity. *Don't be a twat. A four-year age gap is enormous at that age, and you know it!*

'There was also an incident with your sister?' Merringer asked.

'Yeah, and that was dropped. She made that up because she was a bitch, and she still is. You can't use that against me.' Jason complained.

'We understand that you know Martin Hancock?' Ruth said.

'Not really,' Jason replied.

'Steven Haddon seems to think that you're friends. That you go to the pub together sometimes?' Ruth said.

'Is that against the law?'

'No. I'm just trying to ascertain what your relationship with Martin Hancock is,' Ruth explained.

'He's a bloke I see down the pub sometimes. People round here don't like him, but I think he's all right. Sometimes we have a chat. That's it,' Jason explained.

'You were at the Royal Oak pub last Monday night, weren't you?' Merringer asked.

'Yeah, I was.'

'Did you happen to see Martin Hancock?'

'I've no idea. I'm at the pub most nights so I can't remember,' Jason said, starting to get irritated. 'Can I go now? I've got a lot to do.'

'Of course,' Ruth said.

Jason walked away without another word.

'I'll get those car keys,' Merringer said and wandered over to Kathy Wright's black Ford Focus.

After only a second, Merringer reappeared from the car. 'Boss?' He waved something at her. It was a small black pay-as-you-go mobile phone. 'It was tucked inside the driver's door.'

Merringer came over and handed it to her. 'Wonder what we'll find on that, boss?' he called as he walked back to Kathy Wright's car.

Ruth nodded and smiled. 'Good work, Luke.'

As Ruth headed slowly back towards their unmarked Astra, she knew the phone they had just found might prove significant. Looking at her watch, they had just enough time to go up to Haddon Farm and revisit the yard and barn before returning to CID at Llancastell for an evening briefing.

Turning back, she saw Merringer searching the inside of Kathy's car.

'Today would be good, Luke,' she called out sarcastically.

Merringer looked over his shoulder at her, shook his head with a smile and gestured, 'Her keys were in the ignition. That's country folk for you!'

He reached in to take them.

Click.

*BOOM!*

A ball of orange and black engulfed Merringer, tossing his body into the air.

A millisecond later, Ruth was lifted and flung onto her back. She couldn't get her breath, and then she lost consciousness for a few seconds.

Everything was silent and dark. Hot black embers and dust appeared before her eyes as she tried to move. She felt paralysed. Maybe she was.

And then falling. A rain of fragments and stones that clattered all around her. But she couldn't hear them. She couldn't hear anything.

*What the hell just happened? Oh, my God!*

She sucked in the hot air but felt like she was drowning.

*I can't breathe!*

Her throat, nostrils, mouth and eyes were burning as she tried to move again. Getting on to her side, her hearing started to return ever so slightly. Her eardrums rang and hissed like she had just walked out of a ten-hour techno rave.

Looking from where she had been flung, the black carcass of the Ford Focus was submerged by thick flames and smoke. She could feel the heat on her face and hands from where she was.

Scrambling to her knees and then her feet, she felt overcome by dizziness. She needed to get to Merringer. She gagged on the thick smoke and spat on the ground as she staggered past the car to where she had seen Merringer disappear.

*Where's Luke? I need to find Luke.*

Losing her footing, Ruth reached for the stone wall for balance. She needed to sit down.

'Are you all right, ma'am?' a voice shouted. It was Bennett.

But her focus was on getting to Merringer. *Where was he? What the hell was going on?* Her mind knew what she had just seen. The car had exploded when Merringer had touched the keys in the ignition. Logic told her that it had been some kind of bomb. But at that moment, she couldn't process the thought with any perception.

And then she saw him.

Merringer's body had been flung over the fence and onto the dirt track behind. Climbing over the steel gate, Ruth thought she was going to faint. Her hands and arms shook uncontrollably as she tried to haul herself over. She didn't care. She needed to get to him.

Running over to him, she saw that Merringer's face was a bloody black mess. She could smell the burnt flesh and hair and gagged. The whites of his eyes were highlighted against the charred skin. They weren't moving.

There was no sign of life.

'I've called for help, ma'am,' Bennett said as she crouched beside Ruth.

Reaching to his neck, Ruth felt for a pulse. She knew it was a futile gesture.

Detective Constable Luke Merringer was dead.

# CHAPTER 15

*Three days, twenty-two hours*

Pulling right off the A434, Nick was getting close to Woodburn Farm where Hayley had said Christian Vasilescu sometimes stayed. He knew Woodburn Farm well, especially from his days as a uniformed officer. The travellers had had some sort of site there for over forty years. The population and people changed and fluctuated, but there were a few families who now went back three generations.

As Nick slowed, he could see the irregular lines of white caravans at the end of the dusty track. Hitting a deep pothole, he slowed the car. He had already been spotted coming down the lane. He felt a twinge of anxiety. Maybe it was a bit reckless to go in without any backup. In the old days, no officer would go in without the help of the heavy brigade: the 'hats and bats' unit.

A flag and hand-painted sign signalled the site's entrance: *We Shall Not Be Moved* and *Trespassers Will Be Shot*. Nick knew they weren't joking.

Pulling over to park up, he noticed children playing noisily, riding bikes and chasing half a dozen dogs. They looked free and happy.

A portly woman in a long purple dress came over, looked at him suspiciously, and then smiled. 'Bloody hell. We haven't seen you here for a while,' she said. Despite being away from Donegal for thirty years, she still carried the accent.

'It's Gwen, isn't it?' Nick had just about remembered her name from his time in uniform. He had been there on a regular basis – truancy, vandalism, petty theft.

'How can I help you, son?' she asked.

Nick got out his warrant card and said, 'I'm with CID now.'

'All grown up, eh?'

Fishing into his pocket, Nick pulled out one of the A4 sheets that carried Rosie Wright's photo. 'I'm looking for this girl, Rosie Wright. She's been missing a few days now.'

'We know about that. It's not the feckin' third world out here. We have televisions and everything,' she chortled sarcastically. 'It's a terrible thing, that. Poor girl. And her family must be beside themselves.'

'You haven't seen her then?' Nick asked.

'No. Sorry.'

Nick then pulled out his phone, tapped on a photo and showed it to her. 'Ever seen this man? Christian Vasilescu? He's Romanian.'

'Romanian? No, doesn't ring a bell.' Gwen gestured. 'Come on, we'll ask some of the lads. See if they know him or if they've heard of him.'

As they wandered past the neat, clean chalets, Nick saw two teenage girls hanging out some washing. They looked at him and giggled.

'Don't mind them. Daft as a brush, those pair,' Gwen said, laughing.

To one side, old televisions, a computer and a washing machine had been heaped together. The dogs had noticed his presence and came bounding over to check him out. A large black mongrel decided to jump up at his leg and bark.

'Elvis! Will you feckin' leave the fella alone!' Gwen yelled at the dog, who immediately retreated and trotted away.

Up ahead, a few older men in their sixties, dressed in open shirts, vests and shorts, sat on deckchairs in the sun. One was on a mobile phone, another read a paper.

'Declan. The officer here is looking for someone. I thought you might know him?' Gwen said.

Declan put his newspaper to one side and stood up from his deckchair. He was a short man, no taller than five foot six. But he was heavy and looked like he could really handle himself. His jet-black hair was scraped back off his dark, tanned face.

'Who you looking for, son?' Declan asked as he came over. His voice was surprisingly soft, Nick thought.

Delving into his pocket, Nick fished out the photo of Vasilescu and handed it to him. He frowned and looked at it intently.

'His name's Christian Vasilescu. He's Romanian,' Nick explained.

'He looks like Roma Gypsy to me,' Declan said.

'Have you ever seen him?' Nick asked.

'No. Charlie has dealings with the Roma and Romanians. Come on, we'll go and ask him,' Declan said as he gestured to the woods behind them.

'Declan?' Gwen said in an anxious voice.

'Shut yer feckin' mouth, Gwen!' Declan thundered.

Something about Gwen's reaction troubled Nick. What was wrong with going with Declan?

'Where are we going?' Nick asked as his pulse started to quicken.

'Charlie lives on his own. Likes the peace and quiet. Come on, we'll go up there now. See if he's seen this fella of yours,' Declan said, moving towards the dry path that led up to the woods.

At that moment, Nick caught a momentary glimpse of something metallic tucked into the back of Declan's waistband. It was mostly covered by his shirt, but Nick knew exactly what it was.

A handgun.

If he had to guess, it looked like an old Beretta.

Clearly, having possession of a handgun was an offence, but Nick was on his own in the middle of a travellers' site that was well known for its disregard for the law. With no backup, he wasn't going to risk trying to make an arrest.

'Come on. What are you waiting for, son?' Declan beckoned Nick to follow.

With the red flags piling up, Nick wasn't about to disappear into the woods with a tough-looking traveller with a hidden handgun. He might never return.

Nick held up the photo. His instinct told him that he was vulnerable and in danger. 'I'll leave this here with my card. If anyone has seen this man, let me know.'

'Ah, come on. What are you scared of?' Declan asked, as if he was offended by Nick's refusal to follow him.

'Have a good day,' Nick said with a wave of his hand.

With his heart pounding and sweat running down the back of his neck, he tried to walk calmly back to the car. What he really wanted to do was run.

—

It was an hour after the bomb had gone off and the area outside the Wrights' house was chaos. Ruth was still numb from the blast and seeing Merringer's body in the adjacent field. Drake had told her to go to hospital, but apart from some hearing loss and a bruised back, Ruth was physically okay. She needed to stay.

The whole area pulsed eerily with the blue lights of police vehicles, fire engines and ambulances. Yet, except for the crackle of voices on police radios, the scene was unnervingly quiet. Conversations were respectfully low.

Resting against a stone wall, Ruth looked at the burnt wreck of the car, lost in thought. Close by, a camouflaged army Land Rover was parked. A bomb disposal unit had been called to check the car was safe and to ensure there weren't any secondary devices. They had confirmed that there had been an explosive device under the driver's seat of the car. From what Ruth had told them, it seemed there had been an electrical circuit linked to the ignition. In his efforts to take the key out of the ignition, Merringer must have turned it one click and engaged the car's battery. That sent a signal to the explosive device under the seat that he was resting on. In the age of bombs being detonated by Bluetooth and mobile phone signals, it was pretty crude. The sort of car bomb the IRA had used in the Seventies and Eighties. It didn't matter though. Luke Merringer didn't stand a chance and would have died before he hit the ground.

Ruth could still hear the faint hiss of the water on the hot metal of the car. Two fire engines had put out the fire within a few minutes of arriving.

Drake, who had continually been on the phone since he got there, came over to her.

'I know you don't want to go to hospital, but you should go home at least, Ruth,' he said quietly.

'I'd prefer to stay for a bit, boss.'

Drake nodded and there was a stillness. They had lost a friend and colleague. They all knew when they left the house in the morning that it might be their last. However, the death of a police officer in the line of duty was still a rare thing.

'I'll go and talk to Mel on my way home,' Drake said. Ruth couldn't imagine how Merringer's wife was feeling at that moment.

'And the poor girls…' Ruth said as she thought of Merringer's daughters.

'My daughters are around the same age,' Drake said. 'It doesn't bear thinking about.' Drake and his girls would have been struggling to deal with the anxiety around Paula's cancer. Losing a loved colleague was merely adding to his already emotionally strained plate.

'I'll give Mel a call later, boss,' Ruth said.

'I've spoken to the media desk at St Asaph. They're going to put out a story that it was an electrical fault and a car fire,'

Drake said. She wondered if the press would make anything of it, being Kathy Wright's car, and try to see if there was a story.

Turning slightly to her left, Ruth could see Kathy Wright watching from her garden path.

'Have you spoken to Kathy Wright yet, boss?' Ruth asked.

'No, not yet. I really think someone should drive you home, Ruth,' Drake said.

Ruth ignored him. 'I'll go and have a word with her and see if the shock jogs her memory on anything.'

Ruth turned and started to walk down the road to the gate that led into the Wrights' garden.

Looking confused and shocked, Kathy stood with her arms crossed. Did she have any remorse for what had happened?

'That was meant for you,' Ruth said sharply.

'I know,' Kathy mumbled.

'I've just lost a friend and colleague. We've got to go and tell his wife. And you're responsible for that.' Ruth virtually spat out the words.

'I didn't know there was a bomb in my car, did I?'

'Don't be fucking facetious, Kathy! Your daughter has been attacked and taken. One of my officers has just been murdered. So, whatever you're mixed up in, it's time you came clean and told us the truth!'

'I've told you already. You're way off on this. And while someone's got my daughter somewhere, you're looking in the wrong place. You need to get your head out of your arse, find Rosie and stop waging some personal vendetta against me,' Kathy yelled at her.

Ruth could feel the anger and bile rise inside her. Merringer's body was on its way to the mortuary at Llancastell University Hospital. Rosie had been attacked and abducted. And Kathy was still fucking them about. If Constable Bennett hadn't been standing nearby, Ruth thought, she could have easily slapped Kathy across her face.

Taking a breath, Ruth walked away before she said or did something that she would regret.

# CHAPTER 16

Having stared death in the face, Nick knew that he had to get himself to an AA meeting that evening. He hadn't been totally honest with Amanda about the events of the afternoon up at Woodburn Farm. He had gone as far as saying there had been 'a few hairy moments'. Amanda was pregnant; there was no reason to cause her any undue stress.

Nick's father, Rhys, was helping set up the room when he and Amanda arrived. Nick usually had a chat and catch-up with his dad during the meeting's fifteen-minute break. It really was a miracle that they spoke at all. Nick had been left to be brought up by his Auntie Pat and Uncle Mike after his mother had died. His father, a sergeant in the Royal Welch Fusiliers, had been posted abroad for much of Nick's childhood. When he was around, Rhys was either emotionally cold, or drunk, angry and unpredictable. The last eighteen months had seen a dramatic reversal in their relationship. And Nick knew that he had AA and sobriety to thank for that.

'And how are you, young Nicholas?' Bill asked with a beaming smile. Catching up with his sponsor Dundee Bill, Nick felt the clarity and calm that came with being at a meeting with his tribe. Even when Bill was dishing out one of his famous bollockings, it was done with an element of humour. There were many inside AA who didn't appreciate Bill's brand of tough love. However, Nick knew that's exactly what he needed. No bullshit, no dishonesty: tell it how it is. Bill had had his reservations about Amanda and Nick's relationship – two recovering addicts embarking on a relationship together wasn't going to be easy. He told Nick to tread very carefully, but if they loved one another, who was he to stand in the way?

The meeting started with various thank-yous and a reading. Sitting together in their usual seats, Amanda and Nick held hands discreetly by the side of the chair and listened as Cockney Rob shared his life story. Rob was usually good value and his 'war stories' were generally hilarious. Nick knew it was good for alcoholics to laugh at themselves and how far they would go to get a drink.

Fifteen years ago, when Rob had been kicked out of the family home for the twentieth time, he found himself living above a pub in Llangollen. Having gone on a week-long bender, Rob found that he had run out of booze and, more worryingly, he had lost the use of his legs. It was called alcoholic neuropathy. Ever the resourceful alcoholic, Rob looked around and spotted a bucket and some rope from the bedsit's recent renovation. He rang the pub downstairs and explained that he couldn't get down. If he lowered a bucket out of the window to street level, could someone come out and put two bottles of scotch and a bottle of vodka into the bucket? He could then raise the bucket up to the first floor. Thinking this was hysterically funny, the bar staff took down his credit card details before duly obliging by placing the bottles into the bucket. This carried on for the next few weeks until Rob's credit card was finally maxed out.

At the break, Nick watched from a distance as Amanda spoke to her own sponsor for a moment. They laughed as she placed her hand gently on her bump. Her dark hair was tied back in a ponytail and the whites of her chestnut eyes looked bigger and brighter than ever. A few seconds later, the women of the group had gathered protectively around her, cooing and smiling. However cheesy it sounded, she really was all he had ever wanted. It wasn't long ago that he mocked the idea of a soulmate. He thought that the person you ended up with for life was totally random. Now he believed the total opposite. He just hoped he could step up and be the responsible adult he had always wanted to be.

A thought occurred to him as he wandered outside for some fresh air. A beautiful, exciting thought.

Glancing over to the usual group of men smoking, he made eye contact with his dad and nodded. As he rolled the cigarette paper and licked the gluey edge, Rhys wandered over.

'Having a good week, lad?' Rhys asked as he popped the rolled cigarette in between his lips and searched his pockets for a lighter.

'I was until this afternoon,' Nick said, but he didn't want to go into details. 'But you know, I'm upright, sober and I'm at a meeting.'

'And you're having a baby,' Rhys said as he lit his cigarette. Nick had told his father, along with everyone else, after twelve weeks. Rhys couldn't hide his joy at the thought of being a grandad.

'And I'm having a baby,' Nick said with a growing smile.

Nick knew what he needed to do. Seeing his life flash before him at the traveller camp that day had brought into focus what was important to him.

'Between you and me, I'm going to ask her to marry me,' Nick said quietly.

'Congratulations. I'm made up for you, son,' Rhys grinned and shook Nick's hand. 'When did you decide that?'

'About thirty seconds ago.' Nick admitted.

—

Ruth had spent twenty minutes trying to wash the smell of smoke and burning out of her hair. As she got out of the shower, she found herself shaking uncontrollably. When she tried to get her breath, waves of a full-blown panic attack hit her like a train. Her heart pounded in her chest. She began to count breaths. In for five, hold for five and out for seven. She continued doing this for over a minute. As her pulse slowed, she slumped onto the wet shower mat and wept.

An hour later, Ruth was in the living room, staring into space. She had tried to numb the shock of the day with two large glasses of wine and had fallen asleep for a while. It didn't touch the sides. Angie Stone played on the stereo, but somehow listening to music seemed ridiculous. Walking over to the stereo, she turned it off and looked out of the open patio doors to the garden and the fields and hills beyond that. The sun had painted the thin, white clouds on the horizon a uniform blancmange-pink. How was it possible that Merringer would not see the sun set that evening? It had only been that morning that he had told her about his daughter Gabby looking at universities for the following year. He was never going to see Gabby graduate, get married, have children – it had all been taken away from him.

Ruth's train of thought was broken by the sound of someone coming down the stairs. It was Sian and she was carrying a suitcase. *Where the hell is she going?* Ruth thought.

'What are you doing?' Ruth asked.

Sian looked a little teary as she came into the living room, sat down and looked over at Ruth.

'What's going on?' Ruth asked, starting to get worried.

'I nearly lost you today,' Sian said, getting choked up.

Ruth nodded. 'I know.'

'And it made me realise that you're the most important thing to me on the planet,' Sian said.

'Of course. I feel the same,' Ruth said uncertainly. *Where is this going?*

'But that's the problem. Because you don't,' Sian said, wiping a tear from her face.

Ruth wasn't sure what Sian was talking about. 'Is this about me meeting Ella's dad?'

'Not really. It doesn't help.' Sian sniffed and wiped away another tear. 'I went to get a screwdriver from the garage and I found your desk and all your stuff. The photos on the wall. The files and the papers.'

The revelation hung in the air as Ruth took it in and felt the bottom fall out of her stomach. She didn't know what to say.

'I wanted to tell you but...' Ruth kicked herself for being so stupid.

'It's all right. I understand. I can't imagine what it must be like to have lost Sarah and not know what happened to her. But it means I can never compete with her.'

Ruth looked at Sian. She loved her so much – why had she put all that at risk?

*You're such a bloody idiot!*

'It's not true...'

Sian pursed her lips as she blinked a tear away. 'But it is. And I feel so sorry for you. But that's not enough for a relationship, is it?'

Feeling like she couldn't breathe, Ruth moved forward and took Sian's hand. 'I love you... I really do—'

*Please God, I don't want her to leave me!*

Sian moved her hand away from Ruth's and took half a step back. 'I know you love me. But I... I think I need to be with someone who... wants just me. Not someone who... who always has one eye on the past,' Sian explained as she sniffed and wiped away more tears.

'It's not like that,' Ruth protested, even though she knew what Sian had said was true. It was so painful to think about what Sian was saying to her. Unbearable.

'You know in your heart of hearts that it is. And always will be. I just feel a bit stupid because I thought me, you and Ella were this tight family unit. The perfect post-millennial family,' Sian said with a teary smile.

Now feeling desperate, Ruth used her palm to wipe her cheek. 'We are—'

'But we're not. And that's fine... So, I need some time away.'

*I don't want you to go!*

Now overwhelmed, Ruth got up as the tears came in floods. 'I do love you – please, I don't want you to go!'

Ruth went to give Sian a hug, but she moved away and took the handle of her suitcase.

'I love you too. I'll give you a call later,' Sian said in a choked voice, blinking through her tears as she turned and left the house.

—

*Waking with a slight start, Ruth thought she must have had some kind of nightmare, although she couldn't remember what it had been about as her heart was beating hard against her chest. Her back was still sore from where she had landed on it when the bomb exploded. Reaching over to the bedside table, she took a glass of water, sipped it and swilled it around her dry mouth. She took a deep breath. It was only just getting light, so she calculated it must only be five o'clock. Too early for a ciggie and a coffee on the patio, even by her standards.*

*She stretched out her right leg and flexed her calf muscle. Her whole body felt taut and uncomfortable. The bed was strangely still. As she replaced the glass, her eyes were drawn to a framed photograph of Sarah. It was the picture of her dressed as a bridesmaid. Her elegant neck decorated with a simple antique silver necklace that Ruth had bought her from Portobello Market the day before. However, Ruth didn't remember digging out that photo of Sarah from the garage and putting it back beside the bed where it had sat when she first moved in. In fact, she was sure that she hadn't. She'd only had a couple of drinks – okay, a bottle of white wine – but not enough to not remember stuff.*

*The duvet moved slightly and then someone pulled it. It startled her.*

Ruth froze. *The bed was empty, wasn't it?*

*Sian had left the night before and Ella was sleeping upstairs. Wasn't she? Unless she had crept down during the night? Shifting onto her back, Ruth then heard the* distinct *sound of someone clearing their throat very quietly. A man clearing their throat very quietly.*

Jesus! What the bloody hell is going on?

She jumped up in bed and saw that there was a man lying next to her, staring up at the ceiling. She recognised the dead blue eyes and thin blond hair. And the smile. That faintly amused smile.

It was Jurgen Kessler.

Kessler looked over at her and said, 'I need to tell you where she is.' His voice was soft with a clipped Germanic accent.

Ruth jumped up in bed and screamed at him. 'I don't want you to tell me!'

Leaping across at him, Ruth put her hands around his throat and began to throttle him, squeezing his neck hard.

'If you kill me, you'll never know,' Kessler said, laughing as though she was tickling him. 'You'll never find her.'

'I don't want to know any more,' she yelled and squeezed until the muscles in her forearms ached. 'I want you to die and leave me alone!'

Kessler stopped giggling and his eyes glazed over. He was dead.

Flinging back the duvet, Ruth leapt out of the bed and headed for the front door. She could see a shadow against the frosted glass. Someone was standing outside.

She opened the door.

Luke Merringer was standing there and he smiled at her. 'Cab for a Ruth Hunter?' he said, gesturing to the car on the drive.

At that moment, the car exploded in a huge orange ball of flames and black smoked.

The force of the explosion knocked Ruth backwards and off her feet.

Ruth woke, heart pounding against her chest. Blinking and breathing deeply, she looked around her bedroom again. There was no one next to her, and the photo of Sarah was no longer on the bedside table.

# CHAPTER 17

*Four days, eleven hours*

There was a stillness and darkness over the incident room as Ruth did her best to prepare for the morning briefing. They had lost one of their own. It might have sounded corny, but she knew that Llancastell CID was really one big family. They didn't always agree or get on, but because of the job they did, they always had each other's backs. Merringer's death was going to leave a big hole in her team. She had already spoken to the Regional Police Federation and the North Wales Police's chaplain about some kind of service in memory of Luke in the coming days.

Ruth tried to refocus on the continuing search for Rosie. Sian sat down over by a computer. They exchanged a knowing look. It would have been easier if they'd had a blazing row and could blank each other childishly.

'Good morning, everyone,' Ruth said as she moved to the centre of the room. She could feel her voice wobbling already. She needed to keep it together for the sake of her whole team. 'I know this is going to be a very difficult day for all of us. Luke was a loyal, dedicated police officer and it was my privilege to have worked alongside him. I know that all our thoughts will be with Luke's family, especially Katie and Gabby. There will be a collection for them going around at some point today. And I'll keep you posted as to when the service of remembrance and funeral will take place.'

Ruth waited for everyone to gather their thoughts. She kept expecting to look to her left and see Merringer sitting at his desk, diligently writing notes. The empty chair was haunting.

'If Luke was sitting here now, he would tell us that we need to get on with the job in hand.' Ruth pointed up to the scene boards and said, 'We need to find Rosie Wright. And we need to find out who planted the bomb that killed Luke yesterday. Although we believe that these two investigations are linked, Luke's murder will be investigated by the NCA. We don't have the manpower here and I think we're all too close to do the investigation justice.' The National Crime Agency was the UK's lead agency against organised crime.

Ruth clicked the iPad and a photo of Curtis Blake came up on the screen. 'This is still our prime suspect for Rosie's abduction. In the past two months, Blake has taken over the illegal trade in drugs and mobile phones at HMP Rhoswen. We know that the smuggling was previously run by Frank Cole with Kathy Wright's help. Our theory, and our main line of inquiry, is that Curtis Blake used intimidation to force Kathy Wright and her team of corrupt prison officers to work for him. For some reason, Kathy wasn't willing to play ball. We think that Rosie's abduction was part of Blake's intimidation, but something went wrong, which is why there was blood found at the scene. For Rosie to be of any use to Blake, she needs to be alive, but we have no idea where Rosie is or if Blake is still holding on to his bargaining chip. Yesterday's bomb was clearly intended to kill Kathy Wright. We assume that Blake now believes that she knows too much or just isn't taking his threats seriously. Last year, we saw just how far Curtis Blake will go to keep any witnesses against him out of court. It's likely that he wants Kathy dead and out of the way before she decides to talk to us. We are installing surveillance in Blake's cell so we can monitor all his calls and all of his visitors in the hope that he makes some mention of Rosie Wright or any connection with Kathy. At the moment, Kathy Wright is under house arrest, but she is shit-scared after what happened yesterday. If I were her, I would be thinking that Blake would get to her one way or another. However, she still hasn't told us anything. She will not admit that she has been smuggling anything into the prison or that Rosie's disappearance has anything to do with that. There will now be an armed officer posted permanently at the Wrights' home.' Ruth clicked the iPad and an image of Hayley Collard appeared on the wall monitor. 'Nick has been investigating another line of inquiry. Nick?'

Taking a breath, Ruth sat back on a table to one side of the monitor. The base of her spine was still painful where she had bruised her coccyx. She looked around. Despite what had happened to Merringer, it had to be business as usual. The grave faces of the detectives looking back at her were full of concentration.

Nick nodded as he moved to the front of the briefing. 'Boss. This is Hayley Collard, aged seventeen. She is a known prostitute working in Rhyl and has a string of convictions for soliciting from the age of thirteen onwards. Hayley is working for this man—' Nick clicked the iPad and another photo appeared '—Christian Vasilescu, a Romanian national who is wanted back in Romania in connection with people trafficking, drug smuggling and extortion. Hayley uses fan sites of various bands to groom vulnerable teenage girls. She particularly targets girls in care, who have been fostered or where there is some kind of abuse or addiction in the family home. She arranges to meet them secretly, knowing that if they turn up, they are worth continued grooming. Once they are hooked in, they are bribed with drugs and alcohol and then intimidated by Vasilescu and his gang. He takes them via Holyhead to Dublin, where they are forced to work as prostitutes for the Romanian gangs out there. There might be some connection between the Irish travelling community in North Wales and the Romanian gangs in Dublin. I tracked down Vasilescu to the travellers' site at Woodburn Farm. They claim they hadn't ever seen him but did admit they had dealings with Romanians and Roma Gypsies. I came across this man—' Nick pressed the iPad and an image of the man with the handgun at Woodburn Farm the day before appeared '—Declan Brennan. Brennan has previous convictions for assault and robbery. He also has a brother, James Brennan, who is serving time for five counts of abduction, assault and holding workers against their will at travellers' sites in Scotland. While I was there, Declan Brennan had a concealed handgun on his person. At the moment, Superintendent Jones is debating whether we go in to retrieve that handgun due to the sensitive nature of our dealings with Woodburn Farm. However, it's worth bearing in mind for any future dealings with anyone at that site,' Nick warned.

'So, our theory is that Rosie Wright could have been groomed by Hayley Collard and Vasilescu?' French asked.

Nick nodded. 'Yes. It doesn't explain the blood in the yard. But if we go for the botched abduction theory, then Rosie could have been taken from Haddon Farm by these people. She might be being held against her will somewhere in North Wales or she may have even been taken over to Ireland.'

'Thank you, Nick,' Ruth said.

'We've got passenger lists and CCTV for all the ferries from Monday evening onwards. CCTV isn't very clear and you don't need a passport to travel, just some form of ID. Rosie could have been taken out of the country without anyone knowing. I'm talking to the Gardaí's Special Detective Unit and National Surveillance Unit in Dublin this morning,' Nick explained.

Ruth nodded and then looked over at Sian. She didn't know how she felt as she looked at her. Regret, pain, anger.

'Sian, what have you got?' Ruth asked, managing to sound professional but feeling anything but.

'Boss. Possible lead on Martin Hancock, who is on the Sex Offenders Register. He was convicted of downloading and possession of indecent images of teenage boys while he worked as a counsellor at the Young Offenders wing at Rhoswen. It seems that he has some contact and even possible friendships with both Steven Haddon and Jason Wright. They claim that they see him at the Royal Oak pub and have a chat, but it's nothing more than that. I'll go and talk to the bar staff and see what I can find out,' Sian said.

'Jason Wright was at the Royal Oak on the evening of Rosie's disappearance, wasn't he?' Ruth asked.

'Yes, boss. I have checked that with the bar staff, but I'll dig around and see what else I can find,' Sian said.

French looked over at Ruth. 'Boss. We talked to Gareth Wright about his fight with Rosie on Monday afternoon. He claims Rosie wanted him to get her and her mates some ecstasy pills for their camp out on Monday night. He refused. She threatened to tell their father that Gareth was dealing again.'

'Is there anything in that?' Ruth said, thinking out loud.

'Gareth Wright was permanently excluded from Llancastell Sixth Form for threatening a student with a shotgun,' Nick said.

'See if we can tie down Gareth's movements on Monday afternoon and evening. His alibi is still very vague,' Ruth said to French.

French nodded. 'Will do, boss.'

There were a few seconds of stillness. The briefing was over and Ruth was glad to have got it out of the way for the day. The lack of Merringer's presence still loomed heavily over the room, and it would do for a while yet.

'Thank you, everyone. It's going to be a tough few days for all of us. Merringer was very proud to be a member of this team. Let's go out today and continue the brilliant work we do,' she said.

Ruth had only experienced the death of a colleague in the line of duty twice before. The first was WPC Sharon Ross, who was based at Lewisham nick with her. They had worked on a couple of cases together and had mutual friends in the force. On 6 October 1997, Sharon was called to an incident of a man who was acting in a threatening manner on Lewisham High

Street. Wayne Lavelle was a paranoid schizophrenic, high on skunk. As she went to restrain him, he stabbed her twice and she died at the scene. It was a wake-up call for Ruth at the time; sometimes police officers went out to work in the morning and never came home.

As the team dispersed, Ruth's attention was drawn to Nick, who had been looking at his phone intently for minutes and was now at his computer.

'What have you got, Nick?' she asked.

'They've sent footage over from the sixth form college. Rosie's form tutor spotted something at the college last Friday afternoon. Have a look,' Nick explained.

Nick looked up at the monitor on the wall, clicked his mouse and the CCTV footage appeared and began to play.

Ruth watched intently as the video showed Rosie walking along an internal corridor towards the cafeteria in the college. She is joined by another female student who has caught her up. They talk but seem to get into some kind of argument. The girl turns and slaps Rosie hard across the face. Rosie recoils and holds her face as the girl leaves.

'Can we get a closer look at the other girl?' Ruth asked.

'Hang on. I'm not very good at this...' Nick said, trying to work the zoom function.

Rewinding the CCTV footage, Nick paused it as the girl turns to go and zoomed in.

It was a face that both of them recognised.

'That's Emma Haddon,' Ruth said.

–

It was the middle of the morning, and Nick and Ruth were at HMP Rhoswen, heading for an accommodation block with DI Lyon and DS Buckley from the RPIT and Prison Governor Gordon Holmes. Ruth had received a call to say that the surveillance team were going into Blake's cell and they needed the SIO on site.

As they went, Holmes explained that the green paintwork had been psychologically proven to have a calming effect on prisoners. Ruth thought of how violence at this prison was statistically higher than average, but she kept the thought to herself.

'Not really a deterrent, is it?' Nick muttered quietly.

'Rhoswen's not about deterrence. It's about *rehabilitation*,' Ruth said, but her tone was a little mocking. She wasn't sure where she sat in that debate.

'X-box in your "room", all meals cooked for you. Gym, classes, footie on the Astroturf. They even have AA meetings in here. This is a doddle compared to rehab,' Nick whispered to Ruth.

As they arrived at Curtis Blake's cell, which Holmes was at pains to stress were 'rooms', the North Wales Police surveillance team were rigging up hidden microphones within the bed frame and under the sink. Given the serious nature of the crimes they were investigating, Ruth knew that the covert surveillance against Blake was covered by the Investigatory Powers Act of 2016. The extension of the police and security service's powers of surveillance was a direct response to terrorist plots and attacks. However, human rights groups such as Liberty felt that these powers were too far-reaching and impinged on people's rights to privacy. They challenged the Act in the High Court. Ruth could see their point, but she was a pragmatist. Anything that allowed her and her officers to gather more information to prevent serious crime or terrorism was okay in her book. She would forgo her right to privacy for her right to feel safe, thank you very much.

One of the officers saw them arrive and approached with an evidence bag. Inside was a tiny burner – a prepaid mobile phone. It was only three inches long.

'We found this in a compartment cut into the heel of Blake's trainer,' the officer said to them as he held up the evidence bag.

'Preferable to the usual prison wallet,' Nick said sardonically. Many prisoners kept their tiny mobile phones up their rectums.

The officer gestured to the phone. 'You can buy these for between twenty and thirty pounds. In here, they'll go for anything from two hundred to eight hundred pounds. I've even heard of them going for a grand.'

Ruth looked at the phone and then at her colleagues. 'If we take the phone, Blake will know we're onto him.'

'What's the alternative?' Buckley asked, looking over at the officer.

'We have the phone's ID, IMEI and SIM card number. We can trace all calls that Blake makes. We can just put it back in his trainer,' the officer explained. 'In fact, we can also use this phone as an extra listening device.'

'Until Blake dumps it,' Lyon pointed out.

'If he doesn't suspect we've been in here, he has no reason to get rid of the phone immediately,' Nick said.

'We put it back, hope he uses it for a couple of days and makes some mention of Rosie or yesterday's bomb,' Ruth said.

–

By the time Sian and French turned off the A55 towards Capelulo, the sky was opaque – a uniform blanket of virtually colourless cloud. It was still hot, but it was getting close and muggy. They were on their way to talk to Emma Haddon and find out why she and Rosie had fought and Emma had slapped Rosie around the face. Although there were two ongoing major lines of inquiry, anything of significance that had happened in Rosie's life in the days leading up to her disappearance could give them a lead.

The atmosphere in the car was quiet. It wasn't surprising. French was young and new to CID, and he was probably still in shock over Merringer's death. So was Sian. They had lost their colleague Mac last year, but that was different. That was a darker, more complicated loss. With Merringer, it was cut and dried. He was a good, honest copper and a family man who had lost his life in the line of duty.

'You okay?' Sian asked French, who continued to be lost in thought.

'Yeah, fine,' French replied unconvincingly.

'It's all right if you're struggling with what happened yesterday. I know I am. We're not robots.'

French took a moment and looked at her. 'I just keep seeing his face,' he confessed.

'Yeah, so do I. Don't buy into all that macho copper bullshit. If you need to talk about it, then you talk about it. Okay?' Sian said to him, leaving him in no doubt that she was being serious.

'Yeah, thanks,' French said.

Sian had spent the previous evening at her brother's house over in Mold. Even though there were three children in the house – her two nephews and a niece – they had a couple of spare rooms. Her brother, Phil, was minted. He ran his own estate agents and a building-development company. Her sister-in-law, Vicky, lived in the gym and fitness classes. It was clear that neither of them really understood why Sian was in love and had moved in with an older woman. She knew they thought it was weird. But they said supportive things and gave her sympathetic smiles when she arrived with her bags. Vicky said she had put clean towels in the 'big' spare room that was en suite.

Sian hadn't slept well. She felt all over the place and knew that she needed a few days to let the dust settle. If she and Ruth had any future, then Sian needed to work out if she could live with all the baggage of Sarah's disappearance.

As they pulled onto the bumpy track, the sun had started to burn away the clouds. The rhythmic chirruping of birds came from the trees that overlooked the yard, and the rumble of a tractor and clatter of its trailer sounded in the distance.

Putting on her sunglasses, Sian wandered into the farm with French. A young farm worker perched on a quad bike gave them a quizzical look.

'We're looking for Emma Haddon?' Sian said.

'Out at the back. In the paddock with the horses,' the young man said with a thick North Wales accent.

The ground was hard and bumpy underfoot and Sian smelt the acrid waft of slurry as there had clearly been some muck-spreading somewhere on Haddon Farm.

Up ahead, they could see Emma Haddon taking the saddle off of a beautiful chestnut horse. Wearing a dark blue riding hat and boots, Emma had obviously just finished riding.

'Emma?' Sian called as they went through the wooden gate and into the paddock.

Putting the saddle down on a nearby fence, Emma gave them a quizzical look as she approached. 'Is it Rosie?' she asked apprehensively.

'I'm sorry, no. We just need to clarify a few things as part of the search to find Rosie,' Sian explained.

'Okay,' Emma said as she unstrapped the riding helmet. Her hair was sweaty underneath and had matted.

'We've seen some CCTV from your college from last Friday, Emma.' French said.

Emma frowned as she pushed her hair off her forehead. 'Okay. I'm not sure what you're talking about.'

'We saw that you had a row with Rosie and that you slapped her,' Sian said.

Emma nodded and began to look upset. 'Yeah. It was nothing. I apologised the next day.'

'Could you tell us what you rowed about?' French asked.

Emma's eyes moved towards the ground. Sian could see that she wasn't comfortable talking about what had happened.

'Anything, however small, could help us find Rosie, Emma,' Sian said. 'Even if you think it's not relevant.'

Emma nodded as she thought about what Sian had just said. 'It was just a joke about my dad. I overreacted, that's all.'

'What did Rosie say about your dad?' French asked.

Sian could see Emma battling with what she knew she had to tell them.

'Emma, please. Whatever it is, you just need to be honest,' Sian said, sensing her hesitation.

'It's nothing awful. Rosie wanted us all to take pills on Monday night. She was going to get them off Gareth. I'd already told her that I didn't want to, but it was her birthday. On the Friday, I told her again I didn't want to. So she said I was really boring and that my dad wouldn't mind because he's cool.'

'Why would she say that?' Sian asked.

'My dad's really chilled about that sort of thing. I know he took pills and other stuff when he was younger,' Emma explained.

'So why did you slap her?' French asked.

'Because Rosie said that me not wanting to take pills was the sort of reason why my dad preferred her to me,' Emma explained, clearly upset.

'What did she mean?' Sian asked.

'It's just what everyone jokes about. Rosie and my dad are really close, ever since she was young. And they talk about lots of stuff. Politics, music and films.'

Sian sensed there was more to this. 'Why does everyone joke about that?'

'My friends say that my dad fancies Rosie. He doesn't. He's not like that. They just get on really well,' Emma explained.

Sian exchanged a look with French – well, that was news to them.

# CHAPTER 18

*Four days, twenty hours*

Sucking the last half-inch of her cigarette, Ruth stood out on the steps at the front of the building in the designated smoking area. She would never get used to the smoking bans. For two decades, her work as a police officer had been accompanied by a ciggie in one hand and coffee in the other. The bloody do-gooders had ruined all that for her.

Ruth's phone rang. It was Steven Flaherty. Instinctively, her stomach tightened.

'Hi, Steven,' Ruth said, answering.

'Hi, Ruth. I imagine you've seen on the news about the rape and attack in Edinburgh?' Steven said.

'Yes, I have. I immediately thought of Kessler,' Ruth said.

'I've been in contact with the police up there. They have two eyewitnesses that saw a man quickly walking away from the scene of the attack,' Steven said.

From the tone of his voice, Ruth already knew what he was going to say next. 'What did they say?'

'The man they described sounds very much like Kessler. I'll call you when I know more,' Steven said before ending the call.

Stubbing out the cigarette butt on the filthy cigarette bin, Ruth now hoped that Kessler had made a mistake. Something that would allow the Scottish police to find and apprehend him.

*Don't get your hopes up, Ruth. Kessler is very good at avoiding detection and disappearing*, she said to herself.

Trying to put all thoughts of Kessler to one side, she turned and made her way inside. DCI Drake came out of the lift that she was waiting for.

'I've spoken to the chaplain. We have a service for Luke at seven thirty p.m. tomorrow,' Drake said and then looked at her. 'You do know you shouldn't be in today?'

'What am I going to do at home? Gardening?' she said, rolling her eyes. She couldn't tell weeds from flowers and ended up pulling everything out of the flowerbeds anyway.

'You got blown up yesterday, Ruth. A day on the sofa watching a box set wouldn't be a bad idea,' Drake said.

When he put it like that, he had a point. But she felt she needed to be at work.

'I think *Game of Thrones* can wait, boss.'

'How did it go at Rhoswen?' he asked.

'Blake's got more surveillance than Watergate,' Ruth said.

'Why is Kathy Wright holding out on us?' Drake asked.

'I don't know, boss. Yesterday's bomb has to be Blake's work. Her daughter is missing. Blake is trying to kill Kathy, but she's saying nothing. Her only option is to go into witness protection, but she's laughing at that suggestion.'

'Rosie's running out of time and so is her mother. Okay, keep me posted, Ruth,' Drake said as he turned and left the building in a hurry.

Ten minutes later, Ruth was back in her office beside Incident Room One. She trawled through her emails and there was something from Technical Forensics. They had found a series of documents and searches that had been deleted from Rosie's laptop. The email detailed how Rosie had built a hole within the program files in the middle of a random game in which the files were hidden as PTA files. Ruth wasn't that interested in how she had done it. Truth be told, she didn't understand 90 per cent of what the email said. What she was interested in was the fact that they showed that Rosie Wright had paid two hundred and fifty pounds for a fake UK driving licence, which had been sent to her three weeks ago. What troubled Ruth was the fact that the licence had a completely different name on it – *Hannah O'Brien*.

Of course, it might just be a sixteen-year-old girl trying to get fake ID to buy drinks or get into a club, but that didn't explain the need for a different name. Given Rosie's disappearance, her need for a fake UK driving licence in a different name might have had a darker purpose.

At that moment, Nick knocked on her open door.

'Boss, something's come over from Rhoswen that you should look at right away,' Nick said.

As Ruth got up, she gestured to the computer. It was still preoccupying her. 'Three weeks ago, Rosie Wright bought a fake UK driving licence online.'

Nick shrugged. 'She's not the only sixteen-year-old to buy fake ID.'

'That's what I thought. But it was also in a fake name – Hannah O'Brien,' Ruth explained.

'Which is Irish,' Nick said as he started to think. 'You can travel to Dublin from Holyhead on a UK driving licence.'

'And if Rosie had travelled as Hannah O'Brien, then we wouldn't have found her on the passenger lists.'

The pieces of their theory that Rosie Wright had been trafficked to Ireland seemed to be fitting together more clearly.

'Just to confuse matters, boss, have a look at this footage from two weeks ago,' Nick said as they went over to the large screen on the wall.

There was footage from the prison CCTV, which showed the staff security entrance at HMP Rhoswen, both outside and inside. It had been paused.

As Nick clicked the iPad, Ruth watched the footage begin to play.

The screen showed a figure get out of a car in the car park. Despite the baseball cap, Ruth could see immediately that it was Gareth Wright. He had a small rucksack over his shoulder as he looked around on his way to the staff security entrance, which was a single door with a video entry phone. Gareth buzzed and within thirty seconds the door had opened. Kathy Wright was standing inside. Gareth handed over the rucksack and Kathy handed him a thick envelope, which he stashed inside his jacket. The door opened and Gareth made his way back to the car park. As Kathy walked past the prison officer, who was sitting behind a monitor and desk, she reached inside the rucksack, pulled out what looked like a sandwich box before disappearing into the staff toilets.

As Nick stopped the footage, he looked at Ruth. 'Now we know where Kathy gets her supply of drugs from,' he said.

'Keep it in the family,' Ruth said as she shook her head.

'I think it's sweet that Gareth pops by the prison every day to take his mum her packed lunch,' Nick quipped sardonically.

'You think this has anything to do with Rosie disappearing?' Ruth asked.

'Maybe Rosie found out what they were up to? Maybe she threatened to go to the police?' Nick suggested with a shrug.

'And they decided to shut her up?' Ruth said, following the line of thought.

'Maybe. I still think it's more likely that Curtis Blake's involved,' Nick said.

'That's because, as they say in US cop shows, you have a "hard on" for Curtis Blake,' Ruth said, raising her eyebrow. She knew that Nick's vendetta against Blake had at times been obsessional and even got in the way of previous investigations.

'The planet would be a safer, nicer place if he wasn't on it, that's all, boss.'

Ruth nodded as her mind turned over the new evidence they had against Kathy and Gareth Wright. The frustrating thing was that with every new piece of solid evidence, the picture of who had taken Rosie and why became murkier and more confused.

'I'll talk to Drake now. We need search warrants for Gareth Wright's house and car. I want SOCO all over them. Go and pick him up and bring him in for voluntary questioning, at this stage. If he resists, nick him and I'll deal with that once he's in custody,' Ruth said, feeling a surge of adrenalin.

–

After about twenty minutes into the drive, Nick watched as the sun began to set in the west behind the dark plum outlines of the Snowdonia mountain range. The low orange sunlight began to tinge with darker auburn hues.

As *A Brief Inquiry into Online Relationships* by The 1975 blasted from the stereo, Nick flicked on the Astra's headlights. He pulled off the A55 and headed for Penmaenmawr, where he was going to pick up Gareth Wright. Finding St David's Terrace, he parked across the small driveway where Gareth had parked his shiny black Golf.

Getting out of the car, Nick tucked his sunglasses into the breast pocket of his blue shirt. He got to the front door and knocked. There was a loud bang from somewhere: the sound of a door closing.

Out of the corner of his eye, Nick spotted Gareth dashing from the side of the house and jumping into his Golf. By the time Nick had reacted, Gareth had already started the engine.

'Gareth, what the hell are you doing?' Nick thundered as he jogged over. Nick had blocked the drive with the Astra. *Where the hell does he think he is going?*

Hearing the gearbox clank, Nick realised that Gareth wasn't going to let the unmarked vehicle stand in the way of his escape route. He was desperate. The car sped forward, ramming into the left wing of the Astra with a loud metallic thud. Revving his engine, Gareth used the Golf to push the damaged Astra out of the way and into the street until there was enough space for him to drive off the pavement and onto the road.

Running to look at the damage, Nick immediately saw that the front passenger wheel and wing were crushed and twisted. He was going nowhere and Gareth was getting away.

'Central from three-six. Suspect Gareth Wright in a black VW Golf, plate unknown, heading north on St David's Terrace, over. Request assistance and a PNC check, over,' Nick hollered into his Tetra radio as he ran into the middle of the road.

A new-looking white Mini Cooper slowed to try to pass the Astra that was jutting out into the road. There were two women in their twenties inside.

Nick flashed his warrant card and shouted, 'Police emergency. Sorry, but I need your car.' He yanked open the driver's door as the terrified woman got out.

'Are you kidding me?' she said, looking astonished.

'Sorry. I'll send a car to pick you up,' Nick said as he jumped into the driver's seat.

Her friend had already got out of the passenger side and looked bewildered. 'This is mental!' she said, shaking her head. 'You can't just take her car!'

Slamming the car into gear, Nick stamped on the accelerator and roared up the road after Gareth.

'Are you kidnapping me, or are you going to let me out?' screamed a female voice from the back seat.

*Shit!* Completely thrown, Nick looked around. There was a terrified young woman in the back whom he hadn't seen when he commandeered the car. He slammed on brakes and skidded.

'Jesus! I didn't see you there. Sorry,' Nick said.

'For fuck's sake!' the woman grumbled as she got out of the back seat and slammed the door angrily.

Stamping down on the accelerator, Nick worked through the gears, pushing the car's acceleration as hard as he could. Fifty miles per hour. Sixty. Seventy.

Gareth Wright had a thirty-second start on him and a very fast Golf. Nick's only hope was that he had been held up at the junction on the main road for a decent amount of time.

Scanning left and right, Nick still couldn't see him. *Where the bloody hell is he?*

'Control from three-six. Still in pursuit of suspect but have lost visual contact, over,' Nick said.

'Three-six, received. Alpha-tango-five-seven is en route to assist. Will advise, over.'

Then suddenly, Nick saw the red blur of brake lights up ahead. It was the back of Gareth's Golf as it zipped out onto the main road. As he had hoped, Gareth had been slowed down by traffic.

*I'm coming for you, you fucker*, Nick thought.

Nick drove the Mini down the outside of the waiting traffic, sounding the horn. He then skidded out onto the main road. He dropped down into third and the engine roared as it strained. Up to sixty miles per hour, then seventy.

*Is the gear box going to take it?* he wondered.

Where did Gareth Wright think he was going to go? He couldn't think he was going to go into hiding. However, if he was in business with his mum, that also put him in danger from Blake. Even on the VP wing on remand, Gareth wouldn't be safe if Blake had people on the inside. And Blake *always* had people on the inside.

As the traffic lights up ahead turned red, Gareth made no effort to slow. Flying across the junction at high speed, the Golf nearly hit a lorry. He was out of control with nothing to lose. And that made him very dangerous.

'Control from three-six. Still in pursuit of suspect, travelling east on the A-three-two-five. Suspect is in a black VW Golf, plate sierra-delta-one-five, yankee-alpha-tango, over,' Nick said into the Tetra radio.

'Three-six, received.'

The Golf pulled out to overtake a tractor and Nick followed. Seventy-five miles per hour, then eighty. Up ahead, the unmistakable flicker of blue lights. Roadblock? Stinger!

Red lights flared from the back of the Golf. Gareth had spotted the blue lights. What was he going to do now? *Give up, mate. You're going nowhere and you're going to kill someone trying to get there.*

And then the Golf hit the stinger. Rubber went flying into the air as the tyres burst. Nick could smell the burnt rubber coming through his air conditioning unit.

Now driving just on the metal of the alloys, the Golf slowed steadily and then ground to a halt on the empty road.

Nick pulled up behind.

The driver door opened and Gareth got out with his hands up. *We're not in a film, you twat*, Nick thought. *I'm not going to shoot you. Bloody American reality cop television has a lot to answer for.*

Getting out of the car, Nick wondered why Gareth hadn't continued to run. Maybe he knew the game was up?

'All right, all right,' Gareth said as he walked towards Nick.

'Gareth Wright, I'm arresting you on suspicion of the supply of class A drugs and resisting arrest. You do not have to say anything, but it may harm your defence if you do not mention when questioned something which you later rely on in court. Anything you do say may be given in evidence.'

'I just need to speak to Mum. Then I'll tell you all about Curtis Blake. But you need to believe me. I don't know where Rosie is. Honest. And while you're chasing me, you're not out there looking for her,' Gareth said with a sombre expression.

# CHAPTER 19

*Five days, one hour*

Downing a large glass of wine, Ruth looked at the garden and the apricot glow of the setting sun outside. It should have been perfect, but she was feeling exhausted. The last couple of days had been horrific, both professionally and personally. The only thing keeping her awake and sane was wine.

Ella had gone to collect her father, Dan, from the airport. He was booked into a hotel in Llancastell until his wife and child arrived a week later from Australia. They were then travelling around the country to see friends and family.

To say that Ruth had mixed feelings about Dan's sudden appearance in their world would be an understatement. Ella and her father were going out for dinner, and it made Ruth feel very uncomfortable. She had brought Ella up on her own with no help until she had met Sarah. She didn't want Dan swanning in as if that was all okay. She knew that was selfish. It was what was best for Ella in the long run and having contact with her father would be good for her. However, Ruth couldn't help feeling resentful.

'Protection' by Massive Attack was playing on the stereo as Ruth tidied up for the third time. She had watched a colleague blown to pieces and had her partner walk out on her in the past forty-eight hours. There had also been a possible sighting of Jurgen Kessler in Scotland. What she really needed was to go and lie down in a dark room for a few weeks. What she didn't need was to meet her ex-husband and have any more emotional scars picked at.

*More wine*, she thought as she poured another glass. Self-medicating wasn't healthy, but she had had more than her fair share of trauma for one week.

Half an hour later, she heard the key in the door and felt a twinge of anxiety. What was going on? Ella was meant to be out for the evening.

'Come on in for a second,' Ruth heard Ella say as the door swung open and her daughter walked in.

Turning to face her mother, Ella shook her head and said, 'I'm such an idiot. I left my phone here. I'll just run upstairs and get it.'

Walking awkwardly over the threshold was a man she hadn't seen in over twenty years. They eventually made eye contact and he smiled at her.

'Hi, Ruth,' he said in his deep voice.

Dan had changed so much that, for a few seconds, she felt quite stunned. In her head, it was still the mid-Nineties and Dan had just turned thirty. But twenty-five years later, his long blond hair had all gone and been replaced by a tanned, virtually bald head. His eyes and mouth were also tanned and lined. A neat goatee was greying on his chin. It was like the moment Dorian Gray stabbed his own portrait and aged decades in one go. At least, that's how she remembered the story. Maybe he just died.

However, Dan looked well and handsome. He had always been handsome. She had to give him that. Maybe he was better looking now he had aged?

'If this is too weird, I'll wait outside until...' Dan said, still showing his uneasiness.

She didn't know if he felt genuinely guilty or embarrassed about how badly he had treated them both, or if he just feared Ruth's reaction to his very presence. She hoped it was the former.

In her slightly drunk jolliness, Ruth made a decision as she looked at Dan.

'This is stupid, Dan. Come in and have a drink,' Ruth said, not quite believing that the words had come out of her mouth.

'Really?' Dan asked, his brow furrowed as though this was some kind of trick.

'Christ, it was a long, long time ago. And I'm starting to realise that life is very short,' Ruth said as she turned and headed for the kitchen.

Merringer's death had given her a lot of perspective. She wasn't immortal, and carrying around toxic resentment wasn't healthy for anyone. Well, that's what she told herself in her drunken haze.

Ella came downstairs and frowned. 'Are we okay?'

Dan frowned and said, 'Er... I think we're staying for a drink.'

Ella's face lit up. 'Brilliant! Mum, where are you?'

Ruth was still trying to work out if this was a good idea, but the very sight of Ella's face as she entered the kitchen told her that she had done the right thing. She knew that Ella wanted her two parents to be in the same room and be civil with each other – even if it was just for an hour. She owed her that much.

'Wine, Ella?' Ruth asked.

'Of course.'

Going to the fridge, she pulled out one of Sian's bottles of San Miguel and showed it to Dan. That had always been his drink – the irony wasn't lost on her.

'Cold San Miguel, from the bottle?' Ruth asked knowingly.

'Bloody hell. You remembered?' Dan said with a hint of irony as he started to relax.

Ruth handed Ella a large glass of wine and asked, 'Ella, did you really leave your phone here by accident?'

Ella looked at them both and raised an eyebrow. 'Of course I bloody didn't!'

The light had faded to a translucent blue by the time Nick reached HMP Applethorn. Tony was sitting smoking a roll-up cigarette at the same table that they had all sat at during their last visit.

Nick was slightly out of breath as he had jogged over from the car park to catch the last half an hour of visiting time.

Nick put his hand up as he approached and said, 'Sorry I'm late, Tony.'

'Not a problem, Nick. I'm not going anywhere,' he said dryly.

Sitting down, Nick caught his breath and looked around at the neat gardens. 'Not a bad little spot here, is it?' Then he regretted it. Why was he talking about a prison garden? It was because he was nervous and wasn't quite sure how to kick off the conversation.

Tony looked at him, reading Nick like a book. 'You've come a long way to talk about the gardens, son.'

Nick smiled and nodded. He was feeling awkward but knew he was doing the right thing. 'I wanted to ask you something, you see?'

'Right. Fire away,' Tony said as he finished rolling the cigarette.

'Amanda is the best thing that's ever happened to me. And we're having a baby...'

'Yeah, I'd noticed,' Tony remarked with a smile.

'And I want to ask her to marry me. But I wanted to ask you before I did,' Nick explained, feeling clumsy.

Tony lit the cigarette and blinked for a second as the smoke went into his eyes. 'Right, very old-fashioned. I didn't think people bothered with all that these days.'

'I've spent my life doing everything the wrong way. And with Amanda, I want to do things properly and the right way,' Nick said, trying to explain.

'Except for her being pregnant before you get married,' Tony quipped with a broadening smile.

Nick laughed and nodded. 'Well, apart from that. I wanted to ask Amanda to marry me and tell her that I'd spoken to you. I think the fact that I had been to see you, and talked about it, would make her very happy.'

Tony shrugged. 'I don't know about that… I've not been around for much of her life, but she seems to think the world of you, son.'

'Is that a yes?' Nick asked.

'I don't think I have the right to say what Mand does with her life. But yes, I do think you would make each other happy,' Tony said as he flicked the ash from his cigarette and began to cough. The cough continued and Tony seemed unable to get his breath.

Nick looked at him. 'All right? You need some water or something?' he asked.

Tony waved his hands to signal he was fine. 'No, no. I'm okay.'

'Are you?' Nick asked and raised an eyebrow in a way that was intended to signal that he knew something wasn't right.

'Yeah, I'm fine. Bloody fags.'

There was silence.

'It's none of my business, but I don't think you *are* fine.'

'Playing bloody detective, even when you're not at work, eh?' Tony asked with a wry smile.

'How bad is your cancer, really?' Nick asked, knowing that Tony had lied to them. That was the problem with the job. It came with an innate instinct for when someone wasn't telling the truth or was hiding something. Sometimes it was a blessing, but not always.

'What d'you mean?' Tony asked, avoiding eye contact and stubbing out his cigarette on the sun-bleached wood of the table.

'Come on.'

'When I was a kid, we called it the "copper's nose", you know that?'

Nick nodded. He just needed to say nothing.

Tony took his glasses and cleaned them on his shirt for a moment. 'You're right. Cancer's fucking everywhere. Lungs, lymph nodes, liver.'

'How long have you got?' Nick asked.

'Maybe a year… if I'm lucky.'

'I'm really sorry to hear that, Tony,' Nick said.

'I don't want you to tell Amanda. Not yet. I want her to enjoy having your baby and getting married,' Tony said.

Nick could see that Tony was adamant, but he felt uncertain. Was keeping Tony's diagnosis from Amanda the right thing to do? How would she react if she knew he had kept the truth from her?

After the events of last December, Nick had wanted them to be completely honest with each other, no matter what.

'I'm not sure that I should be keeping it from her.' Nick said.

'I will tell her. But please, let me find the right time. Allow me that, eh?' Tony asked, looking directly at Nick.

Nick nodded. 'Of course.'

–

It was heading for midnight, and Ruth had been talking with Dan and Ella for hours. The fact that they had all consumed a huge amount of alcohol had probably eased things along. 'Deep Inside' by Masters at Work was playing on the stereo – '*All we need is love…*' It was a mid-Nineties house music classic and one of Ruth's favourites. It reminded her of when she and Dan had first got together and went to clubs like Garage City, Bagley's and the Ministry of Sound when it first opened and before the tourists found it.

'Drink?' Ruth asked them. She knew it was a mistake to be this drunk, but she didn't care. She was numb, and that's how she needed to be tonight. Laughing and talking about old times had distracted her from all the darkness and pain of the week.

'Why not?' Dan said with a grin.

'I need to go to bed,' Ella said putting her hands up in surrender.

'Lightweight,' Ruth said as she zigzagged towards the kitchen for more booze. 'Oops,' she giggled as she lost her footing for a moment. *Bloody hell, I really am drunk.*

'Mum, you're hammered!' Ella said.

'Wait, what about the time your mum nicked some teenagers for going through a red light? She found a bag of snowballs on them and confiscated them…' Dan said laughing.

'Snowballs?' Ella asked.

'Ecstasy pills. Actually, they had a bit of smack in them, so if you licked them, they went brown,' Dan explained.

'Ew, that's grim,' Ella said.

'They were bloody strong though,' Ruth said as she returned with drinks and stumbled again. She got a flash of how carefree those days had been.

'You took them?' Ella asked.

'We went to that mad club. "Pump your Sporran" or something. Everyone in kilts with eyes like saucers. Brilliant!' Ruth said. She remembered the rushes from the ecstasy were so strong that night she could hardly get her breath.

'Oh, yeah, I forgot that. Used to take half the week for my brain to recover,' Dan said, shaking his head. 'I'm surprised we've got any serotonin left!'

'Mum, I can't believe you confiscated drugs from someone and then went out with Dad and took them!'

'It was twenty-five years ago and I was still a probationer.'

'You confiscated pills off someone at Gay Pride on Clapham Common as well!'

'And if I remember correctly, you had your top off and your hair in a ponytail,' Ruth said mockingly.

Dan patted his stomach and grinned. 'Wouldn't get away with that now.'

From where Ruth was sitting, Dan looked like he didn't have an ounce of fat on him. And his arms were still sculpted, with a Native American tattoo on the right and an Aztec symbol on the left.

In the rose-tinted haze of alcohol, Ruth smiled at the thought of those years. She knew she fancied women, so she thought she was bisexual. And Dan was a real catch. Everyone said so. He was cool and fit. He had tattoos when they were still the preference of hairy bikers and old sailors. He knew everyone. They were guest-listed everywhere.

'Right, I'm going to bed,' Ella said waving. 'Dad, you getting a cab to your hotel?'

'Yeah, I'd better sort that out,' Dan said sitting up and getting his phone. 'Don't suppose you have Uber round here?'

'Joking, aren't you?' Ruth said. 'You can crash on the sofa if you want? I'm going to bed now too.'

*God, I'm so drunk,* she thought.

'Yeah, it would be great to crash here if that's okay?' Dan said.

'I'll see you in the morning then, Dad,' Ella said as she disappeared upstairs.

Ruth went to the hall cupboard, grabbed blankets and two pillows before returning. *How the hell have you allowed this to happen?* she thought as she marked Dan standing by the sofa.

'There you go, twat!' Ruth said with a grin as she threw them at Dan.

'Hey… You used to be so ladylike,' Dan smirked.

Looking at the sofa, Ruth came over and started to remove the side cushions. 'If you take these off, there's more room. I forgot how tall you were,' she said, aware that her words really were slurring now.

'Cheers for this, Ruth,' Dan said, putting his hand on her arm for a second.

As Ruth moved away from the sofa, she nearly bumped into him. For a moment, they stood facing each other, inches apart.

'Oops! I seem to have a balance issue,' she laughed.

They looked at each other and smiled. In her drunkenness, Ruth held Dan's gaze and twinkling grin for longer than normal.

Before she knew, they had leant together and kissed.

*Oh, my God! What?*

They stopped for a moment, looked at each other and kissed again. This time passionately, tongues searching and fighting.

And then, simultaneously, they moved apart.

'I think I should go to bed,' Ruth mumbled, drunk and confused.

'Okay, night then,' Dan said.

Climbing the stairs slowly, Ruth closed her eyes for a moment.

*What the fuck just happened?*

# CHAPTER 20

*Five days, eleven hours*

As Ruth walked into the heat of the incident room, her head was pounding and she was feeling a little sweaty around the edges. She also had the guilt and sober shock of her drunken tryst with Dan. How did she let that happen? How did her brain process that thought and deem it to be an okay thing to do?

She caught Sian approaching and instantly panicked. Hangover guilt was the worst.

'You hungover, boss?' Sian asked knowingly.

'Yes, very,' Ruth replied, closing her eyes for just a moment.

'I can smell it from here,' Sian said with a worried look on her face.

'Don't. Not having a great week, so I decided to self-medicate last night,' Ruth explained. Talking to Sian was making her squirm. She needed to get through briefing, drink water and coffee, and put the events of last night out of her head for a few hours.

Sian touched her arm for a moment. 'We'll find some time to talk.'

'Not today,' Ruth snapped as she grabbed her files and headed for the front of the room. She couldn't deal with how uncomfortable being in close proximity to Sian was making her feel.

Sian looked a little hurt as she turned and walked away.

'Good morning, everyone. Today we have a memorial service for Luke at St Mark's Church at seven thirty. His funeral is to be at Llancastell Crematorium at the end of next week for family and close colleagues. Superintendent Jones has spoken to Luke's family. We will provide officers for a guard of honour and six pallbearers to carry the coffin, which will be draped in a North Wales Police flag...'

From nowhere, the image of Merringer's coffin appeared in her head, followed by an unstoppable surge of emotion and grief. It caught her off guard and she had to take a breath as tears welled and blurred her vision. 'Sorry... erm... we can talk about volunteers for this... at the end of the day.'

Ruth took a deep breath. *Keep it together, Ruth. Get back to business.* She cleared her throat as she pointed to the photos on the board.

'Okay. Rosie Wright has been missing for over five days. Usually, we would now take the view that she is unlikely to be found alive. But given the nature of our investigation, it may be that Rosie is being held as a way of gaining leverage over her mother. We suspect that Gareth Wright has been supplying his mother Kathy with the drugs that she then smuggled into HMP Rhoswen. Gareth's car has already been impounded and a forensic team are due to check it out this morning. SOCOs are also due at Gareth Wright's home. Kathy and Gareth are to be questioned after this briefing in separate interview rooms. We'll compare what they have to say. Gareth seems to be willing to give evidence against Kathy and Blake in return for some kind of deal from the CPS.'

Nick sat forward. 'That makes sense. The messages that Rosie had sent to Hayley on the fan site mentioned that she was horrified by the sort of people her mother and brother were.'

'What if Rosie had found out what Kathy and Gareth were doing?' French suggested.

Nick nodded. 'If Rosie then confronted them with what she knew?'

Sian frowned. 'Sorry, I don't buy Kathy Wright harming her own daughter.'

'Really? I've seen worse,' Ruth said, then realising that it sounded like she was patronising Sian. She avoided looking at her.

Nick said, 'If Rosie threatened to blow the whistle on what they were doing, that puts her in a very dangerous position.'

'Anything else?'

French looked down at a printout, 'Tech have traced a mobile number on Blake's burner phone to the Capelulo area. It was a pay-as-you-go, but it had been triangulated to the area of Haddon Farm. But it doesn't match the burner phone that Merringer found in Kathy's car.'

'Kathy could have several burner phones,' Sian suggested.

'It does establish a direct link between Blake and someone in Capelulo,' Nick said.

'When was the last call made to that number?' Ruth asked as she tried to piece the facts together.

French ran his finger down the printout. 'Last Monday, ten fifteen in the evening.'

Ruth looked at them all. 'Which was two hours after we think Rosie disappeared.'

–

Ten minutes later, Ruth had requested to look again at the CCTV footage of Kathy Wright in the supermarket car park with the man she claimed was Andy.

Clicking on the files that Merringer had been emailed, Ruth brought the CCTV footage up onto the large monitor on the wall.

Nick came over to see what she was looking at and pulled a face. 'Kathy Wright must have done some serious airbrushing if she found someone on a website.'

Ruth rolled her eyes and then played the footage forward to the point where the man in sunglasses gets out of Kathy Wright's car. She paused the image so that they could see the blurred image of the man.

'She wasn't on a dating site and this wasn't a date,' Ruth said, looking at the man in the image.

'How do you know that?' Nick asked.

Clicking on some files that HMP Rhoswen had sent over, Ruth brought up some CCTV footage of the prison's visiting area that she had viewed earlier. As she played the video, they could see Curtis Blake sitting at a table to the left of the screen. A moment later, a thickset man came over and sat down. He had the same Oakley wraparound sunglasses as the man in the supermarket CCTV, but perched up on his shaved head instead.

'Same man?' Ruth asked.

'Same sunglasses, same build, same hair. Yeah, could well be,' Nick said.

'On the afternoon that Rosie was taken, Kathy Wright wasn't lying about her whereabouts because she was having an anonymous shag.'

'She's lying because she's meeting one of Blake's associates,' Nick said, joining the dots.

'Have we got the visitor records?' Ruth asked.

'Yeah, somewhere. Although it could well be a false ID,' Nick said.

'What about the recording of their conversation?' Ruth asked.

'Bollocks,' Nick said. 'It's the day before we put the surveillance equipment into the tables.'

'If we send it over to Merseyside Police, they might be able to ID him,' Ruth suggested.

Nick was still looking at the still image on the screen. 'Can you play the supermarket CCTV again, boss?'

'Yeah,' Ruth said, intrigued by what Nick was thinking.

Clicking the iPad, she rewound the CCTV and played it again.

They watched the blurred images of Kathy Wright and the man talking in the car.

'Can you zoom in a bit?' Nick asked.

Clicking on the screen, Ruth clicked again. The image was bigger, but the resolution was poor.

Walking to the monitor, Nick looked closely and gestured to the image. 'He's pointing his finger at her. Can you play it again?'

They watched the CCTV again, now zoomed in. Nick was right – the man was jabbing his finger at Kathy Wright.

'He's threatening her. And this is a few hours before Rosie goes missing,' Ruth said.

*That makes sense*, Ruth thought. Blake's associate met Kathy Wright in the car park to give her a final warning. Play ball, and do as you're told, or else.

Three hours later Rosie had been taken.

–

Sian looked at her watch as she and French walked into the Royal Oak pub in Capelulo. It was dark, old-fashioned and smelt of wood and beer. There were a few scattered customers at tables and two elderly men sitting at the bar nursing pints. They looked like men who did this all day, every day, Sian thought.

Carrying the emotional hangover of moving out of Ruth's house, Sian was trying to keep preoccupied and busy. Having told Ruth that she needed time to think, the irony was that it was the last thing that she wanted to do. Her thoughts went to and fro like a frenetic game of tennis. She loved Ruth more than anyone she had ever met. She wanted them to share everything and to grow old together. But she feared Ruth would never get over what had happened to Sarah because there was no resolution. She didn't blame her. How could she live properly with the knowledge that Sarah might still be out there? It was like living your life on pause. But that meant there was always a part of Ruth's mind and heart somewhere else. Didn't Sian owe it to herself to be with someone who could be entirely present?

Taking her warrant card from her pocket, Sian went over to the young female barmaid who was stacking glasses. She had a little name badge on her polo shirt: *Seren*.

'Hi there, Seren. DC Hockney and DC French from Llancastell CID. We're investigating the disappearance of Rosie Wright,' Sian explained.

Seren – thick blonde hair in a ponytail, no make-up and fresh-faced – nodded solemnly. She couldn't have been more than eighteen.

'Oh, yeah. Horrible,' Seren said.

'Do you know Rosie Wright?' French asked, leaning slightly on the bar.

'Not really. She was a couple of years below me at school. Then she went to the sixth form college,' Seren said. 'Her dad drinks in here.'

'Could you tell us who was working here last Monday night?' French asked as he pulled out his notebook and clicked his pen.

Seren thought for a moment as she wiped her hands on a tea towel. 'I was on. And so was Robbie?'

'Robbie?' Sian asked.

'Robbie Milton. He starts at lunchtime today if you want to speak to him?' Seren explained.

'You had a band playing last Monday night, is that right?' French asked.

'Yeah. The Bombardiers. Out in the garden,' Seren said as she pointed to a press clipping from a local paper that was up on the wall.

'What time did they play?' French asked.

'Started at seven. Finished about nine, nine thirty.'

Sian nodded, took out her phone and got a photograph of Martin Hancock up on the screen. 'Do you know this man?'

'Yeah. Martin,' Seren said.

'Was he here on Monday night?' Sian asked.

'Not sure. I think so,' Seren said.

'He's a regular, is he?'

'Yeah, a few times a week. Weekends, you know?'

'Sian?' French said, shooting Sian a meaningful look.

Sian followed his gaze up to the newspaper article that had been pinned to the wall. French went over close and pointed to the large photo of the Bombardiers that was central to the article.

'What am I looking at?' Sian said as she joined him.

French pointed to one of the wooden tables in the pub garden that were in the photo of the band. Sitting around one table were Steven Haddon, Jason Wright *and* Martin Hancock.

'That all looks very cosy,' French said sardonically.

'Puts paid to the idea that Steven and Jason hardly know Martin Hancock, doesn't it?' Sian said before she turned to Seren. 'Have you ever seen Jason Wright drinking with Martin Hancock?'

'Yeah, all the time,' Seren said as though this was a silly question. 'This time of year, they sit at the far table out in the garden,' Seren explained.

'Can you tell me what time they all left the pub that night?' French asked.

'Quite early. Actually, it was about fifteen minutes after the band started to play. I assumed they didn't like the band or thought it was too noisy, you know?' Seren said.

'So just after seven then?' Sian asked.

'Yeah. That sounds about right.'

Sian shot French a look – so where did they all go just after seven o'clock?

–

It was nearly three by the time Ruth and Nick walked into Interview Room One. Both Kathy and Gareth Wright had been brought in for questioning under caution, but were being kept apart so the detectives could get the full story.

Kathy looked tired and drawn. Ruth wasn't surprised. How would anyone sleep knowing their daughter was missing and fearing that Curtis Blake wanted you and your son dead?

Ruth sat down decisively. The hangover was gone and she was starting to get into her stride. She also wanted to know what the bloody hell Kathy Wright was playing at.

'Kathy, I need to remind you that you are still under caution,' Ruth said as she shuffled through her files.

Reaching into an envelope, Nick pulled out a still image from the CCTV they had seen at the staff security entrance at HMP Rhoswen.

'For the purposes of the tape, this is item reference five-six-T-G-five. It is a still image from CCTV footage that we have obtained from HMP Rhoswen. It shows your son Gareth Wright arriving at the staff entrance to the prison. He hands you a small rucksack and you hand him an envelope,' Nick stated.

'So what? This has nothing to do with the fact that Rosie is still missing and you two clowns are doing fuck-all to find her. Don't you get that?' Kathy growled at them.

Her duty solicitor, a middle-aged man, balding, thickset, shifted and gave her a quick look as if to imply that she should tone it down a bit.

'You know what I think? I think that Gareth was supplying you with drugs that you were distributing to your colleagues and Frank Cole. The rucksack that Gareth gave you had the drugs in. The envelope that you gave Gareth was his payment,' Nick said.

'Prove it,' Kathy said.

'Hold on a second, Kathy. Let me finish,' Nick said sarcastically. 'So, you and Gareth have a nice little family business going. It pays for the ten-thousand-pound car that your son drives around in. You keep some of the money hidden around the house. And everything is hunky-dory until Curtis Blake arrives at Rhoswen. He wants to take over the drug and phone market in the prison. He puts Frank Cole into hospital. He intimidates you so that you now have to work for him. Maybe he threatens your family? You don't want to work for Curtis Blake.'

Taking out another photo, Nick slides over an image from the supermarket car park. 'For the purposes of the tape, I am showing the suspect item reference seven–eight–T-Y-five. You meet with his man on the day of Rosie's disappearance and from what we can see, he clearly threatens you.'

'You told me that this man's name was Andy and you met him for anonymous sex on a website?' Ruth asked.

'Yeah?' Kathy said. 'That's what happened.'

Ruth pulled out a photograph of the man, late forties, shaved head, and showed it to her. 'For the purposes of the tape, I am showing the suspect item reference nine-three-R-T-four. This is the man that you met in the car park and the man we can see in the CCTV.'

'So what?' Kathy said.

Ruth and Nick knew that they now had Kathy on the ropes. She was tired and frightened and not thinking clearly. Otherwise she wouldn't have agreed with Ruth that the man in the photo was the man that she met.

'Would it surprise you to know that the man in the photo is Tony Kelly, a well-known associate of Curtis Blake?' Nick said.

'No. I… didn't… know who he was,' Kathy stammered.

Ruth leant forward and delivered Kathy her well-rehearsed, compassionate performance. 'Kathy, did Tony Kelly threaten you or your family?'

Kathy had nowhere to go. Ruth could see that the walls were closing in on her and she was terrified. Eventually, Kathy looked at the floor and nodded.

'Did Tony Kelly threaten to hurt Rosie, Kathy?' Ruth asked again.

'No, no. Not directly. He just said I needed to do what I was told or there would be major repercussions,' Kathy said quietly. She started to tremble.

'Did they take Rosie?' Ruth asked.

'I don't know, I swear I don't know. She's my daughter and I just want her back,' Kathy whimpered as she began to sob. It was all too much for her.

'Did Rosie know what you and Gareth were doing?' Nick asked.

'No. How would she know?'

'We have phone calls from Curtis Blake's prison phone to a burner phone close to your house, Kathy?'

'Blake just wanted to know when I was coming back to work. He said it was messing up his business 'cos he couldn't get the drugs and phones into Rhoswen without me,' Kathy said, wiping tears from her face and sniffing.

'Did he mention the car bomb?' Nick asked.

Kathy nodded, but she was now sobbing again. Ruth could see that she was breaking with the strain.

'What did he say to you, Kathy?' Ruth asked gently.

'He said… he'd… he'd heard there had been a nasty accident outside my house. He said it was lucky that… I didn't get hurt.'

'Are you willing to testify to any of this, Kathy?' Ruth asked.

'I can't, can I?'

'Why not?'

'What, and go into witness protection? How's that going work? Relocate to some shithole in the Outer Hebrides. No thanks.' Kathy wiped her eyes and nose with a tissue.

'Reduced sentence?' Nick said.

'I wouldn't make it as far as the court doors. You know that,' Kathy said quietly as she looked down at the floor and shook her head.

Ruth shrugged and said, 'You and Gareth are still both going to serve time. And that makes you vulnerable.'

Kathy looked at her. 'I'll just have to take my chances.'

Ruth waited for a few moments of silence to allow the tension to build again.

'Kathy, you need to tell me what happened to Rosie. Where is she?' Ruth said gently.

'I swear I don't know. I would give anything to see her and know she's safe. She's my little girl. I promise I don't know where she is or what happened to her.' Kathy's shoulders began to judder as she sobbed again. 'Rosie's… just my little girl.'

# CHAPTER 21

*Five days, fifteen hours*

It had only taken Sian and French five minutes to drive up the hill to Bluebell Cottage where Martin Hancock lived. Sian wanted to know why he had lied about his whereabouts on the night of Rosie's disappearance. It was a strange decision to claim that he had been at home all night because that gave him no witnesses to his alibi. Instead, Hancock had been at the Royal Oak pub. They had photographic proof that he had sat with Jason Wright and Steven Haddon. They would have provided a secure alibi for him. So why did he lie about his whereabouts? Where did they all go at seven o'clock when they left the pub?

A moment later, Hancock opened the door. He didn't look particularly fazed to see them and ushered them both into the living room, where they sat on the immaculate blue sofa.

'Mr Hancock, there are a couple of things that we would like to clarify with you as part of our investigation,' Sian explained.

'Fire away,' Hancock said with a disarming smile. Sian really didn't like him – there was something creepy about him. She knew that was hardly the basis for a conviction, but it was her copper's instinct.

'You told us you were here late afternoon and all evening last Monday,' Sian said, reading from her notebook.

'That's right, I was,' Hancock confirmed.

French frowned for effect, and then looked at his notebook. 'Which is strange as the barmaid at the Royal Oak distinctly remembers you being in the garden with Jason Wright and Steven Haddon.'

'Oh, gosh. Yes, that's right. I'm sorry. I was at the pub for a while that evening,' Hancock said in an unflustered way.

'Why did you lie to us, Mr Hancock?' French asked.

'I didn't lie. It was a genuine mistake. I just forgot,' Hancock said with a shrug.

'How well do you know Jason Wright?' Sian asked.

'Not that well. I see him at the pub. We have a chat.'

'The staff at the Royal Oak seem to think that you spend a lot of time together at the pub. Is that right?' French asked.

'You seem to be making more of this than you need. I have a drink once in a while at the pub with Jason Wright. There's no law against it. He's a nice bloke, that's it.'

'What about Steven Haddon?' Sian asked.

'And sometimes I have a drink with Steven as well. I think you'll find that having a drink and a chat with locals at the pub is very common in this country,' Hancock said sarcastically.

'What time did you leave the Royal Oak?' French asked.

'I have no idea. Not late, I don't think,' Hancock said.

'The staff seem to think you left just after seven o'clock?' Sian said.

'That seems about right.'

'And Jason and Steven stayed at the pub?' Sian asked, seeing if Hancock would trip himself up with another lie.

'No, I think they left about the same time as I did,' Hancock said.

'Where did you all go?' French asked.

Hancock frowned – he clearly didn't like the question. '*We* didn't go anywhere. I went home. I assume that Jason and Steven did the same.'

Sian had been dying for a wee for about an hour. She would have waited but she also fancied a quick snoop around Hancock's home. He was hiding something.

'Mr Hancock, could I use your toilet for a second, please?' Sian asked.

'Yes, of course. Up the stairs and straight over,' Hancock said.

Getting up, Sian felt the plush carpets under her shoes. The landing was bright with tasteful pieces of modern art on the walls. As she made her way to the bathroom, she saw the door to Hancock's bedroom was ajar. Pushing it gently, the door opened a little more. It was exactly as she had expected. Clean, chic and impeccably tidy.

Her eye was drawn to the distressed wooden bedside table that had been painted eggshell blue. A photograph in a frame sat at its centre.

The photo was of a carefree sixteen-year-old girl in a T-shirt. She was beaming at the camera.

It was Rosie Wright.

–

Having organised for Kathy Wright to be taken back to Cape-lulo and kept in protective custody with armed officers, Ruth and Nick made their way to interview Gareth Wright.

When they entered the room, Gareth was in the middle of an animated conversation with his duty solicitor. It was clear Gareth Wright had been discussing a full confession with his solicitor. He was clearly terrified that Blake was going to have him killed and he was going to admit to everything.

Ruth got through the preliminaries quickly before the duty solicitor made it clear that Gareth was willing to cooperate in return for some kind of witness protection.

Ruth looked at Nick and then down at her notes.

'Where's your sister Rosie, Gareth?' Ruth asked.

'I don't know. I swear down, I don't know. I wish I did know... Jesus, she's my little sister...' Gareth looked a little teary and wiped his eye with the cuff of his jacket.

Ruth waited a moment. She needed to start asking questions about the stuff that Gareth was happy to talk about. Once he started to talk, maybe he would reveal more.

'Gareth, is it correct that you supplied you mother with drugs and phones to be smuggled and sold in Rhoswen prison?' Ruth asked.

'Yeah…' Gareth said as he looked down at the floor and nodded.

'What kinds of drugs did you smuggle in, Gareth?' Nick asked.

'Everything… weed, cocaine, smack, spice. Whatever they needed. Sometimes there were special orders for prescription drugs. Benzos like diazepam, or sleepers.'

'How many officers were helping your mother distribute these drugs?' Ruth asked.

'I don't know. Three or four from what she said. I haven't got any names though, except a bloke called Doug. That's the only one she talked about,' Gareth explained as he jigged his left leg nervously.

'What about Frank Cole?' Nick asked.

'Frank sorted out all the orders and all the money. Everyone was scared of Frank, so there were no problems. Or if there were, they got dealt with.'

'Until Curtis Blake arrived,' Nick said dryly.

'Yeah… you could say that,' Gareth snorted.

'And your mother wouldn't do what Curtis Blake wanted, is that right?'

'Yeah.' Gareth nodded.

'And that's why Rosie was taken?' Ruth asked.

Gareth looked around at his solicitor. 'No. I've told you, I don't know what happened to Rosie. Why would I lie about that?'

'But Blake made threats to your family if you didn't do what he wanted? Is that right?' Nick asked.

'Listen, I'm not saying anything else now until I see details of what is on offer for me to give evidence against Curtis Blake.' Gareth looked over to his solicitor.

'My client has made it clear that he will cooperate in this investigation and give evidence if he is required to. However, we have no details or anything in writing. My advice to my client is he should wait until we have direct contact with the UKPPS via the National Crime Agency.'

The UK has a nationwide witness protection system managed by the UK Protected Persons Service, and it is responsible for the safety of around three thousand people. The UKPPS is part of the National Crime Agency that dealt with investigations into organised crime.

'It would be prejudicial for him to continue answering your questions. My advice to my client from here on in would be to give a "no comment" interview.'

Ruth and Nick exchanged a look – the interview was effectively over and they were no closer to finding Rosie Wright.

—

Having spent half an hour upstairs with Jones and Drake, Ruth was starting to feel that the search for Rosie had hit a brick wall. They had released Hayley as there was no evidence to hold her or charge her. They had no tangible leads and the search for Rosie had slipped right down the national news agenda and had been replaced by the plight of a beached whale that had become stuck upstream in the River Avon. It was that time of year.

As Ruth headed back to her office, Sian and French arrived.

'Boss, I've got Martin Hancock in a holding cell downstairs,' Sian said.

'What for?' Ruth asked.

'He lied about his alibi. He was sitting talking to Jason Wright and Steven Haddon in the garden of the Royal Oak pub until around seven o'clock last Monday. And then they all left the pub together,' Sian explained.

'That's weird,' Ruth said.

'Not as weird as having a framed photograph of Rosie Wright on his bedside table,' French said as he took out his phone to show them a photograph he had taken of Rosie's framed picture.

'What? What the hell is that about?' Nick asked.

A slight feeling of uneasiness came over Ruth. A convicted paedophile with Rosie's photograph at his bedside, meeting with the girl's father and neighbour.

'We thought his interest was in teenage boys,' Sian said.

'Are we missing some other connection here? Paedophiles don't normally have photos in frames by their bedside. They tend to hide their sick fantasies,' Ruth said.

'He lives on his own. He doesn't need to hide anything from anyone,' Nick said with a shrug.

'It does explain him striking up a friendship with Jason Wright. We've seen paedophiles groom the parents before,' Ruth pointed out. 'Daniel, while I go and have a chat with Mr Hancock, can you dig out everything we have on him on the PNC?'

French nodded and turned to go. 'Boss.'

Nick looked at an email on his phone and then over at Ruth. 'Boss, we've had a hit on ANPR for a vehicle belonging to Christian Vasilescu. The vehicle is somewhere in Bangor. Tech have also triangulated Hayley Collard's phone to a road in Bangor. It can't be a coincidence.'

Ruth nodded. She looked at Sian and they held each other's glance for a moment.

'Nick, go with Sian to Bangor. And put your foot down.'

# CHAPTER 22

Striding into Interview Room Two, Ruth could see by Hancock's face that he wasn't remotely fazed by being held in the police station. He had lied about being at home on the evening that Rosie had disappeared, so technically he could be charged with perverting the course of justice. However, unless he had lied to cover another crime or help someone else commit a crime, it was unlikely that the CPS would take it any further.

Beside him sat his duty solicitor, a thin man, balding with thick glasses. At a glance, Ruth thought he looked almost Dickensian.

The most viable line of inquiry into Rosie's abduction was the link between her mother and brother to the smuggling of drugs and phones into Rhoswen and the likely conflict with Blake. This was made all the more likely as Blake's MO was often to target the families of those he needed to intimidate. And car bombs were a particular favourite of Blake's cousins, Craig and Graeme, who had helped him take over the sale of class A drugs in Glasgow. A rival drug dealer had been blown to pieces in Tollcross in 2017.

Ruth looked across at him, sat forward in her chair and started the voice recorder. There was a long beep followed by a moment's silence.

'Mr Hancock, Martin, can I just remind you that you are still under caution?' Ruth said as she sat back in her chair and opened her file.

'Are you going to charge me?' Hancock asked.

Ruth wasn't in the mood for Hancock's bullshit.

'Martin, can you tell me why you lied to one of my officers about your whereabouts last Monday evening?' Ruth asked.

'I didn't lie. I made a mistake, that's all.' Hancock looked over at her. His air of arrogance was annoying her already.

'A teenage girl goes missing from your village and you forget where you were that evening. I find that very hard to believe,' Ruth said.

'It's the truth. I don't work, so one day is very much the same as the next.'

'Except this wasn't just any day, was it?' Ruth looked at him, trying to gauge what he was hiding. When a crime like Rosie's abduction takes place, people tend to make a mental note of where they were and what they were doing at that precise moment. It is human instinct. So Hancock was lying. Why? 'What are you hiding from us, Martin?'

'Nothing. It was a genuine mistake. And you know as well as I do there is no chance of you charging me with perverting the course of justice.' Hancock looked at her. His pulse hadn't altered since they started and, even though it was hot, there were no traces of sweat. He was a cold fish.

'What is your relationship like with Jason Wright?' Ruth asked.

'I don't have a relationship with Jason Wright. He's someone that I bump into at the pub. We have a drink and chat.'

Ruth looked down at her notes. 'The bar staff at the Royal Oak seem to think that you and Jason spend a lot of time drinking and chatting?'

'I wouldn't say "a lot of time". There is nothing clandestine about mine and Jason's chats at the pub. We talk about cricket, music or Brexit. That's about as racy as it gets, I'm afraid,' Hancock shrugged with a bemused smile.

'You and Jason were together with Steven Haddon at the pub on the evening that Rosie disappeared, weren't you?'

'Yes, that's right.'

'Why was that?'

'As I have already explained, they were at the pub. We had a drink together.'

'And then you all left the pub together?'

'It wasn't like that. There was a band playing in the pub garden who were very loud. Jason said that he was leaving as he couldn't hear himself think. Steven and I decided that was a good idea.'

'Where did you all go?'

'We all went home. Separately.'

'And you were home on your own for the rest of the evening?' Ruth asked.

'Yes. I have been through all this with another one of your officers,' Hancock said, shaking his head.

'Can anyone vouch for you being at home?' Ruth asked.

'I wish they could, but I'm afraid not.'

Ruth pursed her lips as she looked down at the file. 'Can you tell me why you have a photograph of Rosie Wright in your home?'

'Jason asked me to take some photographs of Rosie a few months ago,' Hancock explained. 'I had told him that I was a keen photographer. I put my favourite one in a frame. I don't think that's a crime, is it?'

For a few seconds, Ruth processed Hancock's bizarre explanation.

'Jason Wright asked you to come and photograph his teenage daughter?' Ruth said in a tone that bordered on utter disbelief.

'Rosie had expressed some interest in doing some modelling. I told Jason that he would pay a small fortune to have a professional photographer create a portfolio. I offered to come and take some photos, that's all,' Hancock said so matter-of-factly that Ruth shook her head.

'Come on, Martin. You offered to take photos of Rosie Wright, the teenage daughter of someone you know casually from the pub? For some reason, you keep a photo of Rosie by your bed. Last Monday evening, Rosie is attacked and abducted. Can you see how that looks?' Ruth said.

'Yes, I can see how it looks. But it's the truth. I'm a homosexual, so I have no interest in teenage girls. And I had nothing to do with Rosie's disappearance,' Hancock said. 'In fact, I feel guilty that you're wasting time talking to me.'

'But we only have your word for that, don't we, Martin?'

Hancock looked at his watch and then at his duty solicitor. 'I've said everything that I'm going to say now. By my calculations, you have eighteen hours to charge me with something. And I am happy to go and sit in the holding cell until you have to release me because the only answer I am willing to give you from here on is "no comment".'

### Five days, eighteen hours

Bangor was the oldest city in Wales and lay on the north coast overlooking the Menai Strait and beyond that, the island of Anglesey. The shadows of Bangor Mountain lay across the centre of the city, so from November to March some parts received no direct sunlight. Another ridge rose to the north of the high street, dividing the city centre from the south shore of the Menai Strait. This area was known as Upper Bangor, and it was where Nick and Sian were heading.

The intel they had picked up was that the car that Nick suspected belonged to Christian Vasilescu had been registered on the ANPR cameras in Bangor. There was a male driver and two young female passengers. Nick assumed one was Hayley Collard. Could the other one be Rosie Wright?

Tech had also managed to triangulate Hayley Collard's mobile phone to a road in Bangor. As Nick slowed the car on the residential street, it wasn't long before he spotted the dark red Audi parked on a drive by a small detached house with a brown pebble-dashed exterior.

'Bingo,' Nick said as he parked discreetly further down the road.

'Irish plates,' Sian said. 'Do we need backup, Sarge?'

'Let's go and have a look first,' Nick said as he unclipped his seatbelt.

The house was dilapidated and dark curtains were pulled at all the windows. The concrete drive and path were cracked and covered in flowering weeds.

Creeping along the outside of the house, Nick peered into the windows. Through a narrow gap in the stained curtains, he could see an empty room in virtual darkness. No furniture, no carpet, nothing. Just bare walls and wooden floors. Even though it was warm in the sun, the peeling window frame smelt of damp.

Glancing over at Sian, who was now crouched outside the front door trying to look through the letterbox, Nick gave her a quizzical look. Signs of anyone inside? She shook her head. Nothing.

Heading down the side of the property, Nick looked over the rickety wooden fence and gate that were about five feet high. Reaching over, he slid the rusty bolt lock and opened the gate to the back garden.

Was this some kind of holding location for the girls before Vasilescu took them up over through Anglesey to Holyhead and then down to Dublin? The garden was wild and over-grown. Thick curtains hid the lounge from view. Nick thought he could hear movement from somewhere inside. And then talking.

'Can you hear that?' he whispered to Sian who had followed him round the back.

She nodded. The talking was getting louder and more urgent. He didn't recognise the language. Had they been spotted?

Nick was aware of a growing smell that had replaced the scent of grass and flowers. Thick and pungent.

Sian shot him a look and frowned. Smoke? Something was burning somewhere, and it wasn't a bonfire.

Glancing quickly up to the first floor, Nick suddenly spotted black smoke pouring from the thin gaps in a window.

And then another smell that he recognised. Petrol.

'Shit!' Nick thundered as he clicked his Tetra radio. 'Control from three-six. We're at number three Orme Road, Bangor. We have a house fire. Request assistance. I need a fire engine, ambulance and uniformed officers, over.'

'Three-six received. Will advise, over,' the dispatch controller radioed back.

Somewhere in the house there was a scream and a woman's voice.

'*Help me! Someone!*'

Nick looked urgently at Sian and yelled, 'Go around the front and see if there's a way in. I'm going in this way!'

'Sarge,' Sian said. She turned and ran out of the garden.

Glancing left, Nick saw a rusty metal base that had once held a garden umbrella. That would do. It was the size of a dustbin lid and weighed a ton.

Heaving it up onto his chest, he flung it against the large ground-floor window. The metal base smashed through the glass pane and disappeared.

Nick kicked at the shards of glass until there was space for him to swing his leg over into the house. As he ducked into the lounge, a remaining blade of glass cut into his neck. It stung like fuck and he could feel the blood trickle down his back, but there was no time to stop.

As he moved urgently into the room, he could hear more shouting and screaming.

'*Help us! Help us!*'

It was coming from upstairs.

Black smoke was everywhere and getting thicker by the second. His eyes, nose and throat stung as he went to the door. He needed to crouch lower where the smoke would be thinner.

It wasn't the fire that was going to kill him, it was the smoke. If he wasn't careful, he would be unconscious and then dead long before the flames burnt his flesh.

Moving swiftly out into the hallway, he could see daylight flooding in through the open front door. Beyond that, through the haze, Sian was manhandling Hayley Collard to the ground outside.

If Rosie was in here, she was upstairs. Was that her shouting for help? Where was Vasilescu?

Nick tried to peer through the thick, sooty air but he could only see two feet in front of him. There was another scream. Someone was locked in a room upstairs.

Crawling up the stairs, Nick was starting to feel dizzy and disorientated. His brain wasn't getting enough oxygen. He coughed, trying to breathe. And now he could feel the growing heat of where the fire was raging on the first floor.

Coughing uncontrollably and gasping, he got to the top of the stairs. There was a door straight ahead. It was closed, but someone was hammering and choking from inside. It was locked. *Shit!* He didn't have time to talk or even shout a warning.

Lunging at the door, he hit it with his shoulder as hard as he could.

Nothing.

His streaming eyes were burning with the smoke. Feeling his lungs struggle to get any oxygen, he knew that he needed to get downstairs and outside soon. Or he was going to die.

Taking a few steps backwards, he could feel his legs beginning to wobble under him.

But he wasn't going to leave and let people die inside.

Running as best he could, he flung his whole body weight at the door. The lock snapped and the door swung open.

Two teenage girls pushed past him as they escaped, coughing and screaming. Retching, he tried he wipe his eyes as he watched them go.

Neither of them were Rosie Wright.

Glancing across the landing, Nick could see that the other bedroom doors were open. He hoped that meant there was no one else inside the house.

The noise of the flames was getting louder. Part of the ceiling crashed down onto the landing, filling the smoky air with plaster. It was time to get downstairs and out.

Then suddenly, he saw a figure crawling out of the front bedroom.

Christian Vasilescu.

Still clinging to a large black petrol can, Vasilescu's face and clothes were charred and burnt. He must have underestimated how quickly the petrol would ignite. More likely, Vasilescu had underestimated how flammable the petrol fumes were. Nick had seen it dozens of times before. Someone standing a long way from where they had poured petrol throws a match or a burning rag only to be hit by the burning flash as the vapours combust like an explosion.

Pushing through the smoke, Nick got as low as he could to try to get cleaner air. He needed to pull Vasilescu out of the house. Not because Nick wanted to save the scumbag's life, but because he might know where Rosie was.

As Vasilescu reached forward, Nick could see that he wasn't holding onto the petrol can. It had merely melted into the skin of his hand. Worse, as Vasilescu dragged himself along the burning carpet, Nick could see that petrol was still spilling out.

There was a whoosh sound like the sudden rush of wind. The trail of petrol and the can lit.

*VUMP!*

Vasilescu was engulfed in a corridor of orange flames. He screamed for a few seconds and then passed out.

The smell of burning hair and flesh nearly made Nick vomit as he crawled away and tumbled down the stairs. He didn't care if he broke a limb.

Someone grabbed him under the shoulder and lifted. Pushing his feet against the floor, his face was lit by sunlight, his lungs gasped and heaved for the fresh air of outside.

Squinting through his singed, sooty eyelashes, he could see blue sky, clouds and Sian's concerned face.

And then everything went black.

# CHAPTER 23

Ruth had released Martin Hancock at three o'clock. She didn't have a choice. He wasn't going to tell them anything more, and there was nothing she could charge him with.

Briefing Drake with developments, Ruth admitted that although there was something strange about Martin Hancock, she didn't think that he had attacked or abducted Rosie. But what was frustrating was that they couldn't eliminate him from the investigation either. She also wanted to know why Jason Wright had kept information from them.

The surveillance team at HMP Rhoswen had reported back that Blake hadn't used his phone since they planted bugs in his cell. Either he was being very cautious or someone had tipped him off.

Sipping at some lukewarm bottled water, Ruth looked out of her office window. A woman with a toddler in a pushchair weaved her way along the pavement before stopping to hand her daughter a sweet. Ruth could barely remember pushing Ella around the streets of South London. That was nearly twenty years ago, and it felt like another life. So much had happened since then. Calculating that she might have another thirty-plus years on the planet, Ruth wondered how she would make it. Life was exhausting. And the idyllic life of rural policing in Snowdonia and seeing out her pension hadn't panned out quite as she had envisaged.

Ruth clicked the BBC News app on her phone, as she had done regularly since the phone call from Steven Flaherty. She was desperate to see if Edinburgh Police had made an arrest. They hadn't.

She threw the bottle into the bin with a frustrated plonk. Was there time to head down six floors for a ciggie? If she wanted to live another thirty-odd years, maybe she really should cut down…

The reports of the house fire in Bangor were just coming in when French approached her office. Knowing that Sian was over in Bangor with Nick, Ruth started to worry if they were safe.

'Boss, I've got some stuff back on Gareth Wright's car,' French said.

'Anything interesting?' Ruth asked, already assuming it would be another dead end. That's the way the investigation was going.

'Yes, boss. I need to show you something over here,' French said, gesturing to his desk and computer.

Following him over, she could see tattoos across his back through his sweat-stained shirt. A swooping dragon across his shoulder blades. Ruth thought it was ironic that it was cooler and more rebellious not to have tattoos in 2019.

'Gareth Wright has a black box in his car to keep his insurance,' French explained.

'And that black box has a GPS tracker of every journey Gareth Wright makes,' Ruth said, remembering her first case at Llancastell CID where they had used a black box to track a suspect.

'Exactly. I've downloaded all the GPS data here,' French said, pointing to the screen. 'We have location, date and time travelled.'

'Where was he last Monday evening?' Ruth asked. What had French found?

'Gareth Wright lied about where he was last Monday,' French said as he typed again and brought up a map of North Wales. He pointed at a place on the north coast and said,

'He was at this place – Gogarth – which is eight miles from Capelulo, just north of Llandudno.'

'What do you know about Gogarth?' Ruth asked. She was still an outsider when it came to local knowledge of North Wales.

'Cliffs.' French gave her a meaningful look. 'It's known for having massive cliffs over the sea.'

–

Sitting on the stone steps of a nearby house, Nick was still coughing up black phlegm from his lungs. His eyes felt red and raw as he dabbed them with a wet surgical bandage that the paramedics had given him. His breathing was laboured but after five minutes of oxygen, he had taken the mask off as it was making him dizzy. His temples throbbed as his brain reacted to all the carbon monoxide he had inhaled.

It had taken two fire engines around half an hour to control the blaze. The black shell of the house now sizzled and smouldered.

Sian came over and squinted down at him. Her face was streaked with black.

'Have they managed to get in there?' Nick asked in a croaky voice.

'Yeah. The only body they found in there was Vasilescu's,' Sian said.

'Thank God for that.' Nick unscrewed the cap off another bottle of water and took a sip. He couldn't seem to get rid of the smell and taste of burning human hair and flesh.

'You saved those two girls' lives, you know that?' Sian said.

'Yeah, but no sign of Rosie Wright though?' Nick was frustrated that after all that, they seemed no nearer to finding her.

Sian shook her head. 'I'm afraid not. The two girls that you got out of there are Polish nationals. They don't speak much

English but they said they had been locked in that house for a few days.'

'What about Hayley? What's she have to say for herself?' Nick asked as he coughed up more black sludge from his lungs.

'Nothing at the moment. She won't talk to me,' Sian said.

Pushing down on the warm stone steps, Nick managed to get himself to his feet. His head was still whirling a little, but he got his balance.

'Where the bloody hell are you going? Sit down,' Sian said, putting her arm out for him to take and steady himself.

Nick smiled and pointed over at Hayley, who was sitting on the adjacent steps in handcuffs. 'I was going to say that I'm going to grill the suspect, but it might be a bit too soon for jokes.'

Sian rolled her eyes. 'Back to your old self, Sarge.'

Nick squinted up at the sun for a moment, reached for his sunglasses in his top pocket before realising that they were now somewhere inside, melted beyond recognition. Taking a couple of steps, he got his balance and stumbled over to where Hayley was sitting.

'Hello, Hayley,' he said.

'Fuck off!'

'Charming. Do you want to tell me what you were doing inside that house?' Nick asked.

'Fuck off. I've got nothing to say to you.'

'Who are the two girls that were locked in the bedroom?'

Picking at her chipped red nails, Hayley ignored him and looked down at the step.

'Were you and Christian taking those girls down to Dublin, Hayley?'

Continuing to chew a broken nail, Hayley gave out a sigh to show that she was bored with Nick's questions.

'Where's Rosie Wright?'

Hayley smiled and looked up at him. 'You're not going to find her, you do know that?'

'Where is she, Hayley?'

Hayley shrugged and shook her head. She still had a slight smirk on her face, which Nick would have gladly slapped off if there weren't a dozen police officers, firemen and paramedics within fifty yards.

'You think any of this is funny?' Nick was getting angry, but he didn't want Hayley to see that she was irritating him. His instinct was that Blake was involved, but Hayley might be telling the truth. 'It wasn't that funny when I watched your boyfriend go up like a tandoori chicken.'

*I hope that hurt, you bitch!*

Nick saw Sian wince. He didn't care. Hayley was holding out on them and he needed to get her attention one way or another.

'Rosie is a long, long way from here. And you'll never fucking find her, pig. And I'm more than happy to serve time rather than tell you anything. So you can go and fuck yourself.'

Overwhelmed by fury and exhaustion, Nick glanced over at the corner shop across the road. *Off-licence* was printed along the top of the window. That's what he needed. A couple of cold beers.

*I've just saved two people's lives and watched a man burn to death! I can have a couple of cold beers, for fuck's sake. It doesn't mean I'm going to relapse. I'm not an idiot.*

Taking an unsteady step into the road, his whole being lit up at the thought of having a drink. Just a couple. He took another step as he squinted up at the sun.

Suddenly, a car zoomed past about six inches away and sounded its horn.

'Shit!' Nick said as he jumped backwards. He hadn't even seen the car.

Someone put their hand on his shoulder – it was Sian.

'Where are you off to, Tonto?'

'Nowhere… I just…' Nick was feeling disorientated.

'Sarge, why don't you come and sit down for a bit?'

Sian and Nick shared a look.

Nick nodded, walked gingerly back onto the pavement and sat down on a step.

# CHAPTER 24

*Five days, twenty-two hours*

Ruth and French had driven along Marine Drive as they approached the cliffs at Gogarth. The sea swept out like a curved mirror to the west, with the rugged east coast of Anglesey to the left and close to the Great Orme.

At the end of the last ice age, retreating glaciers had left behind many strangely shaped rocks around the headland. It was also said to be the home of the Welsh Atlantis. The prince of Tyno Helig, Helig ap Glannawg, who lived in the sixth century, had a kingdom that stretched from the east of Conwy all the way to Flintshire in the west. Legend had it that Helig's turreted stone castle, some two miles from today's coastline, still lay preserved under the waters of Conwy Bay.

As the road steepened, the craggy rocks loomed over them. Spots of yellow flowers dotted the uneven stone surfaces.

Ruth was trying to hypothesise why Gareth Wright had driven out to Gogarth on the evening of Rosie's disappearance. As they pulled into the flat concrete car park and observation area, she was filled with a sense of unease.

French turned off the engine as Ruth looked out across the black sea that seemed to stretch out before them for ever. Unclipping her seatbelt, Ruth opened the door. The cold sea wind was refreshing as it blustered and chased itself around her.

Walking towards the grassy edges of the clifftops, she looked down. Her stomach lurched with vertigo. It was nearly seven hundred feet down to the sea, which swirled and crashed aggressively against the sharp rocks.

'The Devil's Cliff,' French said.

'Sorry?' Ruth asked. *What is he talking about?*

'This section of Gogarth is called the Devil's Cliff,' French explained.

Ruth looked down again – she could see why.

'Remind me, what time did Gareth Wright arrive here?' Ruth asked as she moved away from the cliff edge and her stomach and head relaxed.

'Eight thirty, boss,' French said.

'Do we think this is all coincidence? Rosie Wright goes missing at around eight o'clock and half an hour later her brother is parked here? Not a bad place to get rid of a body,' Ruth said, thinking out loud.

French nodded. 'Yeah, worst-case scenario, the body washes ashore somewhere with all forensic evidence destroyed by being in the sea. At best, the body is dragged out to sea and never seen again.'

Ruth nodded. French was spot on with his summation. She was impressed.

Walking along the clifftop, Ruth looked down into the grass. At this stage, it was all hypothesis so she couldn't order a fingertip search of the area or get SOCOs involved. It was too expensive.

'If there's more rain, we're going to lose all our forensics up here,' Ruth said in a concerned voice.

They both crouched, looking into the grass. If there was anything there, they needed to find it now.

*We really are looking for a needle in a haystack*, Ruth thought sardonically. She moved stones and bird feathers as she gazed across the area slowly. Something silver caught her eye – only the remnants of a chewing gum wrapper.

The noise and strength of the wind oscillated rhythmically. Moving forward, and clearing leaves from the grass, Ruth felt a sudden blast of wind and watched as leaves and feathers danced and swirled away.

Ruth stood up in utter frustration. 'Bloody hell. This is hopeless!'

'Boss,' French said, as he crouched by the small wall that separated the parking area from the grass.

'We'll have to get Uniform here in the morning and hope there's no heavy rain,' Ruth grumbled.

'Boss,' French said again.

'What?' Ruth asked and then looked over at him.

*Bloody hell. He's not found something?*

French looked up at her as she approached.

'Got something?' Ruth asked hopefully.

'I don't know,' French said as he raised up his pen. On the end of the pen was a tiny silver hoop. 'Looks like an earring?'

Ruth shook her head. 'It's not an earring.'

'No?' French said with a shrug.

'And it's too small to be a ring for a finger.'

'Toe ring?' French suggested.

Ruth took the pen from French and looked at it. The silver had a slight pink sheen to it.

'It's a trainer eyelet,' Ruth said.

'A what?' French asked.

'The metal ring where the laces go,' Ruth explained. 'How the bloody hell did you see that, Mr Hawk-eyes?'

'It was under some leaves that blew away. Bit of a fluke, really.'

'Can't have been here long. It's virtually unmarked and not rusted.'

Ruth held the eyelet up closer to her eye and into the light. On the underneath, there was something tiny that had been stamped onto the silver metal – *Converse*.

'It's from a Converse trainer of some sort,' Ruth said. Was it significant? It could have come from anyone's shoes. And then she had a thought.

Taking out her phone, Ruth skipped to the photo of Rosie that Kathy Wright had texted to her the morning after her disappearance. Using her fingers to enlarge the photo, she scrolled down to the shoes that Rosie was wearing.

Pink Converse All Stars.

Ruth glanced up at French and gestured to the photo. 'Rosie Wright was wearing these shoes when she went missing.'

She could see the reaction on French's face. 'It has to be hers, doesn't it?'

Getting up and heading for the car, Ruth continued to hold the pen and the eyelet. She delved into the boot, pulled out an evidence bag, dropped the eyelet inside and sealed it.

'It's not enough at the moment. We don't have Rosie's shoes, so we have no way of establishing if they're missing an eyelet. Gareth Wright could claim he drove out here to have a look at the view,' Ruth said.

French nodded as he opened the car door for her. 'Maybe Blake told him to get rid of Rosie? Or abduct her and put pressure on his mother?'

'Maybe,' Ruth said as she went through the possible scenarios herself.

Her phone buzzed. It was Drake. Surely, he didn't want another bloody update.

'Boss?' Ruth said as she answered.

'Where are you?' Drake asked.

'Gareth Wright drove out to the cliffs at Gogarth on the evening that Rosie was abducted. The timings fit exactly with when she disappeared. I've found a trainer eyelet that might have belonged to Rosie,' Ruth explained.

'Ruth, I want you to get that whole area taped off as a crime scene,' Drake said. His tone sounded urgent, which confused her.

'Boss, we don't really have enough to warrant that kind of manpower, do we?' She didn't want to challenge him directly.

'We got a message from Forensics. They found traces of blood in the boot of Gareth Wright's car. It's human and they're testing it against Rosie's DNA overnight.'

'Christ!' Ruth muttered.

It looked like Gareth Wright was out on these clifftops with Rosie Wright on the night she went missing and never came home.

*At last! We've got a breakthrough in the case. And we've got a prime suspect.*

However, it did also mean an acceptance that Rosie Wright was very likely to be dead.

—

The sun was setting behind the main steeple of St Martin's Church, which had been built in the eighteenth century. Stubbing out her cigarette, Ruth looked around as the last few police officers trundled respectfully into the church for Luke Merringer's memorial service. As she went in, she could see that most of the officers were in uniform. She hadn't had time to change, but she didn't think that Merringer would have minded.

A figure gestured to her as she walked across the back of the sombre church. It was Nick. His face was still red raw from the earlier fire. He was pointing to a space beside him and Sian. That would be too awkward, so she shuffled onto a nearby pew close to Drake and Jones.

The police chaplain began to talk to the congregation. 'Detective Constable Luke James Merringer carried out his duties with selflessness and integrity. He was an officer willing to take risks for the sake of others, something that police officers do, consciously or unconsciously, practically every day of their lives. Luke believed that the job of police officers was to defend the rights of ordinary citizens and to prevent crime and lawlessness and in pursing those goals. They put their lives at risk, sometimes with tragic consequences. And that is what we are here to mark today in an act of remembrance and thanksgiving to God for Luke's life.'

Ruth couldn't help but get caught up in the emotion of what had happened. Wiping a tear from her eye, she looked at the order of service that carried a photograph of Merringer beaming in his usual geeky way.

As the service continued, there were a few of Merringer's favourite readings and a poem. At the end, they played 'Always Look On The Bright Side of Life' which Merringer had requested. It allowed everyone to smile at his sense of humour.

And then the chaplain brought proceedings to an end.

As Ruth shuffled out, she saw Sian approaching. She wasn't in any kind of mood to talk to her. It wasn't the time or the place.

'I'm going to come and get the rest of my stuff tomorrow,' Sian said. She could barely make eye contact with Ruth.

'I thought we were going to talk?' Ruth said. She felt like she had been punched in the stomach. When Sian had moved out, she assumed it was just temporary. They would iron out whatever problems they had and move on together.

They walked out of the church and into the sunlight, moving to a quieter part of the church yard. Ruth knew this wasn't the place for a conversation. Some of her colleagues knew about her and Sian. Others had their suspicions. But a full–blown domestic was highly unprofessional.

'We can talk. But it's not going to change things. There's always going to be a third person in this relationship. I don't blame you,' Sian said in a virtual whisper as a tear rose in her eye and she blinked it away.

Ruth ushered her around the side of the church and out of everyone's view.

'It doesn't have to be like that. I can move on,' Ruth said, feeling overwhelmed.

'You can't. How could anyone move on? It's my fault. I thought that I wouldn't care about it, but I do.'

'And that's it?' Ruth asked as she gave way to the pain inside her. She didn't want Sian to answer the question. She didn't want it to be over. Sian was the best thing that had happened to her in years.

'I don't know. I can't see how it's going to change. And I don't want you to lie about how you're feeling. No one knows what happened to Sarah, and I can't imagine how that feels. But I don't want whatever's left over.'

Ruth looked at her for a moment. 'Please. I promise it will be different,' she said, knowing that she sounded desperate. She didn't care.

'I'm sorry. I do love you but it's not about that,' Sian took a breath and gave her a hug for a second. Ruth put her arms around Sian's back and pulled her closer to her. She could feel Sian resist and move away.

'I'll put in a transfer request,' Sian said, wiping a tear away with the palm of her hand.

'No, you don't need to do that.'

Sian took a decisive deep breath to compose herself. 'Right, I need to go.'

Watching her walk down the church path, Ruth felt detached, as though it was too much for her to bear. And then the anger and self-pity arrived. How had she let this happen? She was so stupid.

Sarah's disappearance had destroyed her. And there was no coming back from that.

# CHAPTER 25

*Six days, one hour*

Ruth had already finished a bottle of white wine and checked the BBC News app three times by the time Dan rang the doorbell. She had also taken strong painkillers, so the codeine and alcohol had numbed her of any feeling. Ella had rung to say that she was running late and wouldn't be back for over an hour.

'Hi, Ruth. Is Ella here?' Dan asked. After their drunken kiss from the other night, Dan was clearly feeling embarrassed.

'Come in,' Ruth said. She should have felt awkward, but she was drunk and her head was all over the place. 'She's going to be late, so you're stuck with me.'

In fact, if she was honest, she was glad of any company that would distract her. And Dan was always good company.

'You don't mind me waiting here?' Dan asked as he walked into the living room.

'As long as you don't try to kiss me again,' Ruth grinned at him. 'Drink? Beer?'

She could tell she was in *that* kind of mood. A bit drunk and childishly reckless.

Dan looked at her and frowned. 'Erm... okay... I would love a beer.'

'Great. I've only got Amstel,' Ruth called as she went to the fridge. The booze was giving her a buzz and it was a relief not to feel anxious and despondent. It was a relief to not feel at all.

'For the record, you kissed me,' Dan said as she walked in and handed him the beer.

'You stuck your tongue in my mouth, Dan,' Ruth chuckled.

'After you kissed me,' Dan said defensively. He swigged his beer and looked at her. 'Are you drunk?'

'No,' Ruth said and then smiled. 'A bit.'

'Nobody drinks any more. Have you noticed that? Ella's generation. Bloody snowflakes. They have a drink or two and that's it. Remember what we were like?'

'That's the problem, I can't remember,' Ruth laughed.

'The Nineties. I went out in 1991 and came back just in time for the millennium,' Dan quipped.

Ruth laughed. That's what she had loved about Dan. His funny, sharp wit.

'Oh, while I remember, Ella found my watch from when I stayed over. She said it's on her bedside table,' Dan said, gesturing upstairs.

'I'll show you where that is,' Ruth said, going to the stairs. 'Come on.'

*Why are you going upstairs with him?*

'Are you inviting me upstairs with you?' Dan said with a grin.

'Fuck off, Dan. I think I can resist you,' Ruth laughed as she turned. 'I'm just making sure you don't steal anything.'

Dan laughed. As Ruth walked up the stairs, she realised that she was now drunk to the point where the light of the day looks different. Where the pattern of time seems to change. One part of her brain told her to be careful. The other part told that part to fuck off.

Having retrieved the watch from Ella's room, Ruth watched as Dan came out onto the landing. He looked at the open door to Ruth's bedroom and beyond that, the beautiful view across the Welsh countryside.

'Wow. Now that's a view,' Dan said as he walked into the bedroom and stood in front of the large window.

Ruth followed him in, slightly annoyed at his lack of manners.

'Help yourself, Dan,' Ruth mumbled as she followed him in.

Now they were in the bedroom together, Ruth could feel the tension rising. What were they doing? Was it just the drink making her brain misfire? For fuck's sake, Dan was happily married and she was gay. *Get a grip.*

Dan looked at the curtain and straightened it.

'Sorry. Force of habit.'

'You know for a straight man, you were always strangely neat and tidy.'

'You mean metrosexual?'

'Or camp and mincing?' Ruth said, and they laughed.

Dan gave her the finger with a grin. 'Aren't you a lesbian?'

'Am I?' Ruth said, smiling and raising an eyebrow back at him. Oh my God, she was flirting with him.

They looked at each other. The tension mounted and Ruth felt herself begin to fizz inside. And then she reached for the corner of the duvet, pulled it back and looked at him.

'Really?' Dan said uncertainly.

'We can go downstairs and sit on the patio instead?'

'Yeah, that does sound boring,' Dan said.

A moment later, they lay on the bed together. Ruth reached for him, putting her hand on the back of his warm neck. She pushed her lips to his. They kissed, first lightly, then more urgently, her tongue in his mouth. She moved so that her hips tilted against his. She felt her breasts against his chest. She felt his weight and strength as he pulled her closer. He nuzzled against her. His lips on her neck as he worked his way up to her earlobe. Arching her back, she closed her eyes.

It was such a relief to let go and allow herself to be taken. That blissful loss of control. Not to care about anything for a few reckless moments.

*It was nearly dark as Nick gazed over the River Dee, which snaked its way past the pub garden where he sat. Over on the other side, the riverbank was wooded and steep. He could hear the twitter of evening birdsong and the mechanical whirr of someone cutting their lawn nearby.*

*Sitting at the far end of the garden, Nick looked around and saw that it had now emptied out. It must be getting late. Or at least too late for children to run and shout as they played on the swing and slide as they had done earlier.*

*Reaching down into a Co-op plastic bag, Nick pulled out a litre-bottle of vodka and a litre of Coke. Glancing around to make sure that no one was watching, Nick poured a good four inches of vodka into the pint glass and topped the rest up with Coke, which fizzed momentarily over the top and dripped down onto the grey wooden table. He couldn't bloody wait. He felt like shit. His face, his lungs, his back were all agony. The only thing that was going to help was alcohol.*

*He put the glass to his mouth, tipped it and opened his throat. With four large gulps, the pint had gone. The warmth began in his stomach as he waited for the booze to do its magic trick.*

*Suddenly, there was movement from a table over by the doors that led from the garden into the pub. Someone was sitting smoking. They were looking over at him. In fact, they were staring at him with a fixed gaze.*

*It was his dad.*

Jolting awake, Nick opened his eyes and looked at the bedside table full of fear and anxiety. The only drink he could see was a glass of water. Thank God. His mind raced for a few seconds until he knew for certain that he hadn't picked up.

*Fucking drinking dreams*, he thought to himself as he rolled onto his back and looked up at the ceiling. He could hear Amanda's slow breathing as she slept beside him. His heart was still pounding in his chest as he took some deep breaths.

Drinking dreams were common for those early in sobriety, and even though it was a relief to wake up sober, they scared the crap out of him.

Rolling onto his side again, he watched Amanda sleeping as she faced him. The skin on the back of his hand was still red and tender from where it had been burnt in the fire. He didn't care. He could have stayed like this for ever.

# CHAPTER 26

*Six days, eleven hours*

It was now seven o'clock and the SOCO team had been working overnight to secure what Ruth suspected was a crime scene. A large white forensic tent had been erected over the grass that led from the tarmacked observation point to the actual cliff edge. They needed to keep the rain and wind off until they had completed a fingertip search.

Having managed to stave off yet another hangover, Ruth sank the remnants of her strong coffee before putting on the white forensic suit, purple rubber gloves and boots. She couldn't even work out if she needed to feel guilty, and she was too tired to process it. In her head, Sian had made it clear that she didn't want to be with her. If Dan wanted to cheat on his wife, that was his business. What she had needed last night was drunken sex with someone she felt comfortable with. So anyone that judged her could go and fuck themselves. Of course, there was a large part of her moral conscience telling her otherwise, but she was happy to live in self-deception for a while.

She glanced over as Nick parked his car next to hers, got out and gave her a nod of hello. She had told him to come in late or even take the day off, given the events in Bangor the day before. However, she knew that he would get restless and bored, so it wasn't a surprise to see him this early.

A male uniformed officer, twenties, tanned and handsome, was standing beside the scene of crime tape. He was running the scene log.

Ruth showed him her warrant card so he could sign her in. 'DI Hunter, Llancastell CID.'

'Morning, ma'am,' the constable said.

'Morning. Has DCI Drake been here yet?' Ruth asked. Drake had messaged her to say that he was going to be there at the crack of dawn.

'Yes, ma'am,' the constable replied, looking down at the timings of the log. 'He arrived at five thirty and left half an hour ago.'

'Thank you,' she said as she turned to wait for Nick to reach her. 'Nick, you're supposed to be taking the morning off.'

'And do what, boss?'

'I don't know. Aren't you meant to be painting a bedroom for the baby or building a cot?' she asked.

Nick grinned. 'Yeah, I've been told to go away as I make the house look untidy.'

'Where's Hayley Collard?'

'We had to release her on bail.'

'Does she know where Rosie Wright is?'

'I don't know, boss. She said some stuff to imply that she did. She said that Rosie was "a long, long way away" and we'd never find her,' Nick explained.

'And what did you think?'

'I thought she was bullshitting. Her scumbag, sex-trafficking boyfriend had just been flambéed…'

'Flambéed? Wow,' Ruth teased him. The hangover was showing signs of going.

'I'm not the Neanderthal Welshman that you think I am,' Nick replied with a smile. 'Hayley's raging with us because we found out where Vasilescu was keeping the girls. He tried to burn the house down with them in it and destroy any evidence. Except he died in the fire.'

'You think she made comments about Rosie to get at you and waste our time?'

'That's my instinct. Rosie Wright might have been taken to Dublin, but my money is on her disappearance being linked to Blake.'

'Your money is always on Blake, Nick,' Ruth said.

'His misery is my life's goal. Anything that sees him locked away for the rest of his natural is good in my book.'

'Glad to see you working a programme of serenity and toler-ance,' Ruth said sardonically.

Ruth and Nick ducked under the tape as chief forensic officer Alexander Travis strode over to greet her. He pulled down his mask and gestured to where they were.

'Glorious morning and a view to die for,' he said.

'Was that meant as a tactless joke, Alex?' Ruth snapped. Travis's jolly mood and clinical attitude to forensics got up her nose at the best of times. This morning she had one shredded nerve left and he was already getting on it.

'Oh, no, sorry.'

'Have you found anything?' Ruth asked. She wanted to get down to business and feared that Travis would try to sidetrack her with irrelevant prattling.

'Yes, have a look,' he said as he replaced his mask and they wandered in the direction of the small wall that separated the parking area from the grass and the clifftops.

Crouching down by the white-painted wall, Travis pointed to a dark spot of something on the paintwork.

'Blood?' Ruth asked.

'Yes. We've tested it here already. We'll get it back to the lab for a DNA match,' Travis explained, 'but it's only been here for a matter of days.'

'Anything else?' Ruth asked hopefully.

'Over here,' Travis said as Ruth and Nick followed him to the cliff edge where the grass stopped and the ground became rocky and dry.

Crouching again, Travis pointed to some marks in the earth only six inches away from the edge.

Feeling her anxiety rise, Ruth knew this wasn't the morning to be looking down the Devil's Cliff – a seven-hundred-foot sheer drop to razor-edged rocks and a swirling black sea. She drew a breath and crouched down to see what Travis was looking at.

'You see these,' he indicated to another set of indentations in the earth that were about three inches wide.

'Yeah,' Ruth said.

'They look like drag marks to me. Maybe from the heels of two shoes,' he said.

Nick looked at them. 'If you were dragging a body to the edge of these cliffs to throw it over, would you expect to see drag marks like these?'

'Yes, quite possibly. I can't think of any other explanation of why they're here.'

'Can you tell how long they've been here for?' Ruth asked.

'There was heavy rainfall ten days ago, which would have washed this dry earth away, so they were made in the last ten days,' Travis explained. 'And over here, we have two partial footprints in the soil.'

'Anything we can use?' Nick asked.

'This one is small. Maybe an adult's size-five shoe. This one is larger. A size ten. We'll make casts of them here and then get back to the lab,' Travis said.

This was music to Ruth's ears. She knew how important an imprint of a shoe could be. Forensics could look at the pattern, size, wear and damage features of a shoe tread and match those to an individual suspect. It wasn't just that they were wearing Adidas Gazelles, size ten. It was the way they wore it, the way they walked that gave the soles a pattern of wear that was completely individual to that particular shoe and wearer. Using powder and special lighting, they could spot microscopic details that were second only to a fingerprint in identifying a suspect.

'So, a woman and man?' Nick said.

'Kathy and Gareth Wright,' Ruth said.

It was unusual to have a briefing halfway through the day, but the developments in the search for Rosie Wright were coming thick and fast. Ruth didn't want any officers wasting their time on irrelevant lines of inquiry.

The air was hot inside the incident room. Having over a dozen CID officers working flat out in one area didn't help.

Sipping at her water, Ruth watched Sian coming in, reading documents and going to her desk. She didn't know if Sian was actually reading or just avoiding eye contact. Now that the hangover had all but gone, Ruth was left floundering as she tried to process what had happened yesterday. Sian had all but said that she no longer wanted to be with her. In a drunken, needy state, Ruth had slept with her ex-husband. All she could conclude was that it was a bloody mess.

Swigging at her bottle of water, she could still taste the cigarette she had smoked ten minutes earlier. That was one bonus, she thought. No one nagging her about her smoking. She still hadn't told Ella what had happened between her and Sian. She was going to be gutted.

And on top of all that, the BBC News app still had no developments in the Edinburgh rape case. Trying to push her chaotic personal life out of her head, Ruth looked up to see that Drake had come into the room and was resting casually on a table at the back. He nodded her an acknowledgement.

'Okay, everyone. A quick update on where we are with everything, please,' Ruth said as she waited for the room to quieten while walking over to the scene boards that were now cluttered with documents, photos and maps. 'The black box from Gareth Wright's VW Golf shows that last Monday at eight o'clock Gareth drove up to this point here on the Gogarth cliffs. This is an observation point over the Devil's Cliff. As most of you know, these are the highest cliffs in Wales. Forensics and SOCOs have been at this area since the early hours of this morning. We found a trainer eyelet out there last night that belongs to a pink Converse All Star, the type of trainer that Rosie was wearing when she went missing. A trace of blood was found at the car park, which is being DNA matched as we speak. There were also drag marks and footprints close to the edge of the clifftops. One footprint belongs to a size ten, probably male. The other, a size five, is likely to belong to a female. Our hypothesis is that Rosie Wright discovered that her mother and brother were smuggling drugs into HMP Rhoswen and confronted them about it.'

'You think she threatened to report her own mother and brother to the police?' French said.

'I don't know, Dan. We do know this could explain the altercation between Gareth and Rosie outside the college on Monday afternoon. Fearing that Rosie would go to the police, Kathy and Gareth Wright went to Haddon Farm on Monday night. Something went wrong and Rosie was injured. She was placed in the boot of Gareth's car and driven out to Gogarth where Rosie's body was tipped into the sea. That does mean that we are now treating this as a murder inquiry rather than abduction. Okay, what have we got?'

Dan shifted in his seat and looked up. 'Boss, I spoke to the coastguard at Conwy. Given the time and tides, he thinks that a body going into the sea would have been taken away from the mainland and out into the Irish Sea. He didn't hold out much hope of it ever being washed ashore anywhere.'

The idea that they might never find Rosie's body was upsetting news for everyone. Being able to bury your loved one, whatever the tragic circumstances, allowed a family some kind of closure and a chance to move on.

Nick looked over. 'Nothing from our surveillance team at HMP Rhoswen, boss. Blake has gone very quiet, which makes me think he's been tipped off. If he's making any phone calls, it's not from his cell or from the mobile phone we found.'

Ruth shook her head. *How was Blake allowed to operate with such complete freedom?*

'Right, first things first. I want Kathy and Gareth Wright arrested and brought here this morning. I need to speak to the CPS to see at what point we meet the threshold for charging them with Rosie's murder. We'll get a better picture when we get the DNA matches back from Forensics. Dan, I need you to liaise with Traffic. I want to see if any other vehicles were in the vicinity of Gogarth cliffs at that time. If we can get a witness to ID Gareth and Kathy in that area, that would be great.'

'Boss,' Dan nodded as he finished scribbling in his notebook. 'I'll look for anything that puts the two of them in the car together that evening.'

'Great.' Ruth walked over to the scene boards. For a moment, Rosie's pretty, innocent face looked back at her and she had a horrible flash of the girl's body falling from the cliffs into the sea. Shaking the image from her head, Ruth pointed to the photos of Jason Wright, Steven Haddon and Martin Hancock that were grouped together. 'I'm not sure what these three's stories are, but they're hiding something. Sian, go and have a chat with Jason Wright. We need to inform him that there have been significant developments in the case, but given that his wife and son are implicated, we clearly can't tell him very much. See if you can dig around and find out why they're lying to us. I want to eliminate them from the inquiry if I can.'

Sian nodded and looked up at her. Her face didn't give away any of the upheaval or upset that was between them.

'There's seems to be some kind of bond between Jason Wright and Martin Hancock, but I don't know what it is. I'll see what he has to say,' Sian said as she gathered her files together.

'I've spoken to the FLO. Nick, if you meet me at Capelulo and we can bring Kathy and Gareth Wright back separately. I don't want them to communicate with each other from now on.'

At that moment, Drake headed for the front where Ruth was standing. It was hot and his shirt sleeves were rolled up.

'Good morning, everyone. I've just chased the DNA results that we got from the blood found in Gareth Wright's car and from the observation point at the Gogarth cliffs.' He paused just for a moment to signify the importance of what had been found. 'The DNA from both samples matches Rosie Wright.'

# CHAPTER 27

*Six days, eighteen hours*

It was two o'clock when Sian watched the cars leave the Wrights' home to take Kathy and Gareth Wright back to Llancastell for questioning. She had remained there to talk to Jason Wright, who was devastated by what he had learnt in the last hour while Ruth and Nick escorted the mother and son back separately. Ruth had told them that they were under arrest for Rosie's abduction and murder. Jason wanted clarification. Did they know that Rosie was dead? Ruth still couldn't confirm it 100 per cent, but they did think there was a strong possibility that, given the growing evidence and the long timeline, it was unlikely she was still alive.

Sian finished making two mugs of tea and went out to the garden patio where Jason Wright sat staring into space.

'Thank you,' he mumbled as she put the tea down in front of him.

They sat quietly for a moment. There was a gentle breeze and the sound of bees buzzing around the colourful flowers nearby.

'They didn't do it,' Jason said as he sat forward at the table.

'Why do you say that?' Sian asked. *The thought that your wife and son were responsible for your daughter's murder must be overwhelming.*

'How could they?'

'I can't go into details, Jason. But we'll keep you informed of what's going on as much as we can. The FLO is here to help you.'

'I don't understand what's going on. What have you found that makes you think that Kathy and Gareth are involved?' Jason asked, shaking his head. He looked on the verge of tears as he massaged the bridge of his nose.

'I really can't talk about that with you. I'm sorry. I know it must be difficult for you to deal with,' Sian explained. *How could he possibly get his head around what he had just been told?*

Jason sipped at his tea as the wind rustled through the leaves of a nearby tree.

'We were a really happy family once. You know that? Really happy. When the kids were younger. We did stuff together. I can't remember when it all started to change,' Jason said as he squinted his eyes for a moment. He looked like he was going to cry. He was broken and exhausted by it all.

'Jason, I need to ask you a couple of questions,' Sian said. 'If that's all right?'

'Yeah?'

'We need to know what your relationship is with Martin Hancock?'

'Why? Why does it matter?' Jason said witheringly. It was curious that he wasn't now sticking to the line that Hancock was just a bloke down the pub, Sian thought.

'We found a photo of Rosie at Martin Hancock's home.'

'So what?'

'Why does a man like Martin Hancock have a framed photo of Rosie by his bedside?' Sian asked gently.

'It's not what you think,' Jason sighed.

'Martin said that he took photos of Rosie. Is that right?'

'Yeah. It's not weird that he has a photo of Rosie beside his bed,' Jason said.

'If Martin Hancock is just a man you know from the pub, it *is* strange and suspicious that he has a photo of her.'

'It isn't because…' Jason stopped for a second.

'Because of what, Jason?'

'Because Martin's her uncle,' Jason said. 'Martin Hancock is my brother.'

Sian took a few moments to take the information in. *How is that possible?*

'Really? We've checked our records, Jason—' Sian said, wondering what Jason was talking about.

'Our parents were killed in a car crash when we were younger. I was seventeen, but Martin was only twelve. He was fostered and then adopted,' Jason explained.

'Why didn't you tell us this when we questioned you?' Sian asked.

'When Martin got out of prison, he wanted a new start. We were back in touch. I suggested he move to Capelulo, but I didn't tell Kathy or the kids. It's not easy to tell them they have a paedophile for an uncle and he lives around the corner.'

'Yes, I can see that,' Sian said. Martin Hancock being Jason's brother did explain a lot about the clandestine way they had been behaving.

'None of this has anything to do with Martin,' Jason said as he put his mug back down on the table.

–

When Nick sat down opposite him, Gareth Wright was nervously jigging his leg. He was dressed in police-issue grey tracksuit bottoms and top because his clothes had been taken for forensic analysis. His solicitor, a slightly sweaty middle-aged balding man, shuffled papers and took out a pen.

'This is fucking stupid! How can you think that I murdered my own sister? That's mental!' Gareth yelled.

Nick watched the duty solicitor touch his client's arm and whisper in his ear. Basically, it was advice to calm down and shut up.

Putting down the folder and papers on the wooden table, Nick moved his chair to get comfortable. All this was carefully engineered to build the tension and anxiety. The more tense and anxious the suspect, the more likely they were to make mistakes or even start to confess.

'Gareth,' Nick said to get his attention. He reached over and clicked the tape machine. 'For the purposes of the tape, I'm Detective Sergeant Evans. Present are Gareth Wright and Duty Solicitor John Needham. I need to read you your rights. You have been arrested under the suspicion of the abduction and murder of your sister, Rosie Wright. You do not have to say anything, but it may harm your defence if you do not mention when questioned something which you later rely on in court. Anything you do say may be given in evidence.'

Gareth just stared at the floor and shook his head in disbelief.

'Did you understand what I just said to you, Gareth?' Nick asked.

'Yes. This is a fucking joke, you know that?' Gareth said as he looked at his solicitor.

*It's not a fucking joke, mate*, thought Nick angrily. *What is a joke is that you murdered your innocent sister and chucked her off a cliff because you and your scumbag mother were dealing drugs inside a prison.*

'For the purposes of the tape, I'm going to show you item reference four-five-Y-H-two-one,' Nick said as he took out a photo of the boot of Gareth Wright's car. 'Gareth, you own a black VW Golf, registration sierra-delta-one-five, yankee-alpha-tango. That's S-D-one-five, Y-A-T?'

'Yeah,' Gareth mumbled.

'This photograph is from the boot of that car. And here you can see a small speck of blood. Can you see that?' Nick asked.

'Yeah, I suppose.' Gareth shrugged as if to say, 'So what?'

'We've done a DNA match and that blood belongs to your sister, Rosie. Could you tell us how Rosie's blood got into the boot of your car, Gareth?'

'No idea. She had a nosebleed or somethin', I dunno.'

'Rosie had a nosebleed in the boot of your car?' Nick asked in a withering tone. It wasn't even a decent attempt to explain the blood away.

254

'I don't know, do I?' Gareth growled.

'So, you don't know how Rosie's blood got there, is that right?'

'Yeah.'

'For the purposes of the tape, I am going to show you item reference G-F-four-nine-J-K. This is the GPS readout from a black box supplied to you by your car insurance company to give you a lower premium. Is that right?'

'Yeah.'

'Last Monday evening, you claimed that you were in the Ship pub with friends and driving around.'

'Yeah, I was.'

Flicking over a computer readout, Nick took a breath. That's what still amazed him. Gareth was still lying, even when he knew he was about to be proved wrong. Like a cornered rat, he was struggling to survive.

'According to the GPS tracker on the black box, you drove out to the Gogarth cliffs at around eight o'clock. Is that right?'

'So what?'

'Why did you drive out to Gogarth, Gareth?' Nick asked.

'It's a nice view, isn't it?'

*Dickhead*. Nick wondered how clever Gareth was going to be when he was sentenced to thirty years for his sister's murder.

'Okay, but that's not what you told us when you were interviewed, was it?'

'Must have slipped my memory. I dunno.'

'For the purposes of the tape, I'm showing you item reference two-one-C-V-eight-three. This is a photograph of the car park wall where you stopped at the cliffs. Can you see the small mark that is circled there, Gareth?' Nick asked, showing him the photograph.

'Yeah.'

'That's blood, which, guess what, is also Rosie's. Do you know how it got there?' Nick asked.

'No. How would I?'

'Was there anyone with you when you drove out to the Gogarth cliffs that evening?'

'No, it was just me.'

Taking a sip of water from his bottle, Nick looked over at Gareth and waited for the tension to mount again.

'Right, Gareth. You need to stop messing me around here. There are footprints in the earth by the cliff edge. One is a size ten, and one is a size five. We have your shoes and we have your mother's shoes. And these days, forensics can match a footprint to a particular shoe. And they're going to match those shoes to you and your mother, aren't they?' Nick growled. He needed to increase the pressure on Gareth and get him to make a mistake.

'No,' Gareth mumbled.

'Stop lying to me, Gareth!' Nick thundered. 'This is your sister we're talking about here. Don't you have a decent bone in your body?'

'I... I don't understand. We didn't go to the cliff edge,' Gareth stammered.

'We? You and your mum, Kathy Wright?' Nick asked.

*Got him!*

'Yeah. We were there.'

'Why?' Nick asked.

'Because...' Gareth's voice trailed off.

'Come on, Gareth. What is it?'

'We had a text message. We were meant to be meeting someone there.'

'Who?'

'We didn't know. That's how it works. We sometimes get a message to meet someone to talk about the drugs. Quantities, types of drugs, special orders.'

'Someone connected to Blake?' Nick asked.

'No. That's how we communicated with Frank Cole. We assumed that he still wanted us to smuggle in the drugs for him. If he wanted to take on Blake, we didn't care. As long as we were making money, that was for them to work out.'

'And you had done this before?'

'Yeah. It's always somewhere remote. When they didn't show, we assumed they'd decided to call it off, so I drove Mum home,' Gareth explained.

'Who messaged you?' Nick asked.

'There's no number. It's always done from a burner.'

'So why was Rosie in the car with you?' Nick asked.

'She wasn't. I swear to you,' Gareth said.

'Her blood's in your car boot and at the car park at the cliffs. Your shoe prints are on the cliff tops. For God's sake, Gareth, just tell me exactly what happened up there,' Nick said.

'I can't…' Gareth mumbled as he put his head in his hands.

'Why not?'

'Because I don't know. The last time I saw Rosie was when we had a row outside college that afternoon. I wish I had seen her after that. I wish we were all sitting at home now and she was safe. But she's not. And I had nothing to do with it, which means that she's still out there, and you're doing nothing about it because you think it's me,' Gareth said as he shook his head and closed his eyes.

–

It was three thirty and Ruth was heading down to Interview Room Two, where Kathy Wright was waiting. Sian had relayed the information about Martin Hancock being Jason Wright's brother, but it needed to be verified through the relevant local authority and that could take days. However, Ruth's hunch was that it was true. Jason would know it was something that could be checked. It also explained why Jason and Hancock spent so much time together at the pub and why Hancock had a photo of Rosie in his bedroom.

A female uniformed officer came in and was clearly looking for Ruth.

'Ma'am?'

'How can I help?' Ruth asked, thinking that the young blonde officer was very attractive. *You've got enough crap going on in your personal life*, she said to herself.

'Something came to us this morning from one of the switchboard operators,' the officer explained, handing her a piece of paper.

'What is it?' Ruth asked.

'A young woman or a girl rang the switchboard last Thursday. She wanted to speak to an officer. The operator asked her what her name was and first of all she said it was Rosie and then she said it was Rose.'

'Did she say what she wanted?' Ruth asked.

'No. She wanted to talk to someone about reporting a crime,' the officer explained.

'Did she elaborate on that?'

'Not really. As soon as the operator started to ask for more details and her number, she hung up.'

'And the operator thought that she sounded young?'

'Yes, ma'am. Could have been a teenager.'

'Someone sounding like a teenager, called Rosie, calls in to say that she wants to report a crime the day before Rosie Wright is abducted and no one puts two and two together? How has this not been flagged up before?' Ruth asked, annoyed. If the caller had been Rosie Wright, then the fact that she was calling to report a crime was significant.

'I don't know, ma'am. You know what it's like down there. Too busy worrying about what's going on in *Love Island*,' the officer said.

'Thank you anyway, Constable.'

The officer nodded and left.

As Ruth took this new information in, she passed the computers to one side of the incident room. French spun his chair around and looked at her.

'Boss, we've got a hit on a car leaving the Gogarth cliffs just after eight last Monday evening. Traffic light cameras on the B-four-seven-three picked it up,' French explained.

'Is it clear enough to get a plate?' Ruth asked.

'Yes, boss. I've run it through the PNC and I've got an address in Llangollen.'

'Go and have a word. See if they saw anyone up at the observation point.'

As Ruth turned to go, she saw Sian approaching and her stomach lurched. She didn't have the emotional wherewithal to have any type of conversation.

'Quick word, boss,' Sian said.

'I'm on my way to interview Kathy Wright,' Ruth explained.

'Steven Haddon is downstairs. He's found something that he thinks you should see straightaway. But he wanted to talk to you,' Sian explained.

Ruth felt deflated and a little stupid that she had assumed Sian was coming to talk to her about their situation rather than the case.

'Right, I'll go and see him now.'

# CHAPTER 28

Interview Room Three was the least intimidating of the inter-view rooms at Llancastell nick and the one that Ruth used for informal meetings rather than the more complex official interviews of suspects.

As Ruth entered, she could feel that the air conditioning was working.

*Thank God for that!*

It was a stark relief to the CID offices on the sixth floor.

Steven Haddon was sitting at the table, his elbows resting casually on its wooden surface. She could see that both of his thick, tanned forearms were tattooed.

'Steven, sorry to have kept you,' Ruth said as she sat down opposite. She wondered what he had found that had prompted him to make the journey over to Llancastell.

'I spoke to the guy on the reception,' he said as he gestured to a plastic wallet that contained printed documents. 'I found these in my printer last night. They must have got jammed, but I thought you should see them.'

'Okay,' Ruth said as she took the documents from the wallet and turned them over to have a look.

The document was entitled:

> What is life like in the UK's witness protec-tion programme? – Linda's testimony put this murderous gang behind bars. Now she lives in a

different part of the country as part of the police's witness protection programme.

'They don't have a printer next door, so sometimes Rosie comes over and uses ours. You know, if her and Emma have got college work to do,' Steven explained.

'You think that Rosie printed this off?' Ruth asked.

'I think so. She came over the day before she disappeared. I asked Emma and she said Rosie was printing some stuff for her media studies course. She was the last person to use the printer,' Steven said.

'Okay, thank you. This is very useful,' Ruth said.

'Once I found these, I went onto the Google page and found out the search history,' Steven said and shrugged. 'I thought it might be useful?'

Ruth nodded. The more clues they had to what Rosie was doing and thinking before she was taken, the better. 'Yes, that's very helpful.'

'I wrote it down for you,' Steven said as he passed her a slip of paper. On it was written a question: *Can you go into the witness protection programme if you are a teenager?*

–

Half an hour later, Ruth launched another question at Kathy Wright – she was on the ropes, but she just wasn't willing to go down and concede.

'You just need to tell us what happened to Rosie?' Ruth snapped. The interview with Kathy Wright had been going around in circles.

Ruth had already relayed to Kathy everything they knew now that Gareth Wright had started to tell the truth.

'Rosie knew what you and Gareth were up to, didn't she? She confronted you and threatened to go to the police. Rosie had researched the police witness protection programme and whether it was applicable to teenagers.'

'I don't know what you're talking about!'

'You needed to keep Rosie quiet or face a very long prison sentence. What happened, Kathy? You attempted to abduct her, but she struggled. Was that it?' Ruth was becoming increasingly forceful as she tried to apply pressure.

'I don't know what happened to Rosie. She's my daughter and she's missing. I'm not lying to you,' Kathy said.

'Explain the blood in Gareth's car and at the car park by the cliffs?' Ruth barked.

'I can't, can I?' Kathy said as she shook her head.

Ruth had come across many criminals who had flatly denied their crimes before. Even in the face of compelling evidence. However, she had never seen a mother so emphatically deny having anything to do with what had happened to her daughter. It was sickening to watch.

'What, so it just magically appeared?' Ruth was riled and wanted Kathy to just do the right thing and tell the truth.

'For fuck's sake, I keep telling you, I don't know.'

'And the footprints at the clifftops? Any minute now, our forensic team will have looked at the moulds of those footprints to see if they match the shoes that we have taken from your house,' Ruth said.

Kathy sat back with a frustrated groan and shrugged aggressively. 'We didn't even get out of the car.'

'Just do the right thing, Kathy. Stop lying to me, for Rosie's sake. There is overwhelming evidence that you and Gareth murdered her, put her in his car, drove her up to Gogarth and threw her body into the sea. You're both going to be convicted of her murder. If you have any decency in you, tell us what happened to Rosie.'

In a split second, Kathy exploded. She pushed the chair back violently, stood up and lunged at Ruth. 'How dare you, you bitch! I've told you the truth!'

Backing away, Ruth glared at her. 'Sit down, right now, or I'll add assaulting a police officer to all the other charges!'

The duty solicitor, who was looking a little shocked, glanced at Ruth. 'I request that I have some time with my client. And that we have a break so that my client can compose herself.'

Ruth nodded. 'I think that's a very good idea.'

–

Nick scratched at his beard. It was getting too long, especially in the summer heat. Added to that, his move from neat semi-stubble to full-on explorer beard had prompted jokes such as 'Where's your ark, Noah?' and general derisory comments about being a hipster wanker.

Beside Nick and his computer, an elderly couple were starting to work through a computer identity parade. Their car had been spotted leaving Gogarth on Tuesday evening. When interviewed, the couple confirmed they had seen a man and woman in a black VW Golf park beside them at the observation car park. They thought they might recognise their faces. They told Nick they had got a good look at both of them.

In 2017, there had been a revision of Code D of the Police and Criminal Evidence Act 1984. Rather than the traditional identity parade of similar-looking members of the public and the suspect, the evidence could be gathered through a computer line up. Nick knew that in the old days, trying to get hold of a significant number of members of the public that looked similar to their suspect took ages. Sometimes weeks. Using the computer database, the process could be done in a matter of hours. It also meant that witnesses were far more relaxed giving evidence, not having to actually see the suspect in front of them.

The couple were going to attempt to identify Gareth Wright first. Giving them his best reassuring smile, Nick clicked his mouse and the first image of a young man in his early twenties.

'Okay, so take your time. There's no rush. I'll go through all twelve images slowly. If you see the young man that was in the car park at Gogarth last Monday, just tell me. Or we can go through all the photos and then you can tell me.'

'What if we get it wrong?' the elderly woman asked nervously.

Nick smiled and leant forward. 'You can't get it wrong. Please don't worry about this. If you see him, tell me. If you don't, there's no harm done, is there?'

'Okay, sorry,' the woman said with a little self-deprecating laugh.

Her husband reached over and took her hand. 'It's fine.'

For the next five minutes, Nick clicked through a series of images of young men in their early twenties who bore some resemblance to Gareth Wright.

Clicking on image number eight, Gareth Wright's face appeared on the screen.

Immediately, the couple's facial expressions and body language changed. They looked at each other and nodded.

'Yes, that's the man we saw last Tuesday. Mary?' the husband said.

'Oh, yes. It's definitely him,' his wife replied.

# CHAPTER 29

*Six days, twenty-one hours*

It was five o'clock as Ruth and Drake walked down the corridor together. They were on their way to meet with the CPS.

'How's your wife doing?' Ruth asked, conscious that even with everything going on with the Rosie Wright search, Drake was still dealing with the emotional burden of his wife's cancer diagnosis.

'Paula? Oh, good. Test results from yesterday were very positive. Thanks for asking,' Drake said, his face lined with concern still showing how relieved he was.

Ruth's phone rang – it was Professor Roy White from the Abel UK Forensic Laboratory. She gestured to the phone as they reached the meeting room. 'Better take this, boss.'

Drake nodded. 'Of course.'

'Professor White. Thanks for ringing me back. What did you find?' Ruth asked.

'Well, I've got good news on two fronts. There is wear on the right side of Gareth Wright's trainer, below the ball of the foot. It's an exact match for the wear that we found on the size ten footprint on the soil at the cliff edge,' White said.

'Great,' Ruth said. 'What about Kathy Wright?'

'Different type of wear. More from the heel on this one. But Kathy Wright's trainer sole is an exact match for the size-five footprint we found too.'

'Brilliant,' Ruth said, giving Drake an encouraging nod. They had conclusive physical evidence that Gareth and Kathy Wright stood on the cliff edge at Gogarth.

'The other match that we examined the trainers for was soil and anything else that was found on the soles,' White explained. 'Cliff tops have a particular make-up due to the soil erosion caused by their exposure to the coastal elements. It leaves the soil thin and close to the chalk and granite of the cliffs. The soil from where the footprints were found, and the soil found on the two trainers are an identical match.'

This was fantastic news for Ruth. Two pieces of hard, physical evidence that directly linked Kathy and Gareth Wright to the crime scene at Gogarth.

'If you put me on the stand, DI Hunter, I will testify categorically that the owners of these two pairs of trainers were standing on the cliff edge at Gogarth in the last ten days.'

Ruth nodded and shared a look of victory with Drake. Kathy and Gareth Wright were evil bastards and were going to prison for a very long time.

'Thank you, Professor. That's very good news.' Ruth finished the call. 'Trainer prints and soil samples match. Kathy and Gareth Wright were on that cliff top.'

Drake gestured to the meeting room they were about to enter. 'Good work... Let's see what Miss Finshore has to say now.'

They entered the meeting room and made their introductions. Zara Finshore, an experienced prosecutor for the Crown Prosecution Service, was sitting waiting for them. Her brunette hair was pulled back into a ponytail and she wore a smart blouse that was cut low. Up to this point, Finshore had been Ruth's point of contact at the CPS each time a significant piece of evidence came in or the investigation changed in any meaningful way. Despite her uber-confidence and Irish accent, Ruth thought Finshore was good at her job. Drake had told Ruth before that he considered Finshore 'very attractive'. She knew what he meant. Then again, Ruth was always attracted to powerful women.

Hoping for a positive outcome to the meeting, Ruth knew that Finshore needed to be satisfied there was enough evidence to provide 'a realistic prospect of conviction' against both Kathy and Gareth Wright. Ruth was confident that it was now appropriate to present charges for the criminal court to consider, but the decision to proceed was now out of her hands.

'As you know, Zara, we've made the decision to arrest both Gareth and Kathy Wright for the murder of Rosie Wright,' Drake said as he leant forward and poured water from a jug for them all. He slid the glass over to Finshore with his best winning smile. *Bloody flirt. And he is married with kids.* In that moment, Ruth noted the irony of her judgement.

'Yes. I was up at the crack of dawn sifting through all the evidence. I've also spoken to the DPP. I've told him that we have now reached the first stage in the decision to prosecute. As you know, I need to be satisfied that there is enough evidence to get a conviction against each defendant on each charge.' Finshore looked over at Drake for a moment. 'DCI Drake, am I right in thinking that both suspects have admitted to the unlawful supply of class A drugs?'

Drake nodded. 'Yes, although Kathy Wright is more reluctant. Gareth Wright is willing to make a deal and go into witness protection in exchange for information against Curtis Blake.'

'But neither of them are willing to admit to the abduction and murder of Rosie Wright?' Finshore asked with a slight frown.

'No. They admit to being at the Gogarth cliffs on the evening that Rosie was taken. But they are both adamant they had nothing to do with it. We have Rosie's blood in the car and at the car park. Matching footprints and soil samples that put them at the clifftop. GPS tracker that shows the journey that the car took,' Ruth said.

'Any positive ID?' Finshore asked.

'An elderly couple identified them from a computer-generated sample this afternoon. They saw Gareth and Kathy arrive and argue. They were both certain it was them.'

'Would they testify at trial?'

'They said that if they needed to testify, they would,' Ruth explained.

'That's great. At the moment, it's very hard to see what a defence counsel would come up with for them,' Finshore said as she scribbled notes and then looked up at Ruth. 'And we have motive?'

'We believe that Rosie stumbled across what her mother and brother were doing at HMP Rhoswen. She was possibly thinking of going to the police with what she knew. We have a Google search and printout that we believe she carried out into the witness protection scheme and whether a teenager could enter into the programme. We also have a call to our switchboard from a Rosie asking to speak to an officer before hanging up,' Ruth explained.

'But this theory is hypothesis?' Finshore said.

'Yes,' Drake said.

'And of course, we don't have a body,' Finshore said as she flicked through her notes.

Ruth could feel herself getting a little anxious, even though she knew this didn't rule out a conviction.

'Zara, there are precedents for this. I worked in the Met when the Danielle Jones case was going on just up the road in 2001. It's very similar,' Ruth said, hoping that she didn't sound patronising.

In June 2001, fifteen-year-old Danielle Jones was last seen walking to the bus stop near her home in East Tilbury, Essex, before disappearing. Within a couple of days her uncle, Stuart Campbell, became a suspect for her abduction. However, CID detectives had delayed his arrest because it might endanger Danielle's life. At that stage, they hoped she was still alive and being held against her will. They hoped that their surveillance on Campbell would lead them to where he was keeping Danielle.

Despite Danielle's body never being found, the CPS brought a case of abduction and murder against Campbell. It was felt that the evidence against him was sufficient to go to trial. Danielle had disappeared without contacting her parents, which was completely out of character. She had also been seen talking to a man in a blue Ford Transit van resembling Campbell's on the morning of her disappearance. Campbell and Danielle's DNA was found during the testing of blood-stained stockings discovered in the loft of Campbell's house. Danielle's lip gloss was also found in Campbell's home. The police had a strong suspicion that Campbell had developed an inappropriate relationship with Danielle that was also unlawful. When Danielle told him to leave her alone or she would tell someone what they had been doing, Campbell abducted and murdered her.

Part of Campbell's defence was a text message that Campbell claimed Danielle had sent to him days after her disappearance. The message was sent in uppercase, however, Danielle always sent messages with the letters all in lowercase. Further analysis of the phone records showed that Campbell's alibi of being at a retail park half an hour away when he received the message was false. In fact, Campbell and Danielle's mobile phones had been within the range of just a single mobile phone mast at the time that the text message had allegedly been sent. This evidence showed that Campbell had written the message on Danielle's phone and sent it to himself at the same location to make it appear that she was still alive. Campbell was sentenced to life imprisonment, but Danielle's body was never found.

'Yes, we've been to trial without a body before. It's just rare. But as far as I can see, we have a very strong case. There are no reasons to question the reliability of the evidence, its accuracy or integrity. We have a very convincing hypothesis and a more than realistic prospect of conviction on all charges against both suspects.' Looking up from her paperwork, Finshore sat back. 'It's my recommendation that Kathy and Gareth are now charged with Rosie Wright's abduction and murder, and that we proceed to trial. We will oppose any requests for bail as I think they're both a flight risk and given the severity of the charges against them.'

Ruth let out an audible sigh and nodded over at Drake and then Finshore. 'Thank you. It's not the outcome we wanted when we started this case, but we have brought Rosie's killers to justice. I just hope they are both put away for a very long time.'

*Six days, twenty-three hours*

It was late in the day, and now that Finshore and the CPS had agreed they'd charge Kathy and Gareth Wright with abduction and murder, Ruth had called in the members of CID who had been working on the case. The word had already got around and so the mood in the incident room was positive. Had it been a different case, there might have been laughter and even drinks, but a teenage girl had been murdered and one of their colleagues killed – no one was in the mood to celebrate going to trial.

Getting up and heading for the centre of the room, Ruth took a moment to look up at the scene boards that would soon have to be cleared.

'Evening, everyone. Some of you already know that the CPS have given us the go-ahead to charge Kathy and Gareth Wright with the abduction and murder of Rosie Wright. There are also the lesser charges of misconduct in a public office, supplying controlled drugs of class A and B into a prison and conveying a list A prohibited article into a prison,' Ruth explained as she moved over and leant against a table. A phone buzzed to one side of the room and Sian answered it.

Looking out at her team, Ruth said, 'I want to thank you for doing a brilliant job on this. I know that Luke's death has thrown us, but you have all continued to be professional and dedicated to the job in hand. And I hope that when Kathy and Gareth Wright are convicted, we have helped get some kind of justice for Rosie.'

Sian put down the phone and glanced over at Ruth. 'Boss, there's a message from the North Wales Coastguard. They've found some clothing floating in the sea about fifty miles out, just south of the Isle of Man.'

'Thank you, Sian,' Ruth said. 'Okay, so Kathy and Gareth Wright will be held overnight at their home. There will be armed officers, as well as the FLO. We have intel from the OCG that their lives would be in danger at any prison in Wales or the North West. So, tomorrow morning they will be transferred by armed guard to HMP Bullingdon, near Oxford, where they will be on remand in the VP wing. Sian, can you go down to Capelulo later and brief the AFOs and the FLO for me?'

Sian nodded but failed to make eye contact 'Yes, boss. Do you want me to stay there overnight for the transfer?'

'No. If you just have a check around and make sure that the place is relatively secure,' Ruth said, before turning back to the other officers. 'So, over the next few days I need you all to type up your notes, statements and evidence logs for the CPS to have before the end of the week. And given the spate of mistrials, you all need to be very careful that we are making full disclosure on everything that we have looked at. Double-check everything, please, as a matter of urgency. Evidence is evidence, and the CPS need to see everything now, not when the defence counsel brings it up at trial and we risk the case collapsing.'

Gathering up her files, Ruth calculated that she had time to go back to her office, drop off her stuff, go out for a ciggie and grab a coffee before going upstairs for a meeting with Jones.

Passing French's desk, she noticed that he was watching a video of Rosie. She was jumping on someone and squealing in laughter.

'What's that, Dan?' she asked.

'Kara Haddon has her own YouTube channel. You know, make-up tips, boys, music,' Dan explained.

'And what's this you're watching?' Ruth asked.

'It's a video of her fourteenth birthday party. It's her and her friends out in the garden. And then this happens...'

Pressing play, Ruth watched as Steven Haddon arrives in the garden with a tray of ciders, which he puts down on the table. There was a handful of teenage girls giggling, messing about and listening to music.

'Bit young to be drinking,' Ruth said under her breath.

As the video continued to play, Ruth watched as Rosie and Steven start to play around in the garden, hitting and chasing each other. Steven picks Rosie up and puts her over his shoulder. From the side, Rosie starts to hit Steven on his behind.

'Oh, you're going to spank me are you, missy?' Steven laughs as he twirls Rosie around.

'Yes, you have a problem with that?' Rosie giggles as she kicks her legs.

'Hey, two can play at that,' Steven says as he begins to spank Rosie's behind as she lays over his shoulder.

'You can't spank me! I'll have you arrested!' Rosie says, roaring with laughter.

'Go ahead. I'll get you the number,' Steven replies before putting Rosie back down onto the grass.

As Steven turns and walks back to the house, the video stops.

French looked up and glanced at Ruth. 'Is it me, boss, or is that a bit weird?'

'I wouldn't have been very comfortable if my neighbour had done that to my daughter when she was fifteen or sixteen,' Ruth said.

'What do you want me to do, boss?' French asked.

'We've got our suspects. And although it's a bit overfamiliar and creepy, there's not a lot we can do. Steven Haddon's not been on our radar. Make a copy and put it on the case file on the central hard drive.' Ruth said. 'Can you chase Forensics and the DNA testing on that Converse eyelet that we found up at Gogarth?'

'Yes, boss,' Dan said as he nodded and went back to the folders and notes on his desk.

# CHAPTER 30

Entering the busy ward, Nick scoured the whiteboard that had patients' names written by each bed number. He was looking for Zofia Mazur, one of the girls he had rescued from the burning house in Bangor.

Ruth had asked Nick to tie up all the loose ends on the investigation into Christian Vasilescu and Hayley Collard before they handed it over. North Wales Police's own dedicated Modern Day Slavery Unit, MDS, appeared to know Vasilescu quite well.

Stopping the ward sister, Nick showed her his warrant card. 'DS Evans from Llancastell CID. I'm looking for a patient, Zofia Mazur?'

The ward sister pointed to a corner room. 'She's in there.'

'Is she up to answering a few questions?' Nick asked.

'I'm sure that's fine. There were some other detectives with her this morning, so don't be too long, please,' she said as she went on her way.

Assuming that officers from the MDS unit had been to talk to her, Nick went over to the door, knocked and went in.

'Zofia?' Nick asked.

The young girl nodded, looking a little nervous, and sat up in the bed. Then she frowned. 'You're the man that got me and Nadia out of the house yesterday, no?'

'Yes, that's right.' He opened up his warrant card and said, 'My name's Nick. Okay if I sit down?'

She nodded as he went over and took a seat by her bed. Zofia was lying on top of the bedding with just a blanket over her feet. Her legs were skinny and bruised, and Nick wondered what kind of nightmare she had been through in recent months. Sex trafficking was an evil, brutal business with no regard for human life.

'Where are you from in Poland, Zofia?' he asked.

'Szczecin,' Zofia replied.

'I'm sorry, I don't know it,' Nick shrugged, wishing now that he hadn't asked.

'It's a small port. Close to border with Germany,' she explained.

Nick nodded. 'And that's where you met Christian Vasilescu?'

Zofia nodded and started to look upset. 'He said he could find me work in UK. Cleaning, maybe a nanny. But he lied to me.'

'Did you come straight to Wales from Poland?'

'No. Christian took me to London. He said he need to sort paperwork for me. But he locked me in room. There were other men there. I had to do whatever they ask. They shout, blaming me for everything. Sometimes they bit me, they beat me. They say to me, "You are just slave, you don't say anything," even though I am a child myself. I was scared all the time,' Zofia said as tears came to her eyes. She wiped them from her face and sniffed. 'I… sorry.'

'You don't need to be sorry, Zofia. What Christian and those other men did to you was horrible,' Nick said. 'And then Christian took you to Wales?'

'Yes. To Wales. Maybe two months ago,' she said.

'Were there others with you?'

'Yes. Eight girls.'

'All Polish?'

'No. Four of us were Polish. Others were from Romania, I think.'

'Did you all go to the house that we found you in?' Nick asked.

'No. Just me and Nadia. Then every day Christian brings the men. He says they can do things without a condom, he says they can beat me because they pay a lot of money for me. I can't decide what I can do, I have no say. When he beat me and I lost the pregnancy, he said that I cannot be pregnant because I was prostitute.' Zofia began to sob, her shoulders shook as she recounted the horror of what she had been forced to do. She then looked up at him, 'I glad Christian is dead. We say, "*Idź do diabła*". That he is going to hell.'

Getting out his phone, Nick couldn't disagree with her. Vasilescu was vile and evil. Swiping through his photos, Nick got up a photo of Hayley Collard onto his screen and showed it to her. 'Do you know this girl?'

'Yes. Hayley,' Zofia said with a sneer.

'You saw her at the house?' Nick asked.

'Yes. She is Christian girlfriend, I think?' Zofia said.

'What about any other girls? In the last week? We're looking for a Welsh girl?' Nick said.

'Welsh? No, I'm sorry I don't think so. Maybe you should talk to Nadia. She was in that house longer than I was.'

Nick got a photo of Rosie Wright up next. 'Did you ever see this girl?'

Zofia shook her head. 'No, sorry. I never see her.'

—

Moving her finger down the condensation on the glass of iced water, Sian sat at the kitchen table opposite Bennett, who was buried in her iPhone. There was just the sound of children playing in the distance and an aeroplane overhead. It was a comfortable silence after a very hot day.

In the nearby living room, Gareth and Kathy Wright were watching television. They had been monosyllabic since Sian arrived. Out of the window above the sink, Sian could see the two authorised firearms officers, AFOs, who Drake had assigned to watch the house, chatting in the sunny garden. They were there just as much to protect Kathy and Gareth as they were to prevent them from leaving.

Sian had briefed Bennett and the two AFOs about the ongoing house arrest and the transfer of Kathy and Gareth Wright to HMP Bullingdon sometime the next morning. There would be two armed response vehicles, ARVs, so that the two suspects were transported separately in case anything happened.

Looking at her watch, Sian decided she would wait for another half an hour before heading back to Llancastell. Typing up statements and notes was her idea of hell.

'I'll put the kettle on,' Sian said, breaking the silence.

'Good idea,' Bennett replied, without looking up from the screen.

Knocking on the window, Sian signalled to the AFOs that she was making tea and asking if they wanted one. They both gave her the thumbs up. They could sort out their sugar and milk when it was made.

Clicking the kettle on, Sian looked up at the photos, drawings and magnets strewn randomly across the large fridge door. Menorca, Tenby, Disneyland Paris. A shot of a much younger Rosie and Gareth on a roller-coaster together. Two children with faces full of unabandoned joy. It was horrible to see their expressions, knowing how things would end for them both.

There was the deep rumble of an engine from outside, which Sian naturally assumed was a tractor. The rumble seemed to stop on the road in front of the house, and there was the slam of doors. Moving to the hallway, Sian peered from the curtains and beyond the hedge.

A BMW X5 with blue-and-yellow police markings had stopped on the road outside. Behind it, a Land Rover Discovery, also with police markings.

Bennett came out from the kitchen. 'Everything all right?'

'Two ARVs out the front?' Sian said. She didn't know what they were doing there.

'I thought they weren't coming until tomorrow,' Bennett replied.

'Neither did I,' Sian said. Maybe she was being overcautious, but her stomach felt a little tense, as though something wasn't quite right.

Opening the front door, Sian watched as two AFOs climbed out of the BMW and opened the garden gate. Dressed in their black helmets, Kevlar body armour, and the short Sig Sauer MCX assault rifles held at the customary forty-five-degree angle, Sian thought they looked as though they had walked out of a sci-fi film.

'Afternoon,' Sian said brightly but confused as she approached, wondering what was going on.

'Afternoon,' the AFO, black and muscular, said with a smile as he audibly let out a breath. It was hot. Too hot for helmets and body armour.

'You guys must be frying in this heat?' Sian said.

'It's all right, we've got the AC on. But what I'd give to be in shorts and T-shirt,' he chortled.

'We weren't expecting you until tomorrow morning?' Sian said. She was still feeling anxious about their arrival.

The AFO shrugged. 'Sorry, love, CPS want the prisoners taken tonight now. You know what they're like?' he said as he rolled his eyes and showed her his warrant card. He turned a clipboard with paperwork around so she could see it. 'These are the transfer papers that we got sent. Kathy and Gareth Wright, is that correct?'

'Yes,' Sian replied, wondering if she should be suspicious that the transfer was happening earlier than planned. But the paperwork looked in order.

'Transfer to HMP Bullingdon tonight,' the AFO said as he pointed to the transfer papers.

As far as Sian could see, everything was correct.

'I just need your signature,' the AFO said, twirling a pen in his hands. Sian nodded and signed it. Maybe it was her suspicious nature, but she also didn't know why she hadn't had a phone call from someone at Llancastell to tell her that the plans had changed.

'How long does it take?' Sian asked.

'About four hours. So, eight-hour round trip,' the AFO explained.

'That doesn't sound good.'

'I don't mind. Day off tomorrow and my son's playing his first cricket game.' The AFO smiled.

'How old is he?' Sian asked.

'Nine. We've been practising his bowling, so I've got a feeling he's going to nail it,' the AFO said with a laugh.

Sian's anxiety was starting to ebb. If there was going to be trouble, something would have happened by now. 'Oh, well, good luck.'

Hearing movement from the door, Bennett appeared with one of the officers from the garden. Kathy and Gareth Wright were beside them, looking thoroughly miserable. Bennett had already put them in handcuffs.

'One in the X5 and one in the Discovery, guys,' the AFO said to them as he turned back down the path.

Sian followed them out onto the main road and watched as Kathy and Gareth Wright were put into their respective vehicles. They said nothing. What was there to say?

Once the doors to both ARVs were closed, Bennett and the AFOs turned, made their way back to the cottage and went inside. Their work there was done.

Still feeling unsettled that she hadn't heard anything from Llancastell, Sian got out her phone and looked up. 'I'm just going to ring my boss to tell her what's going on,' Sian said, gesturing to the phone.

'You don't need to do that,' the AFO grumbled. 'Come on, I need to get this lot on the road.'

'Won't take a minute,' Sian said as she pushed the button to ring Ruth. It was still awkward, but she had to be professional.

Getting a transfer to another police force seemed to be the sensible thing to do.

Looking at the top of her phone, she could see that the signal was flicking between 3G, 4G and no signal at all. She could see the AFO was starting to get impatient as he moved a step towards her.

The AFO put his hand on her shoulder. 'Come on. You can do all that when we're gone.'

Her phone flashed up Ruth's name. 'It's all right, I've got a signal now so I can run it past my DI,' she said.

Suddenly, the AFO snatched the phone from her hand and she felt something hard jab into the right side of her ribs.

*What the bloody hell is he playing at?*

At first, she thought it was the AFO's fingers, but as she looked down, she could see that it was a Glock 9mm handgun.

'You should have left it,' the AFO said quietly. 'If you make a sound, I will blow a hole in your side. Now get into the fucking car.'

With her heart now banging like a drum, Sian couldn't quite believe what was happening. She took a breath to steady herself as she was marched at gunpoint to the back door of the BMW.

The AFO opened the door, pushed her roughly into the back seat of the car where Gareth Wright was sitting handcuffed and looking totally confused.

Jumping into the passenger seat, the AFO turned to the driver. 'Right, let's get the fuck out of here.'

The driver stamped on the accelerator and they sped away.

The AFO turned around and pointed the Glock at them both. 'Either of you move, I'll shoot you in the fucking head, got it?'

'Where are we going?' Sian asked. Her voice trembled.

*These men work for Blake.*

Sian felt her stomach tighten hard with anxiety.

Blake had used fake police uniforms and cars before. She should have trusted her gut when she felt uneasy earlier.

Sian felt the pounding of her heart against her chest. What were they planning on doing with her?

*I've seen their faces. I can identify them all.*

Sian felt a sweep of sickness as she tried to get her breath.

*They are going to kill me too.*

# CHAPTER 31

*Seven days*

Nick had gone to the other side of the ward where Nadia Kowalski was in a private room, recovering from her ordeal. The nurse said that not only was she suffering from smoke inhalation, but she was exhausted and malnourished too. He needed to keep his time questioning her to a minimum.

Having run through the preliminary questions, as he had done with Zofia, Nick wanted to move onto what and who she had seen in the house.

'Zofia tells me you were in that house for longer than her?' Nick asked.

'Yes. Three weeks,' Nadia said.

'I'm looking for a girl who might have been taken there. She was Welsh,'

'Welsh?' Nadia said. He could see the word didn't mean anything to her.

'Welsh. It means she comes from Wales. But to you, she would have sounded English,' Nick explained, hoping that he wasn't coming across as patronising.

Nadia's eyes widened as she processed what he had asked her. 'Yes. Two girls in the room next to us. They were English, maybe Welsh. I don't know difference.'

Wondering quite what he had stumbled upon, Nick clicked his phone to bring up a photo of Rosie.

Leaning over, he showed it to her. 'This is the girl I'm looking for.'

'Okay, I don't know.'

'Did you ever see the English girls?' he asked.

'Only once. At the top of stairs,' Nadia explained.

Nick found another photo of Rosie and asked, 'Think carefully, Nadia. Was this one of the girls you saw?'

Nadia peered at the photo. 'Maybe. It was dark. This girl had all her hair down so I not see her face. But it could be her, yes.'

'When did the girls leave the house?' Nick asked.

'Two days ago. I heard them screaming when Christian opened the door.'

'What about Hayley? Was she there?'

'Yes. Hayley went into the room to talk to them a lot. Maybe she knows who this girl is that you look for?'

Nick nodded. *Maybe she does.*

—

Ruth pulled off the main road and headed for Capelulo. The sky overhead was a patchy grey and she saw the first spots of rain on the windscreen. She had some questions for both Jason Wright and Steven Haddon before handing on the case files to the CPS. Even though she trusted Sian, Ruth also wanted to make sure that everything was secure at the Wrights' home. She was the SIO, and it was her responsibility if anything went wrong.

Her phone rang. It was Drake. She took it on her Bluetooth headset.

'Boss?' Ruth said.

'We have a situation at Capelulo, Ruth.' Drake's voice immediately made her feel nervous.

'What is it?' Ruth asked as her mind began to play over various dark scenarios.

'About fifteen minutes ago, Blake's men took Kathy and Gareth Wright from the house.'

'How?' Ruth asked, but she was really thinking about Sian. She was down there checking everything with Bennett and the AFOs. Was she all right?

'They were dressed as police officers. No one was harmed but—' Drake paused for a split second '—they took Sian with them, Ruth.'

Ruth pulled the car over as her anxiety went through the roof.

*Oh God, no.*

'Jesus!' Ruth said as her heart raced.

'I've got armed units out and a helicopter. We'll find them and we'll get her back,' Drake said. 'I just need you here.'

'Yes, boss. I'm on my way back,' Ruth said and then hung up. Her mind was whirring. All she cared about was finding Sian safely.

Pulling the car out, Ruth headed back towards the main road to Llancastell. As she waited to pull out, she tapped her fingers nervously on the steering wheel. Her heart thumped noisily. It was difficult to concentrate on the road.

The tension in Ruth's stomach was getting tighter. And there was the added guilt at having driven Sian away. She would do anything to get her back safely.

For the next ten minutes, Ruth was lost in her thoughts and the panic of what had happened. If Blake's men knew Sian was a police officer, why take her with them? Was that a good sign? Did it mean that they weren't prepared to shoot her in cold blood? Why weren't the AFOs alerted?

Ruth's whirring brain was broken as the Tetra radio crackled. 'Control to three-six, over.'

'Three-six, received,' Ruth said after a moment. She prayed there was good news about Sian or the kidnappers.

'Ma'am, we have a report of two burnt-out vehicles two miles east of Capelulo, on the intersection of A-three-four-five and Corwen Road, over,' the operator said.

'Three-six, received. En route now,' Ruth said as she punched the location into her satnav and spun the car around at speed. Her pulse started to quicken.

*'Burnt-out vehicles' doesn't sound good.* Blake's men knew that they would be spotted in their fake police cars very quickly. Maybe they had 'clean' vehicles waiting for them? What would they have done with Sian, Kathy and Gareth Wright? Taken them with them? Or worse? Got rid of them there and then? Ruth felt sick.

Two minutes later, Ruth sped around the bend and saw blue lights and smoke rising from a field to the left of the road. Pulling onto the uneven track, she could see that there were already two patrol cars and a fire engine in attendance.

Her car bumped and jolted over the rough heathland. Looking into her wing mirror, she spotted Nick arriving and parking beside her.

*What's happened? Where is Sian?*

A uniformed police officer, muscular, young and mixed race, arrived as she flashed her warrant card, anxious as to what had been found.

'What have you found, Constable?' Ruth asked, finding it hard to hide her concern.

'Two burnt-out vehicles, ma'am,' he replied.

'Nothing else. No sign of anyone around?' Ruth said.

'No. We've had a scoot around and that's all we could find,' the constable explained.

'Thank you,' Ruth said as she turned. About fifty yards further along the farm track were two burnt-out cars. Uniformed police officers were examining the ground for tyre tracks. They would have to wait for the metal to cool down before they could take a look at the charred vehicles themselves. Ruth could still see some of the police markings on the paint-work that hadn't blackened, and from the shape, she guessed it was a BMW X5 and a Land Rover Discovery.

There was only one conclusion to draw. Blake's associates, dressed as police officers, had taken Kathy and Gareth Wright before they could turn any evidence against Blake. What terrified Ruth more was that Sian was with them. What were they planning on doing with her?

As Ruth got closer, she could smell the acrid smoke, which took her straight back to the car bomb that had killed Merringer. The orange flames and his body being tossed like a burnt doll high into the air. The recall of it startled her and her pulse began to race. Taking a breath, Ruth was scared she was going to have a panic attack.

She turned to see Nick approaching.

'Any sign of Sian yet?' Nick asked.

Ruth shook her head, taking another long breath, and pointed at the burnt-out shells of the two fake police vehicles. 'They switched cars and then torched these.'

'Why would they have taken Sian with them?'

'No idea. My guess would be that she realised they weren't real police officers and they couldn't risk her raising the alarm,' Ruth said.

There was a heavy silence as they both looked at the smouldering vehicles.

*Where the bloody hell are they now?*

'We'll get her back, boss,' Nick said.

'Yeah, I know,' Ruth said with a forced smile. She wished she shared his confidence. She was keen to change the subject. 'What happened at the hospital?'

'Nadia Kowalski says there were two English girls at the house in Bangor. I showed her a photo of Rosie Wright and she said one of them could have been her. She said that Hayley Collard spent a lot of time talking to the two girls in their room,' Nick explained.

'Maybe it's worth having another crack at Hayley. It's a long shot but we don't want to go to trial only to find that Rosie is in Dublin,' Ruth said. 'Anything from the Gardaí?'

'Nothing concrete, boss.'

The officer who briefed Ruth earlier approached them. He had clearly found something of interest. 'Ma'am, there are tyre marks heading away from this scene. Big tyres. Off-road. I would say the vehicles they switched into were four-by-fours.'

'How do you know that?' Nick asked.

'My dad owns a tyre yard, sir. I worked there a lot when I was younger,' the officer explained.

'Don't suppose you know the make of tyre or vehicle yet?' Nick asked.

'Not really,' the officer hesitated, but Ruth knew he could be pushed to make some kind of guess.

'But your hunch is?' Ruth asked. They needed something to go on and fast.

'They looked like Pirelli Scorpions. Ten-inchers,' the officer said.

'Does that help us with the vehicle?' Ruth asked.

'They're fitted as standard to all new Range Rovers,' the officer said.

'Which happens to be Blake's vehicle of choice. And always black,' Nick said.

'Thank you, Constable. That's brilliant work,' Ruth said with a smile.

She clicked her Tetra radio. 'Three-six to Control. All units, the suspects are likely to be in two Range Rovers. Possibly black. Suspects are armed, so approach with caution. We also believe that Detective Constable Hockney is in one of the vehicles.'

'Control received.'

At that moment, a black-and-yellow H135 helicopter from the National Police Air Service thundered overhead and then skimmed away over the fields in the ongoing search.

Suddenly, two uniformed officers in high-vis yellow jackets shouted over and put an arm up to signal that they had found something. They had been searching the undulating heathland that led down to a wooded area.

Turning on her heels, Ruth ran past the black, sizzling shells of the burnt-out vehicles and over the gravel track. She was starting to panic. *What have they found?*

For a moment, everything seemed very quiet and the wind stopped. It felt unnaturally still. Her boots made a rhythmic swish through the grass and in the distance a chainsaw on a farm reverberated with an angry snarl.

'What have we got, Constable?' Nick asked.

'It's a body, sir,' the officer, young, blonde and pasty, said. 'A woman.'

Casting her eye into the undergrowth, Ruth felt sick in the pit of her stomach.

*Oh God. Not Sian… please, not Sian.*

Ruth hesitated for a moment before forcing herself to focus on the body that was slightly hidden by thorn bushes and brambles.

She saw the legs, then trainers. It was Kathy Wright. *Thank God.*

From the unnatural twist in the legs and the torso, Ruth assumed that her body had been flung into the undergrowth after death.

Ruth moved so she could see Kathy's face clearly. There was a neat black-and-red hole in her temple with a smear of blood across of her forehead. Kathy's once blue eyes were wide open – they were opaque. Blake's men hadn't even allowed her the dignity of closing her eyes once she was dead. Cold and callous didn't cover it.

Nick wasn't saying anything. Ruth knew that he was worrying about Sian too.

'Ma'am!' the other officer called over from further along the undergrowth. 'There's another one here.'

This was unbearable. Ruth's stomach twisted again.

Had Blake's men swapped cars and shot all three of their victims? Ruth's mind was rattling with overwhelming scenarios.

'Male body,' the officer shouted.

Again, a huge wave of relief.

Moving down the bushes, Ruth and Nick could clearly see Gareth Wright lying face up with an identical shot to his head.

Where was Sian? Would they have shot Kathy and Gareth and spared Sian? Was killing a police officer a step too far? Ruth hoped that Kathy and Gareth had been the targets for the hit and that was it.

Scouring the undergrowth, the next few minutes were agonising. For a second, Ruth saw what she thought was a boot, only to realise it was a fallen piece of wood. As they moved further down the field, the bushes and undergrowth stopped by a dry stone wall and a steel gate to a field.

Sian wasn't to be found anywhere.

# CHAPTER 32

The air inside the cloth hood was getting increasingly warm. As Sian sucked in air, the cloth moved back and forth in rhythm with her breath. The plastic ties around her wrists were cutting into her skin, so she had to try to use her tongue to push the black material away from her mouth to get more air. She was claustrophobic at the best of times. Ruth used to tease her when Sian would gasp for air and struggle under the duvet when it went over her head. It felt like she was drowning.

It had been quiet inside the Range Rover for the past ten minutes. Having been taken from the fake police BMW, she had been hooded and her hands tied, but not before spying the looming black Range Rover that was waiting for them. As she sat in the heat and darkness, she heard a strange sound. When she smelt the petrol and the smoke, she knew the gang had torched the fake police vehicles. Then the sound of two gunshots about a minute apart. She could only assume that Gareth and Kathy Wright had been killed. Was she going to be next?

However, the car doors slammed and the vehicle she was in sped away.

Hearing some mutterings from the front about a landing strip at Llandegla, Sian wondered if the gang were flying out of Wales. What were they going to do with her? If they were going to kill her, why not do it earlier when they had stopped? Maybe they assumed that having a police officer in one of the vehicles gave them some protection if they were located? The police weren't going to smash the vehicle off the road or fill it full of bullets while they had her.

And then a darker thought occurred to her. If the gang got to the airfield undetected, what did they plan to do with her then? She thought it wasn't likely that they would just leave her there.

At some point, they were going to kill her.

–

Nick had driven over to HMP Styal in Cheshire to interview Hayley Collard in the Young Offenders wing. He made Ruth promise to keep him informed about the hunt for Sian. Nick had naïvely assumed that when Blake was sent down for life in 2018, his quest to bring him to justice was won. Secretly, Nick wanted Blake dead, but a life spent rotting in jail would have to do. Except everyone had underestimated Blake's power from within prison. And now Sian had been caught up in his power struggle from within HMP Rhoswen.

Although Llancastell CID were convinced that Rosie had been murdered by her mother and brother, Nick still wanted to find out the identities of the two girls that Zofia had seen at the house in Bangor. He wanted to rule out any chance that Rosie had been taken by Vasilescu, however remote the possibility.

Hayley was sitting in the prison's interview room when he arrived. It was painted in a cheerful primrose-yellow with large windows that let in the burning sunlight from outside.

With her blue hair pulled back off her face, Hayley looked tired as she inspected her chipped nails.

Sitting down at the grey table, Nick could feel the sweat from his lower back against the chair.

'Hi, Hayley. I need to ask you some questions as part of our investigation. Is that okay?' Nick asked.

Hayley looked up at him and shrugged. 'I suppose.'

'I've been told that you've already spoken to detectives from MDS? Is that right?' Nick asked. He knew that Modern Day

Slavery would be interested in the intel that Hayley might be able to provide about the smuggling of girls from North Wales down through Holyhead to Dublin.

Hayley nodded and sat back in her chair with a sigh.

'I'm only here as part of the investigation into the abduction and disappearance of Rosie Wright,' Nick said as he fished out his phone.

'Yeah, I know who Rosie is, don't I?'

'Okay. I've spoken to Zofia, who was being held at the house in Bangor. You know Zofia?'

'Yeah, course.'

'She tells me that there were two girls at the house the day before the fire. She says one was English and one was Welsh? Is that right?'

'It might be,' Hayley said. Nick, aware that the Polish girls hadn't been able to specify the Welsh accents of the girls in the next room, could see that the question had got her attention as she leant forward onto the table. His tactic had worked.

'What does that mean, Hayley?' Nick asked.

'What if there were two girls in that house. And what if one of them was Rosie? What then?' asked Hayley.

Nick could feel his pulse quicken. Was this bullshit or was Hayley telling the truth? They were already 99 per cent certain that Rosie was dead.

'What are you telling me, Hayley? Was one of the girls Rosie?'

Hayley said, 'I told you that yesterday.'

'What?' Nick said trying to recall their conversation. 'You said we would never find her.'

'I'm going to spend the next few years in this place. If you want me to tell you about Rosie, then you need to offer me something in return,' Hayley said.

Nick wasn't convinced. 'The proviso of any deal that we offer you would be that we find Rosie safe and well.'

Hayley snorted. 'I don't know if she's alive and well, do I? All I can do is point you in the right direction.'

'Dublin?'

'Get me an offer where I don't serve any time, then I'll start to talk to you.'

'Before I start negotiating anything on your behalf, Hayley, I need you to confirm that Rosie was abducted and taken somewhere. Otherwise, I'm walking out of this room and you'll never get this chance again,' Nick said.

Hayley looked at him for a moment as she weighed up his last comment.

'Yes. Rosie was taken and I think I know where she is now,' Hayley said.

—

As the car took another corner at speed, Sian felt herself helplessly pushed against the door behind the passenger seat. Moving her forearm against the door, she began to move her left hand slowly over the inside.

She could feel the door panel and the padded armrest. Sliding up the inside, she felt what she assumed was the switch for the electric window. As she ran her fingers away from her along the panel, she came to the button that locked the door. It was raised about half an inch.

It was unlocked.

Maybe they thought that if she was hooded with her hands tied, she was going nowhere. She was aware that she was alone in the back but there were two men sitting in the front of the car.

Running through what she needed to do to get out, Sian began to listen carefully to the sound of the engine. Could she hear anything outside? She needed the car to be going slowly enough for her to jump without risking terrible injuries. However, it would be best that she jumped when other vehicles were around. If they were on a deserted stretch of road and she jumped, they could get out and bundle her back in or just shoot her. If it was busy with traffic, they might decide to leave her and make their escape. That was her best hope of getting away.

The engine began to slow. She could hear the sound of cars passing in the other direction. They were coming to a junction. *This was it!*

As she felt the brakes move her forward, she braced herself.

For a moment, the car almost stopped. Then with a quick jolt, Sian was pushed back as they accelerated and turned right.

*This was it. Now or never.*

She felt the car begin to straighten. Reaching left for the lever, she manoeuvred two fingers behind it, ready to pull.

She shifted in her seat. She tensed the muscles in her thighs and calves.

And then *clunk*.

She pulled the lever, sprang against the opening door and rolled out onto the road below.

Falling over and over again, she was completely disorientated.

And then an incredible pain as the road tore through her shirt and at her skin. The wet of blood on her back. Her left hip felt like it had been hit with a hammer. Her knees repeatedly hit the tarmac and pain shot down her legs.

Gritting her teeth as she started to slow, she could hear the sound of cars braking from somewhere. Had Blake's men stopped to get her or kill her? She couldn't tell.

Something hit the base of her skull, which sucked the air out of her, and darkness enveloped her.

# CHAPTER 33

As she marched down the hospital corridor, Ruth felt a mixture of emotions. Part relief that Sian had been found an hour ago by the roadside, alive. But Sian had been injured while trying to escape and had been admitted unconscious.

The corridor was stuffy and the air had an undertone of detergent, chemicals and hospital food. It was that time of day. The magnolia walls were scraped bare in places where trolleys and equipment had bumped them. Landscape pictures of Snowdonia were on the walls to try to lift the spirits of patients and visitors alike. As she pushed on through the double doors, large blue plastic signs and arrows showed the wards on either side.

Gazing up, she saw that the chapel of rest was on the left. It was only a few days since Merringer had been lying in there for his family to identify.

The sign for the critical care ward loomed into view, and Ruth took a right without breaking stride. The whole time, she had been avoiding the guilty thoughts that were nagging away at her. She had slept with Dan within a day of Sian moving her stuff out. She could come up with excuses for why she had done it, but it was a selfish, shameful thing to do.

Ruth also knew that Sian had accepted her with all her baggage. A daughter from a marriage was one thing. But the unsolved disappearance of Sarah – something Ruth promised she would try to move on from. Sian had trusted Ruth to attempt to build a life with her, to give it her best shot. But in truth, Ruth knew she hadn't. She couldn't let go of the memory of Sarah or the irrational hope that one day she would turn up alive. The two parts of her mind wrestled to and fro with hope and then rational pragmatism. It was bloody exhausting.

And now what? Sian was lying in a hospital bed with critical injuries. Why had it taken this for Ruth to realise how she actually felt about Sian? Why was she so immature and stupid? Ruth was sometimes so intuitive and wise when it came to giving others advice, but when it came to her own mind, most of the time she was miles off. She lacked perspective or the confidence that what she felt was correct and rational. Looking around at others in her life, she envied how they seemed to breeze through, making correct decision after decision. It was like they'd been handed some handbook, but no one had given her one, so she had to copy others until she got it right.

Coming back to reality as she entered the CCU, she pulled out her warrant card and looked at the nurse behind the nurse's station. She was laughing loudly, and for a second Ruth thought how bloody inappropriate she was being. Then she checked herself. Police officers were the worst for black humour to get them through the horrors that they had to deal with on a daily basis. *Don't bloody judge the woman, you idiot!*

'DI Hunter, Llancastell CID. I'm looking for Sian Hockney?' Ruth asked with her best smile.

'Actually, they've just taken her down to the trauma assessment unit, but I think she might be okay to go onto a ward soon,' the nurse explained.

It took Ruth a few seconds to realise that what the nurse was saying was that Sian was out of immediate danger.

'That's good news, isn't it?' Ruth asked, looking for reassurance that what she suspected was true.

'Yes,' the nurse said with a smile. 'It's on the ground floor.'

'Thank you,' Ruth said, feeling the tension begin to drain from her body.

As she got to the stairs, Nick was running up them full pelt.

'It's all right, Usain, they've moved her downstairs,' Ruth said gesturing that he needed to turn around.

'That's good, right?'

'Yeah. She's not critical any more,' Ruth said as they got to the bottom of the stairs and opened the door to the hospital's ground floor. 'What happened with Hayley Collard?'

Nick gave her a look as they continued to stride towards the TAU. 'She claims that she knows where Rosie Wright is.'

Ruth stopped in her tracks. 'What? How is that possible?'

'Hayley is implying that Rosie was trafficked out through Holyhead down to Dublin after she was abducted.'

Ruth rubbed her face as she tried to weigh up what she had just been told. 'Did she tell you that?'

'No. She wants to make a deal with us. I'm guessing she wants some kind of witness protection and to get a new life.'

'Do you think she knows where Rosie is?'

Nick squinted for a second as he thought about it. 'My instinct says no. I think she's hedging her bets. The only thing she has in her favour is that she knows we're desperate to find Rosie.'

'You think we got the right people?'

Nick nodded. 'Unfortunately, I think we did. I think Rosie's body is somewhere out in the Irish Sea, and that's a tragedy.'

Ruth pursed her lips as she looked at him. 'I think we're right too.'

They continued to walk and a moment later found themselves in the TAU. Ruth showed her warrant card again and explained that they wanted to see Sian.

A nurse took them over to a single room at the far end of the ward. As she opened the door, Ruth could see Sian propped up on pillows. Her eyes were closed. There was a drip into her nose and various monitors and drips attached.

'You can stay for a bit, but she needs as much rest as she can get. She's on very strong painkillers so she may just sleep for a while,' the nurse explained.

Ruth's attention was caught by a doctor arriving. He looked at Ruth.

'How's she doing?' Ruth asked.

'Are you relatives?' the doctor asked in his cut–glass accent. Just once it would be nice for a doctor to open his mouth and have a thick Cockney or Brummie accent, Ruth thought.

'I'm her partner,' Ruth said in a way that showed the doctor that she didn't mean in the Cagney and Lacey sense.

'Couple of broken ribs. Concussion. Bruising. And I want to x-ray her neck where she struck the kerb.' The doctor looked at Sian. 'She's lucky to be alive.'

–

The atmosphere inside the incident room was strange and quiet. Ruth knew that the case had been a roller-coaster ride, but it had left a dark atmosphere over CID. It would take them all a long time to get over Merringer's death. It would also haunt some of them that Rosie Wright's body would never be found. As for Kathy and Gareth Wright? There would be many who thought they got what they deserved. However, Ruth thought that Rosie's friends and family deserved to see them stand trial for her murder and get some kind of formal justice.

Nick came over with some sense of urgency and gestured to his computer. 'Boss, I think we can forget any idea that Rosie Wright is in Dublin.'

Following Nick over to his computer, she looked at the CCTV footage. It was marked *Holyhead Ferry Terminal*.

'There are nearly four thousand passengers travelling from Holyhead to Dublin a day. So, I looked through the passenger lists. Each family, couple or single passenger are recorded as a separate entry on the list. You know how many entries there were for two teenage girls travelling on their own?'

'Surprise me,' Ruth said.

'Thirty-five. And I've looked at them all. No sign of Rosie Wright or her fake ID, Hannah O'Brien.'

'So, Hayley Collard was lying to us?' Ruth asked.

Nick nodded as he then brought up an image of two teenage girls on the screen and pointed to them. 'These two girls travelled to Dublin together on the ferry the day before the fire at Bangor. They gave an address in Flint. I've checked with social services and the police in Flintshire. This is Caitlin Marsons and this is Tracey Stone. Both seventeen, both runaways from a care home in Rhyl and both with drug and soliciting convictions.'

'The two girls who were being kept at Bangor?'

'Yeah. My assumption is that Hayley Collard was doing whatever she could to keep out of prison and maybe start a new life,' Nick explained. 'If that meant lying and leading us to believe that she knew where Rosie Wright was, then so be it.'

'And who would blame her? We've seen her file. Girls like Hayley don't stand a chance from the time they're conceived,' Ruth said to no one in particular.

'We got the right people for Rosie's murder,' Nick said. 'That's something.'

# CHAPTER 34

Even though it was eight thirty in the evening, the setting sun was still bright and immense in the sky over the Gogarth cliffs. Friends and family of Rosie had gathered for a service of thanks and remembrance of her life. Ruth and Nick were there to represent the North Wales Police. Gazing down nervously from the cliffs, Ruth could see that the sea was uncharacteristically still as it stretched out before them. She squinted at the shimmering light, took her sunglasses from her hair and put them on. She looked at Nick beside her as he gazed up at the perfect clouds that were just beginning to tinge with oranges and pinks. Even the wind seemed to have calmed respectfully.

It was now two days after Kathy and Gareth Wright had been murdered and loose ends of the case were being tidied up. There was no longer a trial into Rosie Wright's death, but there would still be a coroner's report. Ruth also suspected that given the complicated nature of Rosie's murder and the absence of her body, there would also be a coroner's inquest. There were many precedents. In fact, there were one or two murder cases in the UK without a body every year.

From somewhere, 'When the Party's Over' by Billie Eilish began to play as a poignant hymn to the scene. Ruth remembered that she was Rosie's favourite singer.

As the clouds deepened in colour, Ruth couldn't help but think of Sarah. How unfair it seemed that they had never been able to have anything like this for Sarah. How could they? As Emma Haddon and other girls tossed handfuls of purple and orange petals into the wind over the cliff edge, others let

Chinese lanterns float up and away into the darkening sky. Ruth watched them swirl and dance in the currents of air.

The music, the sunset, the petals, the lanterns, the grief. It was too much for Ruth. Scrunching her toes for a moment, she could feel the pain sweeping through her. She took a breath and pushed her front teeth together, but it was no use. Her eyes welled as she brought the image of Sarah's beautiful face into her mind's eye.

The blue eyes that twinkled with such essence and life. Blonde, feathered hair that framed her face. Lips parted with an uneven smile. That thing she did when she looked to the side and then brought her eyes back with a mischievous glint.

The Billie Eilish song played on, '*Let me let you go...*'

Ruth wiped away a tear and blinked behind her sunglasses. She felt a hand on her arm. Glancing right, she saw Nick giving her a smile of recognition. He knew what she was thinking about, and he understood.

# CHAPTER 35

It was pouring with rain outside as Ruth came into her office. Her sleep had been restless, but the hospital had confirmed that Sian was stable but exhausted. The noise of the rain suddenly increased as the wind threw it against the panes – it was a summer storm. And then from somewhere in the distance, the faintest rumble of thunder.

Listening to the patter of water on the window, Ruth thought about Sian. Could they ever get back what they had only a couple of weeks ago? She would also have to live with the fact that she had slept with Dan, something she had already decided not to tell Sian. There was enough baggage between them and that could alienate her for ever.

Lost in thought, she walked along the line of CID officers who were deep in concentration. A noise from French's computer caught her attention.

Pausing momentarily, she saw that French was watching Kara Haddon's YouTube channel again. The video showed Emma Haddon doing some rehearsals in the main college hall. A caption came up at the bottom of the screen: *My sister Emma in* Grease *rehearsals! 'You're the one that I want…'*

'What are you up to, Dan?' Ruth asked.

'I'm just whizzing through these to make sure there's nothing featuring Kathy or Gareth Wright,' French explained.

Ruth gave him a knowing smile. 'It's almost as if you're avoiding writing up all your notes and evidence, Dan,' she said sardonically.

'Me, boss? I wouldn't do that,' French replied, matching her sarcastic tone.

'Well, don't waste too much time, eh?' she said as she turned to go. She didn't blame him for coasting for a day or two. The investigation had been full-on and the CID officers were knackered.

Out of the corner of her eye, she spotted something. It was Rosie Wright sitting on a table watching her friend rehearsing. At first, it was a poignant reminder of the type of girl Rosie Wright had been. It was so sad to see her sitting there, watching on from a distance.

But then something else unsettled Ruth.

'Can you pause that for a moment, Dan?' she said. Something didn't look quite right.

Ruth noticed that Rosie was sitting next to a young man. In fact, she was sitting far *too* close to the young man – they were virtually touching. He was bearded and looked to be in his twenties. Too old to be a student, but the only teacher that Ruth was aware of was Rosie's form tutor, George Xavier.

Clocking Nick at his computer on the other side of incident room, she looked over at him.

'Nick, you met George Xavier a couple of times, didn't you?' she asked.

'Yes, boss.'

'What's he like?' she asked.

'Young, beard, good-looking. Wannabe hipster. If I was a teenage girl, then I would have a very big crush on him,' Nick said and then frowned. 'That came out wrong.'

'Can you come and have a look at this?' Ruth asked.

Wandering over, Nick looked at the screen. 'Yeah, that's him. And he's looking very cosy with Rosie Wright.'

'Dan, can you zoom in a bit on that for me?' Ruth asked. She thought she had seen something else.

'Yes, boss,' French replied as he enlarged the video.

And there it was.

Nick frowned as he shared a look with Ruth. 'They're holding hands.'

'We always thought Rosie Wright was gay, didn't we?' French asked.

'Call me Sherlock Holmes, but I think there is something going on between her and her form tutor that's distinctly *not* gay,' Nick said.

Had they missed something? Whatever it was, a fifteen-year-old holding hands with her adult form tutor didn't sit comfortably with Ruth.

'I think we should go and talk to George Xavier,' Ruth said.

–

By the time they pulled into the main car park at Llancastell Sixth Form College, the sun had blazed away the grey clouds. The temperature had risen quickly and it was noticeably hot as Ruth got out of the car. Nick took off his jacket and put it on the back seat of the car as he put on his sunglasses.

'Seems very quiet?' Ruth said, looking around the car park that was only a quarter full.

'Maybe they've broken up for summer?' Nick suggested.

They hurried to the entrance and main reception.

A woman in large glasses and bobbed blonde hair sat behind the reception desk that had a sliding glass window. Putting down the phone, she gave them a smile and slid the glass back.

'Can I help?' she asked in a sing-song voice.

Ruth and Nick flashed their warrant cards. 'DI Hunter and DS Evans, Llancastell CID. We're looking for George Xavier?'

'We break up for the summer today so I'm pretty sure he's already gone.' She looked down at her computer and tapped to bring up the computerised signing in and out. 'Yes. Mr Xavier left a couple of hours ago.'

At that moment, a woman entered the reception area and gave them an inquisitive frown. 'Hi, I'm Mrs Beatie. I'm the headteacher here. Can I help with anything?'

Ruth showed her warrant card that was still in her hand. 'We're looking for George Xavier. But he left a few hours ago.'

'Is this to do with Rosie?' Mrs Beatie asked, lowering her voice.

'It's part of our investigation, that's all,' Nick explained.

'George was Rosie's form tutor, wasn't he?' Ruth asked.

'Yes, that's right. It's been such a horrible few weeks for everyone,' Mrs Beatie said as she began to look upset.

'We wanted to ask George to clarify a few things for us,' Ruth said.

'Yes, of course… I think the whole thing has taken its toll on George, which isn't surprising. It's really shaken his confidence as a teacher. It's such a shame,' Mrs Beatie said.

Ruth thought there was a subtext to what she was saying. 'Is there something we should know?'

Mrs Beatie thought for a moment. 'George came to see me this morning and handed in his resignation. He won't be teaching here next academic year. In fact, he said he was going to do some travelling with his wife. What happened to Rosie has really affected him. Poor man.'

Ruth and Nick shared a look. 'We're going to need George Xavier's home address.'

–

Pulling down the sun visor, Ruth smoked the last of her cigarette and blew the smoke out of the window. They were on the suburban outskirts of Llancastell. Detached, newly built houses with drives, garages and front gardens. Someone was mowing a lawn somewhere and the air was full of the smell of cut grass. What a lovely place to live and bring up children, she thought. A lot nicer than some of the places she and Ella had lived in South London. It made her feel guilty, even though she never had the money for this kind of lifestyle in London.

'We went through Rosie's phone records, social media, talked to her friends. There was nothing to suggest that she and Xavier were having any kind of affair,' Nick said.

'Some people are very good at hiding it. She was fifteen and he was her form tutor. That's a criminal offence, a prison sentence and he never works as a teacher again.'

'He can just deny it because Rosie's dead,' Nick said.

'I know, but we still have to follow up the lead. We can't just ignore what we saw in that video, can we? We have to go and talk to him.'

'So, it's just coincidence that they're having an affair and she goes missing?' Nick asked, thinking out loud.

'Normally that would have been a major line of inquiry, wouldn't it?'

'That's what I mean. I just don't like coincidences,' Nick said.

'Neither do I. But you've seen all the evidence.'

Nick nodded. 'The evidence is overwhelming, boss. It just goes against all my instincts as a copper, that's all.'

'Mine too, Nick.'

'Here we go,' Nick said, pointing along the road to a driveway where a Honda Civic was parked. Its boot was open.

A glamorous-looking woman in Sofia Loren glasses, boho hat and fashionable sundress walked up the drive and back into the house.

'Mrs Xavier?' Ruth said rhetorically.

'I guess,' Nick said as he stopped the car across the drive. They didn't want Xavier doing a runner when he saw them.

Getting out, the heat of the sun burnt down on Ruth's face as she and Nick reached the neat, tarmacked driveway. Ruth could see that inside the car's boot was a sky-blue suitcase.

'Someone's going on a trip,' Ruth muttered.

Next door, a pensioner, who was tipping cut grass into a green wheelie bin, looked over at them.

'You looking for George?' the man asked.

'Yeah. Does he live here?' Ruth asked as she reached for her warrant card.

'Oh, yeah. Not for long though. Him and his wife are moving out. He told me they're off travelling,' the old man explained.

Nick gave him a smile. 'Thanks.'

As Ruth turned and began to walk up the drive, the front door opened. A man whom she assumed was George Xavier came out holding a large suitcase. Nick was right. He was dark and handsome, with regulation hipster beard, plaid shirt, turned up jeans and Wayfarers.

He didn't see them at first and took two steps down the path.

'Mr Xavier?' Nick said.

Xavier froze for a second as he panicked. He glanced around but Ruth could see that he had decided that running was pointless.

'Can we have a word, please?' Ruth said.

Putting down the suitcase, he pulled the front door so that it was nearly closed and then walked down the steps towards them.

'How can I help?' Xavier asked, pretending to be breezy, but the shock of their arrival had clearly made him very nervous.

'We need to ask you about the nature of your relationship with Rosie Wright?' Ruth asked.

Xavier frowned. 'I went through all this with Sergeant Evans. I was her form tutor, that's all. I was very fond of her.'

'We've seen a video, George. Rehearsals for the school musical. And you and Rosie are sitting together on a table, holding hands,' Nick said.

Xavier's eyes widened and he looked back at the front door. Ruth could see that he was terrified that his wife would come out and ask what was going on.

'It was nothing. She was going through a difficult time at school, that's all.'

'You had an affair with her?' Ruth asked.

'No, no. Nothing like that,' Xavier said.

Ruth took a step forward and gestured to his house. 'Shall we go inside? Rather than do this in front of all the neighbours?'

'My wife's inside,' Xavier said nervously.

'If you've got nothing to hide, that's not going to be a problem, is it?' Nick said, ushering Xavier back into the house.

As they went into the hallway, Ruth could smell coffee and the hint of coconut suntan lotion.

Mrs Xavier, still in her sunglasses, came out of the living room and looked startled to see them.

'We're just going to have a chat with your husband,' Ruth explained as she looked at the woman. She was smaller and younger than she had looked on the driveway.

Gazing down at her feet, Ruth saw that she was wearing pink Converse trainers. For a moment, she wondered how it had ever become fashionable to wear trainers with a dress.

Then it came to her in a sickening wave.

The left trainer was clearly missing an eyelet at the top where the laces were fastened.

Her eyes travelled straight up to the woman's face.

Except it wasn't a woman.

Ruth slowly reached forward and gently took the large sunglasses from the woman's face. 'Hello, Rosie.'

–

*Rosie suspected that there was something going on between her mother and brother for ages. They would stop talking when she came into the room. They planned to meet at strange times. They both lied about where they had been and with whom. They guarded their mobile phones with their lives and they had a lot of money most of the time. All cash. To say they were acting suspiciously was an understatement.*

*Rosie didn't care. She was having a passionate relationship with her form tutor, George Xavier. And why wouldn't she? He was totally fit, only twenty-five, and she was nearly sixteen. If he was forty and she was thirty, no one would bat an eyelid, would they? Anyone that* judged her could fuck off. She had lost her virginity at his home six months ago. Amazing. She was glad it had been with an experienced man, rather than some moronic, spotty sixteen-year-old boy from college who would have fumbled and cum in about ten seconds. No, thanks. Since then, their relationship had been exciting and magical, and by far the best thing that ever happened in her life. Ever. Swear down.

And then one Monday morning, it happened. Rosie's mum had left her phone unlocked on the kitchen table while she was upstairs in the shower. Rosie couldn't help but look through it. After twenty minutes of scrolling through messages, Rosie could see that her brother was supplying drugs to her mum and she was taking them into prison to sell. At least that's what seemed to be going on. And it would explain why they were being so weird – and all the cash. What the hell? She was shocked and really upset. She felt let down and totally isolated. She couldn't go to her dad – he was a prick at the best of times. She wasn't sure if it was something she could share with her best friend Emma either. It was too big. What the hell would happen?

Seeking comfort in George more than ever, they talked about what she could do. George told her at first to ignore it, but she didn't want to ignore what her mum and brother were doing. They were bloody criminals. She knew one thing. She didn't want to live in that house any more. Plus, Rosie and George were both worried that if anyone ever found out about them, George would go to prison. It wouldn't even matter if she was sixteen. That was the law. It was the whole teacher and student thing. Bloody stupid, if you asked her.

So, they hatched a plan. Run away. Disappear. The only question was how to stop people looking for them? George was okay. He was twenty-five. If he quit his job and went abroad, no one would be suspicious. Rosie was fifteen. She couldn't just disappear without turning herself into some Madeleine McCann-type figure. And then the whole world might start to look for her.

While watching a film, George and Rosie realised the answer to their problems. They needed to fake Rosie's murder. It was just a matter of planning, focus and detail. If everyone thought Rosie was dead, no one would look for her. If they could find some way of demonstrating that her body might never be found, even better.

So first, they needed to invent a plausible story, providing someone with a motive for her murder. If people knew she had found out about her mum and brother's smuggling ring and threatened to go to the police, that would give them a clear motive to murder her. Perfect.

For a month, Rosie collected blood from small cuts in her wrists and legs and kept it in a metal water bottle in the fridge. Hanging a rainbow flag in her room, she came out to her closest friends and said she was gay. That created a nice decoy and deterred anyone from looking for boyfriends or male partners. She made friends with Hayley just to show that she was looking for female friendships online.

The day before Emma's party, Rosie went to the Haddons' home, researched teenagers in witness protection and left a printout to be discovered. She deposited a tiny spot of her blood in Gareth's car boot while he watched TV.

The afternoon of the party, Rosie engineered a row with Gareth in the full glare of the college's CCTV. It couldn't have gone any better. He grabbed her around the throat.

On the evening of Rosie's disappearance, George picked Rosie up at eight. They all but emptied the bottle of her blood onto the yard while Emma and her friends drank and sang on the other side of the barn. It was risky, but it paid off.

Next, Gareth and Kathy Wright were lured to the observation point at the Devil's Cliff at Gogarth with a cryptic text message from a burner. Rosie had already seen the sort of messages that her mum had got about orders, meetings and drugs. Once they were certain that Kathy and Gareth had left Gogarth, George and Rosie arrived and planted the necessary evidence – the missing trainer eyelet, the spot of blood on the car park wall and the footprints from shoes that Rosie had taken from home.

They went back to George's house, waited for Rosie to be declared missing, and then all hell broke loose. They couldn't believe the press coverage. Everything had worked like a dream. The ceremony on the top of Devil's Cliff was the icing on the cake. Rosie had been brutally murdered and her body lost to the sea. She was free to live her new life however she wanted.

*And the plan was only minutes away from working when Ruth and Nick turned up. If only she hadn't reached for George's hand while watching the dance rehearsals, they would have been heading to the airport by now.*

# CHAPTER 36

It was the day after Ruth and Nick had found Rosie Wright alive and well. She was still reeling from all the repercussions. Rosie and Xavier would be charged with perverting the course of justice. The maximum possible sentence for this was life and Ruth couldn't see how they could be given anything less. The pain, misery and stress they had caused was incalculable. The financial cost ran into millions.

Ruth headed for the single room where Sian was still recovering from her injuries. The ward was a hive of early-morning activity. Nurses doing the rounds and handing out medication. Breakfast trolleys clanking and the smell of toast.

Sian was still wearing a neck brace as there had been some concerns about the injury to her neck, and the previous day she had been for a CAT scan and another x-ray. They were waiting to see the consultant that morning.

Ruth and Sian had spent the previous evening together as Ruth filled her in on the bombshell of Rosie Wright being alive and well. However, they never really moved past the case. Never really got to talk about what had happened between them.

As Ruth reached the door to her room, she could see that Sian was sitting upright in bed, gazing at the television. She watched her. That magical feeling of watching someone you love when they haven't noticed your gaze. It reminded her of when she used to watch Ella sing to herself while drawing when she was very young.

Feeling overwhelmed, she could feel her stomach twist. She knew what she had to do. If the last week had taught her anything, it was that life was fragile and no one was immortal. She had someone who was willing to share her life and she was throwing that away.

Sian turned slowly towards the door, as though she had sensed Ruth's presence.

'Why are you standing there?' she asked with a smile.

'I was just watching you,' Ruth said, looking directly at her. She wanted to set the tone. She was done with skirting around how they felt.

'Creepy,' Sian said, raising an eyebrow with a grin.

Moving around the bed, Ruth pulled the chair close to the bed and sat down.

Sian gestured to the television. 'I know everyone says it, but Piers Morgan is an utter twat, isn't he?'

Ruth sat forward, took Sian's hand and looked at her.

'Oh… Okay…' Sian said as she winced.

'I have a few things to say. And I want you to listen. And then at least I know I've said how I feel. I can't change how you feel, but I can be honest,' Ruth said. She could feel her pulse quicken a little.

'Okay, that sounds fair,' Sian said as she shifted on her pillows and squeezed Ruth's hand.

'You know I love you?'

'Yes, I do.'

'But that's not the issue. Every day that I sit and have my life on hold because of what happened to Sarah is a wasted day. I'm a police officer. I know how this works. A young woman goes missing from a train six years ago. Sarah's not going to turn up alive. It doesn't happen. So, I have to move on.'

'Can you do that though?' Sian asked.

'Yes. I have to. We're all going to die one day. When I'm on my deathbed, I'm not going to look back and think that living in this weird, dark limbo was a good use of my life. However, when I'm on my deathbed…'

'Can you stop saying *deathbed*?' Sian smiled.

'Sorry. I want to look back and think how lucky I was to spend it with this beautiful, funny, sexy woman that I met at work.'

'What about me?' Sian quipped.

'Sian! I'm serious,' Ruth said.

'Sorry.' Sian looked at her for a moment and frowned. 'It's one thing saying it. It's another feeling it.'

'I know. And why should you trust me? But I've never said any of this before. I have to take my life off pause and get on with fucking living. And I want to be with you,' Ruth said. She could feel the surge of excitement as she gave voice to what she wanted.

Sian nodded as she reflected on Ruth's words. And then a tear welled in her eye as she squeezed Ruth's hand. 'Okay...' she whispered.

'Okay...' Ruth smiled, leant over and kissed her. The neck brace got in the way, but she didn't care. Relief, happiness and joy.

'Let's just get on with living life, eh?' Sian said. 'And that means you have to stop smoking.'

'Hi, there,' Ella said as she appeared at the door. 'How are you feeling, Sian?'

'Yeah, I'm okay. Better now your mum's here. Come in...'

Feeling tired and a little washed out, Ruth realised that she needed some coffee.

'If I walk up to the machine, who wants coffee?' Ruth asked.

'Definitely,' Sian said.

'Shall I come with you?' Ella said.

'No, you can sit and keep me company, thank you,' Sian said with a smile.

Turning to see Ella and Sian together, Ruth was overwhelmed with joy that she had got her family back.

She didn't need anything else in the world.

As she stepped outside the room, the consultant, a tall Asian woman, had stopped by the door.

'Are you part of the family?' the consultant asked as she looked at her notes.

'I'm Sian's partner,' Ruth replied.

'Right. If you could come in for a moment, I need to talk to you both.'

'What is it?' Ruth asked anxiously. The phrase had made her stomach turn.

'If we could go in...'

'I'd rather know and have a few seconds with whatever it is so I can support her when we're in there.'

'Okay. The x-ray shows some damage to the spinal cord in the neck.'

'What does that mean?'

'I can't say at the moment.'

'Worst-case scenario?'

'Worst case is that her walking is restricted or... that she struggles to walk ever again.'

As the consultant went in, Ruth took this information on board.

Suddenly, she felt the buzz of her phone. Clicking it open, she saw it was a missed call from Steven Flaherty and a text message.

> Ruth, I don't want to get your hopes up, but Edinburgh Police have arrested a man in his forties in connection with the rape and attack in the city centre. I don't have any other details yet. I will give you a call this evening and I can tell you anything else that I find out in the meantime.
> Steven

Ruth's mind was swirling with thoughts. Kessler was in his forties. She clicked her BBC News app:

Edinburgh Police have arrested a man in connection with the attack of a young female student
in the city centre two days ago. A spokesperson
said that the man was helping them with their
inquiries, but this was a significant development
in the case.

–

The evening was warm and Amanda sat on the patio as Nick
pottered around the garden and then went into the rickety old
shed. He had told her about how they had found Rosie Wright
and the story that she told them about faking her own death.
Amanda couldn't believe it and said it would make a great film.

There was the sound of things clattering and Nick came
hopping out on one leg, hamming it up to get a laugh.

'I think I need to give that a bit of tidy,' Nick said.

'Yeah, you've got to make room for all Junior's stuff. Goal
posts, football…' Amanda said.

Nick frowned. 'Erm… what if she's a girl?'

'I meant if she's a girl, you knob. Female footballers. They
earn a fortune too,' Amanda said with a laugh.

Ducking his head back into the shed, Nick rattled around a
bit more and then came out triumphantly holding some kind
of contraption.

'I forgot that I had this bloody thing in there,' Nick said
shaking his head with a smile.

'What the bloody hell is that? It looks like an alien hoover!'
Amanda chortled.

'It's a metal detector, obviously,' Nick said with a wry grin.

'You know, I'm not surprised, but just for the record, why
have you got a metal detector?'

'In some drunken stupor, I decided to buy it online.
Thought it would be great fun to take it down the beach,' Nick
explained.

'What, and discover treasure? You're such a geek, Nick!'

Fiddling around, Nick checked to see if it still worked. He put the headphones over his ears and turned it on. It burst into life with a high-pitched squeal that hurt his eardrums.

'Bloody hell, that's loud!' he said, turning down the volume. 'Here we go…'

Nick began to sweep the lawn with the detector to and fro, all the while playing the clown. Amanda just laughed at him.

Wandering over to where Amanda was sitting, Nick gestured to her.

'Fancy a go?' he asked.

'Erm… fuck off.'

'Come on. Using a metal detector has got to be on your bucket list, surely?'

'Yeah, it's up there with learning how to wallpaper,' Amanda quipped.

Nick carried on using it for a moment. 'Hang on. That sounds like a Bronze Age sword under there. Half a million quid from the British Museum,' he joked.

'You're hilarious!' Amanda said.

Nick smiled, 'Come on, Mand. Give it a whirl! It'll make me happy.'

Rolling her eyes, she held out her hand. 'Oh, all right. If it will make you happy, then give it here.'

Nick clamped the headphones onto her ears and pointed to a patch of grass just by the patio. 'Try that bit. Might find a body under the patio.'

'Well, that's no good. They'd have to dig up our garden and we're about to have a baby,' Amanda said.

'We just won't report it,' Nick joked.

'I feel like a right twat!' she said as she swept the lawn. And then she stopped in her tracks. 'Ooh! What was that?'

Nick came over and listened. There was definitely a high-pitched buzz.

'There's something metal under there. Let's have a look.' Nick bent down and moved the grass out of the way where the noise was coming from.

'I can't see anything.'

'There!' Amanda crouched down as best she could and saw that half buried in the earth was a small silver metal box. It was about two inches square.

'Have you found something? Can we both retire?' Nick asked as she stood up, looking quizzically at the box.

'What is it?' Amanda asked.

'I don't know. Open it,' Nick said with a shrug.

Opening the box slowly, she clicked back the lid. Inside was a diamond ring.

Amanda frowned at Nick – and then the penny dropped.

'What do you think?' Nick asked with a smile as he dropped to his knee.

'It's beautiful,' Amanda said as she started to choke up with emotion.

'Will you marry me, Amanda?' Nick asked.

She shook her head and pushed him playfully. 'That whole metal detector routine! Oh, God, you are such a bell-end!'

'A romantic bell-end?' Nick grinned as he got up.

Amanda moved closer and they hugged tightly.

'Is that a yes, then?' Nick asked as he moved a stray piece of hair away from her face.

'Yes, of course I'll marry you,' Amanda said as they began to kiss.

–

Ruth was sitting watching the BBC News channel intently. She had tried to ring Steven Flaherty, but there was no reply. The arrest in Edinburgh was on a half-hour cycle, but there was no new information. She had already decided that the arrested man was Jurgen Kessler, even though she knew this was a dangerous assumption.

*It has to be Kessler, doesn't it?*

Sitting back, Ruth processed what the consultant had told them about Sian's injury. Ruth felt guilty about watching for news from Edinburgh after all she'd said to Sian, but she couldn't help herself. Kessler was the key to finding out what had happened to Sarah.

The news anchor looked at the screen. '*Police in Edinburgh have now confirmed that a man has been charged with the rape and attempted murder of a woman in the city centre two days ago. Although no details of the suspect have been released, police have confirmed that the man is local to the area and well known to them.*'

*No! Jesus Christ! Why did I let myself believe it was Kessler?*

Ruth's heart sank and she felt sick.

*I'm so bloody stupid!* she said as the anger and frustration built inside.

*When is this nightmare ever going to stop?*

Head in her hands, Ruth knew what she needed to do.

Marching into the garage, Ruth lifted boxes and kicked a garden chair out of her way in sheer frustration.

*I'm not doing this any more! It has to stop.*

Her mind was now full of Sian's diagnosis. That's what mattered. Nothing was conclusive, but there was a possibility that she would never walk properly again, and that was a tragedy. They would have to get the ground floor of the house converted – or move to a bungalow, maybe?

Picking up a large, empty cardboard box, Ruth moved over to the table and chair where all the stuff to do with Sarah and her disappearance were laid out or stuck to the wall. It was time to stop all this and move on. Or at least try to draw a line under what had happened.

*I've got to start living.*

Taking photos from the wall, Ruth's eyes filled with tears as she stacked them neatly in a folder. There was part of her that doubted she could really put all this to one side and leave it in the past. But she had to try or she would be trapped in the past for ever.

Looking up at the photo of Sarah at Glastonbury, Ruth stopped.

*I'm so sorry. I will find you. I promise. And I will find out what happened to you… one day. But I just can't do that right now.*

## AUTHOR'S NOTE

Although this book is very much a work of fiction, it is located in Snowdonia, a spectacular area of North Wales. It is steeped in history and folklore that spans over two thousand years. It is worth mentioning that Llancastell is a fictional town on the eastern edges of Snowdonia. I have made liberal use of artistic licence, names and places have been changed to enhance the pace and substance of the story.

Your FREE book is waiting for you NOW

THE THEATRE STREET KILLING
PREQUEL

South London 1995. A brutal murder.

Find out about Ruth Hunter and her move
from Uniform to being a detective in CID.

Get your free prequel at

http://www.simonmccleave.com/vip-email-club

and join my VIP Email Club.

Do you love crime fiction and are always on the lookout for brilliant authors?

Canelo Crime is home to some of the most exciting novels around. Thousands of readers are already enjoying our compulsive stories. Are you ready to find your new favourite writer?

Find out more and sign up to our newsletter at
canelocrime.com